AVALON PRESS

THE STONE OF TANTALUS

CLANCY WEEKS

Copyright © 2013, 2018 by Clancy Weeks

Published in the United States by Avalon Press.

Avalon Press and its logo are trademarks of Avalon Press.

Title: The Stone of Tantalus
Names: Weeks, Clancy, author
Descriptions: First edition. | Tomball: Avalon Press [2018]
Identifiers: ISBN-13: 978-1-7321220-0-0 (paperback) |
    ISBN-10: 1-7321220-0-8 (paperback) |
    ISBN-13: 978-1-7321220-1-7 (e-book) |
    ISBN-10: 1-7321220-1-6 (e-book)
Subjects: | Science Fiction. | Suspense Fiction.

First Paperback Edition

ACKNOWLEDGMENTS

Way back in 1991 (sometime before the dinosaurs ruled the earth) I picked up a copy of *The Emperor's New Mind* by Roger Penrose. Other than the standard European affinity for exclamation marks, the book was an engaging and accessible explanation of much of the physical universe, even delving into a bit of quantum theory. After reading this, and especially the last chapter (which I leave to you to find and explore) the germ of an idea had formed, and is the basis for this novel. I am thoroughly confident I've managed to mangle Penrose's ideas beyond any hope of recognition, but that's the nature of fiction, right? Any errors in the science are all mine, and are in no way the fault of the brilliant minds quoted within these pages.

PART ONE

"Observe constantly that all things take place by change, and accustom thyself to consider that the nature of the Universe loves nothing so much as to change the things which are, and to make new things like them."
—Marcus Aurelius

PROLOGUE

"TELL ME, MILES... JUST BETWEEN YOU AND ME," FLINT SAID, leaning closer from the cot across the cell. "Why did you kill him?" One of the fluorescent lights buried in the ceiling flickered and buzzed, turning the small room into a 3D version of a kinetoscope.

Miles turned his head in slow motion, tilting it—a praying mantis considering his next meal, then shrugged his shoulders. "I don't know who you're talkin' about." He returned to staring at the gray cell door.

"The *Fed*, man." Flint sat on the edge of his cot, his right leg bouncing like a sewing machine.

Miles smiled. He remembered everything about that day, but he sure as hell wasn't going to tell Flint about it. He was pretty sure the guy was an informant, anyway. The bulls brought the twitchy little man in last night and threw him in the holding cell with Miles. The room was small, but large enough to hold more than two, and Miles was sure a normal Saturday night would see at least ten stuffed in the cramped space. But more than anything else, what pricked Miles' radar was the way the man sat—spring-tight nervous energy restrained through sheer force of will. It bubbled up like an old percolator, at once rhythmic *and* random. Like a junkie in dire need of a fix, but without the sunken and sallow appearance, the man's eyes darted from Miles to the door beyond and back before each sentence he spoke.

Flint tried again. "What are you in for, then?"

Miles snorted and sneered. "Denver cops dragged me in a couple of days ago on a 'drunk and disorderly'." *Tell the idiot only what he already knows*, he thought. It was a trick he learned dealing with his daddy. Never, *ever*, answer more than the question required.

The other man raised an eyebrow, "Then why ya still in here?"

Miles chuckled and shook his head. "I was pretty fuckin' disorderly," he said.

Flint snickered. "Yeah, I bet you were. The cops said you sent one of 'em to the hospital." He said it weird… hos*Pit*al, like a kid would say it. Miles hated kids—hated worse the way they talked. Hated most of all the *adults* who spoke like children.

Miles pursed his lips and narrowed his eyes at Flint. "What did they get *you* for?"

"Ah, you know," he waggled a hand, "a little o' this, a little o' that."

"I hear ya." *Definitely an informant*, Miles thought. It never ceased to amaze him how stupid cops were. He shook his head. *As long as they don't find the gun, they don't have nothin'.*

"You've come a long way, man. I heard you was a congressman or somethin'."

Miles peered at him, eyes boring a hole through to the back of Flint's head, his face a mask of pure bland.

Flint took a breath and let it out in a slow stream. The bouncing of his right leg was joined by his left. "Yeah, I heard whoever got that guy up in the mountains plugged him in the chest with a 45," he said, his voice cracking.

"Do tell…" A picture flashed through Miles' mind—his hands around this fool's throat, carotid pulsing under calloused fingers, eyes bulging as the idiot's smile became a rictus of pain. He tempered the grin threatening to split his face.

His outward calm masked the constant anger that seethed within, buzzing in the background like a swarm of cicadas. A well-practiced skill, it wasn't born of hate, not even for his daddy. The anger was a part of him, applied to everyone equally. That changed the day the bastard from the FBI took his life away, frog-marching him in handcuffs down the Capitol steps in front of every camera the media could muster. Sure, he could sidestep this reality for something more to his liking, but that wasn't enough. It would never be enough. If he were patient, the time for *enough* would come.

And Miles knew how to be patient. Forged by boot and lash, and honed by years of observation. "Miles," his daddy would whisper as they watched the game trail from their deer stand, "be still. Listen." Sometimes this was followed by a sharp slap to the back of his head. "You make one damn sound, you'll scare 'em off." *Slap.* "Do that, an' I'll mount *your* head on the wall." Miles never made a sound—never even *moved*. Not after that first time. His feet dangling over open space, the ground an infinite distance below to an eight year old, his father holding him by the throat.

Miles knew how to be patient.

It took years, but the opportunity arrived, and he followed his prey to the cabin in the woods, boots crunching against the gravel driveway. The man was vacationing alone in the mountains, and when he opened the door, recognition and surprise fought for control of his face. His eyes grew large and round as Miles shot him in the chest, his mouth forming the word "oh" with no breath to voice it.

It took him a while to die, too. Miles watched the whole time, memorizing every second as life ebbed. When it was over, Miles smiled.

I should go back and do that again, he thought. *But why? Why not go back in the dance and get the fool earlier? Make something new.* He could sidestep to a similar reality, and *then* go back to set things right. *I don't have to live this life. I can get it right on the next try!* He grew hard at the idea, and reached down to rub the throbbing distraction. Flint recoiled, and Miles rubbed faster, bringing himself to the edge of climax while he grinned at the little man. He stopped, denying himself, breathing heavy and lustful, the muscles at the base of his stiff member clenching and relaxing in a rhythm guaranteed to hold back the flood.

The look on Flint's face was priceless—a mixture of shock, disgust, and maybe a little desire, and Miles snapped his fingers in front of the man's face to draw his attention up and away from Miles' crotch. He slapped the other man on the leg, and said, "Thanks, officer. You've been a lot of help." Miles tipped an imaginary cap, and said through a tight smile, "Gotta go now."

His eyes lost focus, and he slumped back on his cot. Flint leaned forward to check on him, and then Miles sat up in a shot and drew a rasping breath. He looked around the room, then at Flint, and said, "Who the fuck are you?"

ONE

I f ever there was a day for skipping class, this was it. The sky was blue without a cloud in sight, a faint chill in the air, and the pretty girls were out in force. Jason Callahan wasn't much for skipping, but that didn't mean he couldn't enjoy the walk across campus. April on the campus of the University of Texas meant the women's shorts were high, the t-shirts tight, and the blond pony tails swayed in rhythm when they walked. From his first day on campus, it seemed every girl was a perfect ten, and even now he still marveled at the sight. Jason smiled, shoved his hands in the front pockets of his faded jeans, and began the long walk across campus from Jester East to Moore Hall. He had at least an hour before his Quantum Three lecture, so he took his time, strolling with his usual lanky gate.

A tall and pretty redhead passed him going the other way, dipped her chin and smiled as she reached up to brush a spray of hair over her ear. He smiled back, *almost* turning, when his cell buzzed once in his back pocket.

Kat always knew. Jason might not stray, but he *was* an unredeemable flirt.

He stifled a laugh, then pulled the phone from his pocket to check the text message.

Lunch after class?

He poked large fingers at the screen, correcting several times, *Only if I don't have questions for the prof after,* then hit send.

Less than a minute later the phone buzzed again with the message,

As if.

This time he did laugh.

Kat knew him better than he knew himself. She was always a step ahead of him in life, and he was grateful for it. There were times he grew complacent his first year, but when she joined him on campus in his second things shaped right up. *He* shaped up. It was the same throughout middle and high school. From the day they first met she was his personal drill sergeant, urging him to "get his shit together." Nothing she said or did ever felt as if she were nagging, though his friends laughed every time she pulled him into line.

Which is often.

The air was dry that morning, the early fog shooed away by a demanding sun, so he parked under a tree and watched other students hurry to their classes. Urgent and earnest freshmen were easy to spot, as were the sophomores convinced they knew everything. Seniors seldom made their presence known outside of class, grinding to finish what they started. *Juniors* were a different breed altogether. Members of the student body long enough to know the ropes, but still just *students* rather than soon-to-be-graduates.

Kat was only a sophomore, but she knew the best places to eat (Conan's), where the best music was on sixth street (a running debate), and when to avoid that area altogether (ROT Rally). An Army brat, she soon adjusted to each new environment, and was already an Austin native while he still felt like an outsider. Coming to Austin was, for him, like stepping on a new planet; every social gathering a First Contact situation fraught with diplomatic danger.

Keep Austin Weird! The shirt, worn by a shambling dreadlocked sophomore, yelled at him in all-caps as the boy passed. *The cannabis is strong with this one,* Jason thought with a smile. He had one of the t-shirts stuffed in a drawer in his dorm, too self-conscious to wear it. The damn thing felt like a statement on his own personality, rather than the odd-ball parts of the city.

"How long you gonna stand there watchin' the girls like a creeper?" Jason's roommate, Dan, slipped in beside him and leaned against the tree.

"Damn, dude. Never saw you comin'."

"Too busy scopin' trim," Dan said, smiling. "If I'd a been a snake,

I'd a bit ya." He waggled his eyebrows as his mouth snapped.

Jason laughed. Dan wasn't as dense as the Central Texas twang led most people to believe. Jason was sure it was a deliberate act on Dan's part—like Jason learning Spanish without ever telling anyone. It made for a major advantage at times. Although with no one to practice on, he was forced to watch telenovelas on the Spanish language channels when no one was around.

"And I'm not girl watching," Jason protested.

"Hey, I won't tell Kat if you don't." Dan grinned again, "I don't want to have to clean the blood off the floor when she cuts yer nuts off."

"True that," Jason said, and lifted a fist to bump knuckles with his roommate.

"You comin' out to play some pool tonight?"

"Nah. Gotta work in the lab until nine." Other than his grants and scholarships, it was his only source of income. He worked hard to avoid the student loan trap that snared so many of his friends, but those programs only went so far. Work-study was a joke in many departments, but Physics seemed to get it. They worked him hard, but with enough pay and hours to make ends meet.

"Too bad," Dan said with mock sympathy. He raised an eyebrow and grinned. "Guess I'll have to entertain Kat for ya."

Jason laughed. "Yeah," he said, smirking. "You let me know how that works out for you."

Dan smiled, then checked the time on his cell. "Shit! I'm late for class. Again." He looked around at the bevy of young ladies, then to the sky like he was beseeching a deity. "Fuck it," he said. "Just Geology anyway." Everyone on campus called it *Rocks for Jocks*, and was famous as the only lab science you could pass without ever setting foot in a lecture. Dan set his backpack on the ground, fished around inside, then pulled out a beat up Frisbee. "Wanna toss it around a while?"

"Damn, Dan, that's some serious old-school shit, there," Jason said, shaking his head. He pulled his cell out of his pocket, checked the time. "I've got exactly twenty minutes."

†††

"If you're that interested, Jason, you know Feynman's lectures are available on the internet." The lecture today didn't answer all his questions, and as usual, he spent the time on the way out drilling the professor for more.

"But what about situations arising from having two independent single spin waves? The energies you calculated on the board seemed a bit off. Here..." Jason took out a pen and looked for something to write on, but Kat stepped away from the wall by the door and took his arm.

"Dr. Harrell probably wants to go to lunch, Jason," she said, steering him with a gentle nudge away from the harried man. "Just like *I* do," she finished with a smile. From the first day Jason met her, it was the smile that bridled him.

"Next week, then," he said to Dr. Harrell, allowing Kat to pull him away. She hooked an arm into his, handing over her book bag for him to carry.

She frowned, looking him over. "Don't you *ever* carry any books or paper to your classes?"

"Nah. I like to travel light."

"How do you take notes?"

He tapped the side of his head with a forefinger, "It's all up here, babe."

"You always took notes in high school," she said, squinting at him. "And don't call me babe."

"That was mostly for you. That and I hated all the other subjects in high school. It was all I could do just to stay awake in class." He smiled. "Here—especially this year—everything I'm taking is something I'm interested in." He leaned over and kissed her on the cheek. "You'll notice I have never taken notes about *you*, either."

She rested her head on his shoulder as they walked. "What day was our first kiss?"

"Uh..."

"Maybe you *should* take notes," she said, laughing.

Part of him wanted to complain that no one kept track of such things, but the rational part knew better than to voice it. That path only led to a full-blown argument rather than playful teasing. Most of his friends had been through several girlfriends in the time he had been with Kat, and they often asked him how—some meaning *why*—he stayed in one relationship so long. *It's all in knowing when to keep your mouth shut*, he thought. *Knowing when to pick your battles, and when to surrender.* Neither of which had anything to do with being right.

"So, where are you taking me for lunch?"

He looked down and smiled. "We could walk back to Jester," he said. "I've got plenty on my meal card. My treat."

"I've got a biology lab in an hour."

"Kismet Cafe, then?" he shrugged.

"Sure. I'll buy, though."

"Hey, I got this," he said, sniffing.

"You got any cash or a credit card on you?"

"Uh..."

"Like I said, Mr. Callahan. *I'll* buy today."

And that, apparently, was that. There was no arguing with her once she last-named him. Jason still bristled at the idea of her paying for so much—his upbringing so steeped in the male mystique—but it wasn't as if she didn't have the funds. She rode in her freshman year flush with scholarships and lots of cash from her parents. And even though she didn't *need* to work, she still put in a few hours every week tutoring local students for extra money. Money he knew would help *him* with his expenses.

Money was fungible, as the economics majors were fond of saying, so he couldn't get shake the idea the engagement ring with the tiny diamond he had hidden in his dresser was paid for with *her* money. *Ah, well*, he thought with an inward sigh, *at least if she says no, she gets her money back.*

"So serious," she said, snuggling close. "What are you thinking about?"

"I'm thinking if we don't hurry, you'll miss your lab and my stomach will eat itself."

She laughed as he picked up the pace, matching him stride for stride.

†††

The Computational Physics lab was as quiet as a library. Most students wouldn't begin serious study for another couple of weeks. Tonight it was just the regulars. Those guys—and a few gals—who never got enough time on the mainframe.

Jason sat at the desk, overseeing the students working at their stations, occasionally helping them with a problem, but mostly reading. That was the *study* part of work-study that most departments got wrong. They worked their students ragged, leaving little time to read or do homework. In Physics, the job was monotonous, but also secondary. The exact opposite of the athletic department.

More than once, Jason thanked the stars he never took *that* bait in middle school. The coaches saw his size and athletic ability, first courting, and then haranguing him to join their programs. Too many of his friends in school fell victim to the pitch, and he rarely saw them after the beast swallowed them up. Most were now working in menial jobs, without a decent education, ground up by the football machinery of the state. A few got athletic scholarships to small universities. There they would again be sacrificed to the football gods for four or five years and *still* not have a marketable education to show for their troubles.

Jason closed his book in disgust after reading the same passage for the third time. It was Hugh Everett's *The Theory of the Universal Wavefunction*, and needed all his attention to understand it. Everett was an early pioneer in cosmology, though he left the field soon after publishing the thesis in Jason's hands. He tossed the book to the desk, and reached for another, more recent book from the stack. This one, Roger Penrose's *Shadows of the Mind*, was one he read in high school. It was only in the last year he had gained enough grounding in quantum theory to understand everything in it.

He was on the right track, he thought, *but Everett's right... I think the wave function* doesn't *collapse to a single state.*

Jason agreed with Penrose on one topic, though—artificial intelligence was a dead end. Most of his friends in computer science thought otherwise, and would debate him on this until late in the night. *Dan thinks we will all one day bow to our robot overlords*, Jason thought with a smile. *Of course, Dan also thinks Hogwarts is a real place.*

He checked the clock on the wall. "'Bout time to call it a night, guys. Start saving your work and shutting things down." There were a few groans from the far end of the room where a group gathered around a single monitor, but most packed their books and papers. He tossed the second book on the desk near the first and stood to stretch his legs.

As he stepped away from the desk, he glanced to where the two books lay and stopped. He reached down and turned them, lining them up side by side and shifting his gaze from one to the other. Back and forth, over and over, while his mind raced.

"Ha!" he almost yelled. "That's it!"

The students looked up to see what the commotion was about, but Jason was already sitting again and grabbing for a pencil and paper. After almost an entire semester of hand-wringing, he now had the subject for his senior honors thesis. Jason had almost given up hope he would find a suitable subject, several of his lesser ideas already rejected by his adviser.

Everyone smiled at him, shook their heads, and walked quietly out of the room. This wasn't the first time they witnessed such a reaction from an upper-level undergrad, and Jason knew each one prayed it wouldn't take *them* this long to figure it out.

†††

"I'm telling you, Dan... this is it!" Back in his dorm room, surrounded by piles of notes and books, Jason sat on the edge of his chair. Dan had just walked into the room from a night of playing pool when Jason forced him to sit and listen.

"Can it at least wait until I'm sober?" Dan whined, sitting on the edge of his bed and struggling to pull off his shoes and socks. After a few tugs the second shoe came off, nearly hitting him in the head, and he dropped everything to the floor. They joined the growing mound of discarded clothes in the to-be-washed pile. He stared at the collection like he expected them to dance.

"Nah. You're in the *exact* state of mind to hear this," Jason said, grinning. "It's pretty out there."

"Dude... it's almost one, and I've got an early class tomorrow."

"Then you shouldn't have stayed out late and gotten liquored up."

Dan eyed Jason for a long time, eyelids straining under some unseen weight, and then scrubbed his face with both hands. "Okay, roomie," he said, waving his hand in a *gimme* gesture, "shoot."

"It has to do with why there will probably never be true self-aware artificial intelligence," he began.

"Ah hell, Jay, are we gonna have that argument again? 'Cuz let me tell ya, I think I'd rather sleep."

"Notice I said *probably* this time. I'll lay out the conditions for it in a bit, but first..." he picked up the two books he had been reading in the lab and held them out to Dan. After a few seconds Dan snorted and snatched them from Jason's hand. "Penrose says there can't be true artificial intelligence because what's happening in the human brain is quantum-related and can't be replicated in silicon."

"I've heard this shit before, buddy. What else ya got?"

"It also means even a quantum computer couldn't pull it off because we are still dealing with algorithms that *mimic* intelligence, and since real consciousness is rising from a purely non-algorithmic collapse to a single state, it won't work."

"And I still say Penrose is full o' shit."

Jason held his hands in front, waving them like a carnival barker as he spoke. "Here's the cool part," he pointed at the second book. "Everett there says the quantum wavefunction *never* collapses to a single state."

"Yeah, I know," Dan said, sobering. "That's the multiple worlds interpretation guy, right?" He sneered and shook his head. "What's one thing got to do with the other?"

"What if they're *both* right?"

Dan tilted his head and raised an eyebrow, almost falling over in the process. "I'm not sure I follow. How can two mutually exclusive ideas be both right?"

"Here's where my genius shines! Because the wavefunction only collapses *locally*." Jason stood, his body quaking with a barely restrained energy. Dan looked up at him, his eyes unfocused and uncomprehending. Jason paced as he spoke. "It's like this... all the quantum realities exist like branches on a tree, each decision marking a new path. The decision that marks the branch is the outward expression of a wavefunction collapsing to a single state, but the branching itself represents the universal wavefunction which *never* collapses!"

"So...?"

"What else looks like branches on a tree?"

"Um..."

"Jesus, Dan. You, of all people should—"

"A network!"

"Got it in one," Jason said, grinning. "Or infinity. Depends on your point of view, I guess," he said, rubbing the two-day stubble on his chin. "Penrose believes there's a quantum effect in the rise of intelligence and consciousness, and he's correct, but wrong in the process. I think maybe it's all about the network. From the day you are born—earlier, really—you make choices, branching off new universes with a version of yourself in each one. A you for every possible decision you could have made. But the branches constitute a network in a massively parallel quantum computer that is the source of sentience." He took a deep breath, "That's where the *you* comes from. Our consciousness arises naturally from the growth of the network."

"Are you sure?"

Jason laughed and sat on his chair again. "Oh, *hell* no. I'm pulling most of this straight out of my ass." He swiveled in the chair to pull some papers off the desk behind him. "Some of these concepts have already been explored in other papers I've found." He held up a sheaf, waving it behind him a Dan, "Albert and Loewer", then another, "H. Dieter Zeh. All pointing to what they call the many minds interpretation." He bent to the desk and snagged a pencil. "I'll have to change my whole schedule for next year, *and* take a couple of extra classes this summer. The math alone..."

Soon he was muttering to himself as he worked out an outline for his approach, Dan snoring like a chainsaw behind him.

†††

"What did you mean last night about the conditions for AI?" Dan was pulling clothes from the "clean" pile beside his bed, taking a sniff, then laying them out for inspection. Occasionally he rejected one after the initial sniff and tossed it to the "to be washed" pile on the other side. Not a single piece had ever seen the inside of the dresser, as far as Jason knew, and the system—while odd and disorganized—worked for Dan.

"So you weren't completely out of it," Jason said with a grin. He had showered and dressed before Dan woke, and was already working on his outline again. The fact he hadn't slept never crossed his mind.

"Not *completely*, no," he said, rubbing his head. For Dan, this was known as "combing his hair." Little more than stubble most of the time, the jet black mat refused to do much more than just lay there. Dan scrounged in the nightstand next to his bed, pulled out a bottle of ibuprofen, and popped two in his mouth. "I clearly remember," he said around the pills, "you saying something about certain conditions allowing for an AI to be conscious."

Jason set the pencil down on the stack of papers and swiveled his chair to face his friend. "If that AI, even algorithm-based, is running in a quantum computer and allowed to make its own decisions, then it's a *possibility*." He tapped Penrose's book beside him for emphasis. "There are physical structures—microtubules—in the human brain that, in *theory*, operate on a quantum level. It's my hypothesis they could be responsible for the network connections throughout the multiverse that give rise to consciousness. If those structures can be mimicked in hardware..." he raised his hands and shrugged his shoulders.

"*Can* they be mimicked?"

"Haven't a clue. It's out of my field."

"Probably out of mine, too," Dan said, shaking his head. "I'm just a computer science geek, and I have a feeling this is gonna be way more complicated than your typical IT troubleshooting."

Jason chuckled. Dan was always selling himself short. *Like he actually believes the image he projects of himself.* "Not every computer science geek has read Penrose or Everett," Jason said.

"I blame you, roomie," Dan said with a short laugh, then grabbed a pillow and threw it like a frisbee at Jason's head. Instead it bounced off his chest and fell to the floor near the "to be washed" pile.

"You're gonna know even more before I'm through," he said with a wink. "I've gotta bounce my ideas off *someone*."

"What about Kat?"

"I try not to talk about this stuff around her. Puts her right to sleep."

"I don't know, Jay," Dan said, rubbing his head again, "Maybe a biology major would be of some use to you, donchathink?"

He hadn't considered that. Physics bored Kat to tears, and was a lousy topic of conversation on a date. After the first few times he tried to talk about his classes, watching her eyes glaze over, he avoided the topic like health-food. Now there was a possibility of overlap. He needed a lot of information in the field of biology—specifically the human brain—and that just happened to be Kat's focus. If nothing else, she could at least guide him to the right sources. Internet searches only went so far.

"I'll take the silence and the stupid look on your face as a yes," Dan said, watching him. "Personally, I think yer full 'o shit, but what do I know?" he said with a shrug. He dressed in slow motion, careful not to move around too much, then sat on the edge of the bed and bent to retrieve a shoe. "Ah, hell," he said, then ran out of the room and down the hall to the communal bathroom. The sounds of retching reached Jason's ears, but none of the odor made it through the door. After several minutes and two or three flushes, Dan staggered back inside. The color had leached from his face, but he stood a little straighter.

Jason gave him an evil grin. "Ready for breakfast?"

Dan's face twisted, turned a dull green, spun on his heels, and ran back the way he came.

"I would feel sorry for you," Jason yelled at his back, "but I seem to remember you serving me runny eggs the last time I was in your shoes."

The retching was louder this time.

†††

Miles Henderson scraped the last of the eggs from the plastic plate and shoved the fork into his mouth. The other students at the table had just begun their meal, but Miles learned early in the Navy to shovel it in fast. He finished his one and only hitch three years ago, but those lessons suffered a slow death.

Something they have in common with my dad, he thought as he chewed. That was long behind him, and if the cops hadn't connected the dots by now, they never would. The fact he joined the Navy two weeks after his father disappeared hung a big red *arrest me* sign around his neck, but small-town Texas constabulary being what it was, they were still trying to figure out how to spell his name.

Keeping his temper in check during his time in the Navy was a simple task after living with his daddy. He mastered early the required attitude of obsequious deference to his so-called "superiors." Mastered it well enough to reach the rank of Petty Officer, 3rd Class—his CO even offering him 2nd Class just for re-upping—but the first four were more than enough for Miles. Enough to sock away as much cash as he could, and earn his GI Bill benefits.

Three years at Lamar University, in that dank armpit of a city known as Beaumont, he had enough left over from the GI Bill stipend and his savings to pay for a Masters. A year from now he would join the class of 2014 and graduate with a degree in Poly-Sci, then slide into a graduate program in Public Administration. For the first time in his life, things were looking up. Volunteering at his local congressman's campaign headquarters earned him the connections he desired most, and there was already a position waiting for him when he graduated.

"Hey Miles, what's got you smilin' today?" Bill Oaks poked at Miles at every opportunity, always on the lookout for the man's temper, and for some unfathomable reason disappointed every time the bait was ignored.

"Nothing you would understand, *Billy*." Miles' grin broadened as the other man stiffened. Bill Oaks hated being called Billy. "Just contemplating world domination."

The others laughed, some at Miles—but a couple at Bill—and Miles gathered his trash and stood. "Sorry boys, I've got a fact-finding tour today at the Exxon plant," he winked. "Can't keep the congressman waiting, you know."

"You still volunteering for that asshole?" another boy asked.

"Yep, and for as long as it takes," Miles said. He walked a couple of steps, then turned and said, "I've got your US History paper ready for you, Billy, if you've got the cash." He smiled down at him, and the boy's face reddened. "Catch ya later."

He wouldn't. The fire at the refinery later that morning would see to that.

TWO

$\int$ ASON WOKE THURSDAY TO THE SOUND OF THE TELEVISION BLARING, Dan's face glued a foot or two away from the set. He was watching the morning news, of all things.

"What's up?" Jason sat up, rubbing the sleep from his eyes.

"Another plant explosion," Dan said without turning. He grabbed the remote and muted the sound.

"In Beaumont?" *Bad news always comes in threes*, Jason thought.

"Nah, that was yesterday morning at the Exxon refinery," he said, turning his face away from the pictures of devastation. "This was last night at a fertilizer plant in West, Texas. Pretty much flattened the whole town."

"Fertilizer?"

"Ammonium nitrate," Dan nodded. "Dumbasses in this state never learn. Fourteen dead, over a hundred injured, a school destroyed, and these morons will chalk it up to an unforeseen act of God," he finished by waving his hands in the air. "Can't go regulatin' bidness outta bidness," he said in a fair imitation of the governor.

Jason rubbed his head, then scrunched his eyes at his roommate, "Hey, that's not far from where you live, right?"

"'Bout ten miles," he said, already watching the news again. "Mom called this morning to let me know dad was ok."

"Your dad?"

"He was helping train EMT's in the area and responded to the call." He turned back to face Jason, bitter tears welling in the corners of his eyes. "Three of the trainees died trying to help." He lowered his eyes. "I *knew* those guys," he said, voice cracking.

"Shit, man," Jason said, lowering his voice.

"Yeah." Dan wiped his eyes and turned back to the screen. "Life's cheap in this state. Especially where *bidness* is concerned."

Jason lay back, one arm over his head. *Life turns on a dime, and there aren't any guarantees.* He wanted to tell Dan it didn't matter. Those people lived on in another universe, having made a different choice that day. He turned his head to watch his friend. *This is the wrong time though. Maybe later.*

"Tell me something, Jay," Dan stood and turned off the TV.

"What's that?"

"Are you ever gonna pull that ring out of your dresser and give it to Kat?" He stood over Jason, lips pursed and one eyebrow raised, the muscles on the side of his neck standing out. His arms hung limp at his sides, but there was a restrained tension in his stance, like a boxer preparing to enter the ring. Jason began to think there was a wrong answer possible.

"Why do you ask?"

Dan's shoulders slumped, the tension leaking away. "I dunno," he said, and shrugged. "Everything now is all about the choices we make, right?" He poked a finger at Jason's chest. "You need to shit or get off the pot."

"I'll be sure to use that exact phrase when I ask her," Jason said, a lopsided grin splitting his face.

Dan smiled for the first time that morning. "See that you do," he said, snorting. "Can I be there when you do that?"

"For the proposal, or me acting like an ass with Kat? 'Cause I'm pretty sure you've seen a lot of the latter already."

Dan laughed, reached down beside Jason's bed, and pulled pants and a shirt from the floor. He looked at them, shook his head, then tossed them at Jason's own. "Just get dressed so we can have breakfast before class."

Jason sat up, rolled the clothing into a bundle, and said, "Mind if I shower first?"

"Please do."

He stood and walked past Dan on his way to the bathroom, then turned back. "Dan... it's *always* been about the choices we make—here and all the way up and down the line, across every branch. We just didn't *know* about it before."

He turned and walked out of the room. "Tell that to my dad," Dan muttered behind him.

†††

The morning air held a distinct chill at just under fifty degrees, but it was the rain that made it miserable. Jason pulled the hood from his sweatshirt up over his head and mentally prepared for the soggy trek to class. A heavy coat was pointless, since the weatherman said it would clear off by noon, leaving blue skies and temperatures in the mid-eighties.

Welcome to Texas. If you don't like the weather here... wait a minute.

The rain wasn't bad, just relentless, like someone left the sprinkler running. He avoided the usual low areas on the sidewalks and streets, but couldn't keep his pants from getting soaked. *I'll have to put my shoes in the dryer, too, when I get back to the dorm.*

Jason hadn't been walking more than ten minutes when a wave of nausea hit him, his head spinning like he'd spent an hour on the Tilt-O-Whirl at the State Fair. His heart raced, threatening to burst from his chest, and he staggered to the nearest tree. An elephant sat on his chest and he leaned against the old trunk, doubling over and attempting to suck in lung-fulls of air.

This must be what a heart attack feels like, he thought, feeling for the carotid along the side of his neck.

He turned and braced his back against the tree, the few people walking in the rain never noticing his distress. When he shifted his weight to lean back, he fell *through* the tree. Or thought he did. Part of his mind knew he was still resting against the old oak, but he was also falling. He surrendered to the feeling for a moment to look below and saw... *nothing.* Blackness, deeper than anything imagined. An abyss as wide as it was deep, dropping forever and extending to infinity in all directions; swallowed by the black, and falling to a *darker* line below. *That's impossible,* he thought, the rational part of his mind grasping for a handhold. It was true, nonetheless. Around him a multitude of voices whispered in a sound approaching awe, but he could make out no words. Coherence was lost. It never existed.

Great, he thought as he fell. *I'm dying and apparently going to the wrong damn place.* Something passed him going in the opposite direction—a relative *up* to his down—and its presence was both familiar and alien. Off to one side, the smell of lilac drifted past, but it was gone as soon as it appeared. The darker line approached, now limned in a faint blue haze. Before Jason registered the distance, it leapt forward and engulfed him.

†††

"Damn, Jason," the voice beside him boomed, "you just got fracked with extreme prejudice, dude." A hard slap on the back, knocking the headset off into Jason's lap.

Jason blinked and squinted, his eyes now unaccustomed to the light. The large screen in front of him showed a battlefield—a game—where small groups of soldiers fought with impossibly powerful weapons. The game controller in his hands felt odd, and he placed it on the coffee table in front of the sofa. *His* sofa. He swiveled his head around *his* apartment, then turned his head to look at the young man next to him, his own game controller in his hand. Without even considering it, a name bubbled to the front of Jason's mind. *Ben.*

"You're Ben, right?"

"Dude, did you blow a fuse or something?"'

"Just feeling a little nauseated is all." Jason tried to stand, but his center of gravity was different. His body felt wrong—top-heavy, and his t-shirt was far too tight. He regained his balance, looked down, saw the cowboy boots on his feet and nearly passed out. He fell back to his seat with a heavy thud and rubbed his head. Outside his window, lightning flashed as today's mild sprinkling of rain turned angry, becoming a full-fledged Central Texas thunder-boomer.

"I think it's more than your stomach, man." Ben put his controller down, pulled the headset off and set it aside. "You're not lookin' too good. Color's all gone from your face." He reached for his cell. "Maybe we should call one of the trainers, or the doc?"

Trainers? "Oh shit. I'm a quarterback." The words leaked from him without thinking. Now he *was* nauseated.

"No, dude... you're *the* quarterback. NFL-bound, my friend!" Ben grinned, straight white teeth gleaming. "After next season, they'll be lining up to draft you, Jay." He poked himself in the chest. "And I'll be there watchin'."

He's not kidding, Jason thought. *This has got to be a dream.* He pinched his arm, twisting the skin as hard as he could.

"Ow!"

"The fuck did you do *that* for?" Ben asked, one eyebrow raised.

"Just checking." *Not a dream, then. The only question left is am I crazy, or...*

"You *killed* it in the Orange-White game, Jay. Mack is an idiot if you don't start next season."

"This isn't right..." Jason began, then noticed the large clock on the wall for the first time. "Shit! I've got to get to class."

Ben tilted his head and pursed his lips. "You don't have any classes this morning, dude."

"Yeah," Jason said, his mouth twisting as his brows beetled, "I've got computational..." But no, he didn't, and the knowledge hit him like a punch to the solar plexus. Another memory rising to the surface brought the news he was *not* a physics major, but a goddamn *kinesiology* major. "At least it's not history," he mumbled.

"What?"

"Nothing." *If this isn't a dream, then something impossible just happened.* The set of explanations was finite, even if the multiverse was not. And that's when he knew. *Somehow I've crossed a threshold. The branching must have occurred pretty early in my life to change things this much. So early, in fact, that...*

"Where's my phone?" He stirred the detritus on the coffee table with frantic hands, shoving most of it to the floor.

"Calm down, dude. I think I saw it on the kitchen counter, charging."

Jason scrambled away from the sofa, bumping his leg on the table, and limped to the kitchen. The smartphone was definitely not the simple flip-phone he always carried, but his fingers flew over it using muscle memory as he searched for the number in the contact list.

"She's not in here."

"Who?"

His hands shaking, he tapped out the number from memory—*old* memory. The ringing from the other end told him the number was at least in service.

"Hello?"

"Kat... uh Kathy Nichols?"

"Yes, " she hesitated, "this is Kathy." A second or two passed as she probably checked the number of the person calling her. "Who is this?"

"Jason... uh, Callahan," he said, feeling like he was twelve years old again. Ben was trying to get his attention, but Jason waved him off and showed him his back.

"Oh, Jason," she said as if she didn't recognize the name. "Um... how did you get my number?"

How did *I get her number? Time to tap dance.*

"I was wondering if you would like to have lunch today," he said. *Lame, but it'll do.*

She was silent for a few seconds, as if considering just how to answer a date request from a near-stranger.

"Aren't you in Austin?"

"Yeah, so?"

"Well, unless you have a private jet and a pilot's license, we might have to make it for later in the week." She paused for effect, then said, "I went to Northwestern."

His eyes opened wide. "The one in Illinois?"

She sighed like a steam press, "Is there another?" He had a clear picture of the look on her face, tapping her foot while talking to an idiot football player.

Considering all the options, there being but one, Jason did the only thing left to him.

"I'm sorry for bothering you. I'll let you go." *Or I could tell you we were in love in another universe. That would go over like a lead—*

"Are you okay?" The concern in her voice was real. He heard it enough over the years to recognize it.

"Yeah, Kat. I'm fine." *No, I'm not.*

"It's funny. Only my dad calls me Kat."

"Sorry."

"No, it's okay. Somehow it doesn't sound silly the way you say it." She was silent then, and just when it stretched to awkward, she said, "Are you *sure* you're okay?"

Still looking out for me, even if I'm not her boyfriend. It's what he fell in love with when they were kids. *When did I mess all that up?* It had to have been soon after they first met. His memory of that day was still clear, but now he saw it through a haze of someone else's. It was like watching a movie through *another* movie projected on gauze. A whole lifetime of memories that didn't include her.

"Again, sorry to bother you." He took a shuddering breath, and before she could say anything else, he said, "Bye," and hung up.

He set the phone back on the counter like he was putting a baby to bed, and turned back to his roommate. Ben watched him with pursed lips and one raised brow—just like Dan would.

"What the hell was that?" he asked, head tilted.

"Nothing," Jason said, and sat with a heavy thud, shoulders slumping under an impossible weight. "Not anymore, at least." Outside, the rain beat against his windows with renewed energy, distorting reality with an ocean of water every second, falling across every universe at once.

†††

"He's been like this for three days, ma'am," Ben whispered into his phone in the living room while Jason lay on his bed. "Maybe you should come see him or something."

He no longer cared what was being said about him, but it was difficult to block it out.

"No, ma'am, I don't know what caused it, but he called someone named Kathy when it started. He's been a basket case ever since." The person—his mom, most likely—spoke, though too garbled to understand. "No. I thought maybe *you* knew who she was."

She *wouldn't* know, of course. Kat and his mom never met in this universe. And this *was* another universe—he was sure of that, now. Throughout the first day of his exile, he waited for the process to reverse itself, hoping whatever cosmic event sent him here brought him home as well. After that first day he worried it might be permanent. Today he knew. Even if it were not, there was no guarantee the next shift would take him to his original reality.

He was stuck here.

While he retained his own memories, those of *this* Jason were now fully accessible—if not fully incorporated. He could act like this Jason, but could never *be* him. Could never be satisfied with this life knowing what he lost from the last. On that first day, he thought about starting over in school with physics as a major. He knew he could pass the department's entrance exam, but he would only have two years left on his athletic scholarship to catch up. After that, he would make do with student loans. Assuming the coaches would allow it.

"Yes, ma'am. I'll keep an eye on him until you get here." Ben set the phone down and walked into Jason's room. "Your mom's coming for a visit in a few days, Jay."

"I know... I heard," he said without turning his head, or even opening his eyes. "I told you, Ben, I'm fine."

"No, you're *not*, Jason. Moping around over some girl is one thing, but you've completely shut down, dude. I don't think you've eaten in two days."

"Not hungry."

"Why don't you just *talk* about it? If not to me, then, you know... *someone*." He threw his hands in the air, and Jason felt a wave of sympathy for his friend. *I would probably feel the same way if he were acting like me.*

"Not in a talkin' mood, either, Ben," he said, still not moving. But he did need to talk to someone, understanding that for the first time. He put his hands behind his head, opening his eyes to stare at the ceiling. This wasn't his life, and it never would be. He had to get *his* life back, even if he had to start over and make it happen here. There was a lot to do—visiting his guidance counselor Monday morning was one— but one thing was sure... when his mom arrived, he wouldn't be here.

†††

"All of it?" The bank teller looked at him with sympathy. This was clearly a young man who did not know how the world worked.

"Did I stutter?" Jason said, tapping his fingers on the little ledge in front of the window. "Yes... all of it."

"Aren't you sure you don't want to leave most of it in savings?"

"Nope," he smiled, "I've handled money before. I think I know how it works." In truth, Jason understood the young man's plight. There was a hefty sum sitting in that account, compliments of an enthusiastic alumnus, and it was the teller's job to keep it tucked safely away in the bank's vault. Once that little tidbit of a memory bubbled to the surface, his path became clearer than ever.

The teller sighed, knowing the battle was lost. "How would you like that?"

"A thousand in twenties and fifties, and the rest in a cashier's check will be fine."

"Very good, sir," the little man said, and then disappeared into the back.

Well, that was easier than I thought it would be, he mused. No, the *hard* part was when he told coach he was giving up his scholarship and leaving school. The old man did everything he could to talk Jason into staying, practically promising him he would start, but his mind was made up. There was nothing keeping him here, and starting over at the same school was a depressing thought. No, he had to transfer... find another school where no one knew him.

The teller appeared again at the window and counted out the cash, then slid it under the glass through the little opening.

"There you go, sir. One thousand dollars. Twenty-five in twenties, and ten fifties." He slid another slip of paper through, "And your cashier's check." He looked up, and in his eyes was something close to envy. "Will that be all, sir?"

"That should do it," Jason said, pocketing the cash, then carefully folding the check and placing it in his wallet.

"Thank you for your business," the teller said, smiling.

"Thanks," Jason said, and turned to leave.

Outside the bank, he stopped to pull his sunglasses down from the top of his head. The sun was shining with a vengeance after the week of unrelenting rain, and the streets and ditches were already dry. The on-ramp to I35 was close enough to see from the bank's parking lot, and he turned his gaze north. *With luck, I'll make it to Oklahoma before I have to stop for the night*, he thought as he walked to his car. Even then, it was a two day trip.

He opened the long door to the Dodge Challenger, looked around one last time, and climbed into the car.

"Two, three days max, and we'll see if there's anything left in the tank for my life."

Firing up the engine made him smile, and he threw the shifter into drive and pressed the accelerator. The car sprang toward the highway, as eager to hit the road as he. The classics radio station powered out "Jessica" by the Allman Brothers, and Jason turned it up as loud as he could stand. Ten miles later his smile melted, the DJ deciding to reach back even farther to spin up Eddy Arnold's "Black Cloud."

Black cloud hanging over my head
Down to my last buck
With that old black cloud hanging over my head
There ain't no such thing as good luck.

It wasn't a cloud hanging over Jason's head, but a stone, rough and massive, poised to crush his soul the longer he stayed. The light faded while he drove north, the sun now low enough to blind him from the left, and he shoved the visor over to that side with an angry slap. "Fuckin' *hate* country music," he mumbled as he snapped off the radio.

†††

Northwestern University wasn't what he expected, the campus looking more like a small town than what he left in Austin. Jason certainly wasn't what *Kat* expected.

"What are you *doing* here?" she said, more amused than worried or angry.

"Transferring," he said, still unsure how she was taking his surprise presence. The crazy part was he hadn't been looking for her when they met. He was just going into the administration building to apply for the summer, and she was on her way out and ran straight into him while she was texting.

"Here?"

"Do you see another university nearby?"

She laughed, a carillon's lower octave. "I guess I deserved that." Kat smiled at him the way she always did when trying to understand something stupid he had done. "I thought you were a big football star at UT?"

"I wouldn't say *star*—"

"But what about your scholarship?"

"Gave it back," he shrugged. "Kinesiology really isn't my thing."

"You always were a little smarter than you let on." She smiled again, brushing her hair over her left ear.

"Then you *do* remember me," he said, grinning. And just like that, it felt right. Standing there, bantering like they always did, the familiarity of the moment comforted him like nothing else had since his nightmare began. *Everything's gonna be okay*, he thought. He would court her all over again, only this time without all the false starts while he figured her out. The sad thing was that the Jason he inhabited had no memories of her at all, invisible to him throughout their seven years of school together. She was a hole in space, darker and less substantial than the one he fell through getting here.

"Hey," he said, "after I get out of here, would you like—"

Her phone rang, and she held up a finger to shush him as she answered it. "Hey, babe," she said, brightening. "Yeah, I'm just catching up at the admin building with an old friend." Jason did his best to keep the hurt from his face, but he couldn't do anything about his eyes. She saw it at once. "Hey, I've got to go, but I'll see you at noon for lunch." *Don't say it, don't...* "Love you too, baby." She hung up, then smiled at him with a look that drew hot blood to his cheeks. *Pity*.

"I'm sorry," she said. "I really have to run, but if you want to join my boyfriend and me for lunch, I'd like to catch up." *That look again.* "Is that okay?"

He smiled back as best as he could, "I don't know how long this will take." He tore a corner from a page in the catalog he held, and quickly scribbled his number. "Text me where you're going, and if I get out in time, I'll meet up with you."

She took it. "Um... okay. Guess I'll see you later." *No you won't. Not today, at least.*

"Yeah, catch you later Kat." He turned away and walked through the doors into the administration building without looking back.

Boyfriend, he thought as he walked the long hallway, *not fiancé. She took the number, and if she texts, it means she's interested.* Better yet, if she texted back, she was giving him her number without him ever asking for it.

Sooner or later, *every* boyfriend screwed up. Like it was a law of nature or something. He'd done it enough times to know exactly how she'd react, but never bad enough for them to break up. Part of him knew this was nothing less than manipulation, but he didn't care. When the inevitable happened, he would be there for her. It wouldn't be easy, but he would get her back. He had to.

†††

Luck smiled on Jason just that once, Summer I registration opening the week he arrived, so he could sign up for two courses. The nice lady at the physics department offices informed him that, while his kinesiology courses were not accepted as creditable classes in their program, he was welcome to take the placement exams in September to earn credit for his first four physics core courses. She also told him, in confidence, that a few professors allowed an informal "credit by exam" where the student only had to pass their final exam. In this way he could sign up for several courses that had time conflicts, allowing him to take up to twenty-four credit hours while only attending eighteen. By the end of his first full year, he would be about where he left off in his former life. At least all the basics he had already taken transferred without difficulty.

Kat never did text him after their first meeting. That was okay, as he was too busy that summer to notice. She did call to invite him to lunch when she got back to school in the fall, having heard the stories around town while she was home on break.

"Why haven't you told your parents you're here?" She sat at the table, her back straight, picking at her salad with a dainty silver fork while she spoke. She had suggested a less expensive location, but Jason knew how she loved places like this one. The linens on the table were white and clean, matching the napkin in her lap, and the light through the windows cast a bright, yet warm glow over both the dinnerware and her face. Kat's eyes shined, reflecting that light as she spoke, and Jason's face tightened as he smiled for the first time in weeks.

"I don't know," he shrugged. "Just didn't want to talk to them about it, I guess." As a lie, it was close enough to the truth he didn't feel bad for deceiving her. Other than Kat, he couldn't face anyone in this reality. The large window they sat beside offered a panoramic view of the street, and he watched people walking along the sidewalks going about their daily lives. All clueless to the greater universe around them.

I wish I was still one of them, he thought, looking into Kat's eyes.

"A pretty big jump from football to physics, don't you think?" she said, dropping her gaze to her plate.

"Don't think I can handle it?" He expected this reaction, but his other Kat would have never voiced it.

She stopped pushing her salad around the plate and looked up. "Someone as dedicated to sports as you were rarely has time for another subject," she said. "Especially something as time-consuming as quantum physics."

"Quantum gravity, actually."

"Specializing already?" she smiled.

"Well... the Many Worlds Interpretation is a special case arising from quantum gravity research. *That's* my area of specialization," he said, grinning back.

"I see," she said, placing her fork on the linen beside the plate with considered motion. She laced her fingers in front of her, then rested her chin on them. Jason nearly laughed at her "tell me more of your silly plans" posture. He saw this many times while they were dating.

"I've got a question for you," he said, changing the subject. "Why aren't we having lunch with your boyfriend?"

"Oh... well," she sat back, "let's just say he didn't handle the separation during the summer very well, and leave it at that."

"Ah," he said, nodding. "Got it." *Boyfriends* always *screw up*, he thought, with no small degree of satisfaction. What he must *not* do, however, is smile about it. He scooped a healthy forkful of his meal, and shoveled it into his mouth before that particular orifice got him into trouble.

"Speaking of not handling things well," she began, then hesitated. "Oh hell, I'll just say it. Your dad went ballistic at work about you leaving UT."

She would know. His dad worked for hers.

He choked the food down, then wiped his mouth with a napkin. "Nothing I can do about that," he said.

"You could talk—"

"No I can't," he said, much harsher than he intended.

"But—"

"Just drop it, okay?"

She stopped and stared at him for a few seconds, then shrugged her shoulders. "Have it your way." She drew her mouth into a tight line. "I guess I can relate to not being able to talk to one's parents," she said, her voice tight.

That surprised him. Her family was, though not wealthy in the classical sense, at least comfortable. In his old universe they always had money for whatever she needed, and spent a lot of time supporting her various school activities. Compared to *his* parents, they were damn near perfect. Sure, they were strict, but this was the first time he'd heard of any discontent in the Nichols household. When he first crossed over, he believed that all the changes to each universe were strictly local; ripples on a pond, flattening as they spread from the central point of change. *Is it possible a single person could have so much effect on the people peripheral to them?* He hoped not.

He opened his mouth to say something, but a noise outside their window stopped him. The sound registered as overtaxed brakes locking four tires to the pavement, rubber squealing as the heavy truck did its best to stop. But there was no stopping this juggernaut, and before Jason's brain processed the sound as a danger signal, the truck slammed into and through the plate glass beside their table. The large sheet of glass and its frame collapsed inward, and the truck pushed through as if it weren't even there, scattering the other patrons and pulling down a rain of ceiling tile. Jason was just outside the area of impact, tossed aside like a rag doll, but Kat took the full force of the beast head-on.

Seconds passed before Jason gathered enough of his wits to call out to Kat. Pieces of the building were still falling, and the truck's horn blaring a single pitch—a child screaming from night terrors. He looked where their table had been, but saw no sign of Kat, and he pulled pieces of ceiling tile and glass shards from the floor in a desperate search.

Hands sliced and bloodied, he found her near the back of the room under what was left of their table. There was no obvious sign of injury, but a single look at her glassy stare and he knew. Jason knelt beside her, then crumbled to the floor like the room around them. He sat and lifted her head into his lap, stroking her hair as he cried. The ripples of causality grew, becoming vast waves crashing against a ruined and crumbling shore. Everything they touched shattered and fell, etching the shores of time and creating new boundaries with the sea of realities. Jason felt a familiar pull, and bent to kiss his love one last time, then welcomed the engulfing darkness as he fell into the yawning abyss.

†††

"Are you with us, Mr. Callahan?"

Jason opened his eyes. The other students in the class were smiling or laughing into their notes. He raised his chin to meet the gaze of the professor standing in front of his desk. "Ma'am?"

"The question was, I believe, what effect does high-stakes standardized testing have on the educational environment."

"Depends on who you listen to," he said, stalling. The last time he shifted, the information held in the new Jason's brain took days to bubble to the surface. This time, used to the experience, he accessed the memories much quicker. "Diana Ravtich, who I happen to agree with, thinks the whole thing is a palliative at best, and distracting from the core goal of education at worst." He could still smell the truck's leaking gasoline and the dust from the drywall. Could still see Kat's face in death. He closed his eyes again and concentrated on the memories of *this* Jason.

"Mr. Callahan is correct," the woman said. "At least in his interpretation of Ms. Ravitch's opinion." She leaned over and tapped once on his desk. "And for the record... I agree with her as well," she said, then her face grew stern. "But if you're going to teach in *public* school, Mr. Callahan, I suggest you keep those opinions to yourself." She walked back to her desk near the whiteboard, and lifted a sheaf of papers. "Speaking of tests," she said, followed by a chorus of groans from the class. "Here are the results from the last exam. We will go over these in detail in the next class, *including* statistical analysis of the answer selections." Another groan.

Like the rest of the students, Jason couldn't get out of there fast enough. He glanced at the "A" at the top of his test paper before shoving it into his pack and scrambling out of the desk. The others, each making a mad dash for the door, bunched at the opening and made it nearly impossible to squeeze out. Squeeze they did, though, like all college students, able to navigate the obstacle course of higher education with aplomb.

Out in the hallway, Jason threw his pack to the floor and fished inside the front pocket of his jeans for his phone. A frantic search through the contacts list, and he couldn't find her name anywhere. Dialing from memory, hoping against hope it was still the same, he leaned against the wall and listened to the ringing on the other end.

"Hello?" Kat answered.

"Oh, thank *God*," he said, sliding to the floor and ending the call with a flick of his thumb. He pulled his knees in tight, hugging himself, and rocked against the wall as quiet sobs racked his body.

THREE

The cabin, dark and silent, chilled in the late fall air. Out-side, wind cut and slashed icy blades between shafts of barren old growth. Inside, at a small table near the rough stone hearth holding the dying embers of a warm fire, Jason took a quick, stuttering breath and his back spasmed, arching like he had been kicked in the spine. He stretched his arms wide, hands flexed and tensed, and dropped the snub-nosed revolver. It tumbled with a clatter to the wooden floor, spun for a few turns, then lay still. He watched it with calm detachment, rubbed the small circular dent the muzzle left at his temple, then stood on shaking legs and looked around the interior of the cabin. Jason knew he should recognize this place, but the memory of where he was or how he got there hadn't yet surfaced. He looked at the gun again, but like the new backpack in the corner, it registered as no one more than invento-ry—one more piece of clutter to add to the puzzle of a new world.

This was his tenth trip down the rabbit hole, as far as he knew, and his immediate concern was how much farther from home this trip took him. He shivered and placed a shaking hand on the chair's back for sup-port, then walked the short distance to the heavy oak door separating this warm haven from the ravening wind outside. His boots pounded a dull tattoo as he walked, and he looked down at the detailed stitching on top of what appeared to be alligator skin. He curled his lip. *Not again*, he thought, rolling his eyes skyward. He took another deep breath, held it, and reached for the handle, pulling the door inward on creaking hing-es. The lashing air, chill and damp, chased the remaining warmth in the room up the chimney, leaving him shivering in the doorway.

Jason surveyed the landscape beyond the cabin. Where the clearing in front of the porch ended abruptly thirty yards out at a stand of trees, a gravel road cut neatly through and away. The tall trees, stolid sentries around a prison yard, they groaned and swayed in the wind, speaking words only they understood. To Jason their meaning was clear—*go away, you don't belong here.*

He stepped over the threshold to the wooden front porch, and crossed his arms to ward the wind, a thick denim shirt his only proof against the chill. Before he crossed there had been a hint of Fall in the air, but nothing like *this*.

Where the hell am I this time?

†††

Joan popped the top on another beer, held the frigid can to her forehead for a couple of seconds, then took a long, sweet pull. The liquid ran an icy trail down her throat that radiated outward, drawing the heat of her body to her core. She sighed and shivered despite the warm weather. Lean, tanned, and still debutante-pretty at forty-one, she sat on an old fold-up lounge chair at the edge of the wood deck of her trailer, dressed for the sun in her favorite yellow bikini. She liked the way the bright solid color contrasted with her dark hair and the light mocha color of her skin she worked so hard to maintain. She especially liked the way the men who passed her by leered, the hunger clear in their eyes. Joan leaned back with beer in hand, crossed her legs, dropped the large-rimmed dark sunglasses onto her nose, and sneered at the world around her. Those wine-colored lenses hid the steel edge of her eyes; battered armor covering a life gone sour.

The one-time homecoming queen, girlfriend of the star running back, and salutatorian of her class with scholarship in hand, reveled in her disgust at the life she lived. Joan lost it all the day she gave herself up to that star, even as he abandoned his dreams of college to join the Marines and accept the role of father and provider. Dale promised her a house with a yard and a fence. Dale promised her a lot of things, but in the end all he gave her was a son she never saw anymore, a lot of lonely days, and this double-wide. Her days weren't *always* lonely, but what Dale didn't know wouldn't hurt him. Or her.

A bead of sweat rolled a lazy tour down her spine, stopping at the small of her back for a single heartbeat before leaping to its demise on the deck below. She grinned and shook her head. "Gotta love Southeast Texas in December. At least the humidity's bearable now," she said to the can in her hand.

Joan swirled her beer while she watched the few neighbors working in the heat of the trailer park, and noticed the can was light. She finished it in one long gulp, and then tossed the empty over the side of the deck in the general direction of the trashcan. The soft thud as it hit the ground told her she missed again. As she fished another out of the ice chest at the foot of the lounger, her cell phone on the plastic table at her side buzzed like a wasp trapped under a teacup. She frowned and looked down at the instrument of her distraction. Not only did she not recognize the number, but she had never seen that area code before.

"Telemarketer, or bill collector. Either way," she offered a thin smile to the phone, "fuck you." She popped the top on the next future empty. After a minute of blessed silence, the phone jittered again, just once, to indicate a voicemail message was waiting.

"That's new. Those guys don't bother leaving messages anymore." She was just about to delete it and turn the phone off when it vibrated again. She looked at the offending little brick of plastic and glass in her hand. *It's the same goddamn number.* "Holy hell, do these guys ever quit?" she grumbled. Joan debated for a second about letting it go to voicemail a second time, then stabbed at the "answer" button on the phone.

"*What*," she snapped.

"Mom?"

Joan's eyes grew wide as she drew in a quick shuddering breath and dropped her beer. There was no mistaking that voice, even if she hadn't heard it in three years. Tears threatened to cloud her vision, and she sat up and pulled off her sunglasses with trembling fingers.

"Jason? Is it really you?" Her voice quivered in spite of her best efforts.

"Yeah, it's me. How long has it been?"

That's an odd question, she thought. "Three years. And where the hell have you been, anyway?" Her voice raised in pitch as she shook her head and waved her free hand. "Never mind," she said. "Where the hell are you now?"

"Um, the Rocky Mountains, I think. Somewhere Northwest of Denver."

"The hell you say!"

"No, really. I'm stuck up here in the cold, frozen wilderness." Jason chuckled on the other end. "At least there hasn't been much snow yet, though the weatherman says a big blast is coming soon."

"Stuck? What do you mean 'stuck'?" She couldn't believe she was having this conversation right now. *Three years between phone calls, and he's talking about the weather?*

"Mom, I'd like to come home."

"Then come home, already. Ain't no one stopping you."

"Well, that's the problem. I don't have enough money to get there." There was a long pause. "I don't suppose you could send me a bit for bus fare or something, could you?"

Joan couldn't help it, and she laughed out loud at the sheer stupidity of the boy. "Son, I love you, but there ain't no way your daddy's gonna send you a dime after what you did."

There was a brief silence. "Oh hell. What did I do?"

Had the kid gone off his nut, or something? "Boy, if you think tossing your football scholarship and leaving UT was no big deal, you should have seen your daddy's reaction." That was a bad time, and getting only one other phone call over the next five years didn't help matters. In fact that last call set Dale off again—a minor rampage that lasted a whole week. "To tell you the truth, son, I'm glad he's at work right now, just so I don't have to listen to him go on about it again."

She heard him sigh on the other end. "Huh," he muttered to himself, "what are the odds?" Then to her, "Well, I guess I could try hitchin' it or something."

"The hell you will! There's too many nuts out there on the roads these days." She drummed her fingers on the table for a few seconds, then sighed. *You know you have to,* she told herself. "All right. I've got a bit of money stashed away for a rainy day. I'll wire you some, but only if you promise not to come knockin' on the door until I have a chance to talk to your daddy."

"Sure. No problem." She heard Jason fumbling with something, then a rustling of paper. "Hey, did you get a job or something?"

"Something like that, yeah." In fact, Walter, a regular customer, would pull into the driveway soon.

"Huh. That's cool, I guess. You got a pencil and paper ready for the address?"

"Hang on. I've got to go dig one up from the junk drawer." As she stood, she stumbled as her toe caught on a warped deck board, then stopped and looked around the trailer park to glare at no one in particular. Satisfied none cared what she was doing, she pulled the handle of the tattered screen door and stepped into her castle.

†††

Football? Again?

Even growing up in Texas, he was never interested in playing football, though he was built for it. The coaches in middle school bugged him every day to join, but his life goals didn't involve racking up a string of concussions. His real interest was *science*. Every former football stars in town ended up working at the Market Basket, or the car dealership, or Walmart. He was tired of living in a trailer. At the age of six he read his first Fantastic Four comic and fell in love with Reed Richards as a role model. The scientist who could solve any scientific puzzle, or create any technology. It was only when he studied science in earnest he realized such a super-scientist was ludicrous, but it didn't matter anymore—the bug bit him hard, and he wanted to know more.

Now, once again, he was a dropout with a football scholarship. Worse, he was wearing cowboy boots. *Again. If God is real, he's got a wicked sense of humor. Not to mention a nasty bully streak.*

Jason waited in the lobby of a dying and decomposing motel. It was backed up against a decaying convenience store, sheltering it from nothing more than sunlight. The store had once been a member of a chain he and his friends referred to as a "Sack Some Shit." The motel's desk clerk let him use the phone, then wait in one of the worn plastic chairs for his mother to wire him the money. He spent his last five dollars earlier at the store on something resembling a sandwich he was sure was just cardboard and cheese. This Jason carried little cash, and nothing in the way of a credit card. He wasn't sure what the man was doing up in the mountains with no provisions or money to buy them, but the handgun he left on the floor was a strong clue. In the years since his first trip, he never contemplated what this Jason had, and he wondered how bad it must have been to push this one over the edge.

"Probably the boots," he muttered.

"What was that?" The clerk peeked over the desk at Jason.

"Nothing," he said. "Just talking to myself."

The clerk made a face, then lowered into his chair, keeping one wary eye on the crazy man in his lobby.

People looked at him like that a lot over the years. Every time he shifted he spent precious days learning about the world he was dumped into, and with his new host's memories drifting into his head like so much fog, he spent a lot of time looking stupid to the people who knew him. He didn't remember it happening before he turned eighteen, so he was reasonably sure his childhood was his own. *At least I hope so,* he thought. There were so many happy memories from those days. In none of the realities he had visited did he find parents as happy as his own.

Jason turned to the window at his back. Daylight was already leaking away, a slow leaching of color from the landscape. He shivered, though he knew the growing cold he felt was mostly psychological. The street in front of the motel saw little traffic, but here and there a few people walked to and fro with purpose, crossing paths in a loosely choreographed dance. Most wore light clothing, having grown used to the weather. The wind outside was picking up, and the cold would follow. He wondered how long before the snow came to Denver, and did the residents still wear shorts when it did.

He checked his watch again as he shivered at the thought, and hoped the money would arrive before the next bus left the station.

†††

Three hours later, after shooing Walter out the door, then driving to the Western Union office to send what cash she could spare, Joan pulled onto the weed infested patch of gravel that served as the trailer's driveway. Dale's truck was already there.

Shit, she thought, her mouth drawstring tight. *That man is completely unreliable.* Every other day he finished work early, he made his way to Granny's Ice House for a few beers before coming home. But not today. *Of course not today,* she thought. *Why would I think I could catch a break? Ever.*

Joan was sure on some level Dale knew how she spent her days while he was at work, but he never came right out and accused her. No, visible signs were repressed anger and depression; and though he never became violent, the arguments over every other topic were epic by anyone's standards. As soon as she walked through the door she knew his ire had been building, sitting in his beer-stained La-Z-Boy, feet propped up, with a Bud in his hand and the evening news on the TV.

He looked up at her and his dark scowl brightened, pretending to just notice her. She wasn't fooled. "Where ya been?" he asked, all sweetness and light, the smile never reaching his eyes.

"Out." Two could play the passive-aggressive game.

He grinned again and took another sip of his beer. "I just wonder because I noticed your stash was a bit light."

Crap. The bastard knows where I keep it. She knew at once there was just one way to short-circuit the major fight that was brewing inside that trailer, and that was to tell him the truth for once.

"I got a call from Jason today." No preamble, no sugarcoating. *Just rub his nose in it and wait to see how he reacts.*

"I figured as much." He raised an eyebrow at what she had to know was a dumbfounded look on her face. "Boss told me some kid claiming to be my son called while I was out on the job site." He considered his beer for a second, then looked up at her, lips pursed. "So how much did you send him?"

"Enough for bus fare. Maybe enough left over for a meal or two."

His eyes narrowed, "So about one day's roll in the hay." He swirled his can a couple of times, then downed the last warm dregs.

"Dale—"

"Shut up." As soft as a goodnight kiss, but it stung like a slap in the face. "I ain't talkin' about it." He took a long shuddering breath. "So the boy's finally coming home, huh?"

"Two days. He's in Colorado right now."

"That so? I wonder what he was doing up there?" He rubbed the graying stubble on his chin, then tossed the empty beer can with more precision than she. The can cleared the rim of the little Dallas Cowboys trashcan by the TV and rattled into the bottom. "I guess we'll find out when he gets here."

Dale stood up and looked into Joan's eyes. He wasn't a big man by any means, but his close-cropped dark hair, and his overweight physique hiding thick slabs of muscle was intimidating in the way only former marines can be. Especially those marines kicked out for decking an officer. *Big Chicken Dinner, he called it. Wore the damn thing as a badge, for Christ's sake.*

"How about we see if we can get supper on the table before the game starts." His eyes narrowed to mere slits, and he reached up to pat her gently on the cheek. "Do you think you can do that for me, babe?"

Joan returned his gaze for a second, then lowered her eyes. "Sure. I think there's meatloaf in the fridge I can warm up." She walked away from him then, hoping he wouldn't think of anything to add. She would keep her distance the rest of the night, and with luck he would be a little better in the morning.

✝✝✝

Twenty miles from downtown Alvin, Miles Henderson hunched over the counter in an otherwise empty diner eating a bowl of soup. The process, mechanical and efficient, offered only two sounds—*scrape... slurp.* The big stainless steel dishwasher in the kitchen shifted to rinse, and Miles' eyes darted to the open door for a second, his spoon paused midway. *Scrape... slurp. Scrape... slurp.* The motions both metronomic and hypnotic banished all thought from his head, keeping the voices at bay for a few blissful moments.

Miles checked his watch. *Have to get on the road soon,* he thought. That was the last clear thought this Miles would have as his eyes rolled to the back of his head, his throat constricting against a scream. Every muscle in his body tensed, turning him to stone, and what remained of his mind flew from him in infinite directions. He dropped the spoon nearing his mouth and lurched back in his seat, gasping a deep, rasping breath. The waitress behind the counter and the small dark-haired boy she appeared to be helping with his home-work turned toward him. *This* Miles, now conscious of the attention, closed his eyes, forced his muscles to relax, and settled back to eating his soup as if nothing happened.

Miles Henderson smoldered inside his new body as he hunched over the counter, protecting his bowl from predators. *I remember this place.* He turned his head this way and that, looking the diner over. *I've actually done it!* Knowing a thing was possible and doing it were two very different things, but for the second time in his life he felt the thrill of controlling his fate. *It's not enough to amass wealth and power—you have to take control of the* levers.

He reached into the pocket of his worn pea coat, feeling for the car keys he knew would be there. He looked across the bar to the mirror on the wall, and with a feral, toothy grin, he admired the shock of black hair on his head. *Not a trace of gray!* It was like watching an old recording of himself.

He took another spoonful, *scrape... slurp. Time to get to it*, he thought. *It has to be here, and it has to be now.* The window was closing even as he sat. If he wasn't on his way to Maryland in three days, everything would change, and there was no way to tell what effect that would have on his future. This was the closest he would pass to his target in any of the timelines known to him; his one shot to clean up the mess he had created upstream. *Maybe one day I'll be able to hire someone to do this type of work for me.* For now he was alone.

Miles turned to the waitress to catch her eye. Blond, young, and pretty, she still carried that look of a short, hard life. On any other night he would have attempted to bed her, but he was pressed for time. "Sweetie," he said, waving her over and stretching his mouth into a wide smile. "Can I get my check now?" She smiled back, said a few hushed words to the boy, and walked over as she pulled the grease-stained check from the front pocket of her apron and placed it on the counter beside the empty bowl.

"That'll be six-fifty."

Miles took out his wallet, counted out eight ones, and placed them on the counter. She reached for the cash, but Miles held the bills firmly in place, his eyes lingering on her grimy name tag. "You got an Alvin phone book behind that counter, Kathy? I need to look up an old friend."

FOUR

J ASON RUBBED HIS EYES, SAT UP, AND SCANNED THE WORLD OUTSIDE
his window. It was three in the morning when the bus passed
the 610 Loop, and Jason got his first glimpse of the nighttime Houston
skyline in over five years. Something about those lights—not to mention
the damn downtown Ferris wheel—always cheered him, and a shiver of
new-found energy crawled up his spine. The bus had at last caught up to
the published schedule, and was in danger of arriving on time.

Deep into the night, sleep had fought for control of his body, but
Jason fought back. Sleep on the road was dangerous for him. He never
knew where or how he would wake. *The last two happened while I was
asleep,* Jason thought as he rubbed the stubble on his cheek. *There* must
*be a connection. Maybe the unconscious mind loses its grip on the physical
world, or the pull from another grows too strong. Maybe...*

Try as he might, he had never found a pattern to the transitions,
much less how or what triggered them. *Maybe I'm just a freak, doomed
to suffer one transition after another until I die.* The one comfort was they
left him in much the same condition as the reality he departed, though
the knowledge he might never return to his original reality was a weight
around his shoulders. While most details of his life—family, friends,
places—remained the same from reality to reality, each new stop brought
subtle differences that reminded him this was not *his* home. Each high-
lighted a wrongness in his presence that compelled distance—the result
was a complete withdrawal from the places and people he loved most.

Early on he felt he was losing his grip on sanity, but he couldn't overcome his fear of discovery enough to consult a doctor. He never spoke of these thoughts to his even closest friends, the danger of discovery was too great. After one transition he woke in a psychiatric ward, held by court order with little hope for release. It was an experience he did not want to repeat, and was a sign his doppelgangers did not all have the same ability to adjust to their new reality.

There were also the dreams.

Jason now believed dreams were windows on other realities, but lately his dreams had taken a stranger turn. He no longer saw glimpses of another Jason's life, only barren landscapes, chill winds, and a face shrouded in darkness. And always a feeling of being watched. Each of these dreams pressed against him like cold earth covering a moldy grave, and each time he woke sweating, never spending more than a few minutes asleep and in that space between worlds.

This transition had been worse than the others, and the memories that flooded him when he awoke were disturbing and jumbled. More than that, they were directly related to the dreams he had been having. There were scenes of thousands dying in flames, large black crows feasting on decomposing corpses strewn about a desolate landscape, the sky a dark gray canopy. The air was filled with thick, oily smoke, muffling screams of pain and anguish.

Then there was the smell. A sickening, sweet mixture of charred flesh and decay.

The driver navigated the bus through the one way streets of downtown Houston, making its way to Main Street, and Jason gathered up his meager belongings. The Jason of this reality carried a small backpack filled with the usual overnight needs—toiletries, extra-strength aspirin, and two dog-eared paperback books—but few clothes, little cash, and no cell phone. He stood in the aisle, ready to exit the bus as soon as it rolled into the station, and the driver gave him a testy look. His mom called it "the stink-eye."

"Have a seat over there until I come to a complete stop." He nodded to the jump seat to the front by the steps, then pointed at the sign overhead that read "Please stay out of the aisles while the bus is in motion."

"Sure," Jason said. He pulled the pack off his shoulder, folded the seat down, and half sat, half stood in the entry well. There were few people left on the bus for this last leg of its run, so even with others gathering up their belongings, it was as quiet as a library behind the front two rows. The only illumination came from the few overhead lights the passengers were using to see what they were doing, each one creating a small pool of light that fell over one or two seats. It looked to Jason like a desert spotted here and there with wan campfires.

"In a hurry to get home?"

Jason turned to the bus driver. The man was watching him through narrowed eyelids. The crisp white shirt he wore, neat stitching over the pocket with the name "Carl" in blue letters, offered a stark contrast to his dark skin. "How'd you know?"

White-haired, with forearms of knotted lean muscle poking out of rolled-up sleeves, Carl smiled at Jason, his one gold-capped tooth in a sea of coffee-stained ivory gleaming in the dashboard lights. The deep lines of his face were a road map of a hard-earned life, and the great grin he offered enhanced the hills and valleys of that existence. "Been driving this bus a lot of years, man. You can always tell when someone's runnin' away, or runnin' to home. You're runnin' *to*." He tapped his head with a gnarled but neatly manicured forefinger, "It's a gift, man."

Jason considered that for a moment, then turned his face front. "Glad you like your gift," he said under his breath. "Wish I could return mine."

The driver frowned and made a rude noise. "A gift's a gift," he shrugged. "It don't make life better or worse. It's only in how you use it."

"Maybe so," Jason smiled without humor, "but I don't really use my gift. It uses me."

The driver leaned over and looked hard into the young man's eyes for just a second, then smiled again. "Them's the best kind, my friend." Carl turned the big wheel with expert grace, entered the main parking area of the bus station, pulled into a bay, and glided to a stop as smooth as a well-oiled elevator. "Sounds like you've got yourself an honest to goodness calling, son." He engaged the parking brake, the loud whoosh of compressed air waking the remaining sleepers, then pulled the lever to open the doors. "Don't waste it."

Jason smiled back, pulled his backpack over one shoulder, and stepped off the bus. He waved once at the driver as he walked away. He got about ten feet before the driver stuck his head out the door. "Don't forget what I said, now," he hollered. "Ya hear?"

"I won't," Jason called back, then walked into the station to call for a cab.

An hour later he sat on the edge of the motel's bed, the top cover stripped off and left on the floor where it belonged. Not even the best hotels ever washed them, and even having grown up in poverty, he couldn't bring himself to sleep under one. In his hand he held the dice he carried with him wherever he went. He had to buy a new pair in Denver because this Jason didn't know enough to apply a simple tenet of chaos theory. He tossed them on the nightstand, waited for them to stop rolling, and then recorded the result on the little notepad by the lamp. Jason did this two more times, collecting a series of numbers to memorize. If the numbers on the pad changed overnight from what he remembered, he would know he was in a new reality. It wasn't foolproof, but the odds were in his favor. If all went well, and the number didn't change in the night, he would call his mom after noon.

Sleep didn't take him at once, regardless of how road-weary he was. Each time he closed his eyes, he saw the images burned into his brain from the last transition. He was sure that in one of his realities a lot of people died because of something he did… or *failed* to do.

Please, no dreams tonight. He closed his eyes and waited. When sleep finally came, the morning sun was already peeking through the worn curtains.

†††

Sleep was a luxury for Miles, and one he had grown to hate. Dreams were no refuge, ghosts and demons fighting for control. Miles lay on his back and stared at the ceiling, a burning fury in his eyes. *I wish there was a fucking Sandman, so I could reach out and strangle the bastard when he comes.* Each time he closed his eyes he drifted off, but it was only a moment—a fractional infinity—before the dream drove him from his slumber. It was always the same, and he always woke sweating, his heart racing.

Miles turned his head and read the clock on the nightstand. Four a.m. *Almost a half hour that time*, he thought. Nights like this, he knew he wasn't really dreaming. He was *there*—in *that place*. And in that place, *they* waited.

He reached for the remote and brushed the half-filled tumbler of water, knocking it to the carpeted floor. The empty blister packet of useless sleeping pills sat there on the nightstand, mocking him. *Dreamless sleep, my ass.* Miles sat up and rubbed his head, grabbing handfuls of thick hair and pulling hard. It was a calming technique he discovered as a child, though he made several bald patches before he learned to control it. *At least I'm not one of those weak-minded cutters.* He stabbed at the power button on the remote with his other hand, and the TV lit up. The volume was just low enough for late-night viewing, so he tuned to C-SPAN to catch up on the happenings in DC. *Fucking talking heads will put me right to sleep, though*, he thought.

As much as he knew he needed it, he didn't *want* sleep. The things in his dreams—in *that place*—were waiting, surrounding him as soon as he arrived. Each yammered both *to* him and *through* him, a cacophony voices, every last one of them straining to be heard. Most wanted him *gone*—and not just from that place. They wanted him erased from existence. He could feel it, like hot acid on his skin—an increasing pressure to leave, while others pulled at him to stay and listen. The way forward was an infinite gauntlet, questions and answers grasping like taloned hands, while the way back was as passing through a cobweb.

Miles' eyes snapped open, waking with a start. He drew a long-denied breath and turned to the clock. Five-fifteen. *Close enough. A lot of driving to do today.*

He sat up and swung his legs to the side of the bed, and said, "Best get to it."

†††

Kathy opened one eye to peek from under the covers. Jay's cherub face turned up to her from beside the bed, dark hair framing round cheeks and deep-set brown eyes. *Just like his father.* Even at five years old, Jay looked so much like his father that her heart ached whenever he smiled at her. Just as he was doing now.

"C'mon," she said as she pulled the covers back and held out her arms to help him to crawl up the side and onto the bed, "it's Saturday, sweetie, and it's still too early for breakfast."

"But I'm hungry now," he said as he snuggled up against her while she pulled the covers over them.

"Just thirty more minutes, okay?"

"Okay, mommy."

She kissed him on the top of his head, inhaling deep the redolence of little boy, and closed her eyes to get just a few more minutes of blissful sleep before she had to greet the world again.

The cell phone on her nightstand vibrated, breaking both the spell and promise of slumber. Her one day off a week, and someone had to ruin her morning before it started. She knew who it was before she even looked at the phone.

"Your phone's ringing, mommy."

"I know, sweetheart." Kathy, irritated as she was, refused to let it creep into her voice. She snaked an arm out from under the covers and reached across Jay to pick up her phone. *Of course it's her.* The name on the screen haunted her every free day. She sighed and pressed the answer button.

"A little early, Joan."

"Good morning to you, too."

"Hi grammy!" Jay sat up, a huge grin on his face.

"Am I on speakerphone?" Kathy heard a hint of worry in Joan's voice.

"Nope. Boy's just got good ears." She knew her son loved his grandmother dearly, and she would never do anything to harm that, but there were times she wished Joan would just leave her be. At least for a while.

"Kathy," hesitantly, cautiously, Joan began. There was a long pause, and Kathy could hear the woman on the other end of the line whispering to herself.

"Sweetie," she looked at Jay, "why don't you go get yourself some cereal. I'll be in to get you some milk in a minute."

He looked at the phone in her hand, then at her, and said, "Okay, mommy." Jay crawled off the bed and padded toward the door, then turned and yelled "Bye grammy," before running out of the room.

After he left, Kathy sat up against the headboard. "All right, Joan," she said. "Out with it."

"It's just that..." Another pause, then just as Kathy considered hanging up, "he's coming home."

She sat frozen in place for several seconds. There was no need in asking who Joan meant. Jason. Jason was coming home. At last, and after so many years. She wanted to cry, but refused to allow it to happen.

"Well?"

Kathy looked at the phone like it offended her. "Well, what?"

Joan sighed like a soap opera star. "Are you going to tell him?"

Kathy shook her head. "I don't think you'll give me the option," she said. "*Will* you?" Joan snorted once as Kathy continued, "Besides, it's not like it's a secret in town, is it? You've paraded that boy around to all your friends ever since you found out."

"My son has the right to know about his boy."

"Yes he does, Joan, but I decide when and how. I made the right decision not telling him before he left for school, but I know things have changed now."

"I'll give you two days," Joan said, then paused. "After that, I'm telling him."

Kathy heard the unmistakable sounds of Saturday morning cartoons from the TV in the living room.

"All right, but please let me do it my own way." She stood up and found her slippers. "Now, if you'll excuse me, I've got a little boy to feed," and she hung up before the woman could protest. She knew from experience that Joan would try to call back just to get the last word in, so she turned the phone off. Slippers on, she walked out of the bedroom toward the kitchen.

†††

Joan's eyes locked on the phone in her hand, the words *Call Ended* flashing on the little screen, and suppressed a scream of frustration. Hitting the call button again, she waited for the chance to give the little slut a piece of her mind, but the call went straight to voicemail.

"Bitch!" She knew there was no point in calling again before noon, so she hit the end call button and threw the phone across the room where it landed on the couch, bouncing one and falling with a clatter to the floor. *Maybe I'll just get dressed and go over there*, she thought, even the voice in her head full of heat. *But Jason still hasn't called for me to pick him up.* Houston was in the opposite direction, and she didn't want to delay their reunion just to give the mother of her grandson another piece of her mind.

Drumming her fake nails on the kitchen table, she seethed as she thought about how Kathy schemed to keep Jay's existence not only from her, but Jason as well. Even after Joan found out, Kathy refused to let her tell Jason. It wasn't as if she could, anyway, as he had already lit out from school without so much as a goodbye. In the meantime, Joan watched the boy grow, becoming more like Jason every day, while she grew to love him as only a grandmother could. And not once, during all that time, would Kathy accept help from her of any kind. Even after her mom and dad threw her out of their home.

"Bitch," she said again, though with far less conviction.

"You're gonna stay out of it. Ya hear?" Dale stood in the hallway, dressed for work and leaning against the wall with his arms crossed.

Startled, she looked up into his eyes. "I don't know what you're talking about."

He straightened, then crossed the living room to the kitchen. "I'm talking about Jason and his family." He poked a weathered finger at her, "Stay out of it. Let the girl tell him her way."

"Sure, sure," she said, though her mind was already racing ahead. She scooted her chair back from the table and stood. "Let me get started on breakfast."

"I mean it, Joan," but this time he was almost pleading, rather than ordering. "Stay out of it."

She leaned over and gave him a soft peck on the cheek like when they were first married, then turned to the refrigerator and reached for the eggs and bacon. Dale sat at the table behind her and waited for his breakfast, but she wasn't thinking about him anymore. Her thoughts were now all about her son and little Jay. *It's going to be okay, now. Jason's coming home.* Once he met his son, he would stand behind his mother and take custody away from Kathy.

That'll show her.

Bitch.

FIVE

M ILES HATED TEXAS. IT WAS THE ONLY PLACE IN THE WORLD WHERE you could drive a thousand miles on a single road and still be in the same damn state. Driving his old Dodge Charger south on highway 35 toward Alvin after spending the morning in Houston gathering supplies, his anger mounted at the thought he would be late to his target. There was a lot to prepare before completing his mission, but the drive times between locations were taxing. *Even* without *the goddamn traffic, the trip will eat up an entire fucking day just getting to the store and back*.

This time of the year the sky was crystalline, and even with the chill in the air, the sun beat down with such vengeance the days were warm in defiance of the season. Miles' daddy used to say there were only two seasons in Texas: Hot, and Wet. The old man would have called this an Indian Summer, but even though the time of year was right, there was no recent killing frost. Days like today, though limited in number, seemed to make up for all the others. It was why Miles took the top down on the car, and was now singing along with the radio to an old Eagles tune while flooring that bastard hard.

The old car was one of the few things he missed about this time in his life. It never failed to cheer him up when he got the chance to wind that motor out, the huge four barrel carburetor sucking gasoline like a calf on its momma's tit—just like God intended! Give him a four-banger any day, and nothing short of a jet fighter could catch him.

As he neared Alvin, though, he pulled it back to legal speeds. There was no sense in getting this close only to be pulled over and have some overeager cop find what he was carrying in the trunk. No sir. That would not be a good day for either of them.

Miles took the bypass around the main part of town, not wanting to encounter more police than necessary, and headed for the south side of town. What he needed now was a quiet place to do some work uninterrupted, so he pulled in to the closest motel on the bypass and parked under the awning by the office door. As he pushed the long and heavy car door open, he thought, *Couple more hours, that's all. Get this shit done, then go back upstream to finish the job.*

He smiled, slid the sunglasses up to bury them in his thick mane, pulled open the office door, and stepped across the threshold to the frigid interior.

†††

Joan watched Jason from the corner of her eye while she drove. His right elbow propped on the car door armrest, hand supporting his head as he watched the passing of the flat landscape. This stretch of the road was notable only for its lack of anything worth looking at, the only vegetation around the overpasses. Even that "nature" took the form of neatly trimmed carpets of San Augustine and the occasional manicured and mathematically spaced clumps of pampas grass.

Neither of them spoke much in the last twenty minutes, though her head was filled with questions. *What made him leave school? Where had he been all this time?* And, *why couldn't he just come home?* These were questions foremost on her mind, though not nearly all of them.

Dale left earlier than usual for a Saturday, mostly grunting his approval over breakfast, but she was sure his mood had not changed much during the night. She also knew, however, that leaving early meant he intended to be home when she and Jason arrived. While there was nothing to be done for that, she could at least delay the inevitable.

She turned her head slightly, her eyes never leaving the road. "You hungry?" she asked.

"Starving." He said without moving. It was an automatic response, containing neither desire nor disinterest, and he stared placidly ahead. She saw this behavior many times during his teen years, but she thought he'd outgrown it by the time he left for college.

"There's a Dairy Queen just up the road, here." She looked at him again for some reaction. "Is that okay?"

He smiled, a wistful look in his eye. "Only if I can get a chocolate shake with it," he said, voice catching, and he cleared his throat. "I haven't had one of those in a long time."

"Sure, sweetheart."

He finally sat up, turned, and looked at her. His smile this time, though crooked, was warm, and he sighed just like he did when he was little.

"Jason, I—"

"Not yet, mom." His eyes pierced the veil of her dark sunglasses with such intensity that she was sure he could see clear to the back of her skull. "There's a lot to talk about, but I'm not ready yet." He looked down at his hands, "Some of it's gonna sound crazy, anyway. I'd rather do it all at once with both you and dad, and not have to say it twice."

"Okay. Sure." He was already closing in again, and she fumbled to get that warmth back in his smile. "I just thought it might be easier to go over it once with me before you try to tell your daddy everything, that's all." She hit her turn signal to indicate her intentions to the cars around her, then pulled onto the off-ramp in a single smooth motion. As she drove down the feeder road toward the entrance, she asked, "Do you want drive through, or go in?"

"I think I'd like to stretch my legs a bit. I'm kind of tired of riding, you know?"

"Yeah, I understand that." She parked the car near the entrance and disconnected her seat belt. "I did the cross-country bus thing once when I was sixteen. My ass hurt for a week."

"Must have been the same bus."

She laughed at that. The boy's humor had always been dry, but it never failed to make her smile.

†††

A half-hour later, Jason watched his mother over his cup as she finished her burger. He was still working out the last of the shake, considering ordering another, but he knew his mom wasn't exactly flush with cash. He made these kinds of considerations from a very early age, somehow understanding their financial straits even as young as six. His parents never talked about money to him, but he was an observant child, and he couldn't help noticing the difference between his Christmas' and those of his friends. The first time he remembered ever making his mother cry was the day, at age seven, he told her to take back a present she bought him because it cost too much. He didn't understand at the time that the only thing worse than being poor is not being able to give what you have to your kids.

That was about the time he decided he would never live in a trailer when he grew up. He would never have to live paycheck to paycheck just to make ends meet. Now here he was, twenty-four and without a job or a place to live, depending on his parents to put a roof over his head. The irony did not escape him.

Jason chased the last of the shake around the bottom of his cup with his straw, noisily slurping up the chocolaty dregs. Finished, he sat back and sighed. Not because of the cup being empty—well, not just that—but because he made a decision. He placed the cup down and wove his fingers together in front of him on the table.

"I'm not your son."

His mother stopped, the napkin she was using to wipe the corner of her mouth frozen in time. Then she laughed. A bell-sweet sound that made Jason smile regardless.

"I'm serious."

"That's cute son, but why don't you save the comedy act for your daddy. It might help his mood." She reached over to pat him on the arm.

"Okay, stop. I'm Jason, your son, but I'm not *your* son." He tapped a finger on his head. "In here. The outside is the same, but the inside is not."

"I get it, Jason. Everyone changes as they get older."

He breathed heavily and his face scrunched up, then his eyes opened wide.

"I went to school on a football scholarship, right?"

"Yeah. And your dad is plenty pissed—"

"No… I didn't. *Your* Jason had a football scholarship, I went on a physics scholarship." He looked at her, hoping for comprehension. "In fact, I graduated magna cum laude with a degree in quantum physics. My specialty is quantum gravity."

"Son—"

"I can prove it. Take me to any physics professor at any university and watch me discuss string theory, loop quantum gravity, or hell, even *twistor* theory." His eyes, wild and unfocused, darted from her to the room and back again. "Did your Jason know about any of that stuff?"

His mother looked around nervously at the other customers in the restaurant. "Keep your voice down, son. You're starting to sound like your uncle Phil."

What the hell did that *mean?*

"Mom, I know what I'm talking about, and I'm not delusional." The look in her eyes clearly said she thought otherwise. If he couldn't convince his own mother, there was no chance with anyone else. Deflated, he continued, "It would take a lifetime to explain it in detail. Hell, I'm not even sure many of my old teachers would understand it. Just know that what I'm telling you is real." He reached across the table and held her hands, "I am not your Jason."

She sat across from him in silence for a few seconds, mouth open and eyes wide. After what seemed like an eternity, the light left her eyes and her mouth closed. Slower than a receding tide, she pulled her hands away from his.

✝✝✝

Dale didn't take the news any better or worse than Joan, he was just far more demonstrative. He had paced the floor as he yelled, waving his hands like a wild man, punctuating each sentence by pointing an accusing finger at either Joan or Jason. It was no worse than she had seen from him before, but this time it was directed at her son. She could accept that her son was losing his grip on reality, but calling him crazy was a step over the line, especially for two people who had never said three cross words to the other. At least Jason managed to remain calm in the face of the emotional hurricane.

"Is this why you bailed on your football scholarship?" Dale finally stopped his pacing to stand in one place, though only to point a meaty finger in Jason's face. "Is that what happened?"

"I think so," Jason shook his head wearily, "but that was a different Jason."

Dale threw his hands in the air and said, "Son of a bitch!" He turned to Joan, his face red, again wagging that finger, "I blame you for this. You, and those crappy genes you carry. Your damn brother was nuts, too, and you went and passed it on to my kid."

"Phil has nothing to do with this. And he's not crazy. He was cured a long time ago." Protesting was pointless, she knew, but she wasn't going to let him talk about her brother like that. *No matter how crazy he was.*

"Then explain why he ain't teachin' no more, huh?" Dale looked at her with something close to triumph on his face. "You don't quit in April unless they *tell* you to."

She turned away from him. *We are* not *going there tonight, and certainly not in front of Jason.*

"Mom?" Jason's brow beetled, and his head tilted to the right a bit, just as it always did when he was thinking hard. "The Uncle Phil in my reality…" he paused for a second, turning his head back, "No one ever mentioned him being crazy." Dale huffed loudly and walked away to stand against the wall.

"We didn't talk about it much, either," she said, happy to move away from the issue of Phil's job.

Dale snorted loudly, "Are you buying into his delusion now, Joan?"

Jason just ignored him, "Did he talk about people not being the same, or maybe claimed that his friends were different somehow?"

"Yeah, before mom and dad committed him it got pretty bad." She looked pointedly over at Dale, "But he's better now."

"Sure he is," Dale said.

"Dad, can you quit passing judgment for just a second," Jason snapped.

"I ain't passing judgment," his eyes narrowed as he raised an eyebrow, "and I ain't your daddy. Right?"

Jason shook his head, then looked back to his mother. "You have to understand that this is how it looks to me when I transition. All the basics are the same, but from my point of view the people around me have changed. You see, every time my universe split—"

"Here we go," Dale said as he threw his hands in the air.

"Dale, stop." Joan, finally having had enough, used *the voice*. It was a tool in her bag of tricks that would work only once or twice in an argument, as it did now.

Jason looked at his father, shook his head, and continued, "Every time my universe split, I took everything with me. In essence, I created my own duplicate universe. Everyone does, and the only difference is the choice I made that created it." He spread his hands in front of him, "It's like each new universe is a branch on a tree, one splitting from the other. Now, if my consciousness jumps to another reality, almost everything will be the same. It just depends on how many branches I skipped."

"But what's that got to do with my brother?" She thought she was finally getting a handle on what he was saying, but it was still too far out there to take seriously.

"Well, if the choice I make that splits the universe is something like choosing not to brush my teeth that morning, nothing much will change if I jump to the branch where I had. But what if I jump to a branch where, say at the age of eleven, I chose to practice football instead of study science?"

This can't *be real*, she thought. *Can it?* Her brother had talked like this—just before her mom and dad had him taken away. He had tried to tell her once that she wasn't his *real* sister, but they were kids, and she thought he was just being cruel. Now she didn't know what to think.

Jason looked in her eyes, his head tilted again, thrust toward her in hope, "So much would be different. My classes would change, my friends would change," he lifted one leg and looked at his boots, "even my style would change."

Joan followed his eyes and frowned. When he was in sixth grade he had told her he would never wear boots. "Scientists don't wear cowboy boots," he said. But that was before Dale and the coaches talked him into joining the football team.

"Oh my God," she put up a hand to cover her mouth. "How would you cope?"

Jason smiled that crooked smile. "I have to tell you guys, it ain't easy," he said quietly,

"Son," Dale said, his voice calm for the first time, "I think we need to get you some help."

Jason looked up at his daddy, shoved his hands in the front pockets of his jeans. "You're right, sir," he said, and turned back to Joan. "I think I need to speak with Uncle Phil."

"It's getting pretty late, son. Can it wait 'till morning?" She was sure that this was, somehow, a bad idea, but could think of no good reason to dissuade him, either. Maybe if he saw his uncle in one of his usual manic states, he might listen to reason and get some help.

"Better sooner than later, isn't that what you always say, dad?"

Dale just grunted. "I'll get my keys," he said.

"That's okay, I think I'd rather walk." He picked up his pack and tossed a strap over his shoulder. "He's still over on Wilson street, right?"

Joan nodded.

"That's only a few blocks. Not even a mile." He walked to the door, opened it, then turned back. "Don't wait up."

Joan looked into his eyes, her own welling with long-held tears. "But you just got home," she said, and heard the whine in her voice. "There's no hurry—"

"I'm *not* home, mom," he said, shoving his hands into his pockets. "And I really *want* to be."

Either way—crazy or sane—Jason needed something she couldn't give. *Maybe Phil* can't *help him, but neither can I.* She walked over to him then, gave him a kiss on the cheek just as she did every night when he was still a little boy. "In case we're already in bed when you come home," she said.

Dale sat in his favorite chair, grabbed the remote for the TV. "Try to keep it down when you get back," he growled. "I've got church tomorrow."

Jason sighed, shook his head with a sad smile, and walked out the door.

Things will be be better in the morning, Joan thought. *All Jason and his daddy really need is some time.* She closed the door behind her son, walked to the kitchen, opened the fridge, and pulled out a couple of beers for Dale and herself. By the time she was back in the living room, curled up on the couch and watching the news, she had convinced herself it was already better. She smiled at her husband with renewed hope. *Couple more days together, and we might even be a family again.*

✝✝✝

Kathy drove in silence, not even the radio playing, as she practiced each scene in her head. There were any number of ways her meeting with Jason could play out, and in her mind each one ended badly. So badly, in fact, that she left Jay at home with a sitter. There was no sense in subjecting him to this, and besides, it was past his bedtime. If all went well, she would introduce the two of them tomorrow. It was that sliver of hope that pushed her out the door tonight, even if it meant spending time with Joan.

The animosity that Joan displayed always baffled her. If anything, the two of them should have been able to find common ground in their shared situations regardless of Jay. The only difference was that Kathy hadn't married the father of her son, allowing him to move on with his life without forcing him to provide immediately for a family. Maybe that was the problem between them after all—both did what they were sure was right for them and their boys. While Kathy accepted that neither choice was superior, Joan clearly did not. Life was all about choices, after all, and to Joan some were better than others.

Kathy's parents agreed with Joan in principle, if not in deed. Their first choice was for her to give the child up for adoption so she could pursue her dreams, and a distant second was to marry Jason. Absolutely *not* on their preferred list was for her to raise the child on her own, subsisting on a waitress' income. Once the decision was made, though, their support ended and she was politely asked to leave. At least they allowed her to pack a couple of bags first. It was only after the door closed quietly behind her that she realized she would never be allowed back—not as long as her child was with her.

She drummed her fingers on the steering wheel as she drove, an imagined tune running through her mind. Passing cookie-cutter homes, doors shuttered on either side of the road at this time of night, an infinite hallway of closed options lay before her. Her path was arrow-straight, and it all led to her son. Even if she told Jason about the child growing within her before he left, nothing would have changed, with the possible exception of Jason giving up college to provide for a wife and son. There were no better doors to open.

Turning onto the gravel road leading to the shabby trailer park, Kathy sighed. Years of giving up her happiness for the sake of Jason's future, and he left school anyway. It was all wasted effort. As she pulled up to the trailer where her son's father was raised, she wondered if things could be put right after all.

She parked beside the chain-link fence in front and turned the key to kill the motor, and sat motionless with her hands in her lap. Steeling herself for the frosty greeting she knew awaited her, she sighed again and reached for her purse. As she got out of the car, she dropped the keys into the purse and snapped it shut with a force matching the clench in her jaw. With her eyes never leaving the trailer, she pushed her door closed and started walking up the driveway. Motion underneath the front deck caused her to shiver slightly.

"Possum just ran over my grave," her grandmother used to say, as a skinny calico cat shot like an arrow out from underneath the trailer. "Yeah, I get it," she said to the retreating animal as she mounted the steps, "I don't want to be here either."

SIX

Philip Carson sat alone in his small two-bedroom home, the glowing television his only illumination and companion. Like his sister less than a mile away, he held a beer in his hand that was one sip shy of empty, and now warm to boot. His life was a rutted wagon track of work, beer, and TV. *Maybe it's time to take another trip sideways,* he thought. Where he went wasn't usually any better, but at least it was different. *Maybe I should have made better choices in my youth.*

A grim smile creased his face. His first choice of any consequence landed him in the nut barn, and it slid steadily downhill from there. It took most of a year to convince the soft-headed doctors he was well enough to leave, and it was only through a massive effort to guard his words he *stayed* out. The weird thing was, no matter where he went it was always the same. *Nothing big ever changes, and it makes no damn sense.* His last two trips were spent walking a prison yard, staring through the fence at a world he would never visit.

His most recent big choice got him suspended from teaching, unable to find any job other than day labor. When he was a pup, fresh out of college, his principal told him there were three things that got a teacher fired.

"One," the flat-topped bulldog of a man said, counting off on thick, callused fingers, "don't mess with the district's money. Two, don't mess with alcohol on the job. And three, don't mess with the kids." He finished with a wink, "If'n ya know what I mean."

Phil knew.

Two out of three ain't bad, I guess, he thought with a sigh. The ceiling fan above his head beat the air with an irregular rhythm, its blades unbalanced and loose. The whole contraption wobbled and creaked, ready to drop at the first opportunity. *I should really do something about that,* he thought.

Phil looked at the warm beer in his hands, considered drinking the rest, then flipped it into the trash with a grunt. *I am the master of my fate. I am the captain of my soul.* What started as a defiant pledge to the gods had become nothing more than a weak nightly mantra. He wouldn't take that trip tomorrow, or the next day, or any day after. Philip Carson was afraid. Afraid of the nothingness he seemed to carry with him wherever he went, and he hated himself for it.

Never a small man, he had packed on over sixty pounds since his suspension; and since he had just signed a new contract before they politely asked him to get the fuck out, they generously offered to pay it out in one lump if he would, seriously, *get the fuck out now.* That left a lot of free time on his hands, with nothing to do but eat and feel sorry for himself. He wasn't an idiot. The superintendent wanted to keep the whole thing quiet, so Phil took the money and left. It would last him until August of next year, but then what? There wasn't a school in the state that would hire him with that on his record.

Sour mood or not, he still jumped when the knock rattled the door.

Three knocks. That's good. Cops always use five—like they learned it in cop-school or something.

The small baggy filled with almost three ounces of weed sat accusing him, undisturbed on the end table to his left. Stifling the impulse to stash the evidence, Phil lifted his bulk from the overstuffed chair, scratched his ass through his boxers, and walked to the door to press an eye to the peephole. A great smile threatened to split his face in two when he saw who was on the other side. He pulled it open with such force that Jason stepped back in fright, and he unlatched the screen door to open it wide for the boy.

"Jason! When did you get back in town?" He looked past the boy's shoulder toward the driveway. "What are you doing here at this hour? And where's your mom and dad? Did you walk here?"

"Hey, hey," Jason laughed while Phil grabbed his hand and pumped it hard in greeting, "one question at a time."

"Okay," Phil said, rubbing the stubble on his chin with his free hand. "Wanna come in and have a beer?"

"That'll do." Jason disengaged from the hirsute paw wrapped around his hand and stepped into the dingy living room.

Phil walked into the kitchen and retrieved two frosted mugs and two bottles of Bud from the fridge. "Here ya go, Jason. Nothin' but the best for my little bud."

"Damn, Uncle Phil. I'm twenty-four now." He grinned down at the man while he took a seat on the sofa. "Not to mention taller than you."

Phil grinned back. "And that'll get you exactly *dick* in a fair fight, son"

Jason laughed, then filled his mug expert precision and took a long sip.

Phil marveled at the perfect head on the beer his nephew just poured. "Glad to see they taught you something useful at that damn school before you got smart and left." He sat in his chair and poured his own, though not as well. He took two sips as he leaned back and observed the boy over the rim of his mug. Jason drank with casual ease, but Phil knew he was holding something back just by the way he sat. Too straight, and the boy's eyes never left his own. The way he tried to sit still, yet fidgeting with his clothes—especially his boots—like someone who was no longer comfortable in their own skin. Phil watched him in silence for a time, but he already knew the score.

"So," he said, "how ya been?"

Jason held the mug in one hand and wiped his mouth on his sleeve. "Oh, you know," he scrunched his face, "not bad."

"Uh, huh." *Yeah*, Phil thought. *Tell me another one. I can see the ask comin' a mile away, boy.*

"How have *you* been?" Jason asked, taking another sip. "Mom said you weren't teaching anymore." His eyebrows furrowed. "How come?"

"Oh, you know"—*no you don't, and you never will*—"sometimes you just need a change."

Jason took another sip, wiped his mouth, then held the mug in both hands, looking into the foam. Phil was happy to let the boy stew. *Jason's been gone for years without even a fucking phone call.*

But that wasn't *this* Jason. Part of him wondered why, but it was clear all the same.

Phil had considered the possibility the day he found out the boy left school without so much as a by-your-leave, and had dreaded *this* day ever since. *It ain't like I have any fucking insights.*

Jason cleared his throat one too many times and looked up. "Mom and Dad also said something about a mental institution when you were a kid."

There it is, Phil thought. *And here it comes.*

"I was wondering, uh… you know," Jason leaned closer, his voice dropping almost to a whisper, "what was that like?"

"Shit, son! Why don't you just ask me what it was like the first time I got laid?" Jason drew back, his face a reddening question mark. Phil shook his head and sneered. "Cuz the answer's the same for either one—none of your goddamn *business*."

Jason held up a quick hand, a traffic cop in the middle of a four car pileup. "I didn't mean—"

"I know what you meant, son," Phil said, breathing like the end of a two-mile run. "You want to know if you're crazy or somesuch bullshit." He smirked and grunted once, his voice now a gravel road. "I don't have an answer to that."

"But back then you told Mom she wasn't your real sister, and—"

"I said a *lot* of stupid things," Phil said, waving that line of questioning away with a casual flip of his hand. He hated himself for what he was doing to the boy, but there was no point in following it to its logical conclusion. When *his* Jason returned, *this* one would go back to where he came from. *Telling him what's happening won't help, and it's just as liable to make things worse.*

Jason's shoulders slumped, and he settled back in his seat, a heartbreaking look of defeat on his face. "I've been away so long," he said, more to himself than Phil. "I don't know how to get back." He looked up, his eyes swollen and heavy. "I hoped you could…"

He doesn't know how to get back? What the fuck does that mean? He tilted his head and studied the young man before him. It was crystal clear the boy was not *his* Jason, everything about him screaming it like a warning siren. Just as clear was the fact this Jason knew he was a traveler, and that meant he *should* know how it was done.

Something ain't right.

If the boy knew what he was but couldn't control it, then he needed the kind of guidance only Phil could give. He ached to offer it, and cursed himself for his fear. He leaned forward in his chair to speak the words that would bring comfort to his nephew.

"I wish I could help you, Jason," was what came out of his mouth.

†††

"What do you want?" Joan's words were a barrier between Kathy and the interior of the trailer, blocking her like a granite wall. The woman stood behind the screen door, making no pretense at opening it.

"I came to talk to Jason," Kathy said with a smile she did not feel. She tapped her foot, then shook her head. *Damn, that woman is stubborn.* "May I come in?"

Joan looked past her like she wasn't there, tilting her head downward. "Where's Jay?"

Kathy snorted, crossed her arms. "In bed" she said. "Where he belongs this time of night."

Her eyes widened, and she brought her hand to her mouth. "You left him *alone*?" she said with a dramatic gasp. *That woman should be in the soaps with her acting*, Kathy thought.

She couldn't help herself, dropping her purse and sputtering, "What the hell is *wrong* with you?"

"Nothing that three fingers of scotch won't cure," Dale said, sliding behind Joan in the doorway. He moved her aside, grabbed the latch, and pushed the door open. "C'mon in, Kathy. Jason ain't here, but he'll be back later." He offered her his hand, and when she reached out, he pulled her gently inside. "Can I get you something to drink while we wait?"

Joan seethed in silence, and Kathy suppressed a grin. It wouldn't help matters to gloat. "I left Jay with a sitter, so I can't stay too long," she said, not knowing why she needed to justify herself. Dale had always been kind to her, regardless of the haranguing he must have endured from Joan about her and Jay. "Just a Coke will be fine."

"Sure, hon. Pepsi, okay?"

In Texas, every soft drink is a Coke. It was one of the many things she had to learn when she and her parents first moved to the state. "That's fine, thanks."

Dale left her at the sofa, shot a stern look at his wife, and walked into the kitchen. Kathy sat, quietly watching the woman who was burning a hole in the back of her husband's head with her glare.

"You gonna shut that door any time soon?" Kathy turned her head to Dale, a can in each hand, and one eyebrow raised in Joan's direction.

Without a word, Joan narrowed her eyes, then shoved the door closed.

"That's better. Now get in here and we can all have a nice little chat." He offered a can of Pepsi to Kathy as he walked by her toward his recliner. "I think it's time we clear the air a bit before Jason gets back, don't you?" he said to no one in particular. He popped the top on his can with a hiss and sat back.

Joan stood like a statue for a few seconds, then her face brightened with broad smile that Kathy knew she didn't feel. "All right, Dale. It's far past time to say what needs to be said."

Dale winked at Kathy over his can of Pepsi, and said with a grin, "Let's git to gittin', then."

†††

Dale watched Joan with a wary eye as she stared at Kathy, waiting for the crinkle in the corner of her eyes that warned of his wife's inevitable explosion. She did her best to hide it—right up to the point of detonation—but that one tell allowed him to contain the damage as it occurred. The only reason she had any friends left in town was his skill at dulling her sharp tongue before she went too far. It was exhausting, but nights like this made up for it. He turned to Kathy and smiled. *That girl can take care of herself.* And she *had*, too. From day one she had been an irritant to his wife that no one ever had been before.

"Well," Joan said, hands in her lap resting on primly closed legs, "how do you plan to tell Jason you lied to him?"

Kathy smiled at her without showing teeth, "I thought I would just tell him." She leaned forward as if sharing a secret, and whispered, "If that's okay with you, that is."

"Listen to me, you little—"

There it is.

"Okay, that's enough sparring for now," Dale said as he stood. It had taken even less time than he guessed it would, but nothing would be served by the two of them getting into a screaming match right now. If Jason were to come home now and find a cat fight in full-throated screeching, he might just light out again. Dale might go with him this time. Instead, he shook his head at Joan. "Can we focus on the boy and his father and leave the rest of the crap outside?" He turned to Kathy, and stabbed a thick finger in her direction. "And try not to get this woman all riled up, okay?" he said, gruff papa-bear, then smiled at her. "I just finished patching the wall from the last time."

Kathy's eyes softened, then she lowered them to watch her hands in her lap. "I'm sorry, sir."

"And stop 'sir-ing' me, young lady. I work for a living, and the name's Dale."

He heard Joan snort quietly from her perch. "She's half your age, Dale. Stop trying to charm her."

His face instantly hot, he turned on his wife. "At least I don't earn my money on my back," he spat before he could stop himself.

Her eyes widened, and the quick intake of air from both women was enough to tell him he had taken one step too far. This had gotten out of hand so quickly, but the woman had always known which buttons to push. Dale sighed, all anger leaking out with that breath, and lowered himself back into his recliner. *Maybe it would be best if Jason never came home. He'll be happier away from all this.*

"All right," he said after a tense silence, "Let's try this again."

"Maybe I should leave," Kathy said as she stood. "It might be better if Jason and I talked," she nodded at Joan, "without an audience."

Quietly, without lifting her head to look up, Joan said, "Please. Sit. I promise not to interfere." She looked over at Dale. "I'll be good."

The odd thing was that he believed her. He knew there were more plans rolling around in that pretty head, but for now she would honor her word. For some reason she needed to witness the reunion, and if she had to be nice to do it, she would.

Kathy looked from Joan to Dale, confusion and hesitation fighting for control of her face. Dale cocked his head, then nodded to the sofa. Slowly, Kathy relaxed and sat once again.

"That's better, I think." Dale forced a smile, "Jason should be home soon, and then we can all work on putting this behind us." His son was in for a big surprise when he returned, but the people who loved him most might come together long enough to make sure his homecoming was a happy affair.

A chill gripped Dale's spine, his heart skipping a beat. *Not a chance in hell*, he thought. *Things will heat up as soon as that boy opens the damn door. If not sooner.*

†††

A half mile from the trailer, Miles found his car right where he had left it, jumped in, and fired up the engine. The walk back was against a cold and stiff wind, but that chill matched his thin smile thinking of what lay ahead for Jason. He even ventured to whistle an old tune as he walked the darkened road.

Miles was fortunate when he arrived at the trailer earlier in the evening, the streetlights out and both vehicles in the driveway. He watched Jason and his mother arrive, and then parked his car far away, carrying his supplies back with him in a knapsack. When he returned to the trailer park, an old woman in a dressing gown stepped out of the trailer next door carrying a trash bag. He had to walk past as she toddled to the curb, dropped the bag, walked back to the side of her home, and *then* dragged a large wheeled trash container to the curb to set beside the bag. She eyed him as he walked by, saying nothing, though raising her hand as if to wave. He continued past as if he hadn't seen her. Behind him she *harrumphed*, then shuffled back to her door. Miles continued past his target long after he heard the door slam shut behind her.

A single bead of sweat formed at his temple, evaporating in the cold and dry air as his heart raced. He hefted the knapsack and frowned. *Old bitch might get some of this as well.* He couldn't risk it though. Miles couldn't come back to do the old woman. Once this task was completed, he had to leave for the East coast, and he didn't have the luxury of hanging around to answer questions. He was going to be President, after all, and the internship waiting in DC was the first step in a long journey. In *this* reality, though, he would get it right.

Miles had been surprised someone pulled up to the fence in front of the trailer so late at night. A minute earlier and the car's driver would have seen him as he worked, but he was already under the deck by the time the car arrived. Squatting like a stone gargoyle, he had almost been discovered when a rawboned cat wandered over. He reached out to grab the thing, but sensing danger it hissed and shot away in leaping bounds. The woman walking up the drive stopped for a second as the cat ran off. From his vantage, Miles could only see her from the waist down, but the curve of her hip told him all he needed to know. His hardening cock ached to plumb the depths beneath those jeans, but it couldn't be helped. He rubbed the bulge in his own jeans, savoring the knowledge this visitor would share the fate of everyone in that trailer. Once she was inside, he made his final preparations and left as quietly as he arrived.

Miles checked his watch and peeled his lips back in a grin at the small flash in his rear-view mirror. From this distance the sound was a dull crump when it reached him—nothing like the thunderous blast you heard in movies—but it was satisfying in its own way. The tires crunched through the gravel of the road's shoulder, and he pulled smoothly onto the road to head north and then east, drumming his fingers on the wheel in a rhythm that matched the rapid beating of his heart.

†††

Dale knew something was wrong the instant he heard the explosion. Not a loud bang like munitions, but more like an incendiary device. That sound was followed in rapid succession by smaller bursts around the trailer, and Dale was out of his seat before Joan and Kathy had time to register the noise as something out of the ordinary. The smell of burning wood from the deck wafted through the closed door even as he reached for the knob, but he pulled it open, anyway. A wall of flame reached for him through the open doorway, and he staggered back as Joan screamed.

"Jason's room," he yelled at the two women, both paralyzed with fear. It was the farthest from the front door, and the window was large enough for them to crawl through. Kathy was the first to move, leading the way as smoke poured in from every corner. It piled at the ceiling, rolling and twisting like storm clouds. *If we don't get out soon*, he thought, *we won't get out at all.* He pushed Joan ahead of him, but she kept turning wild eyes at him, mouth working to speak with no sound coming out. She tripped over an ottoman, and he had to haul her up by one arm, hooking his other around her waist. He glanced behind as she shoved her through the door after Kathy, the first tendrils of fire licking through the front door, tasting the jamb and crawling to the ceiling.

"What's happening?" Joan yelled, barely audible over the now-roaring fire. Dale didn't answer, pushing her forward, and hoping they weren't already too late.

He stopped just as he barreled into Joan's back inside Jason's room. Kathy stood by the bed, bathed in orange and yellow firelight as the far wall with the window burned. She turned to him, tears in her eyes, and stepped back from the growing heat. The air was thick with heavy smoke and rank fumes, and she coughed, one hand held over her mouth. The heat beat his exposed skin in waves, the tang of singed hair invading his nostrils.

"Fan out," he yelled, then coughed into his arm. "Find an exit." He ran into the bathroom, pulled three washcloths from a cabinet, and wet them in the sink. "Put these over your mouths and breath through them." *It won't help for long, but long ain't the amount of time we have left.*

Joan ran for the back door, Kathy to the kitchen, and Dale to the other bedroom. The one he shared with Joan, the only woman he ever loved. The woman who gave him a son. The woman who cheated on him, tortured poor Kathy, and had more anger than hope in her heart.

He knew what they would find. The other noises had been smaller explosions, each at a different exit point. When he reached the bedroom, flames had already taken the wall with the window, and were now consuming the bed.

There would be no escape.

Dale ran back to the short hall as Kathy and Joan approached, each holding the other up in a tight hug. Joan's eyes spun, tracing each finger of flame around the trailer, but Kathy's were wet and fierce. He pulled both into the hall bathroom and into the tub where they knelt. Joan bowed her head and prayed softly as he reached around her to turn on the shower.

"If the fire department's on its way, this will buy us some time," he said, trying to make himself believe it. Kathy didn't, and her eyes said so. Dale smiled at her, brushed the strands of wet hair from her eyes. *I know why that boy loves you so much,* he thought with a sigh. *You're as strong as Joan wishes* she *was.* He kissed Joan on the cheek, and she buried her head deeper into Kathy's neck, sandwiched between the two people she hurt the most.

He encircled both with his arms, hugging both to him, a last shield from the beast that hunted them. The last sounds he heard were the crackling of burning timbers, and the siren from the fire truck that would arrive too late.

†††

Inside the little house, neither Phil nor Jason heard the explosion. Only later did they hear the wailing of the fire engines and ambulance. Like most people near large cities, though, they ignored such things unless they occurred on their own street.

Jason left a few minutes later, walking home with both hands shoved in his pockets, eyes clouded and dark. *Uncle Phil's a dead end*, he thought, frowning. He had been so sure when he went to visit his uncle that the man could help. *Why? What the hell made me think things would finally make sense?* The walk back seemed to take much longer than he remembered.

With each street he passed, he came closer and closer to the sounds of fire trucks, and every step his legs grew heavier. *Please... not again*, he thought as he turned the corner and stopped, the heat from the fire pushing against him like a pounding surf. He knew without asking that his parents were gone, and the weight of that loss drove him to his knees. In every way that mattered, they *were* his parents.

Lights flashed from emergency vehicles and fire trucks on either side of the road, and he stood and walked this red hallway in a daze. There was only a single exit, and that was the driveway to his parents' home. His legs were lead as he reached the end of that hall and surveyed what was left of his world.

The trailer was still in flames, though burned almost to the ground, and neither the car nor the truck in the driveway had escaped the fire's wrath. Another car parked on the road by the fence had also been touched by the intense heat, the paint bubbled and roof warped. Nothing of his home remained, and it was clear no one escaped the blaze. Neighbors on either side were hosing down their own homes in a desperate attempt to protect what little they had from drifting embers. Thick smoke swirled and crawled in lazy tendrils over the entire area, burning noses and lungs as it passed.

Mrs. Blaine, his mother's only friend in the trailer park, walked over and threw her arms around him. "I heard an explosion and called the cops," she said between sniffles and coughs. "The place was gone before the trucks got here." She looked up into his eyes, her own red and wet with tears, "I'm sorry, Jason. Your mom and dad never got out. And Kathy..." The woman broke down into sucking sobs, burying her head in his chest, and could say no more.

Kat? Turning to the car by the road, he tried to ask who it had belonged to. He couldn't speak. Even if he had the words, his mouth wouldn't work. *And Kat was here, somewhere. But where? Had she been in the house when...?* He stood immobile as stone, slack-jawed, eyes unfocused, and tears running down hot cheeks. *Someone did this. Someone bombed my house and killed my parents...and Kat. Who would do that? Why?* There was no reason to suspect foul play, but he knew it was true just the same. He sifted through this Jason's memories, but there was nothing about anyone wanting him dead. Instead it was as if he had witnessed this scene a thousand times before, and he knew with the same conviction that the person responsible would never be caught.

An officer was taking statements from the locals, and one of them pointed at Jason. The policeman finished what he was writing, closed his notepad, then turned and walked toward Jason. Firefighters crossed back and forth in his path, but he strode with a single-minded determination. Jason saw the man approach through a bereaved haze, the officer drawing no closer, when he felt the familiar tug at the center of his being.

No, no, no...

But it didn't matter what Jason wanted. The transition was happening right here and right now, and as he watched the officer recede, the darkness surrounded his field of vision, compressing it into a thick, inky-black line. The sensation of motion, lasting only a second, pulled him into that long dark tunnel and poured him head first toward a new reality.

SEVEN

M ILES' DREAM BEGAN THE SAME EACH NIGHT. FALLING INTO THE depths, a stomach-churning drop into an abyss with neither beginning nor end. The surrounding darkness was near total, the thin line to which he fell a black beyond black—an absence of not only light, but reality itself. No wind rushed upward to greet him, yet he knew he fell. Nothing to see, though his eyes were open. No sounds, no odors. It was as if his senses received no input. There was no sensation to tell him he approached the line from one moment to the next, no manner in which to judge his speed, but he knew with conviction he would pass through that Stygian darkness soon enough.

Something's changed.

He should have awakened by now; he always had by this point in the dream. Covered in sweat he would rise from his bed and reach with shaking hands for the bottle of scotch he always kept on the night-stand. Not this time though. Worse than the dreams he had of his father, this one was working to a conclusion—a resolution that always eluded him before—and the thought oddly comforted him. For more nights than he could count, he fell toward that inky blackness without ever passing through, but tonight would be different. Tonight Miles would find what waited for him on the other side.

The thought filled him with dread, even as it exhilarated him. He opened his mouth to scream just as the line of black reached for him.

†††

"Get up you little shit!" Frank Henderson kicked the side of Miles' cot with a booted foot, rattling the rusty springs and instantly waking the eight-year-old from what had been a fitful slumber.

Miles sat up and moved as far as he could from that boot, pulling his knees to his chest and the single cover to his chin like a shield. Most kids his age wielded a blanket as proof against the monsters in their dreams, but Miles knew real monsters had no respect for such things. He kept his eyes low, a tactic he had learned from years of brutal lessons.

"Look at me, boy," his father snapped. Miles knew this trap. To follow the instruction was to be labeled as defiant, but to *fail* to do so was to invite the same. He raised his eyes only as far as his father's chin.

"Got some chores for you to do, and after you finish those, we're goin' into town for a bit." Miles nodded. He knew what that meant. The bar. Always the bar. The *men* would be there, too. They always were. Most days his father had him wait on them as they drank and played cards. Sometimes he had him do... *other* things. Miles pushed the instant spark of rage down, burying it deep within before it had a chance to flare. *I won't think about that—I won't.* He certainly couldn't let his father know he was thinking about it. It might give him ideas.

"Do I bathe first, daddy?" he asked, pulling his chin down to his chest, one hand rubbing a sore elbow. Questions were dangerous, but as questions go, this one was less so.

"Nah," he stroked his chin, "too much to do today."

Miles allowed the tension in his shoulders to leak away. No bath meant he wasn't being cleaned up for *later*. Safe for another day.

Frank narrowed his eyes as he watched his son, then kicked the side of the bed again. "Throw on some pants and go get my coffee started."

"Yes sir." Relieved, Miles lowered the blanket with reluctance and crawled off the bed, wondering if his old man would taste the rat poison he always thought of using instead of sugar. *Some day, old man*, he thought. *And then what?* Miles tried to think of life without his father, and couldn't. At his worst, Frank Henderson was the kind of monster that inhabited every kid's nightmares, but at his best he was the dad Miles still loved.

Miles looked at the pile of mostly clean clothes in the corner of his room, then walked over and pulled out the least offensive pair of bluejeans. While he shrugged them on and buttoned up, he remembered this was a school day. He thought for a second about reminding his father, but then he rubbed his jaw in memory of the last time he did that. Instead, he found his shoes and socks and pulled them on. School would wait for another day.

†††

The line dumped Miles out in the old shed, the dull interior blinding by comparison.

Why the shed?

Passing through was like swimming through molasses, as the darkness pulled at him in every direction at once. Just as he thought he would never get through, he was standing in the shed, sunlight shining weakly through the dirty window above the workbench. Everything was just as he had left it all those years ago, his *tools* still gleaming, their keen edges showing no hint of corruption. He reached out to touch each one in turn, caressing the smooth surface of the unblemished metal.

"Hello Miles."

He turned smoothly at the sound behind him, sweeping his eyes around the small structure while simultaneously selecting a single implement from the workbench. He held it at the ready behind his back, careful with the blade, while he searched for the source of the voice. Confusion and recognition struggled for supremacy across his face when he found it.

"You won't need that," the boy said. "Wouldn't do you any good, anyway."

The child he faced could not have been older than six or seven, but he spoke like a grown man. Miles narrowed his eyes, drew the filleting knife from behind his back and leaned forward, pointing the weapon at the boy's chest, "I know you."

"You should," the boy said as he grinned without mirth, and pointed at the older man. "I'm you."

It made sense. Miles knew other versions of himself must have passed through the in-between on their way to other realities. Until now, though, he had never met one. What didn't make sense was why this one was so young. Maybe he had learned to time travel much earlier in his life, but it still didn't explain the adult demeanor of the child.

Miles relaxed the arm holding the knife, resting the blade against his thigh. He looked around the shed, inhaled the scent of aged wood and decay, felt the heavy warmth of the still air, and frowned. "Why are we here?" he said, head tilted toward the boy.

"Because it's the only safe place I can remember."

Miles understood that. Throughout most of his childhood, this had been the one place where he was in control. At first it was nothing more than a place to hide from his father. Later it became less a haven and more a fortress of solitude. By the time he was nine it was much more than that, but at this time in the boy's life, he hadn't even thought along those lines.

"Did you bring me here?"

The boy's eyes, so bright and knowing a moment ago, darkened as he dropped his gaze to the floor at his feet. "It's… complicated. *You* brought us here. I just created the space and sent the invitation."

"I don't understand."

"No, I guess you wouldn't." The boy looked up at Miles again, earnest expectation and no small amount of awe shining from his face. "We don't have much time," he said, melancholy weighing his eyelids.

"Time for what?"

The boy threw his arms wide. "Well… for *everything*. I've been here so very long waiting for you, picking bits and pieces from those who passed through." Profound sadness radiated from his body in waves that crashed against Miles' own with dull energy. "There are so many of you, and so few of me," he said, lowering his head, his voice fading to a whisper. "We don't have the strength to hold you here for long. Even now the others are trying to take you away—*keep* you away from me."

"Others?"

"Like you." He sighed a little boy sigh, and looked up with eyes older than redwood, "I'm not your twin, but I am the first spawned from him." He watched confusion grow in Miles' eyes. "There's no time to go into details," the boy said. "Just know that all of us who died when daddy beat us that day we broke the window… um… we're different from those who lived."

Miles remembered that day well. There was a scar—and underneath that scar, a *dent*—on the top of his head where his father had hit him with the bat. He also remembered the fear of a little boy as the man's face grew red with anger and he ripped the baseball bat from the child's hands. His father had used it to shove him in the chest several times for emphasis as he screamed; and when Miles cried, he only became angrier, finally pushing him to the ground. It wasn't enough. It was never enough, and the last thing Miles saw that day was his father winding up to send one to the cheap seats. He awoke in his cot two days later with a bandage on his head, and a worried father sitting in an old straight-backed chair beside him. It was the first, and last, time he had seen that particular emotion on his father's face. He wondered at the time why the old man hadn't taken him to the hospital, but he was just happy to be able to wonder at all.

Miles shook his head to clear the tendrils of memory. "So, why are we here?"

"We just wanted you to know it's not too late to stop."

"I don't know what—"

"Don't be an idiot. I know what you know." The boy straightened, confident as a man again. "You have the potential to be a great man, but you are on the wrong path."

"I think I'm the best judge of that, boy," Miles said through a thin smile.

"Stay on this path, and no matter what you do, the ending is bad for you. Win or lose, the ending is the same."

"Everyone dies, boy."

The eyes, large and round, softened. He shook his head in sad defeat and sighed again. "There *are* worse things."

†††

Miles jolted awake, icy sweat covering his forehead, his heart pounding in his chest. He remembered cranking up the motel air conditioner before he went to bed, and the room was now cold enough to hang meat in. He had driven non-stop since leaving Houston, and by the time he got to the outskirts of Charlotte, there was just nothing left in him to go on. Miles would still make it to D.C. on time, so he could afford to stop for the night.

He sat on the edge of the bed and pulled his hair. His heart rate slowed as his breathing became less ragged. Awake, he never felt fear. It was only in his dreams he even remembered what it was like. The dreams about his childhood were the worst, and now were all mixed up with his visits to *that place.*

Miles forced himself to stop, then looked at the small mass of hair in his hands. He was sure those memories were being drawn forth intentionally. Someone—some*thing*—wanted him to feel the terror only a child knows; the terror of an animal trapped in an abattoir. The fear of a *victim*.

There had been many of those in his path. Born a victim, he changed sides the instant he was able. Victims were weak—disposable goods to be used up and discarded. Technically, his mother was his first victim. *Does it count if you kill her in childbirth?* he wondered. It didn't matter. He paid for that—with interest—for the next sixteen years at the hands of his father. Miles smiled thinking of the last time he had seen the old man. He was sixteen years old, and fully a head taller by then. *That was a real good day.* His mouth turned down as he thought of the look on his Daddy's face, the light in his eyes slowly fading.

He turned to look at the clock on the nightstand. "Shit." He had only slept for two hours. Not nearly enough for the day ahead. Miles stood up and took a single step to the other bed in the room where his small toiletry bag lay. He fumbled inside until he found the little bottle of sleeping pills, popped the top, and shook two in his mouth. He looked around for something to wash it down, and found the half-empty bottle of scotch on the writing desk.

"That'll do," he said to the room and the chorus of voices in his head, grabbed the bottle by the neck, and twisted off the cap. He gulped the cheap burning liquid like a pro, then replaced the cap and set the bottle back on the desk. While he wiped his mouth with the back of his hand, he settled back onto the bed and pulled the thin covers up to his neck. These were useless against the monsters. They barely kept out the chill of the room.

†††

"When you're through there, come with me," his daddy said, then turned and walked away from the boy and his breakfast without another word. *Obedience* to Frank Henderson meant never having to repeat your orders.

Miles finished the last of the milk in his bowl and dropped the dish into the sink. More accurately, he set it precariously atop the pile of other filthy plates, cups, and bowls that were already there. At some point in the week this chore would be added to his list, but for now he waited until his daddy got around to it. Experience told him that the larger the chore, the longer the old man left him alone. He wiped his hands on the dirty dishtowel hanging off the edge of the sink, then followed the man outside.

Sunshine filtered through the old trees surrounding the house, a beautiful day in the making. Early spring, and the birds were already nesting and raising a racket. Grackles, mockingbirds, and cardinals all competed against the pulsating whine of the cicadas. Here and there came the unearthly calls of the bluejay, while a lone woodpecker hammered high in the large pine on the south side of the house. Miles, his bland face pointed upward to catch a stray shaft of sunlight, watched it all in detached indifference. He caught his father watching him, smiled briefly, then slipped on the mask of humanity he wore as an accessory.

Frank Henderson stood by a tall ladder he leaned against the side of the house, the thing reaching all the way to the roof.

"Stop your gawking and get over here, boy."

His old man knew Miles feared heights—or, at least, he used to. Miles continued to play the part long after the fear disappeared. It kept his father from looking for other ways to instill discipline.

"Climb up there and clean out those gutters, boy." He smiled down at him, watching for the first signs of defiance.

Miles looked at the rickety old ladder-shaped bundle of sticks, the thing held together by layers of old exterior paint, and wondered if it would hold even *his* weight. He lifted his eyes to the gutters far above, overflowing with pine needles and leaves, and tried to remember the last time he cleaned them out. Years, at least.

"Y… yes, sir." Stammering was always a good touch. He watched his daddy smile. "Can I get some gloves?"

"Afraid to get your hands dirty, boy?"

"No, sir. It's just…"

"Just nothin', boy. Get on up there. I'll check back on you in a couple of hours."

"Y… you're not gonna hold the ladder for me?"

"Don't be a pansy-ass. I got other stuff to do. I can't spend all day holding your hand."

Miles knew that "other stuff" was mostly just having a beer and watching TV, but saying it out loud was a bad idea.

"Yes, sir." Miles reached out, grabbed the sides of the ladder, and climbed. He got about half-way up and then pretended to shake. This would satisfy the old man for a time, but if he stayed there too long, there would be a beating. Finding that sweet spot of a show of fear versus defiance had taken him a year to get right. Miles counted silently to himself, then continued up. He could see the old man turn red and open his mouth to yell at him before he restarted his climb, and Miles congratulated himself for having stymied him again.

Once at the top, he reached into the gutters and dragged out the first handfuls of wet muck. Frank watched for a time, but soon bored and wandered inside. The screen door slammed shut behind him, bouncing once before stilling, and Miles was left alone for the first time that day. From his perch he could see all the way to the stand of trees behind the work shed, and he smiled as he saw furious movement in the underbrush. It was the telltale sign that one of his snares had caught something for him. From the sound of it, he guessed it was one of the bluejays that nested nearby.

Miles smiled again. He grabbed another handful of needles, tossed them to the ground, and wondered what the other kids were doing in school today.

†††

Another gray day. He had been awake for hours, but stubbornly clung to the bed far longer than he should have in hopes of a few more minutes of dreamless sleep. All that did was give himself a headache. The headaches were stronger these days, and came with increasing regularity. He knew he should have seen a doctor by now, but without health insurance he couldn't afford even an office visit.

Miles stood at the window, one hand holding the tatty curtain to one side while the other held to his lips a mug of something pretending to be coffee. As long as caffeine was involved, the taste didn't really matter to him. Just another gray day, like every other in his life, but coffee made everything marginally better. Scotch was better still.

"Maybe a little blood-thinner *will* help." He reached for the nearly empty bottle on the desk and poured the rest into the mug, bringing the surface dangerously near the rim. "That should do it."

He raised the mug and toasted the day, then released the stiff curtain and allowed it to settle back to its original position. The room was still and dark, the cheap bulbs sitting unused in their lamps. The darkness helped. Only the light leaking around the edges of the curtain and the glow from the alarm clock on the nightstand offered any illumination to the gloomy and dank room. In the shadows he felt safe, a velvet cloak wrapped about his shoulders protecting him from all intrusions. True safety was a function of the amount of control he had in his life. Everything came down to *power*. The power to own the machineries of joy, pain, and everything in between.

On the desk by the scotch, lay a manila folder. In that folder was the first step in his plan to take control of his life. One of two reasons for his return to this time, it contained everything he needed to insinuate himself into the life of one of the most powerful men in Washington. The information—the proof—was ridiculously easy to acquire, as long as you knew where it was and how to get it. That knowledge he gained at the expense of a life farther up the line. The beauty was in the fact that, coming to the now as he did, the beautiful things he did up the line from the before didn't yet—and now would not—happen. His record was clear, and in the now he held the information in his hands. Miles grinned as he looked down at the folder. *There really* is *such a thing as a free lunch*.

Get moving, you little shit. His father's voice was as clear as if the man had been standing beside him. Miles didn't jump at the sound, however. The voice had become a comfort over the last few years, and spurred him to do the things he needed—the things that must be done. The memories of his father, strong and demanding, hovered over his shoulder like a specter, urging him ever forward. There was no denying that commanding presence. After everything he had done to rid himself of the man, here he was controlling his actions as if he had always been there.

He always will be, Miles realized. All that remained was a voice. And the voice never stopped.

EIGHT

No, no no…

THE VERTIGO WASA BRIEF, JARRING, STOMACH-CHURNING DISORIEN-tation, but the crashing waves of déjà vu would take days to sort out. It didn't happen every time. Sometimes Jason entered a body devoid of memories, but that had happened only twice before. This mind, extravagant with fulsome tangles of recollection, threatened to crush his own into a singularity of trapped information. Jason struggled to maintain his self; the core of his meaning. His eyes shut tight against the world, he pushed back the waves that threatened to swamp his psyche. It was only then he realized he was not alone inside his mind. He wasn't swapping bodies with another Jason. This one was still here, and he was clearly insane.

Beads of sweat dripped from his forehead as he fought for control, and as the droplets followed their chaotic paths down his face, the pain and confusion ebbed. Jason sat on the floor, knees hugged tight against his chest, rocking forward and back in a steady rhythm. The position was very familiar; he had done this every time he heard his parents arguing when he was a child.

But I'm not a child. And I'm not that Jason.

He stopped rocking, muscles relaxing, and he opened his eyes. All around him was white. White on the walls, the floor, the ceiling—even the thin clothing he wore. The slippers on his feet were also white, and the only break in the bleached environment was the small window on the door a few feet away. On the other side was a dark face, concern in the eyes. He couldn't tell whether those eyes belonged to a man or a woman.

Jason stood, willing himself to calm, and waited in front of the door. After a few seconds of inspection, he must have passed some kind of test. The person turned and nodded to an unseen individual, and the door lock clicked as a buzzer sounded. The slab of white swung outward and a man much older than Jason stood in the opening—two large and hairy men in white close behind.

Jason tilted his head a shallow angle, and his eyes narrowed. "I know you," he said. A little more meat on the man's bones, and no gold-capped tooth, but it was the same bus driver he met in the other reality.

The man smiled, straight white teeth shining. "Of course you do, son," he said. "I'm Carl Ambrose. I took over your case yesterday." He turned his head and spoke to the men behind him. "I don't think you gentlemen are needed. I can take it from here." As he said this, he waived his thin hand, and Jason watched the orderlies faces darken. Each squinted disapproval, then turned as one and left Jason and Carl alone.

The doctor stepped inside. He continued to watch Jason, but his relaxed manner suggested familiarity beyond simple doctor and patient. He gestured toward the small cot by the far wall, then walked over and took a seat on one corner. His back remained straight and true while he sat, his hands resting in his lap. After a moment or two, Jason joined him there, leaning his back against the padded wall behind the bed.

"You had a really nice break, there, last night."

"I bet," Jason said. "I'm guessing I'm pretty nuts, huh?"

"Well, that's not exactly the technical term. I prefer dissociative identity disorder."

"Everything's gotta have a name."

The doctor smiled again, warm and kind, like a kindergarten teacher. "You've apparently been cheeking your meds for the past week. Once it became obvious, we got you lined out." He leaned in, and gave Jason's knee a light pat. "You probably shouldn't do that anymore," he half-whispered.

Jason bristled at the too-familiar behavior and pulled his legs closer. "When do I get out of here?"

The doctor straightened again. "We should move you back to your regular room later today. We just have to make sure you're past this."

"No," Jason shook his head and waved his hand in a wide arc, "I mean *out*."

"Jason, you need to understand... you're here to rest." The doctor sighed, and he relaxed his shoulders. "You've had a very bad shock recently, and you need time to recover and process everything." He reached out to pat Jason's knee again, who pulled it out of reach. "I want to make sure you're ready before I toss you out in the world again," he said, pulling his hand back.

Jason lifted his chin, looking at the reflected a halo of light bouncing from the other man's head. "Ready for what, exactly?"

Ambrose shook his head and blew out a long breath. His shoulders slumped from the added weight of untold years of labor, "Oh, son, if you only knew."

†††

"It's not so much the dream as a feeling I have while dreaming," Jason said, shaking his head to clear the cobwebs. The medications helped him keep the other personality in check, but at times that Jason fought for control. The dreams were the hard part. Asleep, both of them resided in the dream-state, though only this Jason had complete control. There was no real interaction, but the other was there, ever-present and waiting for an opportunity to express.

"Tell me about the feeling, then." Dr. Ambrose watched him from his plush chair across the coffee table in his office. Jason was never sure what the man was thinking. He would have cleaned up at the poker tables in Vegas.

"It's... it's like hands... hundreds... thousands, pulling me in different directions at once." He shook his head again and spread the fingers of both hands before him, "Not like real hands, but that's the best description of it."

This was his third session with the doctor since coming to this reality, but he already felt comfortable talking to him. As long as he didn't reveal too much, he knew he could at least appear sane.

"Is that uncomfortable for you?"

Jason nodded and dropped his hands into his lap, "It was... at first. Now it's almost like being welcomed by an old friend."

"Is that why you distance yourself from the others here? All your friends are in your dreams?"

Jason's brow beetled, and he lifted his chin, "I don't distan—"

"It's not a negative assessment, Jason. Just an observation."

"But—"

"Name three people other than me that you've met here."

"Uh…"

Dr. Ambrose smiled, not in triumph, but in honest good humor. "It's okay, son, I don't think I can name more than four or five myself." He settled back into the chair and crossed his legs. "But you do keep your distance. I think it's a defense mechanism." He steepled his hands in front of his mouth, then drew in a long breath. "The question is why?"

Jason knew the answer, he just couldn't tell him. Every friend he ever made disappeared the instant he changed universes. Sure, they often existed in the new one, but just as often he and they had never met. He couldn't take his friends with him. The only people he could count on were his family. Not having a suitable answer, he sat in silence.

The doctor sat in silence as well for long seconds, frozen and waiting. Without warning he sighed, checked his watch, nodded once, and stood. "Well, that's it for today." He walked to his office door, then held it open for Jason. "I'd like to start seeing you daily. At least for a while if that's okay."

Jason stood, the transition as unsettling as slipping between universes. "Uh, sure," he said, offering a lopsided grin and a shrug. "What else do I have on my schedule?"

Ambrose clapped him on the back, shooing him out into the corridor, and laughed. "That's the spirit." He looked into Jason's eyes, and as he closed the door, he said, "Tomorrow, then."

The heavy door closed with a loud clack from the latch, and Jason was left alone in the hall, stunned at the speed and precision with which he was ushered out. He frowned, shrugged his shoulders, and turned to head to the common area. There was a Twilight Zone marathon on TV today, and he didn't want to miss it. Assuming he could get the remote from the guy with the oral fixation.

†††

The added sessions were productive in a way that never produced positive results. Jason at least grew stronger in his ability to control the other, but that was a minor issue at this point. That Jason learned it was better to control himself, this one only occasionally reigning him in. Reaching an accommodation with a separate entity inside your skull was not the purpose of the sessions, it seemed. Dr. Ambrose kept pushing Jason about his dreams, his relationships with others, and the boundaries surrounding his sense of right and wrong.

Jason made it a point after his third session to get to know the people around him. He hoped this would impress the doctor, but he never seemed notice the effort. Once, while playing chess with Oralman, Jason saw Dr. Ambrose watching him from the nurse's station. Jason smiled and nodded, but the doctor sniffed and turned away. At the next session the doctor never mentioned the event, and when Jason brought it up, he turned the conversation to why Jason felt the need to be so obvious.

"Tell me the man's name." Ambrose's eyes piercing through a veneer of confidence Jason didn't feel.

"I call him Oralman. You know, because the dude always has something in his mouth."

"Fine, but what's his name?"

"He doesn't really talk very much."

"Exactly." Jason cocked his head, and raised an eyebrow. "Son, he's your favorite around here because he doesn't talk. He's safe. You might as well create a friendship with that chair."

"Why is it so important?"

"Because you need a goddamn anchor, boy!" Ambrose said, slamming his open hand on the coffee table. Jason leaned back as far as his chair would let him.

The doctor saw Jason's reaction, relaxed, and his eyes softened. He took a deep breath, let it out slowly. "You need something to care for," he said, calmer". Something to live and die for."

As Jason relaxed, the doctor sighed again. "Son, you need to understand not just why you're here, but how to move on." He leaned back in his chair and crossed his legs. "You have to invest your whole self into something so you can appreciate what it means to lose it."

"I don't understand."

The older man pursed his lips for a second. "Not yet," he said, "but you will."

†††

Six weeks of talk therapy, meds at regular intervals, and long stretches of boredom, and Jason was electric with a desire to travel. If he was indeed here to rest, he'd had enough, thankyouverymuch. He saw how some might see this life as restive, but for him it was hell. Jason had become accustomed to the new. An overload of sameness was threatening to unravel the tapestry of his memories—if not his mind— and he needed to move on. More than ever before, he was desperate to find his original reality.

The realization came the day he found out this Jason's parents had died at the same time as his psychotic break. Jason, shocked and broken, nearly allowed the other out of his mental cage, but Doctor Ambrose was always there to coax him back. The man gave him the time he needed to heal. Jason, though, only wanted to leave; to find a reality where he was happy, and the people he loved were all still alive.

Jason sat on his bed, legs crossed, back straight, meditating while he searched inward for some switch or trigger to initiate a jump.

"It's not going to work, son."

Jason opened his eyes to see Dr. Ambrose standing in his doorway. He cocked his head, raised an eyebrow. "What do you mean?"

"Just that the answers you're looking for are not from within."

Jason snorted. "Odd approach for a psychiatrist."

"I mean you'll have to talk to someone about your... problems. Someone else might have the answers you keep searching for."

"Someone like you?"

The old man put his hands up, palms out. "Oh, no, son," he said. "I'm just an observer. I listen and occasionally toss out a useless tautological comment."

"I've noticed that about you," Jason said, grinning.

"I am what I am."

Jason laughed. Ambrose watched him for a few seconds, then nodded in a way Jason knew the man had reached a decision.

"I think you'll be ready to leave soon."

Jason's face clouded. "If only there were someplace to go." *Or get back to.*

The doctor scratched his chin. "I've got something in mind already," he said. "Think of it as a half-way house."

†††

Fire filled Jason's view. All around the flames licked and darted, his skin blistering in places where it was unprotected. The smoke billowed and swirled around as water rained from above. It wouldn't be enough, though. The trailer was lost. His parents were gone. There was no way to reach them through the inferno blocking his path. And yet he pressed on. He ran inside... hands... clutched and clawed at him from behind, pulling him back and onto the ground. Water attacked the flames crawling over his body.

Then there was pain.

Jason woke, a soft whimper escaping his lips. He knew at once the dream had been real... it had happened to this Jason. Once again, he had slipped between the ways during the night. The pressure from the other Jason—the less sane one—was gone. He lifted his arms and saw the scars there as proof. The pink new skin was still tender and painful to touch, but he had healed in this reality.

He sat up and looked around the darkened room. A real hospital. Not the sanitarium where he had spent the last six weeks. In the corner was a narrow open wardrobe, and the clothes hanging inside were not the colorless coverings he had become accustomed to, but real civies. He looked at the floor and snorted. *The goddamn boots again.*

Morning sun, still cool and distant, filtered in around the edges of the heavy curtains. Jason stretched his arms as much as the new skin allowed, and turned to dangle his legs off the side of the bed. As he contemplated standing, the door burst open.

"Finally up, I see." The nurse, compact and full of energy, walked with crisp strides to the window and threw the curtains aside.

Sunlight flooded the room, and Jason shielded his eyes. "Hey, warn a guy next time!"

"What next time? We're kicking you out today. Don't you remember?"

Out? Sure, that sounds great, but where? My parents, my home... everything is gone.

"Are you at least going to let me get dressed first?"

The nurse, barked a laugh, the sound not exactly pleasant, but it was efficient. "Sure, hon. Just be careful getting that shirt on. I told your people something soft, but they brought that damn knit piece of crap, anyway."

My people?

"I think there's a cotton t-shirt in that pile with his underwear."

Jason turned his head at the sound of the newcomer. He knew that voice.

"Dr. Ambrose."

"Good morning, Jason." The old man walked into the room, stopped in front of the bed, and lifted the chart with one hand while donning reading glasses with the other. He scanned the pages one at a time, then pulled a pen out of his pocket and signed the top sheet.

Jason waited patiently, then nodded toward the nurse. "I hear I'm being released today."

The doctor raised an eyebrow in the nurse's direction and cleared his throat, "Well, I'm still waiting on your last test results," he said, "but that's the plan." While he spoke, his eyes never left the nurse, and she lowered her head and found something very interesting on the floor to look at.

Dr. Ambrose set the chart back in its holder. "Open your shirt, please." He reached down and placed the earpieces of the stethoscope in his ears, then warmed the other end with his breath. Jason unbuttoned the pajama shirt, and gave a short gasp looking at the mass of scars on his chest.

"Never stops surprising you, does it?"

"No, sir."

"You're lucky to be alive, you know that?"

"I'm beginning to."

The doctor placed the end of the stethoscope on his chest and listened, moving it around several times, directing Jason to "take deep breaths," or "now breathe normally." Finally, he stepped back and screwed up his mouth for a time. Then he nodded once.

"I think you're ready."

"For that 'half-way house'?"

"Excuse me?"

"Uh… nothing."

"It was touch and go there for a while. Trailer home fires are the worst. So many dangerous chemicals in the smoke." He looked up at Jason and smiled that same warm smile from the last reality. "But you're a trooper, boy. You'll be a little shorter of breath for the rest of your life, but nothing to worry about. Other than the scars, no one would even know you ran into that fire."

The doctor turned to the nurse. "Why don't you bring those clothes over here, and then we can leave the young man to get dressed in private." He leaned over, patted Jason's knee. "Not that we haven't seen everything already," he said with a wink at the nurse. She returned a bashful grin, but Jason was sure it was an act for his benefit.

"Thanks, doc." Jason shook his head and chuckled.

"Don't mention it. We'll leave you alone while I fill out your release papers. Unless I get something negative on your other test results, you should be out of here by noon."

As the two left the room, Jason began the painful process of changing clothes. He refused, however to look in the mirror. Seeing what the fire did to his arms and chest left him in no mood to see his face. With luck, he might leave this reality before he ever had to.

†††

"Hey, little buddy!"

Jason turned from the TV in the corner of the room to where Uncle Phil stood in the doorway. The man smiled broadly, but his eyes displayed no humor.

"Hey, Uncle Phil." Jason tried to sound cheerful in return, but couldn't bring himself to pull off an acting job even as bad as his uncle's. "What are you doing up here?"

The man's brows met in the middle, and the hurt in his eyes was clear now. "I figured I was takin' you home today." He looked around the room, then back at Jason. "Aren't they lettin' you go?"

Jason grinned at the big man. "The doctor told me that this morning, but I haven't seen anyone since. He said I should be out by noon, but as you can see," he nodded toward the empty food tray, "that train has already left the station."

"Hey, at least they're still feedin' ya."

Jason smirked. "If you can call it that."

Phil stepped closer to the tray, and leaned over, poking one item. "What's that blue stuff?"

"If it's wiggling, it's Jell-O™." He leaned closer and pursed his lips. "If not, it's probably the meatloaf."

Phil laughed, then grabbed the little cup, held it to his mouth, and sucked the whole thing clean, John Belushi style. "Huh. Now why would they color raspberry blue?"

Jason laughed for the first time in weeks.

Phil's eyes softened. "Good to see that again. Thought you had forgotten how."

He watched his uncle for a few seconds, then sighed. "Yeah," he said, frowning. "Me too."

Phil looked him over, raised an eyebrow, then nodded at the door. "How about we get you out of here? You're already dressed for travelin', and we've got a car waitin' outside."

"We?" Jason tried to access the memories of the body he was inhabiting, without success. Still, it was better than sharing a head with a nutcase.

"C'mon, little buddy. Let's make a break for it." He reached over, grabbed Jason by the one good spot on his arm, and pulled him to his feet.

"Don't you think we should wait for the doctor?"

"Why, so he can charge you another hundred bucks to say 'get out?'" Phil snorted and shooed him toward the door. "No way, son. They've bled you for enough cash already." At the door, he poked his head out of the room and looked in each direction down the long hallway. He pulled his head back in, and turned to Jason. "The nurse's station is empty, so the coast is clear." He pushed Jason out of the room. "Get moving, boy. Quick, before they catch us!"

The hallway, darker than his sun-filled room, was long and empty of traffic. The elevator at the end seemed an impossible distance away, but Phil pulled Jason by the arm as they both dashed for the exit. Even though he knew better, it still felt as if they were escaping from captivity, and he smiled at the thought. For the first time since high school, Jason felt as young as his years. They were almost to the doors when the voice behind them brought them to a sliding halt.

"It's a good thing your test results are normal."

Jason turned to see Dr. Ambrose watching them over the rim of his reading glasses, a thick file in his hands.

Phil smacked him on the back of his head. "See, boy, I *told* you we were supposed to wait for the doctor."

Jason rubbed his head and looked at the goofy grin on his uncle's face. "Yeah, because that's *exactly* what you said."

Phil screwed his mouth up and looked at the ceiling.

"If you boys are through playing around, maybe Jason can sign these forms and check out properly." He smiled at them both and handed the file to Jason. "I'm told you already have a car waiting for you out front."

"Sure," Jason said. "Got a pen?"

The doctor pulled one from his pocket and handed it to him, and turned to watch Phil, who was still counting ceiling tiles. He pointed at the man's chest. "You two take care of him, okay? I want to see him in a month for to evaluate his progress."

"Sure, sure," Phil said without looking at the man.

Jason watched them both for a second, then sighed and signed the papers. He handed the file and pen back. "Can we go, now?"

"Of course. Just take it easy for a few weeks, okay?"

Phil reached across, offered his hand, and the doctor shook it. "Don't worry about the boy, doc. He's in good hands."

Ambrose narrowed his eyes, looking for something in the man's face, then nodded. "I believe you're right." He turned back to Jason, taking his hand. "Take care, son."

"Will do," Jason said, pumping the doctor's hand, then he and Phil entered the elevator. As they rode it down to ground level, he turned to his uncle and tilted his head. "What did he mean 'you two'?"

Phil grinned. Then he tapped his chin with a meaty forefinger. "Three, actually."

As Jason opened his mouth to ask him what he meant, the elevator pinged, and the doors opened. Phil waved him through first, and Jason stepped into the lobby.

"Daddy!"

The little boy running at him was familiar, in the way a mirror is, but Jason still turned to look behind him to see who he referred to. When he turned back, his eyes widened to see his beloved Kat trailing behind the boy, her face shining bright as starlight.

NINE

WHEN PHIL SAW THE BURNED-OUT TRAILER ON THE NEWS THAT night, he threw on a pair of sweatpants and jumped in his beat-up F-150. Several near-collisions later he arrived at the scene, tumbled out of the cab, and wove his way through what remained of the crowd of onlookers. The reporters were packing up, Jason was sitting on Ida Blaine's front porch with his head in his hands, and a young cop stood over him with a notepad. The old woman stood by in silence, holding a glass of water in her trembling hands. One look from her and Phil knew with certainty that his sister and Dale were both dead.

As he ran up to them, the officer looked up from Jason, and held up a hand. "Sir, you need to stay back."

"Outta my way, Captain America," he growled. "That's my nephew." He pointed at the remains of the trailer. "And that was my sister's house."

The policeman bristled, but closed his notepad and wandered a few feet away. Phil noticed he remained within earshot, however.

Sitting beside the young man, Phil waited. He hesitated, then wrapped an arm around his nephew. Jason looked up, clear confusion and pain in his eyes. Phil knew at once this was not the same man he spoke with earlier. This was a completely different Jason, and he had no memory of the conversation the two had only an hour before. That Jason was gone.

"I just got home, Uncle Phil, and everything is just… gone." His eyes were red, but the tears had dried.

Phil looked up at the old woman. "Do they know what happened, Ida?"

She shook her head. "I heard an explosion…" Her voice cracked, and she seemed to just notice the glass she held. She took a sip, then nodded at the car by the road. "Kathy was visiting." Ida leaned over to Phil and whispered, "I… I don't think the boy was with her."

Phil let out a breath he didn't realize he was holding. He recognized the car when he drove up, but wasn't sure what it all meant. Now he knew.

"They tell me Kathy's dead, Uncle Phil." Jason was looking at the trailer, lost in his grief. He turned to the only family he had left. "I always thought there would be time for us. You know?"

"Yeah, son. I do," Phil mumbled. There was more his nephew needed to know, but now was not the time.

"Sir?" The police officer, one hand resting on the weapon on his belt, held up his notepad and stepped closer. "Unless you have anything to add, I think we've got everything we need for now." He looked down at Jason. "I would like him to come in tomorrow or the next day to give us a complete statement, though."

"Sure," he looked up at the intruder, allowing the irritation to show in his face and voice. "I'll bring him by tomorrow afternoon." He turned away, dismissing the man with a wave of his hand.

"Thank you," he said, then nodded at Jason. "I'm sorry for your loss, son." He looked up at the woman. "Ma'am," he said, tipping his cap, and walked away.

Phil watched him go, almost wishing he could go with him. *Shoulda gone with the* other *Jason, you goddamn coward.* That one was adrift, lost in the tangle of realities without hope of finding a friendly shore. *I made damn sure of that, didn't I?* All Phil had to do was teach the boy to find his way in the in-between, and he was too afraid to do even that. *Maybe I can make up for some of that here.* He snorted at the thought he could ever help *anyone.*

He wasn't good at this stuff. Most days he couldn't console *himself,* much less a kid he rarely saw. He thought about shifting over; let another Phil sort this out. But he couldn't do that. He couldn't leave another man to do his work, even if it was still himself.

He looked over at his nephew. This Jason had some hard days

ahead of him, that was for sure. Soon, Phil would have time to grieve for his sister, but today—today he had to help his nephew.

Phil struggled to his feet, knees creaking, and put a hand on Jason's shoulder. "C'mon son. I've got a spare room you can use for as long as you need," he said, then turned to Mrs. Blaine. "Can you make a few calls for me?"

Ida frowned, then tried to smile. "Sure, Phil. I think I know what you need. I've got the numbers inside." She looked down at Jason, who still hadn't moved. "You just take care of him for now."

Phil nodded. "Thanks, Ida." He reached down and pulled at Jason's arm. The young man didn't resist, but rose slowly to his feet. Phil put an arm around his shoulder and led him to the old truck.

†††

Phil spent that night and the next day trying to help the new Jason come to terms with what had happened. This one wasn't a traveler—that much was clear—so he didn't have the advantage of knowing his family still existed somewhere in another reality. He also didn't have to live knowing that other realities meant nothing was *better*, and that the grass wasn't always, or even *sometimes*, greener. This Jason only knew his parents and Kathy were gone, and he would never see them again.

The second hardest part was getting the man out of bed the next day to drive to the police station. The *first* was telling Jason about his son.

"You mean everyone knew but me?" If Phil had been any smaller, he would have recoiled at the restrained energy in that quiet question. *Open carefully. Contents under pressure.*

"I think she was at your parent's house to tell you," he said.

"Oh," was all he croaked out. Jason, pacing the floor like a jungle cat, stopped and faced his uncle. He stood for long seconds as memories and lost futures crawled across his face. Phil braved to reach across the void and place a heavy hand on the boy's shoulder. Jason's shoulders slumped as he looked down at the worn carpet in his uncle's house, and said, "How do I tell him about his mom?" He looked up again, eyes moist, but refusing to spill over, "I'm just some guy he's never met, Uncle Phil. How am I supposed to comfort him? What do I do?"

"You be his daddy, son." Phil sniffed, then lowered his hand. "If I had the answers, I'd have a family myself," he said. "You do what you can, and let the rest take care of itself," he added, shrugging his shoulders.

Well, that's crappy advice. No wonder I ain't married.

Phil shook his head, then reached out and gripped his nephew's shoulder again, giving it a strong squeeze. "C'mon, son, let's go see your boy."

†††

Phil left the last two members of his family in a fierce embrace in Dorothy Anderson's living room. Kathy's landlady had been watching the boy since Phil had called her after the fire, and she waited outside on her porch while Jason and his son met for the first time and shared their grief.

"Those two gonna be okay?" She looked up at Phil from where she sat on the porch steps.

Phil tilted his head, then sat beside her. "I think so. Just gonna take time."

"They can stay in Kathy's place until Jason gets a job and decides what he wants to do."

He turned to her and nodded. "Thanks, Dotty. I think that might be best. I was thinkin' they could stay with me, but the kid hardly knows me, and it might be better for him to be around the things he knows for a while."

Dotty wrinkled her nose, sniffed, and nodded down the road. "I doubt that Kathy's parents will be much help."

"No, I don't imagine. They never did take to the boy."

She turned her head to look at him, and said "I can put them up, Phil, but I can't feed them for long."

"No need to worry about that. Dale told me once he took out a huge life insurance policy on him and the missus." He grinned, but the corners of his mouth fell almost as fast as they rose. He tried again, almost succeeding this time. "Jason's not gonna have to worry about money for a while," he said.

The woman nodded. "At least the man got one thing right."

"I guess he did, at that." He hooked his thumb over his shoulder. "Two, if you count that young man in there."

"They're both good boys, Phil." She rose with a grunt, patted Phil a couple of times on the shoulder, and walked back into her home. The screen door bounced twice behind her before it stilled. In the silence that followed, Phil looked east. There, beyond the trees, a thin filament of smoke still drifted up and away. He squinted his eyes and shaded his brow with a shaking hand. Probably just somebody grilling some steaks. Images he never saw flashed into his head, and the gorge rose to meet them. He struggled to keep it down, mind fighting instinct, and won a reprieve.

He sighed, stood on crackling knees, and walked back into the house.

Life goes on.

†††

"I don't like leaving Jay alone right now." Jason pressed against the door of Phil's truck, his right arm hanging out of the window, pounding a methodical rhythm on the side.

"First of all, he ain't alone. He's with Dotty. And second," Phil turned and smiled at Jason, "congratulations, son, you're already thinkin' like a daddy." He watched his nephew for a second or two, then turned his attention back to the road while the smile melted from his face. "Besides, I don't think the kid needs to be with us at the police station."

"No," Jason hung his head, "I guess not." The young man stared out the window as they drove, then closed his eyes and tilted his head to let the breeze blow his hair back. "Do we really have to do this today?"

Phil considered it. "Best to get it over with, son," he said. "You know officer crew-cut will just hunt you down… and probably at the worst possible time." He looked over at Jason, and caught his eyes with his own. "We've got a lot to do between now and the funeral."

Jason swallowed once, then nodded.

"Besides," Phil nodded over Jason's shoulder and turned the wheel, "we're already here."

Jason gave him a feeble lopsided grin. "I forgot how small this town was."

"Yeah, son, we've got the 'welcome to' and 'now leaving' all printed on the same side of the signs." He pulled into the nearest parking space and jammed his foot on the brake, throwing both men against their shoulder straps as the tires slid and finally grabbed the pavement.

His nephew looked at him and smiled in real humor for the first time that morning.

"Yeah, I hear there was a major traffic jam last week when the stop sign was stolen."

Phil laughed and clapped Jason on the back. He held his hand there a few seconds, then gave his shoulder a squeeze. "Let's git to gittin', son."

†††

"Thank you for bringing him in, Mr. Carson."

"No problem, officer…" Phil leaned in to read the name tag on the man's chest, "Cole."

"David, sir." The officer put out his hand, and Phil grasped and shook it once. The man looked at Jason, and nodded to the straight-backed chair in front of the old desk across from himself. "If you will have a seat, this shouldn't take too long."

Jason sat, back straight as the chair, hands in his lap as Phil looked around and found another chair across the narrow aisle. As he pulled it over to the desk, the chair's legs screeching a loud complaint against the floor, the officer looked up from his paperwork.

"Sir?" He knit his eyebrows, the two tufts nearly meeting in the middle. "This is just a formality. You can wait for Mr. Callahan in the lobby."

Phil's eyes widened, then narrowed to slits. In a voice just as narrow, he said "Listen real good officer Friday, I ain't leavin' that boy to anyone's tender mercies." He sat down hard in the chair and crossed his arms, letting them rest on his ample belly. "You got a problem with that?"

Jason bit his tongue, as did the rest of the people in the room, watching both men. There was a slight grin on his face, but otherwise he kept his own counsel while Phil and the officer engaged in a staring contest. After ten seconds, the officer looked down at the papers on his desk, pulled out his chair, and sat.

"Fine, sir, but Mr. Callahan will do his own talking."

Phil nodded once and turned to his nephew. "Boy ain't got nothin' to hide. He can speak for himself just fine."

Cole looked at each man, then said "All right. Let's get started." He pulled out his notebook, flipped through a few pages, then looked up again at Jason. "Do you remember what time you left the house last night?"

"I think it was around nine."

"And you went to Mr. Carson's home?"

"Yeah."

"What time did you arrive?

He turned to Phil, forehead wrinkling. "About nine-thirty, right?"

Phil nodded as he watched the officer. "Yeah, give or take."

Cole flipped a page or two again, then back to the first. "I thought Mr. Carson lived only a few blocks away. Why so long to get to his place?"

"I walked."

The officer nodded, then made a notation on one of the forms on the desk. "I figured as much, but we didn't cover that last night." He tapped his pencil eraser on the desk, looking back and forth between his notebook and the form. "What time did you leave Mr. Carson's home?"

Jason looked at Phil again. "Around ten-thirty, I think."

Phil said, "Closer to ten forty-five. Local news had already finished up while we were talking." He leaned forward, "Is there some reason you need to keep track of the boy's whereabouts?"

The officer's eyes grew wide for a second, then narrowed. "Oh, no. It's nothing like that, sir. I'm just trying to get a timeline of the events." He tapped the pencil on the desk a few more times, then read from his notes. "Fire department received the call at ten seventeen and arrived on scene at ten twenty-four. Near as we can tell, the fire must have started sometime around ten fifteen." He looked up at Jason with soft eyes, still tapping the pencil. "It was completely out of control by the time the trucks arrived. Those older trailers burn very quickly, I'm afraid."

Jason nodded, and he dropped his gaze to the hands in his lap. "So now that you know when, do you have any leads on who started the fire?"

The officer sat back, clear confusion on his face. "Who?"

Jason looked up, his head tilted. "Mrs. Blaine said she heard an explosion."

Cole nodded and checked his notes again. "That was most likely the propane tank. We think the fire started in the trailer, then spread to the tank outside."

"Bullshit!" Phil couldn't help himself. He pounded one meaty fist on the desk. "That tank was empty. Dale went all electric about five years ago."

"Well, no tank is completely empty—"

"That one was! That valve's been open since he capped the line."

"Sir, you need to calm down." He placed his hands flat on the desk. "There's no sign of foul play. Besides, who would want to kill your family? What enemies could they possibly have had?" he said, shaking his head. "If there is a motive, the only person we know who *might* have one is Mr. Callahan here." His eyes narrowed at the big man. "Are you suggesting he killed his own parents?"

Phil felt his whole head heat up, but he fought to keep control of his emotions.

"Worthless," was what he said at last.

"Sir?"

Phil turned to Jason, and jerked a thumb at Cole. "I remember this guy, you know." He turned back to the officer, still speaking to Jason, "Linebacker in high school while I was coaching the running backs." He snorted once and shook his head. "Little Wendall Davis used to run right over him in practice. The defensive line let Wendall through just to watch him do it."

The officer stiffened as his ears turned red, the muscles of his jaw working furiously.

Phil smiled at Cole, then laughed softly. "Got so bad it looked like you had a target painted on your chest." He leaned forward, settling his weight on one arm on the desk, and said "Worthless then, worthless now."

Cole looked at him for a few seconds, eyes flaming, then closed his little notebook with a snap. He grabbed a pen from his shirt pocket, signed the bottom of the top-most form, slid it across the desk to Jason, and offered him the pen. "I think we're done. Sign on the bottom where your name is printed, please."

Jason looked up, mouth open and eyes wide. "That's it?"

"That's it. I told you this was just a formality. The official report will list this as an unfortunate accident." He tried to smile, but as he looked at Phil, he couldn't complete the action.

Phil shook his head and turned to Jason. "Might as well sign it, son. It's the closest you're gonna get to police work around here." As Jason signed the form, Phil stood, looked around the room, drawing every pair of eyes.

"Worthless."

†††

Before Phil dropped him off, Jason was silent the entire trip back to Dotty's. Phil wanted to take care of the all the funeral arrangements without the boys around. They had enough on their plate just getting to know one another.

Police report in hand, he first visited Dale's insurance agent, then the funeral home. Thankfully, Dale had kept his life insurance current, and the payout was gonna be a godsend for Jason and the boy. Added to the standard policy he had at work, and the boys would be set as long as Jason was careful with it. Dale had also bought a family plot beside his parents years ago, so even the funeral expenses would be minimal.

"Thank you, Lord, for small favors." Phil blew a soft breath between his teeth as he drove. "I don't think I could have handled taking care of both of them."

Later that day, the worst of the awful chores behind him, he went back to the smoldering remains of the trailer. The police tape marking the area as off limits flapped lazily in the light breeze, and he stood there looking past it like it was a solid barrier. *It was amazing*, he thought, *how people respected such flimsy lines*. Even a simple yellow line painted on the ground was enough to keep most at bay.

"Fuck it," he breathed, then snapped the yellow plastic in two and walked into what he was sure was a crime scene.

He stepped as lightly as his bulk would allow across the blackened lawn, stopping in front of the old propane tank. The surface on the far side had a single round hole, metal bent outward signifying a small explosion. The near side had what he knew would be there: a thumb-sized bullet hole in a direct line from the exit on the other side. He reached down and placed a finger inside, remembering the day it was made.

"That thing's dangerous, Dale," he said as he waved at the tank. "You should just list it in the classifieds and get rid of it."

"Aw, hell, Phil. It's empty, and startin' to rust. It ain't no more dangerous than you are."

"Maybe Phil's right, hon." The worst thing Joan could have done at that point was agree with her brother.

"For fuck's sake, people." Dale stalked into the house, and Phil and

Joan were just about convinced he had gone in to sulk when he slammed through the screen door and down the front steps carrying his Remington 700. Before they could stop him, or at least get to a safe distance, he shouldered the rifle, took aim, and fired. The Lapua .338, full-metal jacketed round punched through one side and out the other like a hot knife through butter. Dale, a wide grin splitting his face, snapped the safety on and allowed the muzzle to drift toward the ground.

"Shit, Dale, that thing could have blown up!"

Dale shook his head. "No, Phil. For a whole lot of reasons, just… no." He turned to go inside and return the rifle to its place of honor, then stopped and looked at Phil. "Go home and look up the word 'stoichiometry'." Phil's forehead wrinkled like a Shar-Pei. "You learn a lot in the Marines," Dale said. "Especially when it comes to blowin' shit up."

Phil might have stayed in that memory the rest of the day, but a stray breeze brought forth another wave of burnt-trailer smell. He wiped his hand on his jeans and stood. He took another look around the area and sighed. There was no way the cops believed the fire had caused the tank to explode. The assholes were just lazy. The victims were too low on the list of "Who's Who" in town for them to make an effort.

No, if the answer was going to be found, it was up to Phil to find it. There was one way he knew to get the truth, but it would require a lot from him. Probably more than he had. He shook his head and sighed. Maybe he should just let it go.

Walking back to his truck, Phil passed through the place where the other Jason must have stood when he slipped through the wall, and the brief sensation of vertigo nearly drove him to his knees. He passed through these types of veils many times before—you couldn't avoid them if you were, like him, sensitive to their presence—but this was the strongest he had ever encountered, and, in fact, left him with a clear sense of a bearing. Though directions, in the Euclidean sense, held no meaning when finding a pathway through the various overlaid walls, he still had a clear picture of which "direction" to pick.

Phil hated the idea of leaving this Jason in his time of need, but fortunately he could be in both places at once. The Phil that would replace him when he slipped through would take over his duties as if he never left. He hated more the idea he left the other Jason alone and adrift, but now he had more than one reason to find him.

He realized at that moment he had already decided to follow the other Jason through the wall.

❈101❈

TEN

Jason stood before the mirror, razor in hand, and couldn't get past the idea he was stealing another man's life. Sure, that man was himself, but that didn't make it easier. Somewhere in the multiverse, the Jason that belonged here was having to adjust to another life—one that might not be as appealing as this one.

Patches of scar tissue—gnarled and twisted, though few in number—peeked through the shaving cream on his face. It had taken a long time to get used to shaving such a topography, but after nearly a year of practice he almost never nicked himself anymore. At least no hair grew in those areas for him to remove. If it had, he would have just grown a beard and called it a day.

"Are you going to stand there all day, or can I get to the sink?" Kathy stood in the doorway to the little bathroom with her arms crossed, a towel in hand, and a smirk on her face. "That mug isn't going to shave itself, you know."

Jason faced her and raised an eyebrow, most of which had grown back. "I was just noticing that I seem to be getting prettier, while you just keep getting older."

With a practiced flip, she threw the towel in his face.

"Aw, man. Now I've got to start over," he said, feigning hurt and dismay, as he cleaned the lather from his face.

"Keep it up, buster, and I'll go on your fishing trip with you guys."

"Oh, *hell* no. There's not enough bug spray in the state to keep you happy, sweetheart." He smiled again and tossed the damp towel back at her, which she neatly dodged.

She watched it hit the floor. "Be sure to pick that up, dear," she said. "And this time put it *in* the hamper, instead of just laying it on top."

Jason smiled back at her and sighed, happy for the first time in years. He picked up the can of shaving gel, squirted a dollop into his hand, and lathered his face once again. He picked up the razor and got to work. After clearing his mostly undamaged neck, he began to tackle the rough terrain of his face. Kathy watched him with a warm smile.

"Who's going with you this time?"

"Jay, of course, and Phil. I talked Dr. Ambrose into meeting us at the docks."

Kathy tilted her head. "Dr. Ambrose is going fishing?"

"Oh he's probably going out, but the man doesn't really fish. He says the only real reason a man fishes these days is to have an excuse to sit quietly, eat sandwiches, and drink beer without the missus bothering him."

Kathy laughed. It sounded like church bells ringing on a clear morning when she laughed.

"He and I have a lot in common, then. I always thought fishing and golf were invented to get away from the wives."

"Can't help it if those places are not your natural habitat." Jason finished raking his face smooth with one last flip of the razor, and grabbed his towel from the hook beside the sink. As he cleaned the last of the shaving cream from his face, he turned to allow Kathy to squeeze by while they exchanged places.

"About damn time," she muttered, passing him. Jason knew she would camp out there for the next half-hour or so, but at least he got in first this time. Going *after*… well, that would put a crimp in any man's schedule. He stood there watching her and pondered something he had been mulling over for some time, even though he already knew what she would say.

"Kat, do you think we need a bigger place?"

She stopped what she was doing and screwed up her mouth for a second, then shook her head. "Bigger place, bigger problems," she said. "We do fine here."

"You sound just like your dad, sometimes."

Her face clouded for an instant, then cleared. "Well, sometimes he's right."

"Babe, don't you think we could be more comfortable in a larger place?"

"Of course we could, but that's not a good enough reason."

"Look, we're both working, and there's some money left over from all the donations we got while I was in the hospital. I just thought—"

"That money is for emergencies… period." She turned to Jason, her eyes soft and her voice husky and deep, "You spend too much time thinking about *now,* and not enough thinking about *tomorrow.*"

She was right. He had always thought about only the now, never about the future. What was the point? Whatever future this Jason had, it would not be his forever. Why not enjoy now? Tomorrow might see him panhandling under an overpass. Or as a vegetable in intensive care. Or spending his days alone, *not* married to the only woman he ever loved.

He couldn't tell her any of this, though. Even if she understood, the decisions he made would continue to impact her life long after he was gone. For the first time he understood real people were affected by the things he did as another Jason, and they had to live with those actions long after he left for a new reality. Each trip sideways washing him clean. *Can the next universe's God grant absolution for what I do in the this one?* he wondered.

"Are you okay?" She leaned toward him, hand outstretched to touch his shoulder.

"I'm fine, babe." He smiled back at her, trying to recapture the humor of the last few minutes. "You're right. If we moved to a bigger place, we would need a maid… and you never know how *that* would work out."

She laughed and waggled her eyebrows. "Don't forget the pool boy. Momma's gotta have a pool boy."

†††

Twenty-fifth time's the charm, Phil thought.

Now that he stood at Jason's door, mind racing as he considered what he was about to do, he wondered if it was even the right choice. His hand hovered near the door bell, finger ready to press, but frozen in place by indecision. *The boy's happy for a change. What right do I have?* It wasn't *right* that mattered, though. It was *responsibility.*

Phil sighed, shook off his doubt, and pressed the button. He had waited until Kathy left with Jay before getting out of his truck, but he wasn't sure Jason was still in the house until he heard him walk to the door. He shoved his hands in his pockets and waited.

The heavy inner door opened, and Jason stood behind the screen door and smiled.

"Hey, Uncle Phil," he said as he worked the latch and pushed. "What brings you here this morning? I thought the our trip was Sunday."

"Uh, it is," Phil said as he squeezed past and stepped into the living room. It was a small house, so there was no entryway to speak of. A step to his right was a large couch, and he dropped himself there.

"Make yourself at home," Jason said with a chuckle, closing the door. His eyebrows beetled, almost touching one another as they always did when the boy was trying to work something out, and he walked to one of the leather recliners and took a seat. "What brings you by so early this morning?"

Phil had dreaded that question—even though he knew it must be answered. He scrubbed his hands over and over in his lap, then leaned forward. "We have to go back, Jason."

Jason's brows knitted again, then his eyes flew open wide. He stood on rubbery legs, backing away from his uncle. "No, n-no..." he stammered, holding a hand out, palm up like a traffic cop. He stumbled, then placed his other hand on the recliner to steady himself. "You fucking *lied* to me back there!"

"Jason—"

"No," Jason snapped. "You don't know what I've *been* through since I left." His breathing was rapid and heavy, like a bull preparing to rush. "You could have shown me how to get home, but..." Jason looked around the room, then closed his eyes, calming himself. When he opened them again, it was as if a stranger stared back.

"So I lied," he said with a shrug, a bridled anger of his own welling inside. "Boy, that ain't even the worst thing I've done this *year*." *Not even a close second*, he thought. "Son," he said, softening his voice, "there's things to do back in my reality, and I need your help." His eyes bored into Jason's. "You don't belong here. This life is someone else's."

"No," Jason said, cutting off Phil's argument as if he were rejecting a third cup of coffee. "I'm finally happy for the first time in years. I—"

"Your parents were *murdered*, Jason," Phil said with hard finality. He never intended it to come out so harsh, but he had underestimated his feelings. "Don't you want to find out who did it?" Jason stood like a statue, his mouth open, eyes confused. "I know *I* do," Phil said. "They were my family, too, you know."

Jason's voice shook as he moved to put the recliner between Phil and himself. "How the hell did you find me?" he asked.

"It wasn't easy," Phil replied through a crooked smile. "Had to trace a lot of paths and deal with a lot of dead ends." He shrugged. "If I didn't know better, I would have thought you were hiding from me. I wasn't sure I found the right you until just now."

Jason's shoulders relaxed, and he moved around to the front of his chair. He had a look in his eyes he always got when thinking hard about a solution to a thorny problem.

"If they were murdered there, then they were here as well. Same event, same guy, right?" Breathing normally, he sat on the edge of his chair. "We can find out in *this* reality as easily as in the other, can't we?"

"Maybe… maybe not," Phil said as he shook his head. "All I know is neither of us belongs here, and there are clues I've found back home that might not be here."

"I don't belong *there*, either," Jason said coolly.

"I know, son, but as soon as we find this guy I'll help you find your real home."

"So now I have to *earn* the right to go home? Is that how it's gonna be?" Jason's chest heaving again, filling with a growing anger.

"That's not what I meant at all." *This is not how I planned on this going,* Phil thought. *What did I think was going to happen? Did I think he was going to jump at the chance to leave this perfect life to help me find a killer?* From the first few minutes after finding Jason in this reality, he knew the boy would not want to leave. Here, Jason had the life he always dreamed of. He might not have the right to stay, but Phil didn't have the right to take it away from him, either. He also didn't have the ability. As soon as he taught Jason how to move between realities, the boy could just come back any time he wanted. What he needed to do was convince him to do the right thing.

"Phil," Jason began, "I've got a wife here. A son who—"

"Whose grandparents were murdered," Phil said, his voice flat and dangerous.

"Dammit, Phil! You're not gonna guilt me into coming with

you!" Jason gripped the arms of his chair, his face burning a cherry red. "You can't make me go."

"You're right. I can't make you come with me," Phil said softly. "But I won't stay here until you change your mind, either." He shook his head slowly, and lowered his eyes to the floor. "I know I promised to show you how to go home, but if you're not leaving, there's no reason anymore." He looked into Jason's eyes. "Is there?"

Jason's face hardened, lips as tight as a bowstring. "I think you should leave, now."

Phil heaved a heavy sigh. He had failed. He knew from the moment he understood this reality the possibility of failure existed, but he began with so much hope. He also knew he would check in periodically—and Jason probably knew it, too—but the boy was too angry to think about it right now.

"Okay," Phil said at last. "I'll be on my way, then." He settled back into the cushions to clear his mind.

"Not *here*," Jason said, clear exasperation in his voice. "Take him back to where you jumped in." Then, in pure Jason form, he smiled that crooked smile. "You don't want to confuse him any more than you have already."

"Right," Phil said and stood. He stuck out his hand, and for a second he thought Jason wouldn't return the gesture. Finally, the other man stood and took his hand. They locked eyes for a time, then Phil said, "I'm glad you're happy, son." He released Jason's hand and walked to the door and let himself out.

All the way to his truck, he kept thinking—hoping—Jason would call him back, but he never did.

†††

Kathy dried her hands on the dishtowel before threading it through the ring that hung over the sink. "Uncle Phil's called twice today about your trip on Sunday," she said while turning back to look at Jason. "How come you haven't called him back?"

"I don't know," he mumbled. "Busy, I guess." Jason was looking over at the stack of papers on the kitchen table waiting to be graded, avoiding her gaze.

"Uh, huh..." There wasn't much point in pushing him on the subject. He would either tell her what was up, or he wouldn't. He was as stubborn as his daddy, and she didn't have the energy to dig it out of him.

"Are you guys still going? Because you better not disappoint your son," she said, shaking an accusing finger in his direction. "He's been looking forward to this trip for weeks."

"I know, Kat," he said, and smiled, still handsome even with the scarring. "Don't worry. We're still going."

She walked to where he leaned against the small kitchen island, and reached up and placed a gentle hand on his face. "You better," she said, giving him a light smack with that hand. "I need the time off."

He laughed, eyes shining. The truth was he did more of the parenting duties than she, and while she was grateful, he also had more time in his schedule.

"So," he began, an obvious attempt to distract her from her initial query, "what are your plans for the day?"

"I was thinking about visiting mom and dad."

"Ah," he said without inflection. "Good idea."

Good idea. What he means is "thank God you're not dragging me and Jay over there with you." Jason hated her family, and, truth be told, she didn't blame him. She wasn't very fond of them, herself. *But they are family, after all.* Before she and Jason married, they had all but disowned her for getting pregnant out of wedlock. They never liked Jason, and he knew it. He was from "the wrong side of the tracks," as people of their social status used as code for "poor." To them, poor meant lazy, conniving, uneducated—*criminal.* The fact Jason was none of those things meant nothing to them. He "came from the wrong stock," and that was all that mattered. More than once, she pointed out her grandparents—*their* parents—started with little more than Jason's family, but they always waved that off. "We *earned* everything we have," they would say, as if he and his parents had not.

"Well," he said with practiced sincerity, "be sure to give them my best." Before she could respond, he started laughing. "Sorry, babe," he said through guffaws. "I couldn't sustain it."

Kathy smirked, and shook her head. "You see? *This* is why I never bring you with me."

"Yeah," he said with a snort, laugh lines still creasing around his eyes, "*that's* why."

The issue with Phil now completely ignored, she decided against circling back. If there was a problem, those two would work it out on their own. They had been thick as thieves since the fire, being the only remaining members of their family, and there was a closeness there she had never experienced with any member of her own. Her sister, Mary—ten years her senior—never bonded with her while they were children. She left at seventeen, never to return. *Mom and dad never even speak about her anymore.* It was if she never existed.

She shook off the melancholy before it could build. "Well," she said with a slight smile, "if you really want to come, we can make a family trip for Saturday."

"No, no," he said, palms up in front, "don't change your plans for my benefit."

"Thought so," said said, shaking her head. "Just be sure to bring that boy back in one piece. You know how he is."

"I make no promises," he said. "He's got a mind of his own." He shrugged. "He's like people, that way."

†††

Jay slammed the car door, hitting the ground at a dead run when he saw Uncle Phil pull into the parking lot. Jason yelled at him to stop, but the boy was determined to be the first to greet the big man. Tires crunched in the loose gravel as the old truck slid to a stop, the added mass of the boat and trailer it towed taxing the worn brakes.

Phil stuck his head through the open window and bellowed, "*Boy*… three more steps and I might have flattened you!"

Jay, almost seven, with the surety of wizened youth, beamed a bright smile. "You weren't even close," he said, as if that explained everything. Even so, he had stopped running at the man's first word, and stood motionless until Phil gave him permission to move.

Jason held his tongue and allowed his nerves to settle. The little imp was always coming within a hair's breadth of catastrophe, but his on-board avoidance system managed to keep him from serious harm.

"That boy's going to be the death of you, Jason." Leaning against the rear of his BMW, arms crossed and wearing freshly-pressed tan chinos, Carl Ambrose looked as out of place as a man could. He was a spare man even in his lab coat, but in short sleeves and neatly creased pants he was a stick figure. The straw pork pie hat he wore merely enhanced the impression.

"Uh, Carl? We're goin' out on Phil's bass boat, not some yacht from the marina." Jason grinned at the man and shook his head.

Phil walked up beside Jason, and said in a stage-whisper, "This is *not* a good idea, boy." He smiled broadly as he said it, and Jason grinned back.

"Don't mind me, Phil," Carl said, stepping away from his car. "I just came for the beer and sandwiches."

Jason dipped his head. "Sorry Carl," he said, looking at his sneakers. "We, uh… forgot the the beer."

Carl grinned, the skin around his eyes creasing as neatly as his pants. "No matter," he said, popping the trunk on his car. He reached in and pulled out a large cooler. "I brought my own."

Phil pushed past Jason and took the cooler from Carl's hands. "Man know's how to *fish*," he said.

✝✝✝

For once, the mosquitoes stayed home and did whatever it was mosquitoes did when not dive-bombing unsuspecting fishermen. The humidity was low for this time of year, and Jason marveled at smooth stillness of the lake's surface. Mirror-smooth, a leap from the boat would feel like falling into the sky.

No one spoke once the lines were dropped in the water, little Jay having learned his lesson the first time he was allowed to join the men. There was a stillness in the air that, on a normal morning, would have the men staining their shirts with sweat in under ten minutes. This morning, however, there was enough of a chill to keep even Phil from complaining.

On the marshy far shore, snowy egrets lifted yellow feet like children escaping a slumber party. Each dipped black bills into the water, piercing the mirror, feeding on insects and small fish they pulled from the other side of the looking glass. Jason hoped it was mosquito larvae. One of the birds tucked its head back and leapt, wings spreading to beat hard against the cool air. Within seconds it cruised over the lake, swooping low to scoop its bill in the water with each pass. He knew egrets fished much like seagulls from time to time, but this was the first time he saw it in action. They were more graceful in his opinion, though that might just be perception based on the long neck.

Carl lounged near the bow, leaning against his cooler and reading a paperback. From experience Jason knew it would be something trashy. Carl had an affinity for romance novels, of all things. He claimed it helped him understand women, but since Jason had never seen the man with a woman, he doubted that was the case. Women were still a mystery to Jason, and he was sure no book could remedy that—least of all a romance novel. Besides, mystery was part of the appeal.

Phil leaned against the little trolling motor in the stern, legs propped up on his own cooler, and the brim of his gimme cap pulled down over his eyes. The pole was held loose in his hands, with the end hanging lazily over the water. Jason assumed the man was awake because the pole swept a slow rhythm back and forth.

Jay sat beside his father in the middle of the boat, eyes alert and scanning the surface of the small lake for any disturbance. He was eager to catch his first fish, and Jason hoped today would be the day. There weren't many good fishing days left in the season, though there were always the canals and creeks nearby where one could fish well into December.

"Hey, Doc," Phil said from underneath his cap, "toss me a brew."

Carl sat up, opened the cooler, and fished around inside for a few seconds. He pulled out a dripping can. "Head's up," he said, flipping it in Phil's direction. The beer tumbled slowly through the air over Jason's head, and Phil snatched it from the air before it could sail over the edge and into the water.

"Thanks, Doc." He set the can down, tapped the top a few times, and popped it open. Pushing the brim of his cap up with the top of the can, Phil tilted it back and drank in noisy gulps, then set the can down and belched.

"Aw, man, Uncle Phil! I can smell that from here," Jay said, holding his nose with his free hand. "What did you have for breakfast?"

"Sausage and onions," Jason said.

"Good guess, son."

"That wasn't a guess, Uncle Phil." He grinned and nodded back at Carl. "The old man behind me will verify that in a second."

"No he won't," Carl said, waving his hat in front of him.

Phil belly-laughed, toasted Carl, and took another drink.

"Now I'm hungry," Jay said. The men stopped moving for two or three seconds, then broke into sustained laughter. Jay looked at the adults in the boat as if they had grown a third eye. "What?" he said, eyebrows knitting like his dad.

Between chuckles, Carl said, "Might as well crack open that cooler, Phil. None of you are going to get any fishing done until that boy eats."

Phil laughed again and pulled four sandwiches from his cooler. He tossed one to each in turn, holding one for himself, then settled back against the motor. Jay opened his first and made a face.

Jason leaned toward his son. "What did you get?" he asked.

The boy closed the wrapper around the sandwich and shook his head. "I don't wanna say."

"C'mon, dude. What is it?"

Jay looked up, a sheepish grin on his face. "Sausage and onions."

✝✝✝

The reel on the little pole whined as the line played out, Jay grinning from ear to ear as he held the pole in a two-handed grip. Every man in the boat offered advice, but it was clear the boy was focused on the task of keeping the fishing pole in his hands. For just a second, the reel stopped spinning as the fish on the other end considered its options, and Jay used that time to shift one hand to the crank. He turned the handle, then pulled the pole back, alternating as he had seen the men do, reeling the line in. Inch by inch he pulled the fish closer to the boat. It was a game Jason understood, and knew the boy was learning. Give it a little slack—room to maneuver—pull back to tire it out, then reel it closer. Over and over again until the beast was in your net.

"Toss me that net, Carl," Phil said as he handed his pole to Jason and scooted over to sit by the boy. Carl picked up the old wood-handled net and leaned across both Jason and Jay to pass it to Phil. The big man reached out and snagged it without taking his eyes off Jay's line. "Thanks, man."

Jason was so excited for Jay he never considered getting the net. Instead, he held the two poles and watched his uncle help Jay with his first catch. "When you see the end of your lead coming break the surface, be sure to lift the fish straight up so Uncle Phil can get the net under it."

"I *know*, dad," Jay said, shaking his head.

"Boy thinks he's a teen already, don't he?" Phil was smiling, but

Jason had grown weary of the attitude Jay displayed lately. An adjustment was due, but for now he let it slide.

Turning the reel, Jay pulled the fish closer bit by bit, and when he saw the end of his lead he stood and set one foot on the gunwale to hold the fish up as Jason had taught him. There were smiles all around as the wiggling fish cleared the surface and Phil reached out with the net. As the fish slid into the net, Phil pulled it back, and Jay turned to watch with a huge grin. He shifted his weight to get both feet under him and the foot on the gunwale slipped. He flailed to regain his balance, instead falling overboard, his head hitting the gunwale with a sickening thud on the way down.

"Jay!" Jason knew at once the boy wasn't coming up on his own, and without another thought dropped his pole and dove over the side.

The water was murky this time of the year, and visibility limited, but Jason knew where Jay went in. *He can't have drifted far*, he thought. *Why did I let him in the damn boat without a life jacket?* Because he wanted to be the cool daddy, that's why. From the first minute he met him in this universe, he wanted to be more friend than father. He searched until his lungs ached, then surfaced.

"You got him?" Phil and Carl leaned over the side, close to capsizing the boat with their combined weight.

"Not yet." Jason took another deep breath, checked his position in relation to where Jay went over, and submerged again. The sunlight filtered from above, but past a few feet it was little help, and Jason thrashed frantically through the water. *Why aren't the others in here helping?* Carl he could understand. He wasn't even sure the man could swim. Phil, on the other hand, should be in the water. *Maybe he's worried he can't get back in the boat.*

Just as his lungs threated to burst, his hand brushed Jay's shirt, and he reached out to grab a handful. He tugged hard and started for the surface, lungs on fire. He pushed the boy in front, both men in the boat reaching to drag him up. They grabbed his arms and pulled him into the boat, but the added weight tipped the boat to the side just as Jason broke the surface. The side of the boat connected with the top of his head with a dull crack, pretty sparkles filling his vision. Jason slid beneath the surface of the lake at the ragged edge of consciousness, the familiar pull drawing him from this body like poison from a wound. *Please, no. I fi-*

nally have a life. The light ran away, the chill of the water disappeared, and nothing but blackness remained. Jason fell through, sliding from this world into the next.

PART TWO

"As for morality, well that's all tied up with the question of consciousness"
—Roger Penrose

ELEVEN

*P*LEASE, GOD, LET HIM STILL BE HERE, PHIL THOUGHT. *MAYBE THIS TIME HE'LL listen.* He lifted the tailgate of the new truck and pushed it closed with a satisfying clang. *Maybe* this *time I'll actually do more than just give up.*

He heaved the loaded backpack over his shoulders and walked to the edge of the woods. Standing at the boundary of the road's shoulder and the trees, he sighed as he thought of the trek ahead. The old guy sporting goods store told him to look for a game trail near a large boulder at this mile marker, and even though Phil wasn't much of a woodsman, he found it easily enough. He pulled the straps of the pack tighter, distributing the weight as best as he could, took one last look at the truck he was abandoning, and started up the trail.

The Phil in this reality seemed to take his health a bit more seriously than he ever had in his others, and right now he was thankful. What he wasn't glad for, though, was the full beard this Phil was partial to. He spent most of his time relatively clean-shaven—or at least what passed for it in his life—and he couldn't imagine what would possess him to grow such a thing. He could have shaved it off, but he liked to make as few changes as possible when wearing another man's suit. Just common courtesy, after all. *I don't like it when the other guys mess with my shit, either.*

There were a lot of miles to cover on foot before he stopped to make camp. At almost any other time of the year he would have taken the dirt road all the way up to the cabin, but this was the rainy season and he was told the unpaved roads on the mountain were washed out. It was also the closest he had come in nearly six years of looking, and he didn't want the boy to go rabbit on him at the sight of a truck pulling up. The last meeting was a disastrous failure all those years ago, and he didn't want a repeat of that. Better to quietly approach and knock on the door.

Twenty yards into the woods, and the sounds from the road below faded into silence. The air was cool and clear, and the smells he associated with hunting pushed away the odors of blacktop and gasoline. Trees towered over him, while the ground cover remained sparse enough that it didn't hinder his progress, and light filtered in through the branches above. It was a good day for a hike, and Phil set a leisurely pace for a time as he enjoyed the nature walk. *The boy's got good taste in hideouts, that's for sure.* He set his eyes on the trail ahead, and thought, *But this time I'll find him before he crosses over. I have to.*

Jason's random jumps had always been one or two steps ahead of him—compounded by the fact that the two men might be hundreds of miles apart in the new reality—and each time it meant Phil had to search out the fading veil to find the next direction.

"Would be a hell of a lot easier if the damn things were colored blue with a name-card attached to 'em," he grumbled to the trees and the birds in them.

And that was the problem. What Jason only suspected, Phil knew with certainty—people slipped through the wall all the time, and each passing left a veil that faded over time; and while each one had its own "flavor," it wasn't always easy to tell them apart. He had followed the wrong path more than a few times, each time having to backtrack and find the correct one. The upshot was that each time he wandered down the wrong trail, by the time he figured it out and returned to the previous point, the correct veil had faded to barely a whisper. Six years ago, he was sure he was hopelessly lost in the web, not knowing if he was following the correct Jason, when he found the strongest signal since that first one. Jason—the right one—was there. The meeting between the two hadn't gone as planned. *Understatement of the century*, he thought. He remembered leaving the boy there, angry and hurt, vowing in his heart to check back in a week or two to see if he had calmed down.

That proved to be a terrible mistake. A few days after their reunion, Jason slipped through again, jumping randomly, but leaving a strong signal behind. Granted, Phil had to jump in a damn lake to find the transfer point where the veil survived, but there were worse things that could happen to a man. Before he found him, though, Jason jumped yet again, and it took Phil weeks to find the next veil. This happened many more times in quick succession, almost as if the boy were running from him. Phil knew that wasn't possible, though, since he never had the chance to teach Jason how.

He couldn't spend all his time searching, however. *Some* time had to be devoted to raising Jay. It took years, off and on, to finally find the correct sequence of jumps leading here, and he was behind Jason by only a couple of weeks. His nephew's parents, still alive in this universe, assured him the boy was headed up into the mountains of Colorado to "find himself." It was bullshit, he knew. Jason was opting out. Trying to stay away from anyone he cared about, or cared about him, to keep the pain levels down when he made the inevitable next transition. Phil, himself, had opted out a couple of times. The last being not long before he met this Jason.

He chuckled lightly, in spite of the effort of hiking the uneven ground. "Gonna have to invent a new grammar to deal with describing this crap."

The cabin he searched for, he was told, was only a few miles away, but far enough up the mountain that the climb grew steeper as he went. He was lucky it wasn't yet winter, as the snow would have reached all the way to the road instead of just the peak past the tree line. The cabin was situated well below that point according to the map he carried, but it was going to get a bit chilly for the Texan nonetheless. Still, the going was slow, and he knew he would have to make camp for the night rather than work his way up to the cabin. He had no desire to stomp around the woods in the dark.

Though growing up in what he lovingly referred to as "Flatland," Phil preferred the mountains—at least when traveling over them in a car as a kid. He wasn't stupid enough to believe he knew what he was doing up here, but he was confident he wouldn't kill himself, either. Find your landmarks, keep your wits, and follow your compass. Simple rules for the wilderness—as well as life.

The sun was already running to hide behind the mountain, and though he was over halfway to his goal, he decided to stop for the night. Far enough up the mountain where he could no longer see even a hint of civilization through the trees, the air grew still and silent. It was the kind of silence that beat against a man's eardrums like a fist. If he didn't make a noise now and then, he would think he had lost his hearing entirely.

He found an area as flat and level as he could, set up his one-man tent and sleeping bag, and then gathered stones for a small fire ring. It had been a dry summer, so there was no point in taking chances on a fire getting out of control. After he gathered a supply of wood, he snapped smaller branches for kindling and soon had a small campfire burning. The weatherman on the morning news show in town said the temperatures on the mountain wouldn't get too low tonight, but what was comfortable to these people would damn near freeze a Texan from the Gulf Coast.

There was a time when little Jay would have loved this outing. The boy once loved to camp, hunt, and fish. Once. That time was long gone, though. As the boy grew, and the Jason he knew as his father withdrew from the world after the death of Kathy, things had not gone well. It didn't help that the Jason inhabiting the body of the boy's father changed with alarming regularity. Phil didn't understand why, but he could see it clear on the man's face. Every new Jason was different in little ways—almost inconsequential—but a boy needed consistency, especially after losing the only parent he had ever known. Phil did what he could to help out, but the battle seemed lost before it began, and the last seven years was hard on both father and son. Just in the past six months, Officer Cole had picked the boy up for multiple cases of vandalism, fighting, and petty theft.

This Jason, on the other hand, knew nothing about any of that. Phil struggled for a long time with what to tell him, but in the end decided not to say anything. It was another Jason's problems, after all, and would only serve to hurt this one. At the very least, it would be a distraction—and Phil couldn't afford any distractions from the task in front of him.

As the last bit of daylight faded behind the mountain, Phil was left with the little fire and his thoughts. After so long, he wasn't sure how Jason would handle his uncle walking back into his life, but he needed to teach the boy how to move through the wall and back, how to spot and follow a veil, and most importantly, tell him what he had learned about the explosion that killed Jason's parents and the mother of his son.

Phil's eyes narrowed at that last thought, remembering the smug asshole's picture in the paper that very morning back in his own reality, and he tossed another branch on the fire. "That boy and me's got some huntin' to do."

†††

Seventeen hundred miles and an unknown number of universes away, Miles sat in his moldy closet of a congressional office working through the night at his desk. A freshman member of the minority party, he didn't have enough clout to secure more environmentally friendly and larger digs, but this would do. He learned a lot during his last pass through this reality, and he planned on making good use of the knowledge. Now he knew where all the skeletons were buried, and there was no one to stop him from using that information. One more term in the House, then a Senate seat—this time without his previous missteps. From there it was but a short hop to the White House.

Country's so fucked up, he thought. *I'll make it great again. I'm the only one who can.* He snorted in derision. *Everyone in this town is either corrupt, weak, or both.*

"*Both* goddamn parties," he spit.

He had already blackmailed leaders of his own party to secure positions on two important committees—even scoring a two-fer when he used the same information to convince a member of the opposition to co-sponsor one of his bills. While his personal staff was small by congressional standards, they were true believers, and ready to perform any task—no matter how dirty—he ordered.

The party leaders had no idea where or how he was getting his intel, but most now feared him. His only problem was the Minority Leader, himself. The man, it seemed, had nothing damaging in his past, and was apparently that nearly mythical government creature—the incorruptible man.

There were other ways of dealing with that category of road hazard. Methods he had used to much success in the past. There were failures, like the night seven years ago when he missed Jason Callahan. Even though the man survived, there was no indication he would become the same problem he was the first time around. Miles ached to finish the job, but had no desire to arouse suspicion by targeting him a second time.

I will if I have to, though. Screw the consequences.

Miles ran a hand through his slicked-back hair, loosened his tie, and plowed into his next bill. This one came from his most prominent backer, and he needed to make sure the language would make it through committee unscathed. And if he was to put his name to the thing, he figured he should at least know what was in it.

†††

The cold of the previous night gave way to a chill morning, and Phil packed everything up just before first light. As he lifted the heavy pack onto his shoulders, he walked to the stone ring and kicked more dirt onto the dead ashes. *Can't be too sure,* he thought. He hadn't been out in the woods in years, so he was careful to check and re-check everything he did. A mountain could kill a man in a heartbeat, and the reverse was also true.

He pulled out the little compass and checked his bearings, then started up the mountain again. Yesterday he walked six hours before bedding down, so that left him with only two or three hours to go. As with any hike, the time to target always depended on the terrain. So far it hadn't been anything worse than a gentle rise, but the grade was getting steeper with every mile.

The last time he set foot in the woods was nearly seven years ago. After each attempt to track "Jason Prime," as he now thought of him, Phil always slipped back to his own universe to check on the boys. He convinced Jason to drag Jay along on a hunting trip in the desperate hope the two would bond as father and son. It was a disaster. Jay loved walking through the woods, learning to track his prey, how to safely hold and fire a gun, and camping out and sleeping under the stars. Jason, on the other hand, hated everything about hunting. *Every Jason Phil met over the years felt the same way.* How his nephew ended up living in a cabin on the side of a mountain was a head-scratcher. *He's trying too hard,* he thought. *Punishing himself for the death of his parents, maybe.* But that didn't make sense. Jason wasn't at fault, and he knew it. At least, Phil assumed this Jason knew it.

Phil opted out several times over the years, but the last time he had done so by spending an entire year in a universe where he had neither family nor friends. He spent all his free time alone in his house playing video games and watching TV. In his head he called it "the ultimate stay-cation," but the boredom and isolation soon dragged him back to the world he knew. To opt out this early in Jason's traveling life, though, was dangerous. Phil worried that, as dark as he had become during that time, Jason's mood might be darker still. There are many routes a man can take to redemption, but they don't all have a happy ending.

Stop it, he thought. *This Jason's not the kind of kid to off himself.* He hoped. At his lowest, Phil never thought to end it. He believed that, contrary to the evidence he saw to date, there was at least one universe where he was the best possible version of himself. Probability said so. Jason was still young enough that he might not see that.

The game trail took many twists and turns through the forest. Phil wanted to take the straightest path, but he didn't know the area well enough to not get lost. Beyond a small rise, though, he heard the clear babbling of the shallow creek he was told would be about two miles south of the cabin. From there he could head straight north all the way to his destination.

He crested the rise, and looked down at the creek. It was indeed shallow—the depth no more than a foot or two in the middle—and it was only a few dozen feet across at this point. The water burbled and flowed over the smooth stones on the creek bed, and Phil walked carefully down the rise to the water's edge. He looked at his boots. They weren't water-proof, but they were water-resistant. They didn't, however, rise high enough to keep him from getting his pants wet. He shrugged, *Oh well, what the hell*, and stepped down to cross over.

The stones, he found, weren't just smooth, but slippery. Some of them were as large as a goose egg, and it was all he could do to keep from falling on his ass. He mentally kicked himself for not picking up a branch to use as a walking stick. Before he had time to complain about the cold, he was on the other side using the underbrush to grab hold and pull himself up and out.

The next two miles were uneventful, but he constantly checked his compass to stay on course. There was a stillness in the air as he hiked the last three hundred yards toward the cabin. Drawing closer, the sunlight shone not only from above, filtered through the thick canopy, but from the clearing he was approaching. The cabin, small and squat with a wrap-around front porch, looked as empty as the stretch of ground around it. He came to a halt at the edge and watched for movement, but there was none. It was only mid-morning, and the dew on the ground sparkled as it waited to be burned away.

Phil stood at the edge of the clearing, just inside the trees and out of sight of the cabin, while indecision clawed at his brain. He saw an old lime-green VW Beetle parked on the gravel beside the main structure, leaves and pine needles piled up beside the wheels. The clearing was, as near as he could tell, a complete circle around the cabin and small shed, and large enough to see an approaching visitor with ease. Phil hesitated at the boundary of forest and clearing. *Jason can't run in that thing*, he thought. *The roads aren't passable right now.* The bug didn't look like it would start, anyway. He took a deep breath, shrugged his shoulders, and stepped into the clearing.

"The boy's just gonna have to deal with a visitor today, that's all."

✝✝✝

Before Phil was halfway to his destination, Jason awoke with the sunrise, dressed in light clothing, slipped on his running shoes, and left the cabin. There was a small stream a couple of miles away that trickled down his side of the mountain, and each morning he stopped there and washed off the sweat and grime of the run and the previous day's activities; and while the water was cold, it helped refresh not only his body, but his spirit as well. His ears pricked as he heard splashing downstream, but from where he stood he couldn't see through the trees and around the bend in the creek. *Probably just a deer.* He hoped. There were other large animals on this mountain—and some weren't very friendly—but they mostly left him alone.

One early morning while washing up in the stream, he looked up and straight into the eyes of a mountain lion not more than a dozen yards away, watching him through narrowed slits. The big cat was huge by his standards, but he knew now it was small—probably a female. The raw power of the animal was unmistakable, and instinct told him running from a predator was a bad idea. Still bent over the shallow stream, he felt around the bed and grabbed a large rock before he stood. The two animals, both recognizing the other as a formidable opponent, were frozen in place, each with eyes locked on the other and considering their options. After what felt like an eternity to Jason, the mountain lion dipped her head back to the stream to drink, dismissing him without another thought. He didn't move again until she had her fill and left. It was only then he realized he had been holding his breath.

Today, during his return walk, the birds were noisier than usual. *A good sign*, he thought, listening to the birdsong. *Jay would have loved this*. A clear picture of the boy as he remembered him flashed in Jason's mind, but he banished the thought as quickly as it was born. The smile disappeared, and he stooped to pick up a fallen branch. He frowned and stripped the dried leaves and shoots off as he moved down the worn path. It was a hardwood of some kind, and he decided to fashion it into a walking stick to take on future journeys. Focused on this task, he never noticed the cabin's door was open. Or that a large and bearded man was standing in that open doorway holding a fully loaded backpack.

"Mornin', boy," Phil said as Jason stopped dead in his tracks. "Please tell me you've got something in that pantry," he smiled warmly, "cuz I'm starved."

TWELVE

You never could tell about a person. How their childhood affected them later in life, or the choices they would make based on how they were raised. Miles, for instance, knew early on that his father was an asshole. For years, though, he believed the sadistic treatment from the old man was *his* fault.

"Why do you make me do this to you, boy?" he would ask, lashing Miles with the wide belt gripped in white-knuckled hands. "Stop cryin'," he'd say. "*My* daddy beat me almost every day, and I turned out just fine!"

If the old man taught him anything, it was that you had to be *hard* to make your point—and a weak man was a powerless man.

Miles pulled up to the mold-stained little building, paint peeling from every surface, and killed the motor. The engine block popped and snapped as it tried to dump its residual heat into the noonday air. As he pulled off the dark sunglasses, he opened the door and stepped out.

Evil men don't they're evil, Miles thought, closing the heavy door with a satisfying *thunk*. They showed strength in the face of fear, or were decisive in the face of uncertainty, or doled out "tough love" to an unruly child. Looking back on his life, Miles knew—in his head if not his heart—his father thought of himself as a good man who needed to train his son right. Especially after the death of the boy's mother.

And after every beating, Miles retreated to the rotting tool shed behind the house, where the weeds grew tall to hide most of the canted structure, and practiced his art. At first it was just small animals caught in homemade snares—a bird, a mouse, or a small kitten—but he soon graduated to the neighbor's pets. Dogs were his specialty, and the little wood behind the house was soon filled with a scattering of unmarked graves. Sometimes, in those hot and humid summer days before he left home for good, he ventured out, spade in hand, and exhumed an old subject to see what state of decomposition it was in.

Did the suffering he inflicted in life show in death? Did their weakness in the face of his anger follow them—haunt them even as his own anger haunted him?

One dull gray day, his father caught him examining an old kill— one of his first—and angrily slapped the blue jay's moldy bones from his hands.

"What the hell are ya doin', boy?"

The young man, still on his knees bent over the tiny grave, calmly turned his face up to his father, eyes wide and unafraid. He said nothing, anticipating the beating he knew would come. Miles remembered closing those eyes and smiling as he waited for the man's fist to connect with the side of his head, the usual beginning to a rain of hammer blows that ended only when the big man grew tired. It was an overture that never sounded. When he opened his eyes, there was something never seen before on the face of his tormentor. *Fear*. The man shriveled to insignificance then and there. A boy of sixteen, almost a man, always confused that look with the one he truly hoped to see—respect.

He knew now, as a man with more than one lifetime's wealth of experience, that for all practical purposes the two were one and the same. Life—both with and after his father—taught him that without fear there is no respect, and without respect there was nothing.

The Miles from this reality had nothing of value before his body was appropriated by a true predator. There were friends, a job, and the love of a woman, but from the first moment after the new Miles jumped into him, he saw in the faces of the others what was lacking. No fear. No respect. He jettisoned those anchors almost immediately. The people in his life, and the feelings he had for them, were a barrier to his greatness.

This body was one of the rare few he encountered over the years of his trips sideways—a submissive. This one took what his father dished out and became *weaker* for it. His choices were all about "ending the cycle." Anger threatened to overtake him as he thought about the times he encountered such broken men; the times he was forced to share a *body* with them when they refused to step aside and go wherever it was the others always went. He didn't understand how a man could have the strength of will to stay while another mind invaded his brain, yet couldn't fight hard enough to keep control of their own body.

I would never allow it, Miles thought, hot blood burning his cheeks. But this *was* Miles. They *all* were. Even the weak.

In this reality, his father was still alive. He was weak. Pathetic. When Miles realized the man was still breathing, he arranged to visit him in the cheap little retirement home where he lived. This reality's Miles came to terms with his father's abuse years ago—at least on the surface—somehow forgiving him and forging a tenuous relationship. The new Miles wondered how that was even possible.

Standing over Frank Henderson in his wheelchair, Miles felt nothing but disgust for the empty husk there in the sterile common room. The hopelessly cheap chandelier tinkled quietly overhead, the footsteps from the floor above vibrating the fixture. Even as the man's face brightened when he saw his son, some of the old fear started to fray the edges. Somehow, the old man knew. Miles smiled inwardly seeing that fear. That respect.

"I know you, boy." The man's voice was pure gravel, a lifetime of smoking and drinking having taken their toll.

"Yes, sir, you do." Miles smiled thinly, the old deference surfacing instantly. *I'm a trained dog*, he thought. *A lot of years at the end of a leather strap went into that training*. "Do you know why I'm here?"

The old man looked up, searching Miles' eyes. He laughed hoarsely, the laugh turning into a coughing fit.

"You here to kill me this time?"

"Excuse me?" The question confused him, knowing the Miles of this universe.

"Show up around here every few months. Every time talking about killing me." The man smiled at Miles, a hint of a sneer at one corner, and said "I don't s'pose you got any more balls than the others." He waved a palsied hand dismissively, "Go on, boy. Get it over with or don't. I don't care anymore."

Miles, surprised, realized his father understood his talent. And then he understood something else, as well.

"You're trying to provoke me."

The old man snorted once. "Ya catch on quick. Most of the others take a bit longer." He motioned to a nearby chair, and said, "Sit down, boy. Yer killin' my neck with me havin' ta look up at ya all the time."

Miles pulled the chair closer and sat. "How do you know about me?"

"One of the smarter versions explained it to me once a while back." He shook his head slightly, "Thought he was nuts, but you guys kept showin' up, and each one with a different personality and holes in their memories."

Miles' rage flared at the dig at his intelligence. His father always could cut him with a single word. What interested him was the presence of so many others in both this universe and this timeline. That was unusual. He knew there had to be other versions of himself who could do what he did, but why would so many be interested in this one universe?

"One of 'em gave me a note for ya," he said with a slight grin. "Wanna see it?"

A note? For me? That's not likely.

"How do you know it's for me?"

"Not sure, myself. The other one said I would know… and he was right, I guess." Frank reached into his shirt pocket and produced a faded piece of paper folded into a tight square. He held it out for his son and waited, the smile never leaving his face.

Miles reached for it slowly, and asked, "Have you read it?"

"Buncha times." He pulled his hand back to his lap as Miles took the paper, "I still don't understand it, though."

Miles unfolded the note, the cream-colored paper's texture rough in his hands. He realized with a wistful smile that it had been torn from an old Big Chief tablet—the kind he used as a kid in elementary school. The scent of it drifted up as he opened it and rubbed his hand along the surface. Unable to help himself, he held the paper to his nose, inhaled deeply, and was instantly reminded of the time long ago when he loved school. A time when learning every new thing was a wonder to him. When learning meant freedom from his father.

"Keep that up, boy, and people are gonna think you ain't too bright."

Miles froze, tamping an anger that would destroy them both if he allowed it, and narrowed his eyes at his father over the paper. "I don't think you're in a position to judge anyone's intelligence, old man," he said through gritted teeth. Still, he lowered the note and looked at his own handwriting, or at least what passed for it in his usual tight-printed scrawl. There was only one sentence: *Stop before it's too late.*

"That's not helpful," he said out loud before he caught himself. He frowned, angry at himself for giving the man more ammunition to use against him.

"Damn. I was hopin' you knew what it meant," Frank said as he shook his head.

Oh, I know what it means, he thought. *It's just not helpful.* He folded the paper and placed it into his shirt pocket. Leaning back in his chair, he crossed his legs and watched the old man. He was sure his father knew more than he was telling, but in the end it didn't really matter. It wasn't what he came for, anyway.

He leaned in, looked the man in the eyes, and said, "Tell me about your son." *Where did this Miles go wrong?*

It was a simple thing, really. When he was seven years old he told the right teacher about his life with an abuser. After a medical exam and a CPS investigation, Miles was taken from his father and placed with a foster family. It wasn't quite that easy—nothing in Texas ever is for children—but that was the short version. Frank never recovered from the loss of his son.

Confident the demon from his childhood couldn't hurt him, Miles rose and left him there. He had already put the man out of his mind by the time he reached his car. The morning's revelations left him in a charitable mood, and he decided to let his father live this time. *Besides,* he thought, *why give him what he wants?*

†††

Jason, though happy to see his uncle, was still surprised. He told his parents he was headed for Colorado, but nothing specific about his final destination. As Phil ate the last of the eggs and bacon, Jason sighed quietly and stuffed the last piece of toast in his mouth. He realized he would have to make a trip into town today, rather than tomorrow, for supplies. The good news, for a change, was that this Jason was flush with cash. Not a fortune, but enough for now.

"How did you find me?"

Phil scraped the last bit of egg from the plate, and shoveled the steaming mass into his fur-covered maw. He chewed thoughtfully for a second, then said around the food, "You told me where to look." He held up a hand to stop the protest already forming on Jason's lips, "The other you. The one that traded places with you when you slipped through the wall."

Jason's thick brows beetled, nearly meeting in the middle, like they always did when he was considering a problem. "I don't understand," he said. "How would he know where I'd be seven years later."

"Oh… well, he didn't." The man's face lit up, clearly pleased with himself, as he explained, "He mentioned that he had come home from a friend's hunting cabin," he waved his arm, indicating the structure around them, "up in Colorado only a couple of days before the explosion. Remember, you entered *his* reality, not the other way around." His uncle smiled at him across the table, a gentle warmth radiating from his face. "When I spoke to your parents in this universe, and they mentioned Colorado and mountains, I just assumed this was where you were headed." He chuckled. "You're nothing if not predictable, son. And a good thing, too, as I had almost given up on finding you."

"Why did you? It should be pretty clear I didn't want to be found." He watched the man hesitate as he gathered his thoughts. "Especially after the last meeting we had."

"First," Phil held up his hand and put a finger in the air, "I made a promise to teach you how to slip across and back; teach you how to maneuver and, one day, find your way home." His eyes hardened, the middle finger joined the first. "And two," he added through a clenched jaw, "we're going back to my universe to hunt down the bastard who killed my baby sister and her husband." He hung his head. "And Kathy."

Jason stared at the man in front of him, stunned. *How could he possibly know who had planted the bomb that killed my mom and dad? Why did it even matter? There were an infinite number of them out there in an infinite number of universes still alive. What was the loss of two? Or a thousand?* In the end, the numbers just didn't matter.

"I know what you're thinkin', son, and you're right. The loss of one person in one universe don't amount to much, but that ain't the point." He grabbed the mug of warm coffee in front of him and washed the last of the food down his throat. He drank with the same abandon that Jason had seen in every facet of the man's life, black streamers of liquid dribbling out of the corners of his mouth and down his chin to mingle with his beard. Jason noticed none of it managed to make it to the floor.

Every damn one of you is the same, he thought at his uncle. *Just like everyone in my life. So what if one dies? I can just slide right over and find more just like them.* His breath was heavy and hot. *What if I don't want to? What if I've had enough of watching the same people in my life die over and over again?*

Phil slammed the mug down on the wooden table, "The man's got to pay for what he did, dammit! There should be consequences!"

Jason's breathing slowed as he watched his uncle, and he realized that, even with the ability to visit live versions of his sister in other universes, his uncle was still in pain over the loss of the sister he grew up with. *I would feel the same about my real parents, I guess.*

"So why don't you just give your evidence to the police back in your universe?" he asked.

Phil pounded on the table, "Bah! Police. What the hell do they know?" He looked into Jason's eyes, pleading with him to join the cause. "Besides, the only evidence I have is my eyes. They would probably have me committed again if I told them how I discovered what happened."

"What do you mean?"

"Son, it took me almost three months of slipping through the wall before I came upon that same event."

Jason's eyes narrowed in confusion. "How...?"

"You've seen it yourself, I bet. Things don't always happen in each universe at the exact same time. Basic chaos theory. Any little change up the timeline can have drastic effects on when things occur." He splayed his hands on the table, and seemed to make an effort to calm himself. "I finally found one where I saw the guy plant a bomb, and followed him back to his hotel. Greasy little sumbitch named Miles Henderson."

"Okay. Then..." Jason stopped. Something nagging at the back of his brain recognized that name. Then it clicked, "You mean *Congressman* Miles Henderson?"

"The very same," Phil said, upper lip curled in distaste.

"But why would he want to kill my parents?"

"He wasn't gunnin' for them, son. They just got in the way." His uncle's face grew dark and hard, and he pointed a finger at Jason's chest, "Man was lookin' to kill *you*."

Jason nearly fell back in his chair as his field of vision narrowed. From what seemed like very far away, he heard Uncle Phil repeating his name, while nausea threatened to bring his breakfast back for a second go. His mind slowly returned to the here and now to find his uncle leaning over the table, and snapping meaty fingers in front of his face.

"You with me, son?"

Jason shifted his focus from the man's fingers to his face. "Why me?"

Phil sat down again, hard, waved his hand, and said, "Don't know. Don't care."

Jason looked around the room, a shiver ran up his spine. "I'm safe here, though, right? I mean, in this universe, right?"

Phil shook his head and deflated. "I don't think so," he said. He took a deep breath, then let it out in a slow stream. "Son, I've done a lot of traveling, and one thing I have found without fail is that, while an asshole is on a sliding scale from universe to universe depending on his life choices, a sociopath is a sociopath in *every* universe."

"So the congressman Henderson in this universe…"

"Probably needs killin' just as much as the other one, yes."

"I can't believe that every—"

"Do you like girls?"

What the hell? Jason sputtered over the *non sequitur*, "What's that got to do with this?"

"Not a damn thing. Your answer doesn't matter, either. I just want to know which way you lean."

Jason shook his head and curled his lip. "Yeah," he said, "I like women."

"Fine," Phil said. "Chicks it is, then." He tilted his head and raised an eyebrow. "You ever been in a universe where you are Gay?"

"Uh… no."

"Do you think it's a possibility?"

"Hell no."

"There's my point, right there. Some things are just set when you're born, before you start making choices. Jason, this man's got something wrong," he tapped his head, "up here. Call it chemistry, faulty wiring, whatever. He ain't right, and he ain't ever gonna be."

"So, what, are we supposed to kill them all? 'Cuz I have to say, I don't think either of us has the stamina to kill, oh, infinity people."

"It's not as bad as all that. Pretty sure the number is small. I took care of one of 'em, myself. The one I saw plant the bomb." His uncle smiled as if he had earned a gold star in kindergarten.

Jason recoiled in horror. "You've already killed one?"

"Had to. He found out he didn't get you on his first try." He shook his head, "I almost didn't make it in time."

"So what makes you think the number is small?"

"Well, most of the ones I've seen never make it past congressional intern, and the ones who do are like that guy we used to have representin' our district. You remember, the one we called 'Stupid Steve'." Phil snorted and smiled at his own joke. "This guy has no power, and is kind of a laughing stock among the other representatives. No one listens to him." His face grew serious, and he frowned, "But the one that tried to kill you is smarter. I know that doesn't make sense, but he is. He's been gaining power almost since the day he took office."

Jason considered this as he stood, grabbed his mug, and walked into the kitchen for a refill. Four sugars, and a heavy dose of cream—his mom used to say it had to taste like a donut for him to drink it—and he came back to stand in the doorway, leaning against the jamb and stirring the steaming liquid.

Phil twisted in his chair and held his mug in the air.

Jason snorted, not unlike the sound his uncle made. "Would you like a refill?"

"Please." The man smiled up at Jason, nodding. "I think we should get started on your training." He waggled his empty mug at Jason. "Right after I've had a bit more wake-up juice, that is."

†††

Phil, lips pursed, nodded in satisfaction. After only three days of training, he was confident his nephew was ready to solo. Granted, the trips were only a single branch or two sideways, with both of them ending up in the cabin—sometimes in the exact same place—but the distance didn't matter. "Distance" simply had no meaning when you slipped through the wall. What did matter, however, was finding your way back.

With just a few tries, Jason could initiate a trip, rather than have one just happen to him.

"It's like falling for you too, right?" Phil had said.

"Mostly," Jason replied. "After I get sucked though a hole in nothing." He scrunched his face. "Does that make sense?"

"Yeah. The trick, then, is to listen for the sound of the universe you're aimin' for."

"Sound?" Jason had said, head tilted.

After several failed attempts, Phil finally understood everyone must have a different perception of the wall. For Phil it was vibration affecting his "inner" inner ear, but for Jason it was a color and intensity.

"Branches close by have a quality to their sound I can't describe," he told Jason. "Kinda like the farther away I go, the more out of tune the sounds get. I'm guessin' it will be similar for you." He shrugged. "Just remember the longer you're in there, the more branches there are to choose from."

Phil sat in a chair at the small breakfast table during each session, threw a pair of dice while Jason made note of the number, then closed his eyes to visualize the same dark line—that fissure in the wall between universes—he would will his consciousness through.

"Short hops should have us both landing right here in this room," he said.

Gently, just as he knew Jason did, he approached that flaw in the fabric of space, then slipped through. Each time felt different, yet each was essentially the same—like walking the streets in downtown Houston. And each time, after opening his eyes, he watched Jason marvel that the dice showed a different total.

"Keep track of your path, Jason," he had said. "You can't get back here without it."

Each session, Phil took his nephew farther and farther out among the branches, laboriously working their way back, the student following the lead of the master. At one point, Jason asked him about an odor he smelled in the fissure, but Phil had no experience with odors while traveling. Besides, perceptions were different. What Jason might smell,

Phil might feel. Or not perceive at all.

"Where were you?" Jason had asked after one lesson, concern softening his eyes. "I was right here in that universe, but you were nowhere around." His hands shook, and there was a bead of sweat rolling down his temple. "It was a short hop. You should have been here, but I couldn't even find your pack."

"Dead spot," Phil said, shrugging. "If it *was* a close branch, I bet you could have found my body out in the woods somewhere."

"Dead...?"

"Yeah. I was dead in that universe, so there was no 'me' to jump into."

It was one of the reasons it took Phil so long to find his nephew—there were a large number of realities where Jason existed and his uncle did not. Phil chalked it up to bad living and his multiple bouts of "opting out."

"Graduation day," Phil said on the fourth morning, a nervous smile creasing his face.

Jason merely looked confused. "Graduation?"

"Solo jump, son. Try to find a branch beyond this cabin, then work your way back." He had said it with far more confidence than he felt. He was, in fact, scared out of his wits for the boy.

Jason squeezed his eyes shut, and took a calming breath. "You sure I can do this?" Maybe he was a bit more so than Phil.

"Not a doubt, son." He smiled as he tossed the die. "Now get it in gear," he said. "We've got a celebratory supper to make, and I ain't doin' that by myself."

Jason opened his eyes, and offered a crooked smile to his uncle. "Get the new Jason to help you. Maybe *he* can keep you from using so damn much salt."

Phil snorted. There were advantages to a form of travel where no one ever actually left.

†††

The diner where the old man ate his breakfast rested just off the main road, backed up against the trees, a wide expanse of gravel for a parking lot. It couldn't be called a "greasy spoon," as the standard diner fare was absent from the menu. This close to Denver, there were such delicacies as Cinnamon Quinoa, Scrambled Tofu, and Tempeh Bacon on the breakfast side of the menu. Even at this hour, it wasn't unusual to see no more than two or three customers brooding over their meal.

The old man looked up from his plate just as Jason shuddered and gasped in the next booth. The two locked eyes for a couple of seconds before the elder man nodded once and lifted a cup of fair-trade coffee to his lips. Jason cocked his head, and his eyes scanned the other face in recognition. He smiled across the distance, and offered a half-hearted wave. The old man smiled and nodded again, and watched as the recognition faded from the other's eyes.

"About damn time," the old man said to himself, and went back to eating his breakfast.

THIRTEEN

Congressman Henderson picked at the fried egg on the fine china in front of him, moving the undercooked pieces around in a vain attempt to get the slimy egg white on his gold-plated fork. Surrendering in the face of overwhelming adversity, he grabbed a piece of buttered toast for tactical support, dragged it through the mess on the plate, then shoved the soggy mass into his mouth. At no time did he think about the task he was performing, or the mindless droning from the speaker beside him on the dais. His mind was a roiling cauldron as he considered the problems from last night's attempted trip.

One of his favorite sources of information was now closed to him. True, he hadn't been in that universe for a few years, so anything could have happened in that time, but this was the second time he hit the wall hard on a trip in the last four attempts. Too high a percentage to be coincidental. Not to mention the fact that both of those realities were where he was a congressman.

Someone's hunting me in other universes. That much was clear, and they just as clearly were targeting his more successful iterations.

Miles sat straight up in his chair at that thought.

Jason Callahan. It has to be. There's a reason everything keeps coming back to him… why he arrested me that first time. And why he survived the fire.

Miles' election to Congress, along with the growing urgency of his dreams, filled him with anger hot and white. Anger that he might lose the control over his life he worked so hard to gain, and anger at the loss of power that entailed. The closer he approached his goals, the worse it became, and he had responded with orders to watch *anyone* who could hurt him. His investigators in Texas, though, assured him Jason—at least the one in this universe—showed no interest in Miles Henderson or a career in law enforcement. *If he were a traveler, he wouldn't have to do so outwardly, would he?* Miles' men had no idea what people like him could accomplish without ever leaving their living room.

Yer not special, his father's voice said. Miles wanted to believe he was the only person capable of moving between realities, but the voice in his head wouldn't allow it. *Oh, there's others*, it said. *Just because you ain't seen 'em, don't mean they ain't there.*

And now he was the prey. How long before they found him? *It has to be Callahan. There's too many loose ends leading to that asshole.*

Oh... he's comin' fer ya, his father said, the sound eating into Miles' brain like a hungry worm.

It was the reason for the trip back to kill the boy *before* he became a threat. Miles never suspected Jason was a traveler; he was just a roadblock to be cleared. He had wanted to jump back up the timeline to correct the error when he discovered the boy survived, but now the universe blocked him at every turn. Nor could he jump back to a time before the bombing—say, to the boy's birth—as he was thwarted there as well. There was a solid wall set in the timeline right at the point of detonation, and there was just no way of breaking through it.

Most disconcerting was the barrier had once been three days *prior* to the explosion. For some reason it was moving forward in time through this reality, and there was nothing Miles could do about it.

Someone's got yer number, son, his father needled.

No, old man, he thought as his blood boiled. *I've got enough power to do what needs to be done.* He just needed to be careful. *I'm on the cusp of my dreams. No sense getting caught inches before the finish line.* The men working for him were loyal, and would follow orders to the letter, but they were too stupid for this. Miles needed a professional. Someone who could do the job and keep his mouth shut. He grinned at his plate even as he clenched his fists.

I know just the guy...

"...Congressman Miles Henderson." The man at the dais, a heavy hitter among political donors, turned to look down at him, a broad smile on his face as he led thunderous applause.

Miles wiped the corners of his mouth with the linen napkin, dropped it on his plate, and stood to wave at the crowd. *One more speech,* he thought. *One more useless "humanitarian" award, and then I can find a bar and pick up some trim.*

He needed to kill something.

†††

Addison Cain sat in his suite at the Hyatt in Arlington, nursing his third scotch and waiting for the confirmation call he knew would come. The first call was always nothing more than a name and a location. He would research the subject, then return the call with a number. After that, it was just the boring wait for the inevitable confirmation call. *They always call.* At no time during his long career in the game did the client *not* make the call. No one made the *first* call unless there was a problem requiring his unique service. And Addison was a problem solver. It was his one true gift.

Addison worked for them all over the last two decades. Senators, congressmen, government agencies—even a president, once—with no regard for which side of the aisle they sat. A true professional, he was interested in only two things: the quality of his work, and the number of zeros on the wire transfer into his account. This job would have fewer, but the client was a regular, and Addison gave the same service no matter the payment. People came to him because they needed him, but they came back because of the customer service.

When the phone rang, he turned to the nightstand, placed his drink on the coaster, and picked up the receiver without a word.

"The word is 'go'. Accident or random robbery. Half now, half on delivery." The line went dead.

He never bothered with trying to place the voice. It wasn't altered, so the caller was likely a cut-out; some guy chosen at random and paid a few bucks to read from a script. He wished all his clients were as careful. It was the care-*less* who put him in the most compromising positions, and he had to eliminate a few when the job went off the rails. Killing your clients was bad for business, but sometimes necessary. Most understood this.

He looked at the notepad beside him on the bed, lifted it, and adjusted the reading glasses at the end of his hooked nose. He picked up the tumbler with his free hand and took a sip, mulling the location of the target. "Huh," he said. "Looks like I'm going back to Texas."

†††

"Arlington, huh. Arlington, Virginia?" Jason turned to look behind him, while Phil struggled to keep up. The boy had set a brutal pace, and Phil was sure he would twist an ankle or knee with every step.

"I don't mean Arlington, Texas, son. Why the hell would we be going back to Flatland?" Phil shook his head. *Brilliant as he is, sometimes Jason doesn't think things through.*

He and Jason slipped through the wall back to Phil's home universe, and were shocked to find themselves in exactly the same cabin they left in the other. This Jason had decided to opt out as well, but Phil couldn't fathom how this version of himself made it up the mountain. As it was, it took all he had in him to walk downhill, following the path to where he hoped a vehicle waited. He really missed that other body. It was a shame he was too lazy to work this one into the same shape as the one he just left. *At least the stupid beard is gone.*

More disturbing, though, was the thought that Jay was home alone. The memories were still catching up, but Phil already knew that his Jason had run off over two weeks ago and left the boy in his uncle's care. After not being able to reach his nephew for more than a week, Phil left Jay with Dotty so he could chase after the boy's father. *Gonna have to do some heavy apologizin' to that lady when I see her again.* His first order of business—if he lived to make it down the mountain and into town—was to give her a call to see how things were going. *That boy better be keepin' to the straight and narrow.* With luck, Jason might go this whole adventure without ever accessing the memories related to Jay, relieving Phil of the burden of discussing it.

Phil struggled to breathe as he waddled from tree to tree, using each for support before moving down the nearly invisible trail to the next. Jason, younger, fitter, and more sure of foot led the way. Though they left early in the morning, their slow progress guaranteed the sun would be well behind the mountain by the time they reached the road. Phil hoped they got there before it was too dark to see; he had no desire to spend another night in these woods. At least not in his current shape.

"So, what's the plan when we get there?"

"Don't have one yet," Phil said around gasps for breath. "I need a rest, son." He stopped, leaned against the nearest tree, and prepared to sit.

"Stay on your feet, old man," Jason said with a side order of venom, walking back toward his uncle. "You probably won't get back up again. Besides," he gazed into the distance on the line of their descent, "it's not much more than a mile from here."

Not much more than a mile, Phil thought as his chest heaved. *He says it like it's nothing.*

"Fine," he said through a tight grin. "But if I collapse, you'll have to carry me."

"Or I could just leave you for the wolves," Jason shot back.

Phil studied the man before him. The stance was aggressive—challenging, in fact—and Jason's face was twisted in barely controlled anger. He stood before Phil for just a second or two, then found his own tree nearby to lean against.

"All right, son," Phil waved his hand weakly in the classic *gimmee*. "Out with it."

Jason sighed, and crossed his arms, but he would not look at his uncle. "Did you really have to kill him?"

On Jason's last solo run, he found himself in a hotel room staring down the barrel of a very large caliber handgun held by one Miles Henderson. Jumping back to the cabin, he told Phil what was happening. Phil decided to check it out, sliding through the wall to that reality to discover he was, as he hoped, staying in the same hotel. It took him only a few seconds to run to his nephew's room, knock on the door, and announce himself as room service. As soon as the door opened he barreled through, bulldozing everything in his path. Henderson never had a chance to react before Phil was on top of him, pounding him into unconsciousness with hammering fists. Jason arrived in that reality only in time to view the aftermath, watching in horror as his uncle wrapped a lamp cord around the unconscious man's body and strangled him to death.

It took *much* longer than in the movies.

"I didn't see you trying to stop me, junior." The memory of the cold-blooded murder haunted Phil, but at least he understood the stakes. "This is a war, son."

"I know. The guy's trying to kill me for some reason, but—"

"No," Phil shook his head, his mouth a tight line, "you don't get it. When I say 'war', I'm not just tossing around a word." He stepped away from the tree and stretched his back. "This war is being fought on every front, all at the same time." Jason's head tilted, a question on his lips, but Phil pressed on, "Near as I can tell, this guy is gunning for you in every reality I've been in where you both exist." Jason closed his mouth, his brow furrowed. "This is a war with an infinite number of soldiers, all fighting to the death," Phil said. "There can be no sympathy, and no quarter given." He looked his nephew dead in the eyes, pinning him to the tree, "It's all of him, or all of you."

"That's insane."

"No, son," he shook his head, "*he's* insane." Phil relaxed a bit, then smiled. "He's also impatient. It doesn't make him any less dangerous, though." He shrugged his shoulders slightly and sighed, "Look… I did what I had to do. You don't have to like it, but I ain't takin' it back, either." He began walking downhill once again, passing Jason, then said over his shoulder, "And I'm gonna do it again, and as many times as it takes."

An hour later, with the sun almost behind the mountain, Phil and Jason reached the truck, right where he hoped, within a few feet of the truck in the other universe. It was a different model than the one that brought him here, but this one was also new. Tossing their packs into the bed, Phil pulled the keys out of his pocket and unlocked his door. As he folded himself into the driver's seat and unlocked the passenger door, he settled into the cloth seat as if it were a lover's arms. Nothing had ever felt so warm and inviting in his life, and he decided then and there not to venture back into the wilderness in this lifetime.

It took a few tries to get the engine to turn over, but once started it roared to life with all the eight cylinder power it could muster.

Phil smiled with unrestrained glee. "Now that's a motor! None of that three cylinder hybrid crap for me, no sir."

Jason just shook his head. "You still watch NASCAR, don't you."

"What you got against NASCAR, boy?" Phil asked as he threw the shifter into reverse.

Jason snorted. "Not a thing, old man. I like watching carousels, too." His wide grin exposed a large number of teeth, and he pantomimed picking his nose. "Oh wow, they're makin' a left tuuurrrnnn!"

"Shut up." Phil backed the truck onto the road, then shoved the shifter into drive. He floored the accelerator, and cried out a loud "Whoop!" as he pealed the rubber from his rear wheels, leaving black tire marks a dozen feet long on the ribbon of concrete.

"Get comfortable, son. This is gonna be a long ride."

†††

The heat was oppressive. It wasn't the weather, though, but the heat from the dying embers of a blackened city. Smoke lifted high in the air in twisting filaments, carrying the carbonized remains of what had been a nation's capitol. Like the dream where Miles stood, the city and it's people were now nothing more than ephemera. The light breeze carried a myriad of odors—some pleasant, and others far less so—to his flaring nostrils. He quickly covered his nose and mouth with the back of a soot-stained hand, noticing the tattered remains of his sleeve. The rest of his clothes were in similar shape.

Standing near the Smithsonian Castle, he looked up at the ragged structure to the bones beneath the facade. Chunks of the building fell in a cascade of brick, mortar, and dust, forcing him back and away. The stones overhead had a weight beyond mere mass, and his head ached as if they had made contact.

"Welcome to our future, Miles."

He spun around at the too-familiar voice.

"Do you like it?" The boy stood a few feet behind him, his clothes shredded and filthy from soot, grime, and… other things. Miles stood and considered his answer for a few seconds while the boy watched him.

He shrugged his shoulders. "As futures go, I've seen better."

"There is still time, you know," the boy said softly. He looked up at Miles with large eyes, orbs deep in soot-covered sockets. He reached up with a dirty hand to wipe sweat from his brow, and accomplished nothing more than smearing the blackened mess around his face. The sweat-soaked hair of his head clung tightly to his forehead in loose curls.

"Time for what?" Miles asked.

The world shimmered. To Miles it was like looking through a block of ice, the landscape melting and changing before him. He had a brief feeling of vertigo, and a nausea not activated by the previous odors now threated his stomach. Then it was over.

"Time for this," the boy said as he waved his arm to encompass the new reality. The buildings were now whole and everywhere there were people, each on their way to or from an important meeting, or simply sight-seeing. A typical day in Washington D.C. "You have an opportunity," he said, "to step off your current path and allow the world to live."

Miles' eyes narrowed. "I don't believe you, boy."

"What? That you can't change?"

He shook his head. "No," he said, waiving his hand at the tableau. "I don't believe that I'm the cause of all that."

"You're a fool, old man." The boy turned to walk away.

Miles reached out and grabbed him by the arm and shook. "How do you know, huh? How do you know that I had anything to do with that? You were never there!" He released the arm and cuffed him once hard across the face. "For all you know, I'm the only person who can stop it!" His voice grew in both volume and intensity as he spoke, warming to the subject. "All you know is what you've been told by other versions of us." He looked down at the boy who was now on his knees, head lowered. Miles leaned in and gave the boy a death's head grin. "You should know by now, boy... we *lie*," he whispered.

The boy looked up, no sign of fear on his face. In fact, what Miles saw was pity, and he had to fight to keep from strangling the boy. "You're right about one thing," the boy said softly, and stood. "You are the only one who can stop it."

Miles watched him for a bit, and he calmed himself with visions of dismembering the child alive. "Bah! You're so full of shit." He leaned back and laughed—a rasping sound not unlike their father. "The only thing you've shown me is that I'm going to win." He jammed a finger into the boy's chest. "I'm going to get the power to do the things I want, aren't I?"

The boy sighed. "The only thing you get to do, old man, is make choices. Power is irrelevant."

Miles laughed again, forced to keep the beast in check. "Power is *never* irrelevant, boy. Power is everything!" Now his hands *were* around the boy's throat, squeezing with all the strength he had.

The boy frowned in weary frustration, drawing circles in the ash with his toe, refusing to acknowledge the violation. "Every time we have this conversation, you reach the wrong conclusion. And *every* time, you make the wrong choices." He looked up into Miles' eyes, and said, "I would give up, but the stakes are too high. For both of us."

"Every time?" Miles eyes widened, and he increased the pressure on the boys throat. "How many times have we had this conversation?" He shook the child like a rag doll, arms and legs flailing helpless in the defiled air.

"Two thousand, one hundred and twelve," the boy said without inflection or distress. "And let me tell you, brother… it's getting old."

†††

"Congressman! *Congressman!*" Miles woke in a hotel bed with a naked, large-breasted redhead straddling his waist. She held his shoulders as she shook him. His eyes snapped open, the dream fading, his fogged head clearing. The woman's eyes widened, and she said, "Oh, thank *God*. I thought you were in a coma or sumpin'! I was just about to call a amb'lance, but…" she looked down at her nude body, and said, "I didn't know how ta explain all this."

"Get off me." His eyes narrowed, and he stared at her until she complied. *Someone should tell the bitch how close she came to death tonight.* Throttling the boy had been unfulfilling, even for a dream, and it left him empty. *Too empty to do to her what I had planned, at least.*

"Hey, no need ta thank me." She crawled off the bed and began gathering her clothes.

"Wasn't going to," he said as he sat up. He reached over the side of the bed, fished his wallet from his pants, and pulled three one-hundred dollar bills from inside. He tossed the money to the whore with the too-red hair and said, "Get out."

"I'm goin', asshole. Just let me get my clothes on."

He stood, then, and grabbed her by the arm. He pulled her to the door and threw it open. "Let me rephrase that. Get out *now*." Shoving her roughly out the door, he closed it in her face. She stood on the other side for a time, screaming curses at him, then apparently thought better of it, and then silently padded on bare feet down the hall to the elevator.

"Redheads," he mused, shaking his head. Even if the color came from a bottle, she managed to live up to the image.

Miles walked to the mini-bar and grabbed one of the tiny bottles of Scotch. He twisted off the cap as he sat back on the bed and downed the liquor in a single pull. As the liquid burned a path down to his stomach, he thought about the dream. Now, more than ever, he was convinced he was going to succeed this time. The only obstacle in his path that could possibly hurt him was an old foe, and that would soon be dealt with.

Jason, he thought. *Why does it keep coming back to that prick every time?* "Should have gone back and finished the job when I had the chance," he said, and then went back to the mini-bar.

†††

"Hang on a second," Jason said as he turned and eyed his uncle. "I have a *son* here?"

Phil sighed. "I was wonderin' how long it would take you to remember that."

"He's alive? Everything's okay?"

Phil raised an eyebrow at his nephew. The man was sitting up, eyes wide, and his hands were clenched. "Yeah… last time I checked."

Jason relaxed, sat back and sighed, and a sad smile crept onto his face.

"Anything you want to tell me, son?"

He shook his head. "Not really, no."

Both men sat in silence for a bit, then Phil turned his body slightly to the right, adjusting his position in the seat while he steered left-handed. "You know now that you can go back and check, right?"

Jason looked at his hands, frowned and took a long, deep breath. "I don't think I want to know." He looked up at his uncle. "It was years ago, and there's nothing I can do about it anyway. Things either worked out, or they didn't." He shrugged. "Besides, I don't know if *I'm* still alive there."

Phil propped his right arm on the pull-down armrest and leaned toward Jason. "Are you sure you don't want to talk about it?"

Jason looked up again and smiled. "Maybe later."

"Sure, son." He offered a sad smile. "The thing you have to remember is that shit happens. There are only a few things that we have any real control over, and a whole lot of things we don't. You just have to know which is which."

"I know," Jason said softly.

"You think you do, but you don't. Not really." He tilted his head and frowned. "Not yet."

FOURTEEN

Jason took over driving after the fourth hour. Phil was exhausted from the hike earlier in the day, and the load of fast food he was currently processing probably didn't help. Jason was sure the man was dead to the world when he belched, scratched his belly, and sat up.

"How long I been out?" He rubbed sleep from his eyes, and blinked them to clear his vision.

"About an hour." *Holy crap!* "Dude, crack a window or something."

"Yeah. Sorry 'bout that." Phil grinned, depressed the window button, and a roar of fresh air filled the cabin. "Where are we?"

"Somewhere on I70 about to cross the border into Kansas." Jason yawned. "I don't know about you, but I'm starting to look for a place to bed down by midnight." He glanced at his traveling companion, "Is that okay?"

"Sure. We're in no hurry."

Another ten minutes passed in silence, and Jason flirted with the idea of turning on the radio, but the last time was a disaster. Texas native though he was, he despised country music. Uncle Phil, on the other hand, was some sort of aficionado. While his uncle sang loudly—and off-key—to each and every little ditty, Jason entertained thoughts of murder-suicide. Phil dodged a bullet when the signal faded before Jason snapped. His uncle's affinity for "woman done me wrong" songs reminded Jason of another question he hadn't asked.

"How come you never got married?" He raised an eyebrow in his uncle's direction, his eyes leaving the road for only a second.

"Probably the same reason you haven't," Phil shrugged. "Guys like us don't get married." Jason winced, and he was sure Phil took note, but the man made no indication he had. Instead, Phil scrubbed his face with both hands for a second, then stretched his back, twisting and turning as his spine popped like someone strangling a sheet of bubble wrap.

"The first few years I slipped through, my girlfriends kept changing; the variety was nice, but I couldn't ever get close to just one. Plus, my various selves had a wide-ranging view of what was my type." He leaned over toward Jason, grinning. "There were a couple that were just plain coyote ugly," he whispered, then settled back in his seat. "Here in my universe, though, I could never seem to hold on to the women I liked," he said, frowning. "That was probably due to all my other selves screwing crap up when I wasn't here."

"Yeah," Jason nodded soberly. "Been there, done that." He remembered one of his first trips, jumping into one Jason just as he was getting his face slapped by a beautiful young woman. He smiled at the memory, as he had been a much better talker, it seemed, than the man he had replaced. He bedded her before the night was over.

None of them ever matched Kat, though. People say you never forget your first love, but Katherine had been so much more than that. He was sure that if he never made that first transition, he would have married her before graduating from college. It was their plan from the very beginning, but in all his years of traveling, she was in his life exactly two times. One of those was a disaster, and the other was almost as bad—an amazing life with her lost to another random jump. Phil said he could go back, but how could he? Even if Jay survived, Jason may not have. He didn't even know which "direction" to search for the flaw that would lead him there. Too much time had passed.

Everything I care about is always just out of reach.

His uncle must have noticed the look in his eyes. "When this is done, Jason, you can find yourself a nice girl and settle down," he said, false optimism dripping from his words. "Even if you slip through in your sleep, at least you know now how to find your way back."

Jason gripped the wheel a little harder, eyes dead on the road, focusing on a point beyond distance. "That's assuming I get through this alive," he said. "*This* Jason, and the original me."

Phil's face lit like a beer sign. "Hey, that's right," he said, grinning. "You haven't been back to your original universe yet, have you?"

"So?"

"I have, sonny," he said with a chuckle. "Our Mr. Henderson doesn't exist there."

If Phil hadn't been wearing a seatbelt at that moment, he probably would have ejected clean through the windshield when Jason slammed both feet on the brakes—hard—steering to a sliding stop on the road's shoulder, gravel flying in all directions.

Jason spun in his seat, face flushed, and chest heaving. "Come again?" he growled.

Phil threw his hands in the air between them. "Whoa, son, calm down. I thought you'd be happy about that."

"What was all that crap about a war everywhere? I'm not in any danger, and you've got me driving all the way across the country to square off against some guy who doesn't even *exist* in my world?"

"I never said this was about you, son!" Phil's said, his voice booming in the small cabin.

Jason stopped mid-rant, shaken and confused. "Then what...?"

"It's about *my* Jason. Him, and all the others being hunted and killed by this nutbar." His face softened, the harsh tone leaking away from his words. His eyes, though, kept their steely hardness. "This guy will not stop. He has to *be* stopped, but the longer we take, the more you lose your other realities." His uncle ran a large hand through his graying mane. "You have to also consider what happens to *this* you," he said, tapping Jason's forehead, "when enough of your other selves are gone, given your theories about human consciousness."

Jason raised an eyebrow at his uncle. Several days ago he had explained his theory about human consciousness arising from the quantum network as best he could. Like every network, signals degraded, or information packets were sent to the wrong address. This happened to everyone, but Jason knew he and Phil were different, retaining memories from one reality to the next. If he were correct, in most people the memories that overlay their own would supplant what they brought with them in the transition, and they would be who they were meant to be in their new universe. They would never know the difference. Jason, though, had the sensation of traveling. Always a stranger in a strange land, but outside of his immediate sphere of influence, nothing changed. Like ripples in a pond, those changes propagated outward from the source, growing weaker the farther in space and time they traveled. No matter what he did in any universe, the changes were localized and contemporaneous. He couldn't make a change and suddenly own Chrysler in a neighboring universe.

And here I thought Uncle Phil hadn't been listening.

"But why here and now? And why me?" He considered all the angles for a moment. "And what makes you think we can kill all of these guys? It's an impossible task, if you ask me."

Phil shrugged his shoulders. "I have some theories of my own about that, but I'm not ready to lay 'em out yet. I do think there's a reason it's you that has to see this through." He turned back in his seat, facing forward, and waved at the road. "Now get moving. I need a beer and a bed."

Jason took another long look at his uncle, then turned his head back to the road in silent resignation. He lifted both feet from the brake, then stepped on the accelerator as he bounced the truck back on the highway, rear tires sliding in the gravel.

He drove for ten or fifteen minutes, thinking to himself about how crazy this was. Now that he could maneuver between realities, he could go home—and be safe—any time he wanted, but he knew he was going to see this through. Even if the madman hadn't killed his real mom and dad, he murdered *this* Jason's parent. That counted for something, and it needed justice. Something still bothered him, though, and he turned to ask his uncle a question—only to find him snoring softly, his head leaning against the door.

✝✝✝

Addison carried only a duffel and a small leather briefcase when he stepped off the small jet chartered for the flight to Houston. While there was a smaller airport closer to the target, he wanted to take his time getting to know the layout and options open to him, along with keeping his travel arrangements under cover. He was a careful man, as such men were in his line of work, and he needed to know there was no avenue leading to failure. He had used this charter service many times in the past, and he was sure no record of his travel existed. The pilot/owner was a professional, not unlike himself, who knew not only how to fly, but how to keep his mouth shut. It didn't hurt that the man also inferred what Addison did for a living, and therefore knew the consequences of loose lips.

The car waiting for him in the parking lot, a silver Honda sedan, was purchased from a classified ad the day before, and the keys were in a magnetic container attached inside the front driver's-side wheel well. He removed his suit jacket and loosened his tie, then opened the door and threw the duffel and brief case onto the passenger seat. Firing up the little engine, he smiled in satisfaction at the quiet hum. He checked himself in the mirror like a preflight inspection. Nondescript dark blond hair, standard cut, no identifying marks visible on his face or hands, and brown eyes set in a tanned face. Even his height, at five feet, ten inches, with a medium build, fell squarely inside the average. All in all, completely forgettable.

It was a carefully crafted and maintained image, one which had served him well over the years. The few people who saw his face during a mission would not remember it for long, and often would confuse him for someone famous. As he pulled out of the parking space and headed for the exit, he turned on the radio and tuned to the only station in Houston worth listening to—PBS. It was the only place he was sure he could get reliable news, and in his business, information was gold. Besides, he hated advertising, and it wasn't yet beg-a-thon season.

Flying into Hobby Airport meant he had to travel through the seedier South side of Houston, but that was fine with him. Any police activity in the area was always focused on the minority population, so he had no trouble driving unmolested to his destination. Prowling the streets at this hour, regardless of the seemingly round-the-clock traffic, only helped to hide his movements. It was easy to be anonymous in this town, and added to that fact was the ubiquity of guns. No one looked twice at a man carrying a gun—even a sniper rifle—in the back seat of his car. Texas was a dream state for the man who trafficked in death. Regardless, he would not be using a gun on this job. *Accident or robbery.* That was the request, and he intended to go with "accident."

When he turned at the intersection of Airport and 35, he considered getting a room for the night at one of the many hotels there, but decided against it. Alvin was only thirty minutes away, and it would be better to take a room at a cheap motel closer to his target. He would get some sleep, then get out early to scout the area and choose his best option. There were always good choices for accidents, but the location was the key. Staging an accident in the wrong place would arouse the suspicions of the police—even the Barney Fife's that seemed to be the standard in this state.

Addison turned up the radio and settled in for the drive, his mind still working over scenarios for tomorrow's activities.

†††

Miles sat on his office sofa reading the summary of a bill for the fourth time. As before, he read only a paragraph or two and then turned his wrist to check his watch. He did this with such frequency that by the time he got to the end of the summary, he couldn't remember anything he read.

Midnight, goddammit! He threw the pages to the floor in frustration. *Bastard was supposed to have checked in by now.*

He left the hotel hours ago, planning to get some work done while he waited for confirmation that his contractor was on the scene in Texas, but his ability to concentrate on the task was hampered by his impatience. Finally at the stage where he could hire others to do his dirty work, he found he hated it. *Too many points of failure*, he thought. *Besides, it's more fun doing it myself.* True professionals were hard to find—and expensive, regardless—so what he was left with was a cast of incompetents and the occasional pro to supplement. Muscle worked in D.C. in more instances than most people would believe, but there was often a need for a lighter touch. The higher he rose in government, the more true that became.

Miles stood and walked to the little bar in the corner. He twisted off the cap of the Johnnie Walker Blue as it sat in the center of the tray, and poured himself two fingers in a crystal tumbler. Before he drank, he held the tumbler up to toast the picture of James Madison hanging over the bar. "Ice is for pussies," he said, and downed the scotch in one gulp. He reached for the bottle again just as the prepaid cell phone rang.

"About goddamn time!" He slammed the tumbler on the tray and walked over to his desk. He answered the phone, and before he could speak he heard, "The man says he's in town."

"Is that it?" While Miles waited for an answer, he drummed his fingers on the desk and listened to the two idiots talking in muffled tones on the other end.

"Nah. He also said he would check everything out in the morning, then give us a call when he was ready." The man hesitated. "Is that okay?" he said at last.

"No," Miles snapped. "You idiots should have gotten more details! What the fuck am I *paying* you for, anyway?" His voice was a low growl, and he forced himself to calm. "Just stay out of trouble and wait for instructions," he spit. "And call me the instant you hear anything. Got it?"

"Yes, sir."

Miles stabbed the "end call" button and tossed the phone on the desk. *At least he's on the ground. Maybe I can get some sleep, now.*

†††

"That man is seriously wound up too tight." Roger Phelps sat on the edge of his bed and placed the phone's receiver back onto its cradle.

"I know, right?" Carlos Hernandez, his partner for the past three months, sat on the other bed across from him and smiled. "Dude's gonna blow a seal someday."

Roger snorted and screwed up his mouth. "What do you know? You haven't been with the man very long."

"Long enough, Rog," he said as he shook his head. "Long enough."

"Yeah, I hear ya, man."

Carlos looked toward the door, then back at the phone. He smirked at his friend. "What I don't get is why we need this other guy. Can't we just, you know… do it ourselves?"

Roger shrugged. "I'm all for bustin' a few kneecaps, but I ain't no killer," he said, then drew his mouth into a thin smile. "Besides, we do what the man says. You really ain't been with him long enough if you think we can do somethin' on our own without clearin' it first." He shook his head. "That man's *cold,* you know?" he said. "I don't know about you, but the boss gives me the willies." As big and mean as he was, Roger couldn't stifle the slight shiver that crept up his spine. "There's some creepy shit goin' on inside that head of his, and it's best just to leave it be."

"Yeah, I guess so. I'm just ready to go home."

Roger snorted at the round faced man. "You and me, both, partner."

Carlos leaned back against the headboard and crossed his legs, relaxing for the first time in hours. "Toss me that remote, dude. Let's see what's on the naked channels."

"Aw, man. That stuff is always crap… and it ain't cheap."

"What do you care? The boss is payin' for the room, right?"

"Sure, but he checks the bills, man. And he doesn't miss anything."

Carlos' face fell, considering his options. He sniffed, the gave a disgusted grunt. "Whatever, man. It's late, anyway. Think I'll just turn in." He peeled the blanket back, dropped his pants, and crawled under the covers. "If you're gonna stay up, just keep the noise down, okay?"

"No problem 'Los. I'm turnin' in, myself." Roger copied his partner's actions, then reached across and turned out the light on the nightstand. He lay there, face up, both hands behind his head, and shivered again at the thought of his boss in D.C. *I saw what happened to the last guy who thought he could cross that man. Don't want no part of that. No sir.* That was the first time Roger worked as a go-between for his boss and "the guy." He didn't know the killer's name, and hoped he never found out. The man the boss had him pick up was tied to a chair in the middle of an old warehouse, and "the guy" strolled in off the street, pulled out a little gun like the kind James Bond used, and popped the poor dude in the head twice before the man could open his mouth. "The guy" could have done it quietly, leaving no trace, but this was a statement hit. The boss *wanted* the right people to know who engineered it. As "the guy" left, all he said was "Clean up the mess."

Roger still had dreams about that.

Outside the room, the wind picked up speed as a cool front moved into the area. The cheap weatherstripping on the door, dry and cracked, allowed the air to move the door in and out as the pressure changed. Roger felt like the room was breathing as the gap in the door frame wheezed and whistled in soft and eerie tones. It was like someone breathing down his neck. Soon his own rhythms matched tempo with that of the room, and he drifted into a fitful sleep.

FIFTEEN

THERE WAS BUT ONE RELIABLE METHOD OF INTELLIGENCE GATHER-ing—even on a soft target—and that was to observe and ask questions. The issue was how to go about it without raising suspicion. Addison, though not chronologically old, was an old hand at collecting intel. *Simplicity in all things*, he thought. *Keep it simple and clean, and act like you belong.*

That last was the most important, and had served him well over the years. Even a moderately observant person could spot it when a man was trying too hard. An overly elaborate lie, forced sincerity, even simply talking too much. All of these preceded failure. The best method was to remain invisible, whether when staking out a residence, or standing in plain sight as he did now.

"So, you don't think he'll mind?" Addison looked up at the small, white-haired woman standing in her doorway behind her latched screen door. "I've tried to come by a couple of times, but he hasn't been home," he lifted the bucket with cans of spray paint and stencils, "and I really can't wait anymore for him to pick his colors."

"It's just a house number painted on the curb, mister," the woman said dismissively. "I doubt if he'll even care that you did it at all."

"Well," he scrubbed the stubble on his chin, "he did pay me already, so he probably would." Addison pulled his worn and tattered jeans up a little. They were a bit large, but the pickings were thin at Goodwill that morning. He looked over at the woman's driveway, then back at her. "If you'll take responsibility for the colors, I'll do yours for free."

She narrowed her eyes at him and held the handle of her door in a tight-fisted grip with gnarled, bony fingers. "Sure, why not? Don't get much free stuff these days, anyway."

He reached up and touched his cap. "Thanks, ma'am." He started back down the steps, then turned and asked, "Any idea on where he's been, lately?"

"Oh, I hear he lit out for Colorado 'bout two weeks ago. I wouldn't have known anything, but his Uncle Phil came around a week back lookin' for him, and then I heard he followed the boy up there. Strange doin's if you ask me." She narrowed her eyes again, then said, "When did you say he hired you?"

Addison ducked his head a bit. "Yeah, it's been a while. I like to line up a bunch so's I can do them all in one weekend, and, well… it took me a while." He looked up at her with wide eyes, and said, "It wasn't as if I was takin' his money and then ditchin' the job."

"Well," she looked down her nose at him and sniffed, "just see that you don't. And make sure you do a good job on mine, too. I'll be checkin' up on you in a bit."

"Thanks, ma'am."

"Do 'em up in navy blue," she said through coffee and cigarette stained teeth. "We're both Cowboys fans here."

"Sure," he said. "Will do." He tried to smile up at her, but the door had already slammed shut.

The problem with such a cover was that you had to follow through to maintain the illusion. He walked down to the woman's driveway and began laying out the stencils.

†††

"What do you mean, gone?" Miles drummed his fingers on the antique desk in front of him as he sat, seething, in the high-backed leather chair.

"I mean gone, sir. As in 'not here'," the voice on the other end of the line responded. "Your guy called to tell us the target and his uncle left almost two weeks ago for some place in Colorado. He sounded pretty pissed about it."

Colorado? "I think I know where they're headed." *That's just fucking great.* "You two see if you can stay out of trouble, and I'll call back later today with the location for when our guy calls you back. Can I use this same number?"

"It's secure enough for today."

"Fine. I'll be in touch." He started to press the end call button when he was stopped by the idiot on the other end.

"Sir?"

"What."

"The guy said there would be an, uh, 'upcharge' for the change of plans."

"Of course there is. There is always an upcharge, you moron. Now stay in your room and wait for my call." He stabbed at the button and slammed the phone on the desk. Then, taking a calming breath, he stopped the rage that was gathering in his mind and settled back into his chair. Those two had been working for him for years; and though the muscle they brought to bear on a problem was a great advantage, they weren't the sharpest knives in the drawer. Worse than being stupid, they had given him critical information that was over two weeks old. That showed laziness in their work. And that just wouldn't do.

Miles steepled his hands in front of his face and made a decision. It would cost him a bit more, but there was no room for incompetence at this stage of his plans. His asset once gave him a code word that, once uttered, guaranteed no loose ends in an operation. He sighed at the thought of losing two loyal servants, but there was nothing to be done for it.

†††

"So? Are you gonna let me in on it, or just keep it to yourself?" Jason, after several aborted attempts at coaxing an interaction through sighs and body language alone, had finally given in and just spoken up. He had been pushing the eggs around on his plate like a spoiled child, but Phil refused to give him the satisfaction of a response until he asked like a man.

"What I'm gonna do, is finish my breakfast. I don't like talkin' with my mouth full," he said around eggs and ham already fighting for space, while shoving in a corner of his toast. "Besides, I could be full of crap here. Just give me a minute, okay?"

Long minutes passed while his nephew allowed him to finish his meal in peace. Phil wasn't a physics whiz like this Jason was, so he wasn't sure he even understood all the issues, but he had been at the game for nearly forty years. In all that time, and all those slips through the wall, he saw the same people doing mostly the same things in every universe. This Miles Henderson, though, was different; and, Phil was convinced, not from this reality. After he discovered who his sister's killer was, Phil spent a lot of time studying as many of the Miles' as he could. To a man, they were unremarkable—even the congressmen. Something was different about this one.

Phil scraped the last of the egg from the plate with his toast and crammed it into his mouth. Pouring the last of his coffee after to wash it down, he then raised the cup to get the waitress' attention. She smiled from the counter, and picked up the coffee pitcher to bring it over and refill his cup.

"Thank you darlin'," he said sweetly and winked at her. Even though she was older than Phil, she returned the smile as her cheeks flushed, then walked back to the counter.

"Well?"

"Impatient cuss, aren't you?" Phil moved his empty plate to the edge of the table, and motioned for Jason to continue eating. "All right. This guy we're huntin' right now is different. I think he's what you might call a 'zero point'."

Jason's fork, filled with cold scrambled eggs, stopped halfway to his mouth. "And that means?"

"He's the original. The Miles that all other Miles' branched from. There has to be one, right?"

Jason chewed thoughtfully for a second or two, then said, "Yeah. I guess there does." He swallowed, then began refilling the fork, "I don't see how that helps us, though. In the end, one is no different from the other."

"You may be right, but I don't think so." Phil saw the look of surprise in Jason's eyes, then. It had probably been a long time since anyone told him he was wrong about a point of science. "I think he's a, what would you call it?" He snapped his fingers, "A nexus. That's it." He smiled across the table, sure that the other man was growing a bit of respect. "Every one of his realities, and their thoughts, have to pass through him to complete this network you've been talking about. Without him, the network falls apart. It's also why he's smarter than the rest."

Jason's eyes grew wide, and he set the fork down on his plate. "Holy crap, Uncle Phil. I think you're right!"

"'Course I'm right, son. Did you think I just sat around all day watching TV in my underwear?" Jason looked up at him and snorted. "Okay... I'll give you that, but at least I was thinkin' most of the time."

His nephew laughed so loud the entire crop of patrons in the diner stopped to stare. He leaned across the table and whispered, "So we might actually be able to end this in one shot?"

"I think so."

Jason sat back and heaved a sigh, grinning from ear to ear.

"Don't get too cocky, son, cuz here's the kicker—I think you're a nexus, yourself."

†††

"Orville?"

"Yeah. He said that after you find these guys, he would send the money to your cousin Orville." Roger placed his hand over the phone and snickered at his partner, Carlos, seated on the other bed, "Who names their kid 'Orville' these days?"

"I don't know, Rog, but I wouldn't let this guy hear you laughing if I were you."

"Yeah, I hear ya." Roger pulled his hand away and said into the phone, "We're done, here, right? You got everything you need?"

"All I needed was the address, and you took care of that." There was a hesitation on the other end of the line. "Thank you. I am certain your boss will be happy with the job you did today."

"Glad to do it, man." Roger was sure the guy on the other end was queer as hell, because the way he talked was just too refined for this line of work. Probably some kind of pervert, too. *One of those guys who got off on pain and shit*. Roger was good at guessing what people did for a living, and it never took him more than three or four tries to get it right. *It's not a secret or anything. I'm just observant. Like how I can spot a queer.*

The line went dead while he was contemplating all this, and Roger looked over at his partner and said, "Dude just hung up. No goodbye or nothin'."

"Some people are just rude, I guess."

"Ain't that the truth." He nodded toward the door of their motel room, "C'mon, 'Los, let's go get something to eat."

"I heard that. My stomach's started eating itself, man."

Roger laughed. Carlos always made him laugh. It's why they got along so well.

"Hey, Rog," Carlos stopped by the door as he shrugged on his jacket, "think we have time for a movie before we have to get to the airport?"

Roger stopped and considered that, rubbing the two day's growth on his chin, as it reminded him of something that bugged him ever since that last call from the boss. "Sure, but I don't recall the man telling us to take a flight back, though. Do you?"

Carlos smiled, and said, "Naw, me neither." Free day! He and Carlos didn't get many of those when they were on a job. "Screw the movie, then," Carlos said. "Let's hit a bar and pick up some trim."

Roger just shook his head, "Dude, there ain't no bars in this burg. We'd have to go all the way back into Houston for that." He grabbed the keys to the rented car, and followed the other man out the door. "Let's just wing it, and see what happens."

"Sounds like a plan."

†††

Addison spotted the two men as they left the little motel they were using as their base of operations. He anticipated the roll-up code and made his last call from there in the parking lot, after he checked the only other two motels in town earlier in the day. The larger of the two men, looking ridiculously out of place in such a town, lumbered to the passenger door of their sedan, looked around, then opened the door and folded himself into the too-small car. He wouldn't be much of a problem, but the other man—the driver—walked with a grace and self-assurance that indicated training. He might not be intelligent, and certainly not as large as his partner, but he probably had some skills. Addison knew he would have to deal with him first.

He needed this to look enough like an accident to fool the local cops. Experience with the police in this state told him it wouldn't take much work for that, though. As soon as the other car pulled out of the parking lot, Addison started the quiet little engine and drove for the exit. He had to be careful tailing the other car. Though they probably weren't bright enough to recognize a tail through the streets of Houston, the lack of traffic in this small town would allow even the dimmest bulb to notice him.

He needn't have worried. The drive was a short one to a local fast-food establishment. After they pulled in, he drove on by for a few blocks, then made a U-turn and came back to park at a closed hardware store across the street. He killed the engine and headlights, and then he settled in to wait for them come back out. Once he had tagged them, it made no difference if he kept them in his sight, but it would keep things simple.

Addison reached over the center console to the passenger seat, grabbed his briefcase, set it in his lap, and opened the lid. Nestled inside individual foam compartments was his "travel toolkit": Two throwing knives, a piano wire garrote, his favored Beretta 70 with a flash suppressor and two magazines, and his choice for the night, the needle-thin steel stiletto. Wielded properly, it was a clean and lethal instrument. Yes, it required close contact with the target, but it did have the advantage of being almost undetectable… if the bodies were handled properly.

After the men had their fill of burgers and fries, they drove a dusty road to a small ice house just outside of town. Lit in garish colors, the place boomed its music to the world, advertising the epitome of drunken revelry. *Nice of them to provide a cause,* he thought. *Saves me the trouble.* He passed by when they stopped, driving another mile before finding what he needed, then parked fifty meters from the huge pine tree that marked the split in the road. On the walk back to the ice house he planned.

It was a small matter to gain entry to their vehicle, and Addison climbed into the back, pressing himself flat against the floorboard. Most people never checked the back seat when they entered a car, and the two men did not disappoint when they opened their doors.

Amateurs, Addison thought, clutching the stiletto in his right hand.

"Told you that bitch had yer number, didn't I?" the one in the passenger seat said. He chuckled and pulled the shoulder strap across his body and buckled in. It took him three tries.

"Fuck you, 'Los," the driver said. "I don't recall *you* havin' any more luck."

The passenger chuckled, the sound turning into a strained gurgle as Addison's stiletto slid under the base of his skull. The driver laughed at his partner's discomfort while Addison shifted the tool to his left hand. He watched as the laughter stopped, and the driver's eyes widened when his partner's chin dropped to his chest and the body relaxed against the seatbelt.

"What—?" he said, and that was all. Addison slid the instrument into the other man's neck, answering the unasked question.

When the body stopped twitching, Addison stepped out of the car, opened the front door, and shoved the driver to the far side into the other man's lap. The air was ripe with the combine release of relaxed bladders and sphincters, and he rolled down his window before starting the engine.

He drove to the fork in the deserted road and parked a hundred meters from the tree. Though the place was remote enough to qualify as rarely traveled, that did not mean it was *never* traveled. Once the road was clear, he pressed his foot hard, pinning the accelerator to the floor, and drove straight at the tree. At the last possible moment, he bailed out, rolled to the shoulder of the road, and watched the car plow into the massive trunk. Large chunks of bark flew in every direction, and a heavy branch high above cracked and fell across the hood of the car.

Addison stood, dusted himself, walked to the car, and arranged the bodies into more believable positions. He retrieved a couple of empty bottles of whiskey from his own car, and scattered them on the floorboard, then doused the bodies with more alcohol. Tugging at the corner of the driver's shirt, he used his lighter to set it aflame. The fire spread quickly through the cabin, and within seconds the heat was unbearable. Even the large pine tree caught and fed the flames, pushing him farther and farther back.

Staying close to the tree line beside the road, he walked back to his car. He drove away, confident there wouldn't be much of an investigation. While the severing of the spinal cords might be detected in an autopsy if the bodies did not burn completely, the entry wounds would be burned away. The men had, he was sure, rented the car under an assumed name, so there would be little to identify them—especially since no one would ever report them missing.

Two hours later, Addison arrived at Hobby Airport. The job completed, he looked forward to getting to his original task. He had already called ahead, his pilot filing a flight plan to Denver. He parked near the same spot as before, wiped down the car for prints, then left it for the cut-out to pick up and sell for parts.

Clean. Just the way he liked it.

†††

Phil let the hood drop on the new truck, and then pounded on it once with a meaty fist. "Goddamn computer-age crap!"

"So, what's wrong with it?" Jason stood off to one side, as far away from his uncle as he could get on the lonely shoulder of the road. Cars occasionally whizzed by, but no one stopped.

"Hell if I know, junior. Nobody can work on this shit anymore." He leaned against the over-powered paperweight and crossed his arms.

The motor stopped running nearly a mile back, and after they coasted downhill to a stop on the side of the road, had steadfastly refused to turn over. Jason was sure it was a problem with the charging system, but if that was the case, not even a jump would help.

"We should call for a tow, then."

His uncle turned to look at him and shook his head. "You got a smartphone on you so we can look one up?"

"Uh… no. How about you?"

Phil just laughed.

Jason turned to look back up the way they came, and said, "I guess we could try to flag someone down."

"Sane people don't stop anymore, son. At least not for two men."

Jason grinned weakly, and said, "Yeah, I guess you're right." There were downsides to a world that was always connected, and everything was at your fingertips. What used to require a phone book or directory assistance… *shit*.

"Uncle Phil? Doesn't plain old directory assistance still work?"

Phil laughed out loud. "Son of a bitch!" He shook his head, still chuckling to himself, and said, "You would have thought I would think of that. That's *my* generation, after all."

Two hours later they were riding in the cab of the tow truck as it pulled their truck to the local dealership for repair. In Kansas there was a whole lot of nothing between large towns, and it took the towing service a while to get there; even longer to find a dealership to work on the truck. The driver had an affinity for country music, though, and he and Phil tortured Jason with every twang and nasally lyric they could reproduce.

Jason retreated as far into his own thoughts as the noise would al-low, and considered the universe he found himself inhabiting. It was the first time he revisited a reality, and the thought of seeing his son again pulled at him. Sure, Jay wasn't the same boy he left behind six years ago, but it was hard—even now—to make those distinctions. To Jason he would be the same, albeit older. It would be no different than seeing the same child after any long separation. Everyone changed over time. Even the old canard that every atom in the human body is replaced every seven years or so had some kernel of truth to it. *Jay is jay is jay is jay...*

There had to be realities, though, where the boy didn't exist—had *never* existed—and in those, that Jason would never know the differ-ence. *You can't miss what you never had.*

Jason reached up with both hands and rubbed his temples. *If you press hard enough, maybe you can turn off that part that lets you remember every life you've lived.* Too many to count, and he knew he only scratched the surface of what was to come. How many lives would he use up? And what would happen when *this* consciousness died? Was death even a re-ality for him, or was it just another universe to inhabit?

"Won't help, you know."

He opened his eyes to see his uncle watching him, concern on the man's face.

"What do you mean?"

"I mean that thinkin' about it doesn't help." He smiled, shrugged his shoulders, and said, "I've found it's best to just keep pluggin'. Keep moving forward. Things have a way of workin' out."

Jason frowned and turned his head to face the man. "I want to see my son."

"I don't think that's a good idea." He said it simply. A matter-of-fact manner that Jason found hard to understand.

"Why not?" As soon as the words were out of his mouth, the look on his uncle's face told Jason he didn't want to know.

Phil sighed and scratched his chin. "Things haven't gone so well for the little guy the last few years," he said. He leaned across and whis-pered, "Let's just leave it at that for now. We can discuss this later, okay?"

Jason looked into the man's eyes, searching for understanding, but Phil only stared back passively. It was a poker face worthy of Vegas, and there was no penetrating that wall. Finally, Jason shrugged his shoulders and said, "Yeah, sure… but soon. I want to know what's going on."

"Don't we all, son." He nodded at the road and the lot full of cars decorated with balloons, and said, "Looks like we're here."

SIXTEEN

PHIL SIGNED THE RECEIPT AS THE CLERK SLID THE KEYS ACROSS THE counter. She was young and pretty in that Mid-Western mold, though her brown hair was cut short in more of an East Coast style. Her smile was huge—all teeth and gums—and he returned the gesture.

"Should be good to go, sir."

"I'm just glad it was all covered," he said cheerily. In fact, though, he was more pleased the repairs took a single day, and that he and Jason spent just one night in town. He looked over at his nephew, watching him sit in the little plastic chair that was bolted to the floor in the waiting area. His right leg was bouncing like a sewing machine.

Phil smiled again at the girl, then walked over to Jason. He folded the paper neatly and shoved it into his shirt pocket, then held the keys out as he looked down, "You wanna drive, or should I?"

Jason's knee stopped shaking, and he looked up. "You can take the first shift," he narrowed his eyes, "I've got some thinking to do."

Phil winced. "Still upset I didn't tell you about your boy?"

Jason snorted once. "A bit, yeah."

"Well, get over it. Right now we've got bigger fish to fry." He turned and walked out of the little room without waiting for Jason to follow.

Once outside, both men climbed up into the truck. Phil jammed the key into the ignition, turned it, and smiled broadly when the engine turned over and roared to life.

"Good girl," he said as he patted the dashboard. "See, bud, Jenny's good as new."

Jason shook his head. "You named it?"

"Of course, Einstein. I name all my kids." He shifted into drive and pulled out of the parking lot and onto the highway. This time of the morning the traffic was light, although the fact they were in Kansas might have something to do with it.

They drove in silence for a few miles before Jason finally spoke up.

"I still don't understand how I screwed things up so much."

"Well, technically—"

"You know what I mean. It's still me. Why is Jay so off the rails? How much do I suck as a parent for that to happen?"

Phil sighed heavily. Ever since he told Jason about their troubles with the boy, he dreaded this conversation. "You have to understand… it's been tough for both of you."

"But—"

"Look, Jason, Kathy's dead here. Got that? His mom—the woman you love—and the only grandparents who gave a damn about him are gone for good. All on the same night. Think about that for a minute, and let it sink in."

Jason closed his mouth and turned back to watch the road and brood. He had been doing that a lot, lately, and Phil saw clearly how every Jason was more alike than not.

"You can't imagine how hard that would be, because you know they're all still alive somewhere. The Jason left here in your place didn't have that information, and neither does your son."

Jason turned back, eyes moist, and said "I think I can imagine it a little bit." He shook his head. "Knowing other versions are still alive doesn't make it easier, you know. Especially when you have to watch it happen over and over again." He looked down at his hands, clenching and unclenching like he didn't know what to do with them. "How did they manage?" he said.

"Like I said… it's been hard on both."

"What about you?"

Phil wanted to say *How the* fuck *do you think I've been?* He wanted to say that, but he couldn't. What came out, instead, was "Been too busy thinkin' about how to get the bastard who did it."

"I call 'bullshit'," Jason said without inflection.

"Fine… let's just say I wasn't much help to the two of you the first couple of months."

"I think that's okay, Uncle Phil. Everyone gets to deal with the crap life throws them in their own way."

Phil let out a short laugh, and said, "That's just what the other you said once." He turned the wheel, aiming toward an exit ramp. "'Course, he was talkin' about Jay at the time."

Jason looked around, then back at his uncle, his mouth twisted and one eyebrow raised. "Why are you taking the exit? We don't change roads for a couple more miles."

"Like I said, I've been thinkin' 'bout how to get this guy, and the first part is loadin' up on some serious cash."

"I don't understand. Doesn't your credit card work?"

"For now, but I want to cover our tracks better than that." He saw the quizzical look on Jason's face and shook his head. "I would have thought you'd have figured this out already." He looked for comprehension, but the only reaction was Jason's eyebrows meeting in the middle. "Look, the dude's a congressman. He's probably got connections that can track us just by using our credit cards, so I want to go all cash until we get there."

Jason smiled thinly, and said, "I think you're being paranoid. There's no way he even knows we're on to him, much less coming to kill him."

"So, then, explain that little dance we had in the hotel room on your first solo trip."

Jason's eyes widened, but he didn't argue.

"Right, junior. Like I said… better paranoid than dead."

He found what he was looking for, and pulled into the parking lot by the little building that served as a branch bank. Jason's bank.

"Hey, I thought you used Wells Fargo."

"I do. It's time you contributed to the cause."

Jason smiled and shook his head, "Yeah, about that. I didn't exactly have a lot of cash the last time I was here."

Phil smiled back, and said, "Why don't we give it a shot? You never know."

†††

Jason's eyes goggled at the number staring back at him from the ATM.

"Have I been cooking meth on the side or something?"

Phil laughed, but to Jason the sound was more of sadness than mirth. "That's your daddy's idea of being responsible." The big man shook his head, "He always said that you and your mom would be taken care of if he died, but I just thought he was talkin' 'bout funeral expenses and his small pension. What he never told any of us was that he took out a pretty big insurance policy on both he and your mom. Payments must have been hell to keep up with."

"Uh, Uncle Phil, that number is more than just 'pretty big'. And why the hell is it just sitting in my savings account? Shouldn't it be at least in a mutual fund or something?"

Jason watched as the man found something suddenly interesting about his boots. "Yeah, well, I don't get into your business that much. I'm sure you've got your reasons."

He watched him for a few seconds, waiting for more explanation, but when none was forthcoming he said, "I guess. Okay, then… how much do we need?"

Phil looked up to his left for a bit and tapped his chin. "Probably not more than five grand."

Jason's eyes flew open wide. "Five thousand?" He took a step back from the machine. "Dollars?"

Phil snorted, "You think I meant pesos? Of course dollars."

He thought about the rest of their trip. Gas, meals, hotels, whatever equipment they might need. And it wasn't like that amount would put even a small dent in the total. "We can't get that out here. They put limits on what you can get out of an ATM." He pointed at the doors, "For that much we'll have to go inside."

"I was hopin' to stay off the surveillance cameras."

"Oh, that ship has already sailed," Jason said as he tapped the lens on the ATM.

Phil smacked his forehead. "I get it… double-o seven I ain't. We're gonna have to do better, though."

Jason took two steps toward the entrance and pulled the door open, holding it for his uncle. "No doubt about that," he said. "I think before this is over we're gonna have to get better at a lot of things."

†††

Phil continued his turn at the wheel as they left Kansas City behind, making it all the way to Indianapolis before giving in to exhaustion. Since Jason was also in no shape to take over, they decided to stop for the night and try to push through to Arlington the next day. They didn't have any plans beyond that, so for now it was just a matter of grinding out the miles.

He reached behind his seat absentmindedly to feel one more time for the locking toolbox. He knew he was obsessing, but the thing had close to five thousand dollars locked inside, and he wasn't used to having that kind of cash on hand. As they drew closer to their destination, it was critical that their movements could not be traced through bank transactions. There was no point in making their target aware of their location, but some businesses did not like to take cash, and many hotel clerks looked at you funny when you didn't use a credit card. It was bad enough that every motel required a driver's license to book a room, but since he never allowed Jason to check in, that might keep anyone after the boy off their trail. He hoped.

A well-connected congressman could have them tracked throughout their trip, but there was no reason to think he knew they were coming for him. Phil was also sure that tracking two nobodies such as themselves would raise all kinds of red flags, and he was confident that even if Henderson knew they were coming for him, he probably wouldn't risk it. Still, it was always better to be careful.

Both men slept until well past ten the next morning, and with eight or nine hours of driving still ahead of them, they packed what little belongings they carried and checked out of the motel. With luck, they would arrive in Arlington by nine or ten that night and get a full night's sleep. There was still a lot of planning to do, and Phil didn't want to do it with his personal battery drained. They drove the entire trip, rather than fly, just to stay off the man's radar, but that didn't mean they should tackle the problem unrested. That was a fool's errand, for sure.

"So, how are we gonna do it?" Phil turned his head to see that Jason was watching him drive. Probably had been for a while, mustering the courage to ask a question that each avoided quite successfully until now.

"I don't know, son," he said, then turned his eyes, if not his attention, back to the highway. "We're talking about killing a congressman. Granted, there are probably a lot of people out there who wished they could do it, but we're gonna *actually* do it." He gripped the wheel a bit harder, and his mouth twisted as he thought about it. "We're not gonna be able to get through security anywhere in D.C. with a weapon, if that's what you're thinking. And while there are any number of ways this can go down, I would prefer if we both lived and stayed out of prison, if you don't mind." Even though they could both slip through the wall if caught, that would only leave another Jason and Phil here in this universe holding the bag. Forget Jason and Phil, though—he couldn't do that to Jay.

Jason nodded in agreement at that, most likely thinking the same thoughts. He shifted uneasily in his seat, stretching his legs. He looked like he was about to say something, then tilted his head for a second and turned to face the road.

Phil watched him for another second or two, scratched his chin, and said, "Probably the easiest way is to get him to come to us."

His nephew turned to him in shock, "How's that?"

"Guy like that, he's all about control. He would need to feel like he had you trapped." *He'd want to play with his prey a little, too. I've hunted with guys like that.* "Plus, he's just sure he's smarter than everyone in the room," Phil said. "He won't like the idea of us being in the same town with him, waiting for our next move." The corners of his mouth turned up. Nothing warmed his heart more than making a bully uncomfortable.

"So then he finds out where we are and comes in guns blazing." Jason made a gun with his fingers and pointed it at his uncle. "Bang, we're dead."

"I don't think so." He saw a hint of fear in Jason's eyes, then, where only a few days ago he had seen determination. The long hours on the road had a way of wearing down a man's resolve. "We've got a few things going for us, I think." He held a finger in the air, "One, there's no reason to think he knows you can slip through the wall, and he sure doesn't know you're a nexus." A second finger joined the first, "Two, he has to be very careful how he deals with us. He doesn't want to call attention to himself in a way that diminishes his power." His thumb joined the other two fingers, "And three, he doesn't know about me," he said as he poked himself in the chest with that thumb. "When he finds out you're in town, his paranoid little brain will jump to the conclusion that you are out for revenge. He would never consider that your being in town is only a coincidence." He snorted once, "Hell, I wouldn't."

"So we get him to come to us," Jason said softly, rubbing his chin as he stared at the road.

"Exactly. On our terms, at our chosen location, with all the advantages on our side of the ledger."

Jason shook his head and grinned. "Sounds easy. So how do we do it?"

Phil grinned back at his nephew. "Haven't a god damned clue."

†††

It took Addison a full day to fly to Denver, secure a car, and drive to the spot on the map where he could begin his hike up the mountain. His destination was a small hunting cabin nestled in the woods not far from a little stream. The map in his hand showed a convenient sheer drop a few hundred feet north of the cabin. It had been his intent to find the two men, dispatch them quickly with an improvised blunt weapon, then toss their bodies over that cliff. It was at least a hundred feet to the bottom, so there would be enough trauma to indicate an accidental fall. A good investigator might wonder why both men had fallen at the same time, but without witnesses it would still be recorded as an unfortunate accident.

That was the plan, at least. The problem with the plan, though, was a lack of potential victims on site. He realized that the men might not be at the cabin when he arrived, so he found a secure location from which to watch the building, and waited. After a full twenty-four hours of nothing, he came to the conclusion that the two managed to elude him again.

"They're either very lucky, or very good." As a professional, one who understood probabilities better than most, Addison chose to believe they were very good. *No one got killed overestimating their opponent.*

Night was coming to the mountain quickly, and the temperature fell just as fast. With no desire to make his way down in the dark, not to mention the cold, he made a decision and left his hide to enter the cabin. He would start a fire, eat what rations he had left, and get a night's sleep before heading down in the morning. Since his cell phone couldn't get a signal up here, he had to wait until he got back to the car to make the call to his client.

"Should have given me better intel to begin with," he said in a low growl as he stirred the little pot of soup on the stove. The soup would do little to sate his hunger, but the tea he brewed would improve his disposition.

†††

"Make the call. Tell him I'm fine with the new upcharge, but he has to be back in town by tonight, got it?"

"Yes, sir."

Miles ended the call and threw the phone across the room. The man on the other end was a new cut-out one of his operatives had hired, and this one didn't sound any more intelligent than the others. Luckily, though, the job was simple this time. All he had to do was relay the message. *Surely, he couldn't fuck that up*, Miles thought.

Those bastards are here in D.C. He had no evidence. *Absence of evidence is not evidence of absence*, he thought. Paranoid thinking or not, Miles knew in his gut they were here to kill him. *No one ever died from being cautious.* His best asset was almost two thousand miles away, and right now, all but useless. There was no one else he could trust enough to do even the most basic investigation into where the two might be holed up. His only saving grace was in the knowledge that they couldn't get at him easily here in his office, and he had spent enough late nights on the couch by the door not to arouse suspicion if he stayed here for a few days.

It was just his luck that when things were finally headed in the right direction for him, something like this would come along to screw it up. He was mere days away from introducing a bill that would make his name in this town, taking the first step on the last leg of his journey to the White House. He had seen the path clearly... it was right there in front of him. But right now, there were two men in his way, and they had to be dealt with. *I'm too close to everything I ever wanted.*

He needed a drink. And a woman. *That's the ticket.*

†††

Jason lay in bed covered only with a sheet, the top covers once again in a heap on the floor. His uncle thought his quirk a bit silly at first, but as Jason explained his reasons, the top cover from the other bed also found itself piled atop the first. On his back, he stared at the lovely brown water stain on the ceiling. Already edged in a white mold, it must have been there for a long time, and he wondered how long since it was last painted. As he considered that, the stain gathered mass, becoming a rough-hewn chunk of granite hanging over his head. The longer he looked, the more detail he saw, and then it started to sway slightly from side to side as if suspended from a cable. He looked away and blinked, and when he looked back it was just a stain. Even though the room was cold, and he was covered with a single sheet, he was sweating.

He calmed his breathing, closed his eyes, and focused on the thin line that marked the boundary of realities. Now that he had become attuned to the veils, it was easier to see each possibility that the different colors represented. He decided to take a trip sideways without telling his uncle, desiring to check for himself what kind of man Mr. Henderson was in another reality. His plan was to take a short jump only one or two branches over, but as he moved toward the fissure, he heard the sound again. It didn't happen every time, but always before he had ignored it. This time, though, something compelled him to turn toward it's bell-like emanation.

As he did so, the sensation of falling for a great distance came over him. This was no gentle slip through the fissure. It was a twisting, wrenching extrusion through a microscopic rend in the fabric of reality—a burning pain without a beginning or end, and as he neared the limit of his endurance, it stopped.

When Jason opened his eyes he was standing on the National Mall, and through a sky filled with dark clouds and ash, patches of sunlight filtered down to pool and merge into a scene of utter devastation and despair stretching to the horizon.

SEVENTEEN

"Congressman Henderson?" The intern stood in the door-way to his office, one hand on the light switch and the other carrying a sheaf of papers bound in a manila folder, looking like she had walked into an orgy by mistake.

"Don't touch that light," Miles growled as he sat up on the couch, elbows on his knees, and running both hands vigorously through his hair. All around the couch on the floor were empty bottles of liquor and a couple of tumblers—one lay in shards in the corner—and the smell that greeted the hapless intern caused her nose to wrinkle.

"Are you all right?"

Miles turned his head to look up at her. The look of concern on her face was genuine, but forced, and it was obvious she wanted to be anywhere but where she was at this moment. He could relate to that.

"M'fine." He shook his head—not too hard—and said, "I just worked through the night is all." He followed her gaze to the glassware on the floor and smiled up at her, "Looks like I had one or two too many, doesn't it?"

She smiled back sweetly and shrugged her shoulders, "It hap-pens."

"Those for me?" He gestured at the folder in her hands with one hand, while the other held his head.

"Yes, sir. Just some notes for your committee meetings today."

He waved his free hand, and said, "Well?"

She tilted her head for a second at the motion of his hand, and her eyes opened a little wider, "Oh, right. Here you go." She handed him the folder and turned to leave, stopping just outside the door to ask, "Will there be anything else, sir?"

"I think I'm good." He smiled at her without humor, then his face went slack again. "Now close the door behind you and make sure no one disturbs me for at least an hour. Think you can do that, honey?" *Hot as hell, but that heat never seems to generate any light. Of course, I didn't hire her for her brains.*

"Of course, sir," she said through gritted teeth, then closed the door as silently as she could before she walked away.

Miles sat on the couch in the darkened office for another minute or two before dragging himself to his feet to walk to his desk. As he sat down, he pulled the chain on the small Tiffany lamp, and opened the folder. The notes were for his meeting at one o'clock with the Appropriations Committee. That was a plum not usually offered to a freshman, but the information he had on the chairman took care of that. He was pushing for a role on the Defense Subcommittee, with his ultimate goal being named chairman. That would require his party gaining a majority in the House, but that was a real possibility in the coming mid-term elections. Everything seemed to be lining up this time.

All night long, he waited for word that his asset was back in town, but with each tick of the clock he grew angrier and more concerned. Dousing his anger in alcohol wasn't a wise move, but it helped him get through the night. He briefly considered taking a trip sideways to see how things were shaping up nearby, but each of the last three attempts left him shaken. Worse, he couldn't seem to go back in time more than a few weeks, now. Something was blocking his trips south, and he didn't have the knowledge required to even guess at an answer.

He was just about to take his mind off his current situation by digging into the notes for his meeting, when his new cell phone rang from its charging cradle on the credenza behind him. He picked it up, checked the incoming number, and hit the answer key.

"Yes?"

"Our man is in back in town. He asked if there were any instructions."

Miles quickly ran over all the options he had before him, and found the list boiled down to exactly one.

"Next time he calls, tell him to stand down and wait for my signal. If I need him in a hurry, I'll contact him through the regular channels."

"Will do, sir." Three beeps, and the line went dead.

He replaced the phone in its charging cradle, and turned back to his work. He needed a shower and a meal, but he wanted to go over the notes before he left the office. Or he could do two things at once.

He hit the call button on his intercom, "Janet?"

"Sir?"

"Be a dear and go down to the cafeteria and bring me back a breakfast tray."

"Anything special?"

"Nope. Just fill it up." He would take that shower later.

†††

Addison pulled a towel from the stack on the table and mopped the sweat from his face and neck. The hotel gym was usually empty this early in the morning, and today didn't disappoint. He pulled the little earbuds of his headset out, then carefully wrapped the cable around his mp3 player. When most people used their smartphones for this function, he still clung to the idea of "one tool for one purpose." His phones were just phones—and always disposable. Not a Luddite by any means— he fully embraced new technology when it suited his needs—but he found that the more complicated a thing was, the more likely it was to fail.

Grabbing his gym bag, he walked to the glass double doors, tossing the towel casually into the hamper off to the side as he did. A short trip up the elevator to his room, and then he could shower, dress, and be downstairs for breakfast when the hotel restaurant opened.

"Mr. Russell?" The bellman—tall, rail thin, and very dark—waved at him from near the concierge desk. Even from this distance, Addison could see the one gold tooth as the man smiled at him. He despised such affectations.

He turned from the elevators just as the man walked up to him, and he said, "Yes, Carl?" The bellman beamed a broad smile. Addison found over the years that it paid to remember the names of servants.

"Sir, a man left a note for you at the desk," he said as he extended the hand holding a small slip of paper.

Addison raised an eyebrow, looked at the paper, then back at the man. Carl stood there smiling and waiting patiently. Finally, he snatched if from the man's hand and unfolded it to find a phone number printed neatly there.

Addison looked up to Carl, the man smiling obsequiously, and he said, "Did the man say anything?"

"No, sir. He just said to give this to you."

"Good, then." Any slip by an operative always ended up in another body to dispose of, and he was thankful that wasn't necessary. *Wetwork is bad enough. Wetwork for free is just wrong.*

Addison opened his gym bag and fished around for a second before pulling out his wallet.

The bellman looked at him with a pained expression, and held both hands palms out in front of him. "Oh, no, sir. This was my pleasure."

For the second time that morning, Addison raised an eyebrow, but then smiled. "You're a good man, Carl."

Carl winked at him, and said, "Hang onto that thought until I carry your bags down, sir."

Addison laughed. "I think I will, at that." He turned back to the elevator, dismissing the man without another thought, and pressed the up button. As he waited for the car to make its way down, he heard Carl whistling softly as the man walked back to his post. Addison tilted his head just as the doors opened, recognizing the tune as the same song he heard last through his earbuds during his workout.

†††

"Come again?" Phil sat on the edge of his bed, rubbing the sleep out of his eyes, and making an effort to understand what Jason was saying. Sure, it was past eight in the morning, but a man needed his sleep.

"I said I think I just saw the future." Jason stared at him across the short distance, wide-eyed, sweat-matted hair plastered against his face. The man was a mess, and Phil looked him over for signs of a breakdown. He knew them well, as he had seen them in his own mirror at least twice over the years.

"You just had a nightmare. That's all."

Jason waved a hand dismissively, and said, "We both know that most dreams are a window into another reality." His hands shook as he reached for the small tumbler of water on the nightstand between them. He ran a hand through his hair to pull it off his face as he gulped the half-empty glass.

"Sure, son. But the future?" Phil rubbed the back of his neck, and stretched his back. "I don't think we can slip into the future." He considered for a moment all his trips over the years, "At least, I never have." Phil stood and studied his nephew for a second, then picked up the tumbler and walked into the bathroom. As he filled the glass with water, he poked his head out of the door and said, "I think we can only go where we are—sideways—not where we haven't been yet."

"Time is nature's way of keeping everything from happening at once," Jason replied.

Phil walked back to the bed, sat down, and placed the tumbler in Jason's still trembling hands. "What was that?"

"Something I saw scribbled on the wall of the men's room of the Pecan Street Cafe back in Austin," Jason said. He took another sip, pouted his lips and raised an eyebrow, then set the tumbler back on the nightstand. "It means that everything that has happened, or ever will happen is all one tangled thread, and it is only time that keeps everything going in a straight line that we recognize as cause and effect."

"You're about to lose me again, son." Many times over the last few days, his nephew had tried to explain his understanding of the wall using his quantum physics jibber-jabber. In every case, Jason had him thoroughly confused after only a few words. "Try to keep it simple, okay?"

Jason smiled wanly at that. "Sure," he said. He thought for a few seconds, and started again, "I think you're right that we can't travel into the future—at least not slip there like we've been doing. Of course, people travel into the future all the time. It's called living. Right now we are five seconds farther into the future than we were five seconds ago."

Phil nodded. *This was easy... so far.*

"But I also think that not only is it possible to travel to the past, but we can at least see glimpses of the future under the right conditions." Jason stared right through him, then. "I think I just got a look over the horizon," he hesitated, wringing his hands. "And it's not going to be pretty."

"But why you? I've never been able to do it, and I've been at it a lot longer than you."

"It might have something to do with me being a nexus. I've told you before about hearing a sound inside the fissure. I think that's my perception of another direction that can be taken. A different kind of veil." Jason pointed left and right, "We, well you, travel only east or west when you slip through the wall, jumping from one universe sideways to another. Always from branch to branch, and only moving forward, or north," he pointed forward, "in real-time."

Phil sat there in his underwear, considering the man across the divide. He didn't look crazy, though a bit haggard, and he was at least sounding coherent. Through all the years of planning and searching, he had done so confident in his feeling that this Jason was the only one who could help him complete the task before them. But why did he believe that? He found other Jasons who knew how to slip through the wall, but he never recruited them. He knew there was something special about this Jason that gave him hope for their success, and he had thought it was just that he was a nexus. Now he thought there might more. A *lot* more.

"So, what exactly did you see?" he said at last.

Jason took a deep breath and let it out slowly, "I think there's going to be a war."

Phil grinned and slapped his nephew on the knee, "Is that all?" His short laugh punctuated the silent stare from the man. "Son, there's a war going on all the time in this world." He jerked a thumb over his shoulder, "Hell I've got buddies still stuck in Afghanistan fightin' a war no one wants to admit is still going on."

"I'm not talking about *a* war, Uncle Phil," he growled, "I'm talking about *the* war." This time his voice was shaking, and he did look a bit disturbed to Phil. "The one no one wins." He was wringing his hands furiously now, though he seemed not to notice. "I was standing in the middle of D.C., looking at a wasteland covered in ash." He looked up into the face of his uncle, "And everywhere there was the stench of death."

Phil leaned away, stunned, the gulf between the two of them becoming more than a physical reality. Couldn't this have just been a nightmare? His gut told him no. This was, or was going to be, real. *And Jason had seen it, somehow.*

"What does this have to do with us, Jason? How are we supposed to stop World War Three?" He stood suddenly and stepped back from the man. The distance offered no protection, he knew. There would never be enough distance.

"Because," Jason looked up and locked eyes, "our Mr. Henderson is the key." Phil started to speak, but Jason interrupted, "I don't know how I know this, but the feeling was crystal clear while I was standing there in that hell. Henderson caused this." Jason stood as well to confront his uncle, "And it's worse than that. Every time anyone has made a decision in this universe since this began, a new one has spun off with the same Congressman Henderson headed down the same path. By now there are an almost infinite number of realities where this is going to happen."

"But the one we're chasing is a nexus, so…," Phil began.

"So we take this one out, and all the others go poof?" Jason shook his head. "I don't think it works quite like that. There will be some ripple effects, but each new iteration will probably continue as before."

"Then what?"

"I think we have to figure something else out."

Phil was not cut out for this. Sure, he could plan ahead and take action when it was necessary, but this science crap was way beyond him. If only he had studied more in school, he might… "Hey. What was that you said about north and south?"

"Hmm?" Lost in thought himself, Jason appeared not to have heard him.

"You said we could see north, but that we could actually travel south." He looked at Jason, hoping for a miracle revelation of some kind.

"Yeah. We can't go into the future, though some theories suggest it should be possible, but we—or I—can slip through the wall south to the past." He twisted his face and squinted, "Hurts like hell, though."

"Then why don't we—you—just go back and kill that sumbitch before he kills your mom and dad."

"Because I didn't."

"Huh?"

"I can't. Because I didn't."

"Yeah, that's not helping." Phil rubbed his face with both hands, and started collecting his clothes.

"If I traveled back in time to kill him, then he wouldn't be here for us to chase, and there would be no reason to go back to kill him. In which case, he would still kill my parents, and we would still be right where we are now."

"Stop it. My brain hurts," he said as he pulled on his pants.

"Hang on, it's about to get worse." Jason flopped back on the bed, seated once again. "I think Henderson, being a nexus, has learned a thing or two about time travel himself. I think he traveled backward in time to kill me, bringing with him the knowledge of future events he needed to gain power in this reality."

Phil, shirt on and half buttoned, stopped and stared at his nephew, speechless.

"Worse," he said, "I think he went back because I chased him there."

†††

Richard Parker—known as "spider" to his friends—only half-listened to his boss rattle on about the inconvenience of waiting for a response from Mr. Russell. Spider hated his nickname. He explained to his friends a hundred times over the years that Spider-Man was Peter Parker—his *dad* was Richard—but they never got it. Instead, they pointed out his lanky frame and the way he moved, and said "who gives a fuck?" He'd been stuck with it since middle school, and no amount of arguing would change it now.

"No, sir, I haven't heard from him yet." Spider stood by the ATM on the sidewalk outside the hotel, holding his cell phone nearly a foot from his ear, and tapping his shoe on the sidewalk while he listened to the man's growing frustration.

"I'm not paying you to stand around. If you don't hear from him in the next hour, you need to get another message to him. Tell him it's urgent."

"I'm sure he understands that, sir."

The man hesitated, then grew unnaturally calm. "I don't pay you to understand, either." Another couple of seconds passed, then he said, "I just expect you to do as I order. Is that clear?"

"Crystal, sir." He stretched his leg out, and rubbed the sole of his shoe on the curb to scrape off a patch of gum stuck to the bottom. "I'll let you know as soon as he calls, or I have to send another message. Either way, I'll call back in the hour."

The line went dead without another word. Spider held the phone away from his ear and looked at it, then shoved it into his front pocket. *That man seriously needs some Prozac. Or he needs to get laid more often.*

He turned his head in time to see the bellman hauling a cart with several suitcases to the curb for a blue-haired woman. The man waved to one of the taxis waiting in line, then efficiently loaded the bags—including the old one who gave him what looked like a one dollar tip. The bellman smiled anyway, a single gold-capped tooth shining in the morning sun, and even waved at her as the cab drove her away. Just before the bellman went back inside, he turned and smiled at Spider. He waved, and then gave a thumbs-up sign, showing no sign of surprise at seeing the man there.

Spider waved back, in spite of his earlier irritation, and thought, *Maybe the twenty I gave him did the trick after all.* He reached into his shirt pocket and pulled out the pack of smokes he kept there. There was only one left, so he dug that one out, then crumpled up the empty pack and tossed it toward the trash container near the ATM. He almost made it, too. Instead of picking it up to try again, he shrugged, pulled the lighter from the front pocket of his jeans, and lit the end of the cigarette. As he took that first sweet drag, he leaned back against the building and waited for the call. A low-rent private dick, most of his jobs involved waiting for something—a message, package, or some guy to tail—and this one was no different. *That's okay. Waiting is what I do best.*

EIGHTEEN

Sitting at a table in the hotel restaurant, Jason watched as his uncle ate with reckless abandon. Neither man said much since their conversation in the room earlier, and neither seemed anxious to revisit the topics that were foremost in their thoughts. Just as Jason decided they would eat their entire breakfast in silence, his uncle finally spoke up.

"I was thinkin' we could take the Metro over to D.C. proper and see the sights." He looked up, "What do you think?"

"Are you sure that's wise? What if we're spotted?"

"By who?"

"I was thinking maybe, oh, the guy we were coming here to see."

Phil waved his hand dismissively, "First of all, junior, I don't think he even knows we're comin', much less here—"

"He knows."

"Fine. I get it. You've had a run-in with him in the future. Whatever. But my second point is that there are almost six million residents of the D.C. area, not counting tourists, so I'm pretty sure we'll blend in." Phil smiled at him, satisfied he had made his point. "We can't stay cooped up forever, and I need to have a look around to see what our options are. We can take the Orange Line to the National Mall, and decide what to do from there."

Jason smiled back, the horrors of his vision already starting to fade. He considered the possibilities and realized he needed to get out to at least stretch his legs, and there was likely no more danger out in public than there was holed up in a hotel room.

"All right," he said. "First, though, you have to tell me how you know so much about D.C. You said the other day you had never been here before."

Phil tapped the side of his head with his fork, and said, "I'm a smart man."

Jason snorted once, then deadpanned, "No, really."

"I read the tour guide in the room, asshole," he said with a laugh. "Why didn't you?"

Jason started to laugh, just as the waitress walked up and placed the check beside Phil. She smiled at the older man, and asked, "Will there be anything else?"

"Thanks, no. We're good to go, I think." He winked at her, and as she walked away he pushed the slip of paper across the table to Jason. "You got this, right?"

Jason reached for his wallet and gave him a gentle rebuke, "Of course. Don't I always?"

"Hey, son. I'm tapped," he pointed the business end of the fork in Jason's direction, "and you know it."

Jason counted the bills out, leaving a generous tip, and returned the wallet to his coat pocket. He was glad to finally be doing something that didn't involve counting mile markers and filling a gas tank. Sure, they still had to figure out how to kill a man in cold blood and get away with it, but that was for later. For now they were just going to enjoy the nation's capitol, and get out in the sun. It was a perfect day for it, too, as the last days of summer were already giving way to fall, leaving the air crisp and the sky a deep clear blue. Jason smiled, breathed deep, and followed his uncle out of the hotel and onto the street.

†††

Addison sat in his hotel room, eating the breakfast he ordered from room service. Since his client was paying the freight, he felt no need to skimp on the comforts, and he was just peeved enough to run up the tab a bit. Get in, do the job, and get out. That was the standard he strove to maintain over the years, but this had become the longest running clusterfuck of his career. Now he was stuck in a hotel room—albeit a very nice one—cooling his heels and waiting for "further instructions." *Stand down*, Addison sneered. *Who did this idiot think he was?* He shook his head as he thought, *This will simply not do.*

He had been in D.C. many times over the years, but always on assignment, and had never taken the opportunity to visit the many landmarks and monuments the city offered. Wiping the corner of his mouth with a napkin bearing the ornate monogram of the hotel, he nodded once to no one, his course already decided. Time to view what the city had for a tourist with time to kill.

Throwing the napkin down on the plate, he stood and retrieved his overcoat from the closet by the door. Shrugging it on over his suit, he grabbed his wallet and keycard, checked himself in the mirror, and then walked out of the room. The ride in the elevator was blissfully devoid of other passengers, and once on the street he turned for the Rosslyn station and the Orange Line.

†††

Phil followed Jason out of the Federal Triangle station, watching his reactions to the sights. He was like a kid at an amusement park, pointing out all the buildings and monuments he wanted to visit. Turning to the right on Constitution Avenue, clearly headed for the Lincoln Memorial as a starting point, Jason set a pace that strained his uncle's ability to keep up. As they approached the Washington Monument and the Reflecting Pool beyond, Phil couldn't help but think about the last scene of that terrible remake of *Planet of the Apes* he wasted his money on.

He smiled as he looked toward the Lincoln Memorial, and asked, "You wonder what this place would have looked like if chimps had evolved the ability to think like us?"

"Moot point," Jason said as he waved his hand. "We wouldn't be able to travel there even if that universe existed. We can only go where we've been, and we wouldn't exist in that universe." Jason paused and turned to face him to allow the older man to catch up, "It's one of the things I like about traveling like we do—very little changes outside our field of influence. I can go to a McDonald's in any universe and order the same thing in each, and it will taste exactly the same everywhere I go."

"Some would call that Hell, son," Phil said through a grin. "Me, I like changes."

Jason stopped dead in his tracks, looking past Phil, mouth slack and eyes locked on the distance back toward the Capitol building. His eyes grew wide and his face drained of color as he looked nervously around him, fingers splayed as if he were trying to feel the fabric of reality itself.

"Jason?"

"It was here," he looked around nervously as he spoke. "Right here, in this very spot," he said as he pointed to the ground.

"Here?"

His nephew nodded as he spoke, "This is where I was standing in my vision of the future." He grabbed Phil by the shoulders, "It was right here." His eyes grew wild, darting from one unseen horror to another, "I can see it right now." He looked into his uncle's eyes, voice rising in pitch and volume as his rapid breathing threatened hyperventilation, "I can smell it. Death. All around me is death and decay."

Jason looked ready to bolt, a coiled spring of potential energy compressed beyond reason. Phil slapped him suddenly and hard, and Jason reacted by drawing back a stone fist, stopping at the precipice of violence. He was frozen in time for a second longer, then dropped his hands to his sides. Jason slumped to his knees before Phil could prop him up, so he knelt in front of him and held him steady. The few people out this early, mostly joggers, paid little attention. Phil didn't care either way.

"Son," he held his nephew's face up gently, "none of that has happened yet. It ain't real," he looked at the weakened and disheveled man in front of him, "and we're gonna make sure it won't be." He locked eyes with Jason, forcing him to focus his attention, "Got it?"

Jason's voice cracked slightly, the sound quivering as he said, "Yeah, sure." He nodded his head a bit, looked up at Phil, and repeated with more intensity, "Yeah."

Phil patted him a couple of times on the shoulder, and said, "Think we can stop the show we're giving these fine people, and carry on with our day?"

Jason smiled weakly, struggled to his feet, and said, "I think so." He put out a hand to help his uncle up. "You're wrong about one thing, though."

"What's that?" Something changed in Jason, then. He could see a shift in his nephew—almost as if he were watching the universe split, each new Jason drifting from the other. He just made a choice, and it was a big one.

"It will happen, whether we stop it here or not." His face was pure granite, now—his voice razor sharp. "It will happen in a near-infinite number of realities even if we stop it in this one, and there's nothing we can do about it."

"Maybe—."

"It's pointless, Phil. The best we can hope for is that the other versions of ourselves are doing what we're doing. Regardless," he said, his eyes narrowed to slits, "I'm getting this asshole, if for no other reason than to save this reality." He looked around the spot where they were standing, as if committing it to memory, then gestured for Phil to follow him. "C'mon. Let's see what there is to see around here before that bastard burns it down." He pointed at the Lincoln Memorial, and said, "I want to start right there."

†††

Addison walked along Constitution Avenue enjoying the clear blue sky, while—as always—keeping a wary eye on the people he encountered. It was a reflex now, like breathing. His bland, humorless face did not invite conversation, so he usually walked unmolested anywhere he traveled. He did not live in fear of confrontation or attack from the shadows, but he knew well that someone would surely take an opportunity to eliminate him if only they knew his face, location, or name. Still, better to be vigilant than dead.

He hadn't walked too far past the Washington Monument when he saw them. Both his targets, standing in broad daylight like they hadn't a care. Jason didn't quite match the photos Addison had gotten off the two men in Alvin, but the older man was almost certainly Philip Carson. Addison tilted his head and marveled at their obvious insouciance. It shattered his perception of the men as competent, though he immediately clamped down on that line of reasoning. Underestimating your target was a sure way to get yourself killed.

Still, the way the two wandered toward their obvious destination, they appeared to be nothing more than tourists. He could easily follow them to the Memorial and eliminate them there without much effort. This time of the year, and this early in the morning, there weren't that many witness around. Still, it was too heavily frequented for his liking, and he had been ordered to stand down.

Addison smiled like a mischievous child. His last instruction had tied his hands in the matter, even though he knew his client would be furious at the missed opportunity. Still, he was a professional, after all. His mind made up, he followed the men from a discreet distance, confident they hadn't noticed him.

This was shaping up to be a better day than its beginning implied.

†††

"Lincoln was always my favorite president." Jason stood before the massive white marble sculpture, staring up at the great man, as Phil studied him from the corner of his eye. The younger man had seemed to calm down, and was even returning to his earlier jovial state, but Phil was unconvinced. Something had shifted in his nephew, and because of that, he wasn't sure what to do next.

"I am taken to understand that Lincoln was the first *real* U.S. president." In this quiet cathedral, the words emanating from behind jarring them both. Phil turned to confront the possible threat, Jason doing likewise. The speaker was a pleasant, though bland-looking gentleman in dark slacks, camel hair overcoat, and expensive-looking shoes. The gloves he wore were also of the expensive variety, and the silk scarf around his neck would probably keep Phil in new jeans for a month. The dark blond hair, cut conservatively, framed his face and somehow made his eyes seem less deep-set than they actually were. The only real distinction was the hooked nose, and the odd British-sounding accent. Phil couldn't place it, though.

"That ain't quite correct," Phil said. "If you count from the signing of the U.S. Constitution, you can make the case that he was the sixth president born in this country." He smiled, warming to the subject, "But if you count from 1776, as Lincoln, himself, did, then he would actually be the twenty-sixth."

Jason turned back to his uncle, looking at him like he was crazy. "Wait... what? He's the sixteenth!"

Phil chuckled, and shrugged his shoulders. "Like I said, it depends on when you start the clock." He turned again and stepped back to address both men. "The first document creating a government for this country was the Articles of Confederation, and it was used for eight years. Under that document, there were ten Presidents of the United

States in Congress Assembled. Not like the office of the president is now, but still, they ran the show for the most part. He was more like a chairman of the board for a large corporation." He turned back to the statue, "Most people count from the day the current Constitution took effect, and that would, indeed, make him the sixteenth president."

Jason stood in awe of his uncle, mouth agape. "How do you know all this stuff?"

"I was a high school history teacher for a while, there. Pretty good at it, too."

Jason tilted his head and raised one eyebrow, "I thought you were a football coach."

He shrugged his shoulders in Jason's direction, and said, "Texas, son. Those two are the same thing." He smiled at both men, wondering if either even got the joke.

"That's all very informative, but I was speaking metaphorically," the newcomer said. "I only meant that he was the one who most radically reshaped your young country." He tilted his head in thought, then said, "Before Lincoln there was slavery, but not after. Before him, the individual state governments did not believe in the supremacy of the Constitution, after he took office that point was driven home with force." The man looked up at the sculpture, "He understood both the nature and proper use of force. He used it to hold together, then mold something new from the ashes of his country." He looked Phil in the eyes, then, and said, "I've often felt that this country was born in its current form the day he won that war."

Phil nodded at the man, "I guess that's one way of looking at it." He stuck out his hand, "Phil Carson." He nodded at his nephew, "And this here's my nephew, Jason."

The man, still wearing his gloves, shook first his hand, then Jason's in turn. "My name is James Newton. Very nice to meet you."

"I can't place the accent. British?" There was something odd about the way the man stood—too perfectly balanced, and yet always on the verge of motion. The calm he presented felt forced, and Phil's eyes lingered on the man's scarf a little too long.

Newton raised an eyebrow slightly, and said, "By birth, yes." He smiled, "You have a good ear. I've spent so much time living abroad since my youth that it has become a bit muddled over the years." The man looked scanned their surroundings, then turned back. "What brings you to your nation's capitol? On a sight-seeing tour?"

Eyes narrowing, Phil grinned. "Something like that. We were in town," he gestured toward the entry and the area beyond, "it was too pretty to stay cooped up inside a hotel." He nodded once at James, "You?"

"Oh, much the same," he said without inflection. "I have business to conduct, but my associate is currently unavailable."

"Hate it when that happens." Phil saw the confusion on Jason's face that was soon to erupt in a question. He tried to stop it with a glare. "Well, we should get moving if we're going to get it all in today," he said to the other man, eyes never leaving his nephew.

"Oh, there's too much to see in one day, I would think."

"I'm sure that's true, but I think one day is all we have."

"That is a shame."

"Isn't it?" He touched Jason on the elbow, getting his attention. "C'mon, son," he said. "Let's go take a look at the Washington Monument before we grab a bite of lunch."

"Sure," Jason said, as both men moved toward the steps.

Phil waved back at the man in the overcoat. "It was nice meetin' ya."

The man tilted his head again, acknowledging farewell. "It was nice to meet you, too," he said, and it seemed to Phil he meant it. "You gentlemen be careful, now. This city is not safe in places."

"We will, James," Phil called back as he and Jason continued down massive stone steps. "As should you." He waved again, then turned toward the monument ahead of them.

They walked in silence for several minutes, Phil feeling confusion from his nephew like waves of heat. Finally, the young man couldn't take it anymore.

"What was that all about? You were really weird back there."

"He said his name was James Newton. The monogram on that scarf was L.R."

Jason shook his head, "So?"

"Well, either he was lying about his name, or he stole that scarf." He looked over at his nephew and said, "I don't think he's a thief."

"Why would a total stranger lie about his name?"

"I don't know, but I'd like to put some distance between us and him if you don't mind." He glanced back over his shoulder, and relaxed a bit when he could see no one was following them. "Let's finish up our sight-seeing, then we'll take the Blue Line over to the mall at Pentagon City. We can have dinner there before finding another hotel."

"Another hotel?" Jason looked at him with one raised brow, and said "Why do we need another hotel?"

Phil rolled his eyes and sighed, "Son, for a smart guy, you can sure be dumb at times. If that guy works for our man Henderson, he'll have our hotel pegged in under an hour." He shook his head, "Hell, it's probably too dangerous now to even go back to the room to get our shit." *Or I could just be paranoid*, he thought. *Better paranoid than dead.*

"Son of a bitch!" Jason looked at him with a pained expression. "The cash box is in the room! I've only got a couple hundred bucks on me." He was trembling, his eyes darting around the Mall, "Phil... we have to get that box."

Phil shook his head. "No way, son," he said, placing a hand on Jason's shoulder. "That thing's a lost cause for now. We can't risk it." He smiled reassuringly. "Don't worry, we'll think of something."

✝✝✝

Stupid! Addison threw his coat onto the bed, as he held the ridiculous scarf in his hands. The monogram sat there accusing him. When in D.C. he always used the alias "Lawrence Russell," but he told these bumpkins the alias he used in Texas. It was that man's accent that distracted him—caused him to slip. He was sure Mr. Carson noticed the discrepancy, too.

After a few phone calls, he found the hotel they were using, and, as luck would have it, the place was two blocks from his current location. A thorough search of the room revealed nothing of any use to him, and there was no sense in waiting there for their return, as he suspected they now knew they were being followed. The irony was he didn't even bother following them once they left his presence, as he would have been all too easy to spot, and would have only confirmed their suspicions.

One thing he was sure of was this incident would not be in his next report to the client. He had toyed with the idea of letting the fool know he had seen his targets today, but that he had been barred from action due to the ill-advised orders he was given. Now, however, to do so would only serve to make himself look foolish. *Or worse.*

Addison needed a drink, and he knew the bar downstairs had a MacCutcheon on the top shelf. *Maybe a couple of rounds charged to the room will make me feel better.* It certainly couldn't make him feel any worse.

NINETEEN

A LIGHT RAPPING ON THE OFFICE DOOR WAS ENOUGH TO REMIND Miles he had slept another night on the couch in his office. Regardless of the discomfort, it was more secure than the building he called home. He struggled to sit up, gathered his wits, stood to cross the room, and unlock the door.

"What?" he said flatly through the small crack he opened between door and jamb.

"Sir, you have an appointment today with a member of the press about your bill. He'll be here in twenty minutes."

Damn. The job was constantly getting in the way of his work. It was a boulder strapped around his neck, threatening to pull him ever downward. If he wasn't careful, that boulder would lash him to the ground, making him... *plebeian.* "When he gets here, tell him to wait in the outer office. I need some time to, um, freshen up."

"Of course, sir." He heard the disdain in her voice. Performance reviews were coming up soon. *Bitch is up for a raise this cycle, but she's not getting another dime*, he thought. *In fact, let's see if I can get her goddamn pay* cut. She stepped away from the door, so he closed and locked it once again.

Three times over the last two days he tried to jump back along this timeline, and each time he slammed into a wall as hard as stone a short distance away. The gap was growing narrower as well. Both subsequent attempts left him farther from his goal than the previous. The impenetrable barrier preventing him from returning to that starting point seven years ago was moving inexorably forward through time. As it was, he could jump less than a day into the past. Something, or someone, impeded his movements within that realm.

"God *damn* it!" he said, slamming his hand against the desk. He needed to get free of this mausoleum—run the alleys and *hunt*. Two local girls had already "gone missing" near his home, and he couldn't afford another so soon. *I'll have to find another release*, he thought, pulling his hair.

His only option was to continue to move forward through time toward that final decision point he knew must be there. Once on the other side, the entire panoply of realities would be open to him again. That thought calmed him a little, and he released his aching scalp.

He raised one hand to pinch the bridge of his nose and rubbed the temple on one side of his head with the other. Clearly, things were going to get worse before they got better. Also just as clearly, wrinkling his nose in disgust, he was in desperate need of a shower. *I've let too much go, worrying about phantoms*, he thought.

Miles gave silent thanks for the small half-bath tucked away behind a door in the corner of his office. He had made use of it on more than one occasion when he needed to show his face to the press. Today would take a bit more work than usual, however, and he began by tidying up the his office, cleaning every surface to a spotless shine. Satisfied, he walked into the bathroom to put a shine on his appearance.

The face that looked back at him from the mirror shocked him fully awake. *You look like ever-lovin' shit, boy*, his daddy said inside his head. He couldn't disagree. There was no way he could meet with a reporter in this condition. With a shake of his head, he took up the laborious task of making himself presentable. He had soap, water, washcloth, and razor. *Enough tools on hand to put a shine on the shell, at least*, he thought.

Too bad you ain't got nothin' fer the smell, the voice said.

†††

Jason lay awake in his bed, listening to the soft snoring of his uncle Phil in the bed next to his own. He knew it had been hours because he stared at the alarm clock on the nightstand for most of that time. The dream—vision, really—that awakened him was not particularly jarring or frightening, but the growing sense of unease left him fully awake.

He was in that in-between state of being—not slipping through the wall, but inhabiting it; and inside that space, all things were open to him, stretching in all directions to infinity. Take a step to the "left" and he would enter one reality. To the "right" lay another. What he saw, though, in every direction, was death and destruction. It was all around him, but couldn't touch him unless he stepped through to the other side. He was in the center of a spider web whose filaments stretched to the limits of the universe and beyond, and on every strand was pain and loss. And always, from every direction, a sense of pressure to go back. *You cannot come here.* From every direction he could feel that refrain, pushing against his will like a wave crashing on the shore.

When he awoke, at first he felt nothing but confusion. He could clearly remember that feeling of resistance to his movements, but there was also something else inside the wall. Acceptance… anticipation. Something was there, inside the myriad possibilities waiting for him. Not just any Jason, but *this* Jason. There was a reason for him being here, the potentials assured him, though what was required of him he couldn't say.

For two hours he contemplated and considered, only moving to turn his head to occasionally check the time. Light was already filtering in through the windows of the hotel room, and he knew Phil would be up and planning their next move very soon. Jason didn't really have a choice, though. There were too many questions, and not enough time. He had to go back into the wall, and he needed to do it now, before his uncle stirred. There were many questions he needed answering, regardless of what the answers would cost him.

Turning away from the clock, he lay flat on this back with arms to his sides. Breathing regularly, slowly, he closed his eyes and slipped easily from this reality into the wall beneath. Immediately, he felt that pressure to return, but he held his ground, waiting for the acceptance to enfold him once again. He could feel it at the edge of his perception, could almost see it fighting for position among veils of potential energy around him. He could both see and feel that presence coalescing—solidifying—into a form before his eyes. At the same time the pressure around him gradually decreased in intensity as, for the first time, he felt the force of gravity pulling him down and pressing his boots against a hard surface. The cold air assaulted his senses, and all around him the pressure lifted as a blanket from a bed. Early morning light, warm and golden, entered through distorted panes of glass. With a touch of vertigo, he recognized his surroundings even before the image was completely formed.

He was back in the cabin. And he was not alone.

"Good morning, Jason."

The voice was familiar, but wrong somehow. The face, however, was unmistakable. Jason's eyes widened and his eyebrows shot up, threatening to leave his forehead entirely, as he stared into the face of his host. The face of Jason Callahan.

The other smiled, a mix of humor and sadness, and said, "I think we have some things to discuss."

"Okay... this is new." Jason studied the man before him. There were a few lines around the eyes, and a touch of gray in the hair, but, overall, the man was a mirror image of himself. The fact that he was an older version didn't seem to matter as much as the fact that he was there at all.

"Why don't we have a seat by the fire and talk a bit," the other Jason said. "I'm not sure how long we have." He looked around the cabin, though the effect was more of looking through the logs than at them, "The consensus has not been fully reached, and may still not fall in my favor."

"Dude, if we're gonna talk, it would help if you started making some sense."

The other smiled at that, then sat on one of two chairs by the fireplace that Jason only just noticed.

"Do you know where we are?" The question was so obviously loaded that Jason was afraid to answer, sure that he would get it wrong.

"We're in the cabin in Colorado."

"Well, yes... and no." *Nailed it*. Jason had too many teachers use this technique in his past not to spot it. Always start with an easy question you know the student will get wrong.

"Fine. So we're not physically there. I get that. What I want to know is why? And more importantly," his eyes narrowed, "who the hell are you?"

"To take your last question first, I am you. At least, a version of you. A bit longer in the tooth, but essentially the same." He gestured to the empty chair before him, "To answer 'why' will take a little longer."

†††

Phil awoke, annoyed almost from the first by the shaft of sunlight peeking in between the heavy curtains shining like a spotlight into his right eye. Shading it with his

.hand, he reluctantly sat up, and scrubbed his face with both hands as he moved his head from the path of the cursed beam. He had a momentary urge to hiss in its direction, but with no one else awake to enjoy the joke, he let it pass.

Across from him on the other bed he saw the sleeping form of his nephew. Laying there on his back and motionless, with his arms beside him, he looked like a corpse ready for burial. It was only from the regular rise and fall of his abdomen that Phil could tell he was alive. He twisted his mouth a bit and shook his head. His nephew could sleep through an earthquake. Standing on unsteady legs, he gathered his clothes and headed for the bathroom. It always took a good long shower to get himself fully awake in the mornings, and he was gonna have a doozy this morning. *There was a lot of plannin' and preparin' to do, and it was always good to start clean and well-fed.*

He turned to wake Jason before he entered the shower, but decided against it. The man had a rough time yesterday, and Phil thought it better just to let him sleep a bit more. He turned back, entered the bathroom, and closed the door quietly behind him.

Nearly an hour later, Phil emerged from the bathroom dressed from the waist down, with one fluffy towel still being rubbed through his hair in a futile attempt to dry it. Even at his age, it was still thick and curly enough to hold a lot of water, and it always took him a while to finish the job. Blow-dryers, on the other hand, were simply not an option. Every time he used one, the mass of hair on his head would fill out to gargantuan proportions, leaving him looking like a disco reject from the seventies.

He tossed the wet towel on the bed, pulled his undershirt over his head, and whistled loudly. It was the kind of noise only a high school football coach ever makes effectively, and it never failed to get the required response. Jason, though, never moved.

"C'mon, son. Quit playin' possum and drag your ass out of that bed," Phil said in full throat. "We've got a lot to do—startin' with breakfast."

As he shrugged on the long-sleeve shirt he bought the previous day and began buttoning it up, he looked down at his nephew. The man was laying in exactly the same position as when Phil left him, and still had not opened his eyes.

"Hey, Jason," he leaned down and shook him lightly, "stop foolin' around and get up."

Still, no movement beyond the regular and shallow breathing.

Phil kneeled down quickly beside the bed and shook him a little more roughly. "C'mon, man," he cajoled, "please wake up."

He reached up and pulled back the lids on Jason's terrifyingly still eyes and saw that the pupils were dilated and not responding to the light. Phil grabbed the lamp on the nightstand, holding it in Jason's face to be sure. He lifted one of the man's arms and let it fall back to the bed. A doctor might diagnose Jason as comatose, or at least in a catatonic state, but Phil knew better. His nephew just wasn't there anymore. He had slipped through the wall. Where he had gone or why, though, was irrelevant. The real question was why wasn't there another Jason here to take his place?

†††

The phone on the nightstand rang with an annoying little sound, but it was enough to rouse Addison from a light sleep. He snaked an arm out from underneath the covers, pulled the receiver off the cradle, and said "Hello" before he brought it close to him.

"Mr. Russell?" The voice on the other end of the phone sounded worried. Most front desk staff sounded worried when waking a guest this early without instructions to do so, but Addison heard a distinct difference.

He held the phone to his ear as he sat up. "Yes?"

"There is a message waiting for you at the front desk, and the envelope is marked urgent. I hope you don't mind me waking you."

"That's okay. Everything is urgent in this town." He stood, still holding the phone, and stifled a yawn. "Please have it delivered to my room immediately."

"Very good, sir."

Grabbing the thick robe from the foot of the bed, he said, "Before you go, connect me to room service."

"Yes, sir." The line clicked over, and within seconds someone from room service answered and took his breakfast order.

As he waited for the bellhop to deliver the envelope, he wondered what his idiot client had gotten into now. Hand-delivering an envelope with information or instructions was dangerous. He was clear on the rules whenever he took an assignment—no paper trails of any kind. Even the room was paid for by a cut-out paying in cash.

This is the second time he's broken protocol, and it had better be damn important.

†††

"It's important that you understand what is happening. There is much more at stake than just yourself or your current reality." The other sat calmly, but Jason could feel the waves of conflict coming from him with palpable force. Not enough to move him physically, but similar to the gentle pressure he had felt before the other's arrival.

"I understand there's a psychopath out there who wants to kill me. He's already killed this Jason's parents, and I know there is something worse coming from him soon."

The other tilted his head, then said, "Then you have the basics. That's good." He smiled warmly, then pursed his lips for just a second, looking through the walls again. "I'm afraid we aren't going to have as much time as I had hoped. Try to hold your questions while I give you what help I can."

Jason started to respond, then thought better of it and clamped his mouth shut.

The other smiled, then grew serious. "We are in a construct," as he waved his hand indicating the cabin, "of all the potential and actual realities where we have encountered this structure." He locked eyes with Jason, "It exists only here, inside 'the wall,' as you call it, because we create it from one moment to the next."

"Who is 'we'?"

The other stopped and raised an eyebrow, "Please, let me continue." He sat there another second, then, satisfied Jason would not interrupt again, continued, "Uncle Phil was wrong in his theory that you are a 'nexus.' Those do not exist, anyway." Seeing the confused look on Jason's face, he pressed on, "The first time a child makes a choice, they split their universe in two, but that means there are two branches going forward for future splits, not branches from a single point. I—we—refer to them as 'perfect pairs'."

The other waited a couple of seconds to see if the information had been processed, then nodded once. "From these perfect pairs come all subsequent iterations of Jason, and with each iteration something of the original is lost—like making copies of copies—and while the differences are infinitesimally small, over an infinite number of iterations they add up."

"So, each new version becomes less viable?"

"Exactly!" The space between them nearly crackled with energy. "But it's more than that. That first perfect pair have access to this," he waved again, indicating the space around them, "but they also have abilities that none of the other iterations have. With each subsequent iteration more and more of those abilities are lost." He grimaced for just a second, "In fact, after only three iterations, the ability to slip through the wall is lost to the line."

"And just what constitutes these 'other abilities'?"

"I think you already know that, Jason."

"Time travel."

"Again… yes and no." He reached over to the stack of logs beside him, picked one up, then tossed it into the fire. "As you can tell, I'm a bit older than you. What you *don't* know, is you and I constitute a 'perfect pair'."

"How is that possible?"

The other laughed, and Jason noticed for the first time how much he laughed like his mother. "The possible becomes probable inside the wall." He stood, drawing Jason to his feet, as the cabin disappeared around them. They were standing in the middle of the road where his parents lived, watching the last smoldering embers of trailer being consumed. He turned to Jason and said, "What do you know about Fred Alan Wolf?"

Jason, unable to tear his eyes away from that scene, answered without turning his head, "Other than he is a bit of a crank, not much. I met him once, and I know about his theories."

"What about Penrose, or Lanza?"

Finally shaking off the gloom that had captured his mind, he faced the other and said, "Penrose I studied, but Lanza was a medical doctor with that biocentric theory of the universe, or some such nonsense."

"Not really all nonsense, brother." The cabin returned, and the other returned to his seat. "This particular construct, everything that is, was, or ever will be is created by us. All the Jasons who ever lived, or will live."

"I created the multiverse. Right." Jason shook his head, then sat down across from the other.

"I didn't say that. I said we created this multiverse. Uncle Phil created his own, and we are connected to that through him. Mom and dad created theirs, and we are connected to those through them."

Jason shook his head, throwing his hands in the air, "I don't see how any of this is helping me."

"What do you think happens, brother, when we die?" A frenetic energy seemed to grip the other as he spoke, words piling on top of one another as he spoke. "You've seen inside the wall. You've seen the web. Do you think those minds just wink out—like blowing out a candle?"

"You know, it really makes it hard to follow you when you jump from topic to topic like that."

"But I'm not! All of this is one thing, tied up in a pretty little bow for you to just grasp and understand." The other visibly calmed himself, then leaned back in his chair. "I'm sorry, Jason. I am being pulled in too many directions."

"Then help me understand," he pleaded. "Stop asking questions and just tell me what I need to know."

"If it were only that simple." Again he looked beyond the cabin. "Jason, I'm dead. I died, by my reckoning, a long time ago... although for you, it is in the future." He stopped, twisted his mouth again, and seemed to be consciously choosing his words. "You did not see the future... I showed it to you. You and I can only travel to the past, not the future, and I was there when the world ended."

TWENTY

P HIL STOOD WATCH OVER HIS NEPHEW FOR WHAT FELT LIKE AN ETER-
nity, legs and back aching from the two hours locked in
place. There was no way of knowing how long Jason had been like this
before Phil first noticed. Every few minutes he took note of the boy's
breathing and pulse, then lifted his eyelids to check the pupils. After
hours of stasis, fear and concern grabbed Phil by the throat, throttling
what hope remained. He knew Jason might need medical attention—if
not now, then certainly soon—but admitting him into a hospital made
him a stationary target. That was a risk Phil was not yet ready to take,
and he knew Jason would agree if the roles were reversed.

Unwilling to leave for even a moment, Phil called for room service
for himself and Jason. It was a waste of their remaining cash reserves,
but it couldn't be helped, as it was simply too dangerous to return to
their original hotel room to retrieve the cash box. Jason still had plenty
in the bank, but as soon as they accessed that, their location would be
pinpointed. Phil wasn't ready for that. *Not yet, anyway.*

He picked at his food, pushing it around his plate like a child pretending to eat. Helpful or not, he was considering calling a doctor when
Jason's eyes flew open, and he gasped for air as if surfacing after a long
dive.

"Holy shit, I need to pee." Jason sat up like a shot, jumped off the
bed, and headed for the bathroom door.

Phil, rousing from the shock of such a quick recovery, shook his
head to clear it. "Nice to see you back," he said. "Did you have a nice
trip?" The door closed before Phil could get the last words out.

He walked to the bathroom and yelled through the door, "I've got you some breakfast from room service in here."

"Thanks," was all he heard from the other side.

✝✝✝

Phil watched Jason shovel the last of the cold bacon and eggs into his mouth, and marveled at the newfound energy of the younger man. The lethargy and despair seemed to have lifted from his shoulders, and the gusto with which he ate was a strong outward indication of the inner determination Phil was witnessing. The story Jason told after exiting the bathroom, though, had him concerned. Nothing like it had happened even once in all of Phil's travels. *Is it possible the pressure has the boy cracking up?* he thought.

"Where were you, son?" Phil stared hard into his nephew's eyes, still not sure what he saw there. Determination, certainly, but for what? There were so many questions. "What you left behind was an empty shell."

Jason tilted his head and considered for a moment, still chewing, then said, "It's hard to explain, but I was essentially cooling my heels inside the wall. Since I didn't actually slip through, there was no extra Jason to inhabit this body."

"I didn't even know that was possible."

Jason looked up, paused, and said, "I don't think it is for you. It's one of the many abilities I share with my 'perfect pair'."

"Yeah," Phil scratched the stubble on his chin, "about that. Why was this guy so much older than you if the two of you were created at the same time?"

"I think it's because time has no meaning inside the wall. Cause and effect are all jumbled up, and people like me can always move in either direction. At least we can go where we've been." Finally finishing the last of his meal, Jason set the fork down on the tray, then wiped his mouth with the napkin. Holding it up by the corners in front of Phil, he said, "Time flows in one direction," he shook the left end, "beginning," then the right, "to end. Inside the wall, however," he looped the napkin, touching the two ends together, "time has no beginning, and no end. At least with respect to each individual's multiverse."

"You still haven't answered my question." Phil's head was starting to hurt again, as it did every time Jason tried to explain things to him.

Jason set the napkin on the tray, "He looks older than me because he *is* older than me. He said he was dead, too, if that helps."

Phil shook his head, "It doesn't."

Jason smiled thinly, in a look approaching sympathy. "He's also been dead for a long time. He kind of just hangs out in the wall, existing in time between his endpoints." Jason eyes lost their focus for just a second, and said, "I think there are others in there with him." He looked back at Phil, "A lot of them."

"Who?"

"Well… me, I guess," he sniffed. "No one can be inside your own wall but you, right? It's why two people can't travel together, only find one another after the fact."

Phil stood up, walked to the closet, and grabbed his jacket.

"Where are you going?"

"Nowhere," he pulled a bottle from one of the pockets, "I just needed an aspirin." He popped the top, placed the opening to his lips, and tilted his head back to shake a few tablets into his mouth. He stood there for a few seconds, eyeing his nephew and crunching the aspirin, then said, "So what does all this mean, anyway?"

"It means I need to go back inside the wall," he said, wide eyed astonishment on his face. "There's a lot more to learn about what's going on, and I get the feeling that not everyone in there is on board with my brother's approach to the problem."

"Your brother." Phil shook his head once.

"Hey, I've got to call him something. Would you rather I give each one of us a number?"

"I would rather you didn't go back in at all, son." Phil walked back to his bed and sat down in front of his nephew, "Jason, we're sittin' ducks here, and the longer you lay there in a coma, the worse it gets."

Jason grimaced at that. There was a hesitation, then he said, "Well, I guess we just have to keep moving then." He looked sheepishly at Phil. "I can always do my thing on the plane ride."

"Plane ride?"

"Yeah, about that," Jason said, lowering his head a tick. "I'm relatively certain what our next move is and where we need to go," he looked into Phil's eyes and gave him a crooked, halfhearted smile. "And I don't think you're gonna be too happy about it."

✝✝✝

Miles tried to work on the bills before him, but the distractions of the morning were too much. After the interview had come meetings with constituents and lobbyists. Those two were usually one and the same in his short experience, but today there was a steady stream of both. Each time he thought there was time to work, another call from his assistant grated over the intercom on his desk.

It didn't help that he had no real desire to do the work to begin with. It was all just for show—a means to an end—and only necessary as one more step on his path to power. He cared neither for the specific means, nor the people involved in those actions. What was important were the results. In fact, he could just as easily work for the other party, but this one made a habit of playing to the fears of citizens, and that was what would serve his ambitions best.

It also didn't help that his mind continually wandered back to the subject of the two men who were surely in town to kill him. His asset still had not contacted him. *I'd* kill *the bastard if he was here.* He stood, threw the papers to the desk and paced, a jungle cat run out of patience. Miles' fingers itched to be around a throat—*any* throat—and he had to force himself to calm before he called an intern to his office.

This is going to cost me, he thought as he sat again at the desk. It wasn't a good idea to keep an assassin on the sidelines twiddling his thumbs. The man he used as a go-between for contact with his asset was nervous, but since "buffer between the boss and the killer" was part of the job description, that was too damn bad. Miles stood and paced again, pulling at his lip. The anger boiled in him worse now than it had in many years, and he beat his fist against his thigh as he paced.

Miles closed his eyes, forcing all motion to cease, sat, and stee-pled his hands in front of his face. Part of his anger was because he had let slip the names of his targets while speaking to his cut-out. The man was too stupid to do anything of *value* with the information, but he was also stupid enough to try. There were other men on his payroll who were paid to do such things, and a freelancer would gum up the works *but good* if they were heavy-handed about it.

"Fuck it! I've had enough," he said as he pulled a piece of letter-head from the stack on his desk. He tore off the header and footer sec-tions, tossed them in the trash, then wrote a short note. Once finished, he called for his assistant before grabbing the cell phone from the credenza and dialing. Appearances meant everything in this town, and he had always been careful with his, but this was too important and he was too impatient.

"Time to take charge of this mess."

†††

"Fucking Colorado?" Phil, waving his arms in the air, voice raised to a volume that shook the room, was definitely not pleased. "Didn't we just spend several days driving from there?"

"I got the clear feeling that everything is riding on us being there at the end of this. Or was, once." He threw his hands in the air. "Or whatever." Rubbing his eyes, then his temples, Jason understood the other man's issues with going back, but there was nothing he could do. "There is a reason that cabin keeps coming up in multiple realities." Phil started to speak, but Jason held up his hand. "No, I don't know why, but there is a reason. I'm sure of it. Maybe locations can be a nexus in the multiverse like people, but it doesn't matter. We're going regardless."

Phil sneered, "So, you've put your foot down, have you?"

"Yes, I have." Jason's eyes narrowed, daring his uncle to argue, then his face softened and he said, "It's a good plan, anyway. We need to get this guy alone and out of the public eye where we can deal with him. Can you think of a better place?"

Phil twisted his face in thought, "Okay, smart guy, how do we get him to follow us?"

Jason's face and mood brightened, "That's the best part. I don't think we have to."

One eyebrow raised, Phil said, "I don't understand."

"We can't board a plane without purchasing a ticket and then showing ID. We don't have enough cash to buy a ticket, so we will have to use my credit card. Both of those should be enough to tip him off as to our departure and destination." Jason smiled at the thought. "That is, if he's trying to track us."

"So you think you've got it all figured out, huh?"

"Oh, hell no," he said, shocked. "I think we're playing it by ear, but it's the only tune we know." Jason placed a hand on his uncle's shoulder, and said more calmly, "I'm hoping my time on the plane will be helpful. I still have a lot of questions, and maybe one of those questions will be the one that gets us the answers we need to survive this."

His uncle stood there motionless, considering all the alternatives—of which there were exactly zero—then sighed heavily. He looked at Jason, still standing in his underwear, and said, "Then I guess you better get your shower so we can get moving."

Jason squeezed the man's shoulder once, then gathered his clothes and walked into the bathroom. After the ordeal of this morning, a shower was just what the doctor ordered.

✝✝✝

Spider checked his new burner phone again as he sat in the old Fiat. All his friends refused to call it anything other than "the spider-mobile," but that was the one thing he liked about it. Unlike his nickname, this one he bestowed himself. There was no resemblance, however, to the short-lived vehicle that disgraced the early comics. This was a boxy, early eighties miniature tank of a car with more primer than paint covering its exterior. One rear window was nothing more than a black plastic bag duck-taped to the door frame, and in a couple of places he could see the street through the rusted floorboard. Still, it was one of the few things he owned outright. Starting it in the winter was a bitch, but once going, it usually got him to his destination with minimal effort. And unlike the shiny new phone in his hand, the car would still be with him at the end of the day.

He checked his watch while he sat in his car across from the hotel, waiting for the phone to ring. *Already after eleven,* he thought. *Can't wait out here all day.* As he was looking at the phone, it buzzed for the first time that day. The number displayed on the phone was from one of the friends he called earlier. He pressed the button and answered.

"What do you have for me?"

The man on the other end whispered like he was some kind of secret agent in enemy territory, "Your guys took a cab from here to the airport about five minutes ago."

Shit, that didn't work out as planned. "Did you hear where they were headed?" On a hunch, Spider contacted several of his informants who worked as doormen for various hotels in the D.C. area to see if the guys his boss was looking for were in town. Even though all he had were two first names, Spider thought that might be enough, and maybe he could cut out the middleman and do the job himself. *I guess that's off the table,* he thought.

"I don't have a specific location, dude, but I heard one of them say something about Colorado." The man on the other end of the phone covered the microphone, but Spider could clearly hear him yell "I got you, miss!" There was some fumbling with the phone, then "I gotta go, Spider. Duty calls," and the line went dead.

He stared at the phone for a few seconds considering his options. The truth was there was only one. He didn't have the network to find two guys in Colorado. Spider tapped in a number, hit the call button, and waited for the phone to ring.

"Wonder what this information is worth," he mused as he tapped a rhythm on the steering wheel of the spidermobile.

†††

Addison read the note a second time, sure he must have misread on the first go.

I am taking control of the situation myself. You will meet me at 8 tonight at your suite, and we will discuss a plan for moving forward. MH

There was just no way to reconcile what was in that note with how he preferred to do business, and to follow the instructions was to invite disaster. Clients did not get involved in either the planning or the operations phase of his work. Contact, assignment, fulfillment, payment. That was the sequence of events, and no trumped-up self-important fool was going to change the way Addison practiced his craft.

The contact for the client was not answering his calls. *Probably already discarded the phone he was using*, he thought. With no way to reach the client, there was no way to keep him from attempting to meet, forcing Addison to check out of this hotel and into a second under another name.

Addison held off on tracking the two targets down until now because he wanted to rub the client's nose in his meddling, but this was just too much. He knew a couple of contacts inside the National Security Agency who sold him information when needed; the costs were prohibitive on most jobs, but he needed them now. He would make the call to have the men located, then fulfill the contract before the client caused further trouble. Barring that, he would return the deposit—minus expenses—and wash his hands of the fool for good.

This one's gone off the rails, somehow, and I have no desire to be caught in the resulting train wreck.

Bad clients created the potential for bad results, and bad results led to bad reputations. In this business, a man could die of a bad reputation. Sometimes it was best to cut your losses and move on. It wasn't the first time Addison was forced to sever ties with a client—nor would it be the last—but this one was going to need a permanent solution.

Reckless, he thought as he gathered his belongings and stuffed them into his luggage. *Reckless, and stupid.*

†††

"Don't worry, you'll be compensated fairly for this information."

Anytime someone told Spider not to worry, that was usually when things started to go south. "Thank you, sir."

"Don't thank me yet," the man on the other end hesitated, "I've still got something for you to do." *There it is. Always one more thing.*

"Whatever you need." *I'm really beginning to hate this asshole.*

"I just need you to deliver another note. Meet my agent at the same place as last time, and she'll give you the note and an envelope. The envelope will contain your final payment, as my need of your services are at an end."

"I'll take care of it." The truth was, Spider was glad to be done with this. This affair was so far beyond his usual experience that he kept waiting for the other shoe to drop. It was time to get back to what he did best, tailing congressman's wives to their boyfriend's apartment. This secret agent crap was for the birds.

"See that you do, Spider." The line remained silent for a few seconds. The man on the other end was waiting to see if the message hit its mark. *He knows my name. How the fuck did he get that?*

"Don't worry, sir."

The line clicked and went dead.

†††

Addison sat at the small desk in his room, facing the bed where his bags—already packed—sat as he waited for word from his contact at the NSA. He held off on checking out, preferring to wait in comfort for the call he knew would be forthcoming. It was nearly noon, however, and he was sure that his targets somehow eluded him again. They had clearly gone to ground the previous night after having met him, and there was no record of them checking into a hotel or accessing their bank accounts. If he didn't get any positive movement before the meeting the client had scheduled, he would have to call this job a failure and deal with the fallout.

At twelve-fifteen the phone rang.

"Yes?"

"Sir, I have another note here at the desk. Should I send it up?"

Addison drummed his fingers impatiently on the nightstand. The effrontery of this man! *Successful completion or not, I am through with this client.* "Yes, of course. Send it up." He slammed the receiver into its cradle.

Five minutes later, having tipped the bellhop for the second time that day, he held the note open in hands shaking from barely-controlled anger.

I have information our friends are heading back to their previous location. I will handle it, myself, there. Keep the initial deposit, but there is no further need of your services. —MH

No, this is definitely *not how I do business,* he thought. Addison packed his travel case, throwing items in with abandon, without regard for necessity. He jumped when the phone rang again. He stared at the offending piece of equipment for a few rings before answering.

"Yes?"

"The two men recently purchased a ticket for a flight to Colorado." The line went dead. And that little piece of useless information had cost him nearly as much as his profit on this farce. He continued to look at the dead phone in his hands in disbelief for a few more seconds, then replaced it on its cradle.

No one had ever fired him from a job before, and no micromanaging fool was going to do it now, either. He finished packing his case, then took some time to calm his breathing. After cleaning every area he had touched for fingerprints, he gave the room one last visual examination, grabbed his overcoat and case, and opened the door with gloved hands.

Riding the elevator alone to the lobby, he made his plans for dealing with this problem. He had two distinct courses of action, one which yielded less than optimal results, but by the time he reached the lobby he had already decided. When the doors opened, he immediately walked out of the main entrance to hail a cab.

A well-maintained black and yellow cab pulled up to the curb, and Addison threw first his case, and then himself into the back.

"Where to?" The cabbie was large, bearded, and definitely not American.

"Reagan National Airport. Try not to hit anything along the way."

Sohrab, according to the displayed license, snorted in laughter, put the car in gear, and shot away from the curb. While Addison held the door in a white-knuckled grip, he dialed his pilot with his free hand.

He's going to love this.

PART THREE

"Every living being is an engine geared to the wheelwork of the universe."
—Nikola Tesla

TWENTY-ONE

Miles stood at the ticket counter waiting for the pretty little blond to hunt and peck her way to finding him a flight. Behind him in line others waited impatiently, but he was a congressman, by God, and he would take as much time as he goddamn needed!

"There's nothing leaving non-stop for another two hours, sir," she said, offering a sweet corporate smile.

It had been years since he last purchased a ticket for himself, and he now remembered why he paid assistants. *A shame I can't use them now. One more thing the asshole will pay for.*

"Fine, sweetheart. Which one's got the shortest layover?"

"Um…" She tapped at the keyboard a few more times, and said, "I've got one with a thirty minute layover, but that one's boarding in about thirty minutes."

"Book it!"

"First class is all I have left on that one, sir."

He pulled out his black American Express card and threw it down on the counter. "Sweetheart, do I look like I fly any other way? Let's see how fast you can get me on my way."

The woman wrinkled her nose, but tapped diligently away at her keyboard while the people behind him in line checked their watches and sighed dramatically. He didn't care. He just needed to get on that plane.

"Do you have any bags to check?"

"No, honey." He waved his hand frantically over the counter, "Just give me the fucking ticket."

"Your ticket and boarding pass are printing now, *sir.*" She watched him with her mouth screwed up like she just sucked on a lemon, and she handed back his credit card. After a few more seconds, she shoved several pieces of paper into an envelope and handed it across the counter. "American Airlines, Gate 49, sir. Have a nice trip." The smile she offered him with the ticket was thin and hard, and it never reached her eyes.

Miles snatched the envelope from her grasp and turned to locate his gate. As he exited the line and began his run for the gate he heard someone behind him say, "He'll never make it." And another, "Serves the bastard right."

As much as he wanted to, he didn't have time to stop and strangle each and every one of them. Instead, he sprinted for the pedestrian bridge leading to his gate. The people he left behind could go about their insignificant lives, while he would make history.

That's when he saw the line for the security checkpoint. *Sonofabitch!* Not high enough in the hierarchy yet to warrant a security detail, he was forced to endure the same security checks as the average passenger. He really might *not* make it. Miles grew deathly calm, seething as he joined the queue. *How many of these sheep could I take out before a cop shoots me?* he thought. *This shit's gonna change real soon for me. In a few years I'll have my own goddamn plane.*

With dreams of Air Force One in his head, he began removing his shoes.

†††

Jason was grateful to be safely on the plane at last. His uncle was almost unbearable the entire time they waited to board, having finally decided to be paranoid about nearly every facet of the trip. Jason tried to make the man understand that traveling openly was now part of the plan, but that only seemed to make it worse. It was obvious his uncle wasn't afraid for his own safety—he was worried about his nephew, and not just because they were being hunted by a psychopathic killer, either. When Jason tried get in line to board the plane, Phil reached out and grabbed his elbow from behind to pull him back. Together they stood to the side of the mass of moving bodies while Phil watched every face that entered the tunnel. Only when the attendants began to close the doors did he reluctantly allow Jason to pass through as he followed closely behind.

For long minutes after they found their seats, Phil peered nervously around the cabin through narrowed eyes, seemingly unaware of anything Jason said. It wasn't until they were in the air with the wheels up that the man finally settled down and began to relax. Both men asked the flight attendant for pillows, and within minutes Jason heard the familiar soft snoring of his uncle beside him. He smiled crookedly at the man, then positioned his own pillow behind his head, trying to get as comfortable as possible. He was sure he would become completely limp once he had entered the wall, so he also tried to make sure he wouldn't fall over. Several attempts later, he settled on curling up against the window on his right, nestling his head into the pillow between.

He closed his eyes, and slowed his breathing. The transition was instantaneous, much faster than before, and soon he was looking into that fracture in the wall, vacillating between going forward and going back. The pressure to retreat was immense, but he knew there was only one course of action, and that was to step forward into the opening. He struggled against a heavy, viscous tide, slowly entering that darkness; and once inside, he waited.

For what seemed like an eternity, he waited. He could feel the presence of a multitude of others all around him, but none made contact, and there was no sense of familiarity. He probably could not have picked his brother from that mass if he tried, but still he waited. Just when he was sure that this was a fruitless exercise, the cabin appeared around him again. He sat in his chair before the fire and waited some more.

He noticed the fire was dying, so he reached for a small log on the hearth and tossed it in. It hit the cherry red logs already there, sending glowing embers rising up the stone chimney and out. Each of the little lights flickered and danced on the up-drafting air, swirling in a floating gavotte. He watched that dance for a time before he heard the voice.

"Beautiful, aren't they?" His brother sat in the other chair, watching the same show, a look of fascination on his face. "Sorry I took so long," he smiled at an untold joke, "but there was a consensus to manage."

"Yeah," Jason said wearily, "I'm still not understanding that."

His brother watched him for a second, then turned his head back to the fire. "What happens to those embers when they fade?"

"Are we doing this again?" Jason shook his head.

"Humor me."

Jason reached for the poker standing by the open hearth, and grabbed it by the handle. He reached in with the iron rod and stirred the coals for a few seconds, watching the embers rise. "Well, they have released all their stored energy—at least what's accessible through combustion—so the carbon that's left eventually falls back to earth."

"To be recycled."

"I would think so."

"Hmmm." He pushed the poker into the fire again, and then prodded the burning logs within, turning and shifting each until the new wood Jason had tossed in erupted in flame. Within seconds the heat from the fire became almost too intense to bear, and the renewed light coming from that birth illuminated the entire room. Shadows cavorted on nearly every wall of the cabin, yet Jason wasn't so sure they were all cast by the fire.

His brother looked away from that impatient blaze, found Jason's eyes, and said, "We all die, are consumed, and are yet reborn, brother." He turned back to the fire, stabbing and stirring the coals at the bottom. "We sacrifice our *self* in so many ways, every day, that when the time comes we give up what we are readily and completely without a thought." He smiled at the fire, "And then we start over."

"So, you're saying that each of us is reborn after death?"

His brother nodded, still stirring the fire.

"That sounds an awful lot like some religions."

"Well, it's not exactly like that." He stopped his movements with the poker, and said, "Remember, your life is a closed loop. There really is no beginning or end, so when we die," he shrugged his shoulders, "we just start over again. The same life, the same events, even the same choices for the most part." He shook his head and grinned in real humor, "Kind of like the old eight-track tapes. Remember those?"

"So why can't we travel to the future on this closed loop? Why can't we just skip ahead to take a look around?"

"Because you haven't been there yet. Well, you have, but *you*," he pointed the poker at Jason, "have not."

"That doesn't make any sense."

"Annoying, isn't it?" He grinned again, though this time the humor was all but absent.

Jason sighed, sat back in his chair, and crossed his arms. "This isn't really helping me at all."

His brother's eyes twinkled in the firelight for just a moment, and he said with renewed enthusiasm, "Oh, but it is!"

Jason snorted in derision. He was rapidly coming to the conclusion that he was wasting his time inside the wall; that there were no answers to be found here other than what he could discover for himself.

"Exactly!"

He turned to his brother in shock and dismay. "Are you reading my mind, now?"

"Of course not," he smiled, a mask of charm and deception, "I just know what you're thinking."

"How the hell is that not the same thing?"

His brother tilted his head back, eyes searching the heavens beyond the roof of the cabin and sighed, "This is going to take longer than I thought."

†††

Addison's pilot took longer than expected to get the flight plan filed and the plane in the air; consequently, he was a full three hours behind his quarry, and he had no idea where his client was at this point. All he was sure of was their final destination, and it was his intention to meet them there for a denouement to this whole affair. What he hadn't decided was the method of that ending. There were a number of options, but all of them culminated in death. It was, after all, his trade.

No one fires me from a job, and no target has ever escaped, he thought. It was now a point of professional pride, and no matter the outcome, it would be *he* who orchestrated it.

"I can cut some time off at the end, sir," the pilot said over the cabin's intercom. "The big boys have housekeeping stuff they have to do when they land that we don't."

Addison pressed a button on his armrest, "How much time?"

"Maybe a half-hour. I know it's not much, but..."

"Better that than nothing." Addison tapped his fingers absentmindedly on the armrest, then noticed the motion and stopped.

"Do your boys have luggage they need to pick up?"

"Sadly, no. Their room looked like they never returned to it before they skipped town."

"I'm sure you'll catch up to them."

"It's not them I'm worried about, Ken." Addison snapped off the intercom and settled into his seat for the long flight. He knew he should get some sleep, especially since there would not be time for that on the other end. Twenty years in this business, and this was the biggest clusterfuck—by far—of any assignment he was involved in. *I'm a professional, goddammit!* There would be no referrals from this job, that was sure. The only thing to do now was to limit the damage to his reputation.

Early in his career, he was forced to kill a client, but that was at the behest of another in what was a layered CIA operation. He hated working for the CIA. While they paid on time, they still paid like a government agency on a budget. *Come to think of it, that was the last time I willingly worked for them.* The last two times they didn't give him a choice, but the target was a joy to dispatch, regardless. If he cared at all about the politics, he might have done that job for free.

Turning his attention back to the problem at hand, he realized that catching up to the party before reaching the cabin was no longer an option. Things would have to be handled there, now, but Addison almost expected that outcome from the moment he first encountered the place. There was a symmetry about this dance that choreographed the motions of everyone involved. He liked that. Others might feel manipulated by events, but he relished knowing that there was something larger at work—a plan that, once set in motion, would not be denied. It was a rich tapestry of actions, motivations, plans and counter-plans, and like the rugs of the Navajo, he was placed here by a higher power as the intentional flaw in the weave.

How else to let the evil spirits out?

Addison looked out the window to the darkening sky and the horizon beyond. *Over there. That's where we will see what we will see.* He looked forward to discovering what lay on the far side of that horizon. The plane banked, straightened, and chased the setting sun across the sky.

†††

Miles sat in the first class cabin, drumming his fingers on the tray in his lap as he waited for his meal. There were, thankfully, only three other people in first class on this flight. He hated people in first class marginally less than the rest of the rabble; these people kept to themselves. To emphasize the point, two of the three were stretched out in their seats with headphones covering their ears. Only the truly obnoxious bothered a traveler thus armored. There was also little chance anyone would recognize the Representative from Texas, and that was a gift. He had no desire to answer awkward questions about an unscheduled trip to Colorado on an open-ended ticket.

There was no time to secure alternate ID in time before arriving at the airport, so he was traveling openly as himself. While it was unusual, it could be explained with a quick side-trip to the capitol to visit the Governor. The bill he was pushing though Congress impacted areas of the state, so he could justify the visit as a fact-finding tour.

The flight attendant approached with the meal cart. Miles adjusted his seat and pulled the tray down, but the plate she placed before him was worse than the typical fund-raising rubber chicken dinner. Not only were meals mostly eliminated from coach and business class, but what was left for first class these days was abhorrent. Greasy slice of brownish meatloaf, a side of potato mush, and wrinkled, overcooked green beans. All of it on a plate too small to keep each item from touching the other.

"Take this back and try again, missy." He looked up at her, checking her name tag, and narrowed his eyes. "See if there's anything back there that resembles food," he said with a ferret's grin. "Think you can do that, Tara?" *What a stupid fucking name.*

"I can see if there is a Kosher meal left. Will that do, sir?"

He looked her over like a dog contemplating a bone, and she flinched and stepped back. "I guess it will have to, honey," he growled, showing his teeth.

Miles leaned out into the aisle as he watched her flounce back to the galley. The only other man in the cabin watched him watching her.

"What are you lookin' at?" Miles waited for a response, and when none came, he sneered and settled back in his seat.

He knew he was too far behind to catch the two men he was chasing anywhere but at the log cabin. That was just as well. Eliminating them there allowed him to do so without chance of witnesses. Besides, he had done it before. There was no reason to believe he couldn't do it again.

†††

"Did you know I have an army?" His brother said without preamble.

"No, but you *are* the master of the non sequitur."

"It's what you might call an 'army of one', but we are all here, nonetheless." He smiled like a madman, and Jason couldn't help but think he might be. His brother raised an eyebrow, then said, "I guess a better verbiage would be 'I am an army of one', but I think that's copyrighted." He stopped to consider for a second, then said, "It's actually more your army than mine. You have been building it bit by bit over the last seven years with every decision you made." He shook his head, "You are hard to deal with in high volume, you know that?"

"I have an army. Right." Jason leaned forward and rubbed his temples.

"Henderson has one, too." His brother twisted his mouth, then said, "But it's much smaller. Psychopaths and sociopaths tend to both work alone, and not be quite so selfless."

Jason stood. "I think it's time for me to leave."

"Almost." His brother stood as well, dropping the poker back into its stand. "How about we take a walk outside first." Leading the way without looking back, the man headed for the door, grasped the handle, then waited. Jason shoved his hands in his pockets, then finally walked toward the door as well. The other turned to him, smiled sadly, and pulled the heavy slab of oak inward. Both men walked onto the porch, two pair of boots thudding against the wooden planks.

Beyond the cabin lay near-total darkness, only the tree line visible as a black silhouette against an inky midnight-blue sky. There were no stars, moon, or any other points of light to give even the illusion of depth. The entire scene could have been painted on the inside of a dome, for all Jason could tell.

His brother shuffled his feet a little as he looked downward, "I apologize. I haven't finished the landscape. I didn't need to, since the cabin was all that mattered." He looked up again into Jason's eyes, then gestured at the land beyond, and said, "Out there, past what you can perceive, is my army. Our army, if you will. Henderson's is out there, too, and soon the battle will be joined. All who fight among those multitudes will do so with one purpose in mind—to give their brothers-in-flesh the opportunity to do what they must." His eyes grew soft, and his face fell. "To do what I must," he said, placing a hand on Jason's shoulder. "What *you* must."

"I don't understand." Jason's eyes searched the other's for something—anything—that would tell him what to do, but there was nothing but sadness.

"When the time comes, you will." He smiled crookedly at Jason, "At least I hope you will."

"Why can't you just tell me what to do? You know our future. Just tell me." If he had been a child, Jason would be stomping his feet. Instead, he just pulled away from his brother to turn his back on him.

"There's no point. All I have seen is what I have done, and that was not the answer. I only know where things will lead if you don't succeed, and that is the death of everything." His brother grabbed his shoulders, and spun him around roughly, "You must succeed where I failed, because I created the man chasing you now."

†††

Miles woke with a start, and looked around the cabin. The dream brought back memories of a sideways future he hadn't thought about in years.

Things will go much differently this time, he thought.

"More than you know."

Miles turned to see the boy sitting alone across the aisle, watching him, still wearing the same tattered clothes.

"Oh hell," he said with a shake of his head. "I'm still dreaming, aren't I?"

"In a way," the boy said. "I just came to let you know I'm not going to try to talk you out of this anymore." He looked sad in a way that only a child can. "Your path is now your own, Miles."

To that, Miles said nothing. *I'm going to win,* he thought. *I know with certainty now, and none of that end-of-the-world bullshit has to come true. It's all going to be mine.*

The boy sighed, and said, "I guess I'll see you later, then."

"Don't count on it," Miles said with a sneer. "I don't plan on doing much slumming after I eliminate my roadblock."

But the boy was already gone. The passenger who had watched him so closely before was now in that seat, leaning toward him. "Pardon?"

Miles ignored him, and leaned back in his seat and closed his eyes.

†††

Phil woke as the wheels of the 737 touched the ground, chirping their irritation at having been stretched and spun. The roar from the clamshell thrust reversers permeated the cabin as each passenger sat up and readied for arrival at the gate. He looked over to see that Jason was still out, and soon began to worry that the cabin crew would take notice and call for an ambulance when they arrived. There was still time for him to come back, but looking out the window toward the terminal, Phil estimated it to be less than thirty minutes.

He policed their small area, and was heartened to hear a short and quiet gasp from his right. Jason sat up and rubbed his eyes, then looked out the window, noticing they were already on the ground.

"You know, I would enjoy being out like that more if there were actual rest involved." He scrubbed his face vigorously with both hands. "I feel like I've been on an eight-mile hike."

Phil couldn't help it, and he laughed hard. "That's what's happening next, junior."

Jason just turned to face his uncle in silence.

"Okay, maybe not that far, but it sure feels like it when it's all uphill."

TWENTY-TWO

Phil drove the rental car as Jason cataloged their small inventory of weapons: Two AR-15's with scopes and two clips each, two pump-action shotguns, four boxes of shells, two nine millimeter handguns with two fully loaded magazines for each, and two very sharp hunting knives. Since Jason had never fired anything other than a hunting rifle in his life, regardless of his Texas roots, the shotguns were a necessity. The Jason of this reality may have weapons training, but that information wasn't in this Jason's database.

The handguns and the knives were for when things inevitably went to hell, and they were required to fight in close quarters.

"For once, Uncle Phil, I'm thankful the gun laws in this country suck," he said as he looked over their stash with a smile.

"Killing another human being is a hard thing, son. Especially when you're lookin' him in the eye," Phil said as he watched the road. "You know, back in the first great war, officers couldn't understand the difference between the shooting scores their infantrymen got in training, and the god-awful kill-rate they saw on the battlefield." He looked over at Jason, then said, "Things improved a lot after they changed their paper targets from bulls-eyes to a human silhouette." He turned back to face the road. "Turns out a man had to be trained to shoot another man."

"I should be okay, then," Jason said. He snorted once, then said, "I've had a lot of practice playing first-person shooter video games."

Phil shook his head. "I've often wondered if that weren't the damn point of those things."

Jason spent hundreds of hours killing zombies, dragons, vampires, and assorted other monsters, but he only knew one other person in his life who had actually taken a life—his Uncle Phil. He wasn't sure he could pull the trigger with a living human on the receiving end of that instrument of death, but he knew he must. Wounding was not an option in this battle. It was obvious their pursuer would neither stop, nor concede defeat. *And if he kills me and Uncle Phil, Jay dies eventually as well*, Jason thought as his face grew hard. Either way, this would have to end quickly—they simply didn't have enough ammunition and supplies for a protracted battle.

Jason looked over at his uncle. The man was focused on the road and his thoughts, driving in the dark on both fronts. There was a light dusting of snow on the road from the year's first fall, and the occasional *pat pat* of fattened snowflakes on the windshield promised more to come. They drove for over an hour after leaving Denver, only recently leaving the highway for that winding road leading up to the cabin. There were no four-wheel drive vehicles available at the rental lot, so Phil's plan was to drive as far up the mountain as he could in the car, then abandon it to hike the remaining distance. He laughed out loud when the clerk asked if he wanted the optional insurance. "Hell, yeah! Gonna see if I can grab some sick air with this thing," was his boisterous response, winking at Jason as he spoke. The clerk blanched, but Jason laughed and shook his head.

"Phil, you know this road takes some nasty twists along the way. Don't you think it's a good idea to back off the speed a bit?" He smiled thinly at his uncle and gripped the armrest in a white-knuckled vise, but the man never even turned his head to look at him.

"I'm working on the assumption that Henderson is following us, and has access to better forms of transportation, junior." His face scrunched in concentration as they hit a bump and, for a fraction of a second, all four wheels spun freely as they left the road. The wheels re-engaged the road with a bouncing *whump*, and Jason checked his shoulder harness for the fifth time. Phil looked at his nephew, and said, "It's possible the guy could be there waiting for us already."

Jason gritted his teeth, and turned back to watch the road. "Then we probably shouldn't be trying to do his job for him."

Phil sighed, and said under his breath, "Pussy," but he slowed the car a bit, regardless.

"Besides," Jason ignored him and continued, "I need to go back in." Phil turned slightly and raised an eyebrow in his direction, but before he could speak, Jason said, "There's a lot going on here, and I just need to be clear about all this."

Phil considered for a few seconds, then nodded once. "Will I be able to wake you up when the time comes?"

Jason made a moue with his lips. "I don't think so," he said, "but I'm not going to stay long."

Again, a short silence, then Phil drawled, "Better git to gittin' then." He turned and smiled at his nephew, then his eyes were back on the road.

Jason leaned the seat back, then settled in to relax and slow his breathing. He closed his eyes, then slipped into the wall as easy as pulling off a silk scarf.

†††

Miles patted the duffel bag full of the "tools" that lay in the passenger seat beside him. After landing in Denver, the first thing he did was rent a car and drive to the nearest sporting goods store to stock up on weapons and ammo. He chose a Barrett MRAD with an attached scope, and it was already broken down and stored in the bag ready to be reassembled when he arrived at the cabin. The last time he fired a rifle like this one was years ago, but he knew he could still handle it. *Just like riding a bicycle*, he thought. It was the first time he had graduated from killing animals to killing people. *The guy was also a fucking animal. Son of a bitch practically parked his filthy ass outside my dorm to beg for food.* Miles simply wanted him gone. *It was easy, too.*

It always had been.

Subtlety was no longer an option, nor was it required. People disappeared on these mountains all the time, and unless a loved-one knew they were lost and called up a search, it could be years before any remains were found. In their flight from him, they led him to the only good place for their safe elimination. Quite considerate, in his opinion, and he grinned—a rictus of pleasure he no longer needed to conceal.

Wheels within wheels turned inside his head as he drove, a small map of the area lay in his lap. He was leaving too much of a trail, but there was no avoiding it. He could clean it up later, if necessary. All that mattered now was the swift and sure elimination of a barrier in his path. Jason Callahan ended his plans once before, but not this time. *Not here, and not now.*

As he turned off the main highway, the road grew even darker, his headlights barely parting the velvet curtain before him. On either side trees appeared as if by magic, drained of all color in the purifying beam of the headlights, then quickly faded into the blackness as he passed. Already the grade was growing steeper, but none of that mattered to him now. He pressed the accelerator closer to the floorboard, heedless of the thickening layer of snow on the ground.

†††

Jason sat once again in front of the warm fire, though this time the cabin was of his own making. Creating in this magical space wasn't difficult, but it required concentration. His first practice attempts were small affairs—a rough wooden end table, followed by other small items. Once he moved to real furniture, he grew ambitious. The chair where he now sat, instead of the straight high-backed version that always inhabited his brother's constructs, was a wing-backed and over-stuffed leather club chair more suitable for serious discussion. An added benefit was that it was also far more comfortable.

"I see you've upgraded the furniture a bit."

Jason turned his head to see his brother standing behind the other chair, identical to his own, with his hands placed on the wings.

"I'm tired of grinding my tailbone into hard surfaces," he said, irritation creeping into his voice. He gestured toward the seat, "If you'll join me, I have a few more questions."

His brother looked through the wall of the cabin to consider or commune—Jason neither knew, nor cared, which—then nodded once, and said, "I guess we have a little time." He walked around the chair to the front, then settled into the soft leather beneath him. Turning to Jason he said, "Shoot."

"Okay... I understand we have to confront Henderson—maybe even kill him—but I still don't get why." He wrung his hands in his lap as he looked into the crackling fire. "What does it actually accomplish other than keeping him from killing me?"

"I told you. I saw the end of the world, and he's the one who causes it."

"But it still makes no sense. Even if this reality is destroyed at the end, there are myriad other realities out there. This is just one line in a very large multiverse, right?"

"Yes, and no."

"Stop that!" Jason pulled at his hair in frustration, and pressed his body hard against the back of the chair. "Will you please stop playing the 'wise master' and just say what you mean?"

His brother sighed, started to speak, then stopped and sighed again. "I could tell you everything that happened in my reality in detail, and it still wouldn't help you. The main thing, though, is that in *this* reality, the body you're piloting in the real world is mine."

Jason shook his head, a short and violent action, trying without much success to clear his thoughts. He suspected as much, but didn't understand how all the pieces fit together. There were too many heres, here, and not enough spaces to place them.

His brother watched in sympathy. "Don't feel bad, Jason, it took me an eternity to begin to understand." He smiled wanly at his double, "And even now I couldn't tell you for sure if I have it all right in my head. It is, though, the understanding of the consensus."

"That's another thing. What is this 'consensus' you keep referring to?"

He chuckled, a boyish sound from an old soul. "I would think that's obvious. It's the averaging of desires, opinions, and knowledge of all the Jasons here in the wall." He grimaced slightly, "Well, all the ones here that you have created over your last seven years. That makes them more your children than mine, and let me tell you, they are a handful."

"Why are they here?"

His brother snorted, "Don't you listen to anything? I told you—they're my army."

"No. That tells me *what* they are, not why."

"Oh… well, they're dead like me. Each one of them killed by their Henderson in their reality."

"How many?" Jason was sure he had an idea of the answer, and was just as sure he probably didn't want to know.

"Millions." He looked away from Jason and into the fire. "And that's just the ones who chose to stay."

"Chose to stay?"

"As I've told you, your entire life is a closed loop. We don't know when it will end, but at that point the loop closes and all our minds, souls, whatever you want to call it, travel back to the point of origin to start over."

"We're born again."

"Just like religion tells you." He leaned forward, arms on his knees, "But not really the same as we're taught. We aren't reborn into Heaven or a new life like reincarnation, we just start our lives over again, living them much the same as the first time around. Chaos theory says that even with the exact same conditions, there will be variances, but like a Mandelbrot Set, even the variances become part of the overall pattern." He shrugged. "Most wouldn't notice the difference even if they could."

"And the army?"

"They are... well, they're postponing returning to their origin. They are sacrificing their reality to stay inside the wall to do what must be done; and while they are here, they plan, consider, discuss, and meld their opinions and knowledge into the consensus."

"Which brings me to why it matters." Jason slumped further into his chair, his energy all but spent. "If every one of us is in a closed loop, and we simply start over when we die, that means our realities will do the same." His eyes widened as he felt the rightness of what he was saying, "Kill Henderson, or don't. Stop his plans or don't. In the end it will all be the same, regardless."

His brother shook his head, eyes closed. "You haven't been listening at all, have you?"

†††

"I can get you within two miles or so, but there's no good place to land any closer than that." Addison's pilot, Ken, recommended this particular helicopter service, but so far he remained singularly unimpressed. The man was ancient—too old to be flying, in Addison's opinion—and didn't look smart enough to give the machine a good wash, let alone operate it. Behind the counter where they stood, an open door revealed a cluttered office where an equally old woman sat flipping through a magazine, lips drawstring tight. The place smelled of cheap, burnt coffee, and even cheaper cigarettes. Overhead, the fluorescent lights flickered randomly, and from the looks of them probably had for years. Ken told Addison this was the best man in the area. *We shall see. He's smart enough to know not to steer me wrong.*

"I've been to this location," Addison stabbed the map on the counter with his forefinger, "there is plenty of room for your helicopter to land near the cabin."

The pilot rolled his eyes skyward for a second, doffed his Broncos cap to scratch his head, as tiny flecks of dried skin took flight, then said, "Sure, there's room for the 'copter, but there's wind shear up there this time o' the year that can whip that little two-seater," he pointed out the window to his helicopter, "right into the trees or the cabin. Maybe I could land you on the front porch, but maybe we just auger in instead." He looked Addison dead in the eye, "I don't like 'maybes' when I'm flyin'. 'Specially at night." He put the cap back on, and pulled the brim down sharply as punctuation.

Addison held his gaze for a few seconds, waiting to see if the older man would give in. When he didn't, Addison took his hand from the map and said, "Fine. Get me as close as you can. Don't bother hanging around, though," he reached down to pick up his duffel bag. "This is a one-way trip. I'll find my own ride home."

"Suit yerself, mister. It's your money, after all." He pulled the map away, folded it, and placed it back behind the counter. Scooping up the stack of bills that sat beside it, he pushed a button on the old cash register and set them inside. Closing the heavy drawer with obvious effort, he said, "Skids up in twenty."

Addison walked out of the little storefront, the bell hanging on the door frame jingling happily as he opened it. As it slowly swung shut behind him, he heard the old man say "Don't look at me like that, woman. Man's payin' cash, and—"

Thankfully, the door closed in time to muffle the rest of the conversation. Addison sat on the wooden bench out front to wait, as a light snow fell all around him. In a few hours the place would get a fine dusting. *Enough to make it look almost clean*, he thought. The pure white flakes could do nothing for a man's soul, however. For the first time since that first time, Addison contemplated retirement.

TWENTY-THREE

"S HE'S BOTTOMED OUT, SON," PHIL YELLED OVER THE DIN OF THE whining motor. "Back tires are spinnin' free. Cut the engine. We're walkin' from here."

After slamming headlong into one dip and hill too many, the little car had finally landed with the frame resting on a small rise, front wheels buried slightly in the dirt, and the back wheels several inches off the ground. At first, Phil guessed he could just sit on the trunk to push the rear wheels down, but the incline and the fact the front wheels were stuck soon changed his mind. There was simply too much weight on the front end to compensate with one large man. Even three of him might not be able to do it. No, a good truck with a wench was required, and they were fresh out.

Jason opened the door, leaned out and looked behind him, "Damn, Phil. When you go muddin', you don't play around."

"Har, har. Now help me get these packs out," he pulled the read door open, "the map says we have at least a mile of uphill walkin' to do."

Phil shrugged one pack over his shoulders, while his nephew worked on the other. He intended to carry the weapons himself, but Jason beat him to it. *Probably for the best. Load me down with too much, and I'll just be a boat anchor.*

He pulled out his compass to get a direction, then noticed Jason grinning at him.

"What?"

"Phil," he shook his head, "the road dead ends at the cabin."

He snapped the lid shut, laughed, and said, "Right. Let's git to gittin'." He hitched his pack again, shifting the weight to a more comfortable position, and started up the road. He set a pace he knew his nephew could match, but one that might leave himself a pile of quivering flesh at the end. He doubted it would matter much in the long run, but if they didn't get to the cabin before Henderson or one of his people in time to fortify their position, all of this would be for nothing anyway. The only good news was that the narrow road was now well and truly blocked by the stalled car they left behind.

They walked easily for a while, though Jason took the lead soon after they began, and made an effort to relax the pace Phil tried to set. The big halogen lamp Phil was holding tossed a cone-shaped spray of light before them that ended about 50 feet ahead. Good enough for hiking up a road at night, but also clearly marking them to anyone who might be following—or waiting. Try as he might, though, he couldn't make out details beyond the influence of the lamp, as the darkness was nearly total, the great swath of gray snow-laden clouds he knew was overhead blocking even the moonlight. With each step, more of the landscape before him was revealed, while everything behind him faded into blackness.

"I've been wondering about something lately, Phil." Jason was now walking beside him, having dropped back a few paces while he was lost in thought. His nephew's brows were knitted, and his mouth was bunched up as he considered his question.

"Yeah? What's that?" Phil, already a little out of breath, hoped this wouldn't be a long conversation. He wasn't sure he had the stamina for both that and the hike.

Jason tilted his head slightly, then said, "How do we know we're not on the wrong side here?"

Phil pulled up short, refusing to take another step while he considered the possibilities. "What do you mean?"

Jason stopped a step or two later, turned and confronted Phil, and said, "I've read a lot of fiction over the years, and in all of the stories where the good guy is roped into saving the day by defeating some dude he had never heard of before the story started, no one ever stops to ask the important question: 'How does he know he's on the right side?'"

"Son," he shook his head and smiled sadly, "I don't think that applies here."

"Why not? Maybe I do something in the future that causes the world to end, and he's the guy trying to stop me. Maybe—"

"That bastard killed your daddy and your momma—my sister—in cold blood, and you think he might be the good guy?"

"I'm not saying he's good, only that we don't know which side is the right one."

Phil threw his hands in the air and glared at his nephew, the lamp throwing it's light in every direction as he gestured, "I don't get you, Jason." He held out a hand, thumb and forefinger an inch apart, "We're *this* close to either finishing this thing, or getting our heads blown off, and now you want to start questioning which side you're on?"

"All I'm saying is that there is a possibility—"

"No, there ain't," Phil said, shaking his head vigorously. "Son, I've known you your whole life—hell, I diapered your ass a few times—and what I know is that you are not a liar. Not to your momma and daddy, not to me, and near as I can tell, not even to yourself."

"So?"

Phil sighed and looked skyward, "You have got to be the dumbest genius I ever met, you know that?" He locked eyes again with the man in front of him and said, "The guy who recruited you for this, the one who's been feeding you all the information and new-age bullshit," he stabbed the light into Jason's chest, "is you."

Jason tilted his head, then stood up a little straighter, "But—"

"Don't 'but' me no 'buts', son. He's you, and I'm askin' ya straight up—would he lie to you?"

His nephew considered that for a moment, then all the energy leaked out of him as his face softened and his shoulders slumped. "I guess not."

Phil watch him for a second, then clapped him hard on the shoulder and said, "Cheer up, son! This way when we get killed at the cabin, we'll at least know it was for a good cause." He smiled hugely at his nephew, all teeth and gums, real cheer in his eyes for the first time in days. "Now can we get back to walkin' before my feet freeze clean off?"

Jason smiled back at the dark humor, nodded his head, and said, "Let's git to gittin', then."

Phil laughed out loud as both men turned back up the road. As they walked, Jason turned to Phil and said through a wide grin, "Besides, I'm pretty sure I saw you buy some of those electric socks back there at the sporting goods store, ya big wuss."

†††

Addison leaned out of the opening on his right, watching the ground grow closer in the circle of illumination from the small belly light on the helicopter, sneered at the pilot and said over the noise of the rotors, "Are you sure you can land in such a small spot?"

The pilot snorted, but otherwise ignored the dig at his skills. "I've been comin' up here a lot of years. Drop hunters off once a week or so in this spot when the season is peakin'." He looked over at his passenger, "Good thing we're in an in-between time for big game huntin', you bein' without a vest and all. Not to mention the dark clothes." The pilot shook his head lightly, and said, "You're an accident waitin' to happen, you know that?"

"That's the plan, anyway," he mumbled.

"What's that?"

"Nothing. Just see if you can land your machine without rattling my teeth loose."

The last twenty feet of the approach looked to be uneventful, then the tail shifted clockwise and they dropped a few feet suddenly as the helicopter tilted several degrees. While the pilot fought the controls, Addison's face remained passive, but his hands were a steel vise holding either side of his seat. Righting the machine with some effort, the pilot dropped the few feet left to land with a mildly jarring thud.

"See what I mean about that wind shear?" He grinned at Addison, vindication in every coffee-stained tooth he showed. "Gets worse farther up."

Already unbuckled and out of the cabin, Addison grabbed the duffel from behind his seat and said, "I'm sure." He pulled an envelope from his heavy coat, and tossed it onto the passenger seat. "That's the rest of the cash, as we agreed." He looked up at the pilot, his face a mask of calm, and said, "No part of this trip is in your records in any way." He nodded once at the old pilot, his eyes never leaving the other's, "As agreed."

The other man looked him up and down. "Yer man made that damn clear when he first called me," he said. He looked on the verge of saying something, then stopped and shook his head. "No, I don't suppose so. I don't want people to know I brought some greenhorn up here to get himself lost and froze." He grinned, tipped his cap, and said, "Think I'll keep that to m'self, if ya don't mind."

"That will do, then." Addison narrowed his eyes at the pilot. "I will know if you don't," he said, a dangerous edge to his voice. He turned his back to the man and walked away, and the helicopter lifted off behind him. He was a hundred yards from the small road leading up to the cabin, with only a small stand of trees in his way. From here, the walk would not offer him much difficulty. He hoped he could say the same for the men at the end of that road.

With just enough light to see the difference between trees and open space, Addison finally made it to the road, then turned right to head uphill. While the air was quite cold, his coat kept him warm enough. The hiking boots he wore were of the highest quality, so his feet would be none the worse for wear when he finally arrived at the cabin. His only issue with clothing was with his trousers. Ken misheard his size, so consequently he was still wearing the jeans he carried in his pack from Washington. He didn't even have thermal underwear to help retain his body heat. Keeping moving, then, was the prescription. As long as he continued to move he was able to generate some body heat, and then he would take time to warm up properly after he finished his business and took the cabin. With luck, one of his quarry would provide the necessary garments for his hike back to civilization.

He walked for no more than thirty minutes when he saw the large shape in the middle of the road, and it took only a second to realize it was a car stuck in a particularly steep section. Stepping off the muddy track, and back into the trees for cover, he watched the car for fully ten minutes before being satisfied there was no movement in or around the vehicle.

Addison approached in careful slow motion, and set his duffel on the ground at the edge of the trees. He pulled the Beretta from his inside coat pocket, and stepped up to the car, keeping below the line of sight of anyone who might be inside. He stopped near the trunk, crouched low and listened for any sign of movement. When he was satisfied the car was empty, he peeked inside the back window. *Nothing*, he thought, releasing a slow breath. He then moved to the side and checked again, before pulling the door open.

Nothing. That was good and bad. Good that he didn't have to use the gun, but bad that they were on foot and ahead of him. He felt the car's hood. *Not much above ambient*, he thought, pulling his hand away. *Can't be more than an hour ahead. Probably less.* Ahead, he saw no indication they were any closer, but decided to stay close to the trees for the remainder of his journey.

He walked back to his duffel, picked it up, and started up the mountain, keeping the Beretta in his free hand.

†††

Miles slowed the car as road grew both narrower and steeper. There was no sense in killing himself when he was so close to the finish line. He smiled at that thought. He was really going to enjoy killing the two men standing in his path to glory. Even though he had already killed Jason once, he was sure the sensation would not be any less satisfying than the first time. His grin turned skeletal and vacant. *The bastard had needed killing after what he'd done to me. Fucking goody two-shoes Fed.*

Jason Callahan, one of the FBI's finest, had the temerity to investigate Miles for campaign finance violations, of all things. *Okay, so I bribed a few people and accepted dirty money for my campaign, but who didn't?* He could have picked anyone at random to investigate and found a crime, but he had locked on to Miles for some reason. Sure, there was a body in the closet, but that couldn't be pinned on him… though Callahan tried.

In the end, Miles was forced to resign his office and scuttle back to Texas instead of serving jail time. As a long and proud tradition in his state, it didn't offer much impediment to his business dealings, but it was a death-blow to his political ambitions. The ironic part was that wasn't even his original reality. He stumbled upon it just as that Miles was offered his first internship in Washington, and he had an epiphany. All his life he had wanted to be something special, but everything always seemed to stand in his way. With access to power for the first time, he was able to systematically eliminate the obstacles keeping him from the power that was his by right.

Then Jason showed up to his office with his fucking badge, his accountants, computer nerds, and investigators, and everything went to hell.

Lost in thought, Miles barely had time to register the stalled car in the road before he hit his brakes. The tires worked furiously to grab the road, but the snow said "not on my watch," and the wheels locked as his car slammed headlong into the back of the other car. If the front end was not partially buried, both cars would have slid forward some to absorb a little of the energy involved. Without that advantage, however, the two cars simply folded along their respective crumple zones in spectacular fashion. Only the reduced speed and airbag saved Miles from certain death.

Miles woke several minutes later, the hood of his car folded in front of him like an accordion, and the airbag in his steering wheel looking like a powder-covered Dali painting. With a sharp pain shooting through his ribcage, he unbuckled his seatbelt, pushed hard on the door to open it, then crawled out onto the cold ground. Kneeling there, taking slow rasping breaths, he saw blood dropping to the snow-covered ground beneath his face. He reached up, felt his broken nose, and realized a few of his ribs were probably cracked as well. As he stood slowly, he checked each movement to make sure there were no broken bones in his legs or arms. Working all his joints, he smiled as realized his luck. He was going to have a hell of a headache later, along with two black eyes, but he was still operational.

He reached into the car to pluck the bag of weapons from the debris, and then he remembered the jacket in the back. *No sense in freezing to death before I get there.* Ignoring the pain, he shrugged the coat on over his shoulders, zipped it up, and then grabbed the bag by its nylon handles and started walking up the road. Confident in his mission, he walked down the center line arrow-straight. *A couple more miles, that's all. Almost done.*

†††

Addison heard the muffled sound of the collision on the road behind him. *Please let that be my idiot client,* he thought. With only the sound of snow crunching under his boots, there was little competition for noises that were out of place in these woods. The other car was no more than a mile behind, so whoever that was, if they lived, was close enough to cause problems. With luck, the fool died in the accident, but Addison knew he couldn't be that lucky. *I'm going to have to make some hard choices, soon,* he thought.

It was time to improve his odds. He pulled the map of the area out of his pocket, and using the small GPS he brought along, calculated his current position. Once he had a bearing, he set off through the woods on a straight line for the cabin. He estimated the direct path would shave almost twenty minutes from his ETA if the terrain did not slow him substantially, though it was sure to leave him more fatigued than if he stayed to the road. He did not like functioning sub-optimally, as this is how mistakes were made, but he was pressed for time.

I must keep moving. Target ahead, complication behind, and no-where to go but up.

TWENTY-FOUR

"**I**'LL GATHER KINDLING FROM THE YARD WHILE YOU CARRY IN AS many logs from the woodpile as you can."

Jason looked at his uncle for a second, then shook his head in resignation. "I see you took the hard job for yourself."

"Yeah, well… you're in better shape," he grinned, "and younger, too." He tossed his backpack of hastily-gathered supplies on the small table beside Jason's pack, and started out the back door. Jason watched him leave, then looked at the meager cache of food they brought with them. It wasn't much, but with the supply of canned goods already in the pantry, it should last a few days. Their last meal was likely to be far less satisfying than your basic death-row inmate gets for his last day. *At least I get to pick my own time and manner of execution*, he thought darkly.

The real question was how long would they have to wait? There was no way to know when, or even if, Henderson would show. They could just as well spend a week out here without ever seeing the man, then run out of food and have to hike into town for supplies.

Or we could die tonight without stopping the man, he thought. He wasn't sure which prospect was worse.

Realizing he still held the duffel full of weapons, he tossed that on the table as well. The food would outlast the ammunition, and that was all that really mattered anyway.

On his second trip inside, a load of firewood in his arms, he saw his uncle had built a small fire from the kindling. Jason dropped his burden atop the others, and watched his uncle pull one piece from the pile and throw it in. The firewood had seasoned all summer, and the little shed behind the cabin where it was stacked kept it sheltered from the elements, so it caught almost immediately. Phil grabbed another piece of the dry pine and fed it to the hungry animal crackling in the fireplace.

"Two or three more loads ought to do it." He looked up at Jason, "I'm gonna separate the pine from the hardwoods, then give you a hand. Make sure when you bring in the next load to do the same."

When Jason looked at him with a quizzical expression, Phil smirked. "That pine catches quick, and the sap inside makes it burn hot. You use that to catch the hardwood, which burns longer." He reached over and began sorting their fuel. "Little pile of kindling, bigger pile of pine, then as much hardwood as we can fit. I think I saw some mesquite scattered throughout the stack, so see if you can get mostly that." He looked up at Jason, flicked his hand toward the door, and said, "Go on. I'll be out there to help you in a sec."

Jason turned to leave, but before he reached the door Phil cleared his throat. "Um… after we get the wood in, I'll, uh, go out and check the shutters," he said to Jason, and this time he kept his eyes firmly on the fire. "Afterward, we'll unpack the weapons and plan strategy over supper." Jason nodded agreement, then stepped outside to grab another load of wood.

†††

Jason was gone only a few minutes, but when he entered the cabin, stomping the snow off his boots, he knew immediately the cabin was empty, a roaring fire his only companion. Phil's heavy coat and pack were gone as well, and checking the duffel, Jason saw that a rifle with both clips and a knife were also missing. He ran to the front door, threw it wide and searched the tree line for any sign of his uncle, but other than the boot prints in the snow leading away from the cabin, there was nothing. Jason knew he shouldn't call out to him. Searching for him in the dark was also out.

Jason dipped his chin and his shoulders slumped, then he closed and locked the door on his uncle. *The man's got his own plans, and he's made a choice.* Jason knew his uncle had probably planned this since before they approached the cabin. He could only wait to see if it was the right choice.

†††

Out of sight, Phil watched Jason come to terms with his decision, and he saw the boy step back and close the door. In that moment he was as proud of Jason as he ever could be. He was sure Jason didn't like it, but he saw the respect. Unguarded, the cabin was a deathtrap. For this to work, someone had to be outside to deal with the attacker while one of them remained safely inside. *I'm expendable, is all. If a man's gotta throw his life away, it should at least mean something.*

He planned to find a decent firing position from the trees on the north side of the cabin. He figured Henderson was the kind of guy to roll in from the road as it approached the cabin from the east, and he wanted a clear line of sight. Elevated would be good, too, but he saw no trees he could climb. *There aren't many of those,* he thought to himself in derision. *Not unless they start growin' 'em with ladders attached.*

Of the two, Phil was the only one with any real hunting experience, so he was the logical choice to take up the role as sniper. This particular rifle was not the best for his purposes, but it had decent range and a scope, and was the best that was in stock. If he were close enough, all he would need was the knife, anyway.

Phil was sure that Jason would never have gone along with his plan had he bothered to tell him about it, so he didn't. Both men were stubborn enough to stand there arguing about it right up until Henderson broke through the door and shot them dead. A trait passed down, no doubt, from Phil's own daddy—Jason's granddad. That old man worked construction his entire life, and once, at the age of sixty-five, fell from a high tower and broke nearly every bone in his body. Not only had he lived, but was he back working on that same stupid tower inside of six months.

Jason was like that. Of course, he got a second helping of that from Dale. That was the one man Phil knew could give his pop a run for his money in the stubborn department. Phil smiled at the memory of the two arguing after the old man found out his daughter was pregnant. *Dale held his own that day,* Phil thought. If his daddy hadn't died suddenly a year later, he was sure the two would have come to an understanding. *Just watchin' Jason grow up the way he did would have seen to that.*

Phil pulled the hood from his jacket up over his head, grabbed the rifle and pack, then headed deeper into the trees to find a good spot.

I wonder how much colder it's gonna get?

†††

Addison smelled the smoke from the fire long before he saw the cabin. It only served to remind him how cold his lower extremities had grown, but he couldn't allow any minor discomforts to interfere with his task. The problem was, though, that the longer he stayed outside, and the more the temperature dropped, the lower his core temperature became. Over time that would affect his ability to function at a high level, and would eventually lead to diminished mental capacity. During his hike up the mountain, the energy he exerted allowed him to keep his temperature up, but once he settled in to wait for a good opportunity to strike, he would shed that heat at an alarming rate.

Tamping down on that line of thought, he crept silently through the underbrush from the south side of the cabin. From here he could see the front door, the small gravel yard, and roughly twenty feet of the last of the road as it wandered eastward and turned a tight corner at the limit of his vision to disappear beyond a stand of trees. He was still sixty yards from the cabin, and fully thirty feet inside the tree line, so he knelt down and pulled the enhanced night vision scope from his pack. The thing had set him back nearly ten grand, but it blended both night vision technology and thermal imaging in addition to being ridiculously compact.

Checking the area around the cabin, he saw no movement. In fact, the place seemed to be locked up as tight as a drum. The heat signature from the fire gave the optics some problems, but he was still able to clearly see a single human-shaped object in the structure. Someone was still outside, but they weren't close to the cabin or the shed behind it. Addison swept the scope around the perimeter of the clearing and targeted a man-shaped heat signature moving east on the south side of the cabin. It could be a bear, but the time of year and the way it moved said "no." Larger than the figure inside, and with his client well behind, he guessed the man was Phil Carson. That meant Jason was the sole occupant of the cabin.

It was complete supposition on his part, though grounded in data, but he still must confirm the identities of the heat signatures. He lowered the scope and leaned against a tree. *This adds a new wrinkle,* he thought. If he was correct, his respect for the two men ticked up a couple of points. Setting up a sniper outside was a good tactical decision considering their limited options. Mr. Carson might have been only a coach and history teacher, but he knew how to plan. *American football is closely related to battle plans and their execution, after all.*

There were a lot of methods for handling this situation, but most of them were messy, and few of them could be made to look like an accident. He checked his watch. He had, at best, twenty minutes before the client arrived.

I could double back and slow him down, he thought. That might require a *permanent* solution, and he wasn't sure that was necessary. There was also the possibility the client might kill *him,* though far less likely. It was also possible that whoever he heard crash into the car was unrelated to any of them.

Addison settled in, pulled an energy bar from his pack, and considered his options.

†††

Miles knew coming straight up the road was a bad idea, so as soon has he came to the last turn in the road, he stepped off into the woods and moved as quietly as he could toward his goal. As he neared the edge of the clearing he saw the rotting corpse of a large fallen tree and lay behind it for cover. Even though he was over fifty yards from the cabin, he was sure he could make a clean shot from this distance—especially with the Barrett and scope he had in the bag.

He surveyed the area around the cabin, and everything about the place was just as he remembered. Of course, the last time he was here was still fifteen or so years in the future. *Places like this don't change much, though,* he thought. *It probably looked just like this the day it was built.* Except maybe for the shed with the generator. *A generator would have got you burned as a witch when the owner first cleared the land around it.*

Opening the bag as he settled with his back against the tree, he began pulling out pieces of his weapon and arranging them on the ground in front of him. Once he was sure he had everything, he began methodically assembling the rifle. The tree would make a good and stable base from which to fire the gun, and appeared to be dense enough to shield him from return fire.

Morning was still eight hours away, and he had no desire to spend the entire night out in the cold, so he began thinking of ways to get them to come out of the cabin. The clearing was too large to try to set fire to the structure, as they would see him coming and shoot him dead long before he closed the gap. He was sure they were watching, too. They had to know he was coming for them. Sure, they didn't know when, but they weren't stupid... someone would always be keeping an eye out.

What he needed were incendiary grenades, but you couldn't just pick those up at your local sporting goods store. A flare gun, even if he had one, wouldn't work either. The flares would bounce right off the walls, or roll off the steep roof. The rifle he held, though, had the muzzle velocity to punch a bullet right through those shutters—and possibly even the door—but without knowing where to fire, it didn't do him much good, and he did not have enough ammo to spray the cabin with abandon like in the movies. No, those men needed to come out, and preferably one at a time.

The longer he watched that cabin, Callahan inside and enjoying a warm fire, the more his blood boiled.

Patience, his daddy said, the voice whispering in his ear all the time now. *Let that deer come to you, boy. Let it think it's safe, alone... and then put a bullet in it's right eye.*

Mile could be patient. He'd had a lot of practice.

I'll wait all fucking night if I have to.

†††

Phil finally settled on a good spot. There was a half-fallen tree with the crown jammed tightly between two large branches of the tree it lay against. The angle allowed him to—with some effort—make his way up that makeshift ramp to a position of twelve to fifteen feet above the ground. He nearly slipped off the snow-covered bark of the tree twice before making it to the top. Once there, he found that the tangled branches made a relatively comfortable seat back. It offered him the ability to relax and remove his pack without worrying about falling or losing his supplies. Laying the AR-15 across his lap, he dug into the pack and removed two protein bars and a blister packet of caffeine pills.

He opened the packet of pills and swallowed them dry, then tore open the wrapper of one of the bars. As he bit into it, his nose wrinkled in disgust. *Cardboard. Why can't they make these things taste good?* He chewed methodically and swallowed the mass, and then repeated the action, determined to finish what he started.

All the while he scanned the trees and the clearing for movement.

†††

Jason stared at the sandwich, his appetite gone with his uncle, so he sat and stared into the fire. He knew he should be keeping watch, but Phil was already doing that, and Jason would probably hear a gunshot long before he saw anyone through the shutters. He had placed one shotgun near the back door where he could reach it in a hurry, another beside the bed in the lone bedroom, and the remaining rifle near the front door. One handgun was in the kitchen, but the other and the knife were in his belt. He was as ready as he would ever be, but clearly all of those weapons—save the rifle— were for a last stand. If he were down to using those, he was likely already dead.

Son of a bitch. It always happened. Every time he played hide-and-go-seek as a kid, the instant he found a good hiding place his bladder picked that time to decide it needed relieving. To this day, he couldn't hide without a simple bodily function betraying him. He was glad there was indoor plumbing in this cabin, but even without it he would not have opened that door. Angrily, he stood up to walk the short distance to the bathroom.

And then the room spun on all three axes at once. Someone added a fourth for good measure. *Oh, hell. Not now...*

†††

Addison scanned the area, sweeping left to right with the scope, and watched the figure inside the cabin stand, then collapse to the floor. He listened for several seconds, but heard no report from a rifle. *So the man was not shot, but* something *had happened.* It was possible he simply fainted, or even just fallen, but even after a full minute there was still no movement inside. There was no discernible loss of heat, so the man had not simply dropped dead, but the fact he had not moved meant that, at the very least, he was unconscious.

This was an opportunity Addison could not pass up. If Jason were unconscious, then Addison could safely eliminate Phil from the equation without worrying about any noise drawing him to the other man's aid. After that, he could still find a way to eliminate Jason—conscious or not.

Addison pocketed his scope, took his Beretta and an extra clip from the pack, and left the rest in place. He needn't carry much for what he had in mind.

TWENTY-FIVE

J ASON SPUN IN PLACE, LISTENING FOR INTRUDERS, BUT THE ONLY sound came from the crackling of the fire. Seconds ago he was sure he felt the familiar stomach-tightening sensation of a transition in progress, but when he opened his eyes he was still standing in the middle of the room. *Except*, he thought as he surveyed the room, *this isn't the real cabin after all*.

"Of course it's real, brother."

"Fine, if you wish," he said. "Not corporeal, then." He thought of the real world. "I need to get back," he said, shifting his weight from foot to foot like a toddler who needed to pee. "Right *now*."

The other Jason appeared before him, and moved to stand by the door. He pulled one curtain aside to peek out the window between the cracks in the shutters.

"No fireside chat this time," Jason said, looking to the window.

The older Jason opened his mouth to speak, then paused. After another second, he said, "I was going to say there's time, but since time really has no meaning for us," he alternated between pointing at himself and Jason, "let's just say we're beyond that, now." Whatever he saw through the shutters seemed to satisfy his curiosity. He nodded once, then stepped back to face Jason. "However, you're wrong in your assessment of this place. Everything you see around you is just as real as the world you think you inhabit."

"Yeah, I understand all that," Jason waved his hand dismissively, "perception is reality, we create our own universe, blah, blah, blah." He looked hard at his brother, "Tell me, can I affect that reality with just my mind?"

"Yes, and no."

"I swear I'm going to strangle you if you don't start speaking in complete sentences." Veins bulging on the sides of his head, he clenched and unclenched his fists in an effort to calm down.

"See? You're finally getting it." His brother relaxed, turned, and opened the door. "Out there in your 'real' world, thought becomes decision, decision becomes action, and action changes reality—just like I opened this door." Suddenly the door was closed again without any intervening movement on his brother's part. "It's just that here," he gestured to the world around him, "we can dispense with that 'action' part altogether." He looked Jason in the eye once again, and said, "Does that make it any less real?"

"But out there, I can't make a door close without touching it."

"Of course you can." He put up a hand to forestall the coming argument, and he said, "You could simply ask someone to close it. Or you could wait for the wind to do it." His eyes softened, and sighed lightly as he said, "Sometimes things that have no visible connections at all can affect reality, and while those things may seem insignificant, they can have profound effects."

Jason walked to the window, and for no other reason than habit, he pulled the curtain aside to take a look. The clearing to the front of the cabin appeared just as he saw it last, though the trees beyond were, again, just black shapes against a dark sky.

He turned to look at his brother again, watching him shift slightly from one foot to the other as he rubbed his hands. "Is there a point to bringing me here this time, or were you just bored for company?"

His brother laughed out loud at that. "Jason, if there is anything I'm not lacking, it's company."

Jason was about to scream in frustration when he saw his brother's face harden, eyes narrowing. "What's—"

"Uncle Phil is about to get himself killed." The other put up a hand again to silence Jason's next question, and said, "You can keep that from happening, and to do so you will end up performing almost the same actions I did in that reality," he leaned closer, "but you have to make that decision."

"Will I die?"

"Probably, but the actions you take will be necessary." He gestured to the ceiling, "We've viewed millions of scenarios as they played out in each reality, and yours is the only one that offers us the chance we need." He smiled wistfully and then pursed his lips, "Besides, you're forgetting that's my body out there, so death for you is irrelevant."

Jason turned to look out the window again, then released the curtain to stand in front of the door.

"Jason, I've told you that Henderson brings about the end of the world, but it's much worse than that. For whatever reason—chance, fate, or cosmic joke—we three trace our line back to the beginning of life on Earth. He and I follow the same trunk, and after you and I split, that same path follows your line. For the same reason, we have an inordinate number of perfect pairs on our branches, and when Henderson kills my reality, there will be a cascade of destruction back through time all the way to the beginning."

"So you're saying..."

"The network that connects each of our selves will fail, and without that we will be no more intelligent than your average monkey. Without intelligence, brother, we suck as predators." He took a deep breath, then said, "Life, at least *human* life, ends on Earth. In every reality."

Jason took a deep breath and let it out slowly. He had known from the day Phil recruited him to hunt down Henderson that dying for the cause might not only be possible, but necessary as well.. Knowing it, and *knowing* it, though, were two different things. Still, it was his Uncle Phil, after all.

"Okay," Jason said at last, squaring his shoulders. He lifted his chin and his eyes narrowed. "What do I have to do?"

†††

Addison, silent and dark, crept slowly around the back of the cabin, never leaving the trees. The clearing on this side was much smaller, so he was in danger of being seen not only by Phil on his left, but Jason from the front—that is, if the man had recovered from whatever caused his collapse. From this angle he was unclear on the man's status, because the heat from the fireplace made it difficult from this angle to discern other signatures that might be in the room.

Once he moved past the northwest corner of the cabin, though, he at least had a clear line-of-sight to the larger man in the tree. The position the man held presented him with a minor problem, though. While Addison could take him out with relative ease and minimal noise by simply shooting him with the Beretta, the whole scene still needed to look like an accident. There was pride at stake here, after all, as well as self-preservation, and there was just no good way to make a gunshot wound look like an accident.

As he got closer, he could see more details through his scope, and these showed that his target had taken up a protected firing position aimed squarely at the road near the edge of the clearing. Obviously the man thought his pursuer would be walking right up the road with no cover, and just as obviously, he thought his adversary was no professional. Addison tilted his head to consider this. He and Phil had met, and he was sure that the other man knew that Addison was a professional; therefore, Phil must be expecting someone else.

The only one he was sure both of them knew and disdained as an amateur was Addison's client. That man was, indeed, on his way, but for some reason Phil was only expecting him. A more experienced man would have planned for others, but it was possible that his target knew exactly what kind of idiot he was dealing with. He must have guessed that the client would be coming for the two of them alone.

It's a shame that a correct assumption will lead to his undoing, he thought.

†††

Phil swept the clearing around the road with the scope of his rifle, looking for any sign of movement. There was a soft rustling to his right, and he swung the rifle in that direction to see a small branch move slightly in the underbrush. For a full two minutes he watched that space for further movement, but when nothing happened, he relaxed and began sweeping the area again. *I'm gettin' twitchy*, he thought, *and that's gonna get us both killed*. Even with the deafening silence of the camp, he was unable to pick up any sounds of human encroachment. Only the wind and the increasing frequency of fat snowflakes hitting his coat impinged on the still tableau.

My whole life I ain't never sacrificed for nothin', he mused. *Not even for love or family. Tonight will be different, I think. That boy's gonna live to be with his son... even if I don't.* He was old, fat, out of shape, and only passably good with a rifle. His hope was to slow Henderson down with a lucky shot so Jason could finish the job, but he was unsure if his nephew could ultimately pull the trigger when the time came. Even though the numbers were in their favor, they would most likely be dead by morning. If what Jason said was true, though, it probably wouldn't matter—they would both just start over from birth and be right back here again in fifty-four years. *A never-ending loop of suffering and death. Good times.*

He wondered how many times they had already done this. Phil shook the dark thought from his head. *Nope, he vowed, this time luck will be on our side.* It was comforting to think they had a chance, but reality was a better line of thought. He remembered the line in the movie, *In the Line of Fire*, where the bad guy said that to kill a man "all someone needs is a willingness to trade his life for the other guy."

Ain't a bad way to die if it comes to that. He continued to swing the rifle around the clearing with clock-like precision. *'Course, it ain't my first choice.*

†††

The assembly finished on the Barrett, Miles eased the barrel up and over the fallen tree and looked through the scope at the front of the cabin. He could see light leaking out of the windows through the shutters, but no hint of movement in or near the structure. That was okay, though—he could wait. Sooner or later they would have to step out, or just take a peek out the window. The clearing was too large for him to run up and set fire to the cabin, and he didn't have the arm strength to throw a torch that far. Even if he had incendiary grenades, he doubted he could heave them far enough to cover the distance.

The position in which he lay against the tree afforded him cover, but the beginnings of a leg cramp told him he couldn't maintain it. The wreck, the long walk, and the cold were all conspiring against his body, forcing movement when he most wanted to be still. He leaned the rifle against the tree, and then rubbed his leg. A few seconds of kneading the muscle through the heavy material of his pants served to relax it a bit, but he realized his discomfort was due more to dehydration than exertion.

Once again, he cursed his shortsightedness for not taking the time to outfit himself properly. He had brought neither food nor water to the party.

I taught you better than that, boy! His daddy's voice, clear as a bell in his head, made him jump for fear someone might hear.

Shut up, old man, he snarled back in thought. *I don't have time to listen to your bullshit.*

Weak, boy. Weak and worthless. You never did hunt worth shit.

Miles pounded the side of his head with one fist. *Shut the fuck up!* He pulled his knees to his chest and rocked back and forth, beating the side of his head in time with the motion. *Go away! Go away and let me do this.*

Get off your ass, boy, and get your eyes on the target!

Miles complied immediately with the demand. Years of conditioning took care of that, and he resumed his earlier position, hoping to end this quickly. *Maybe that will shut the old man up*, he thought.

He knew it wouldn't, though. Nothing he ever did, would.

†††

Addison was behind and almost directly below the large man sitting in the tree. Carson was so intent on watching the road, he never heard the quiet approach of his doom. The position the man held was precarious at best, and leaning forward as he was, his center of gravity was just inside of open space. It wouldn't take much to push that past the point of no return, sending him falling to the forest floor. Once on the ground, there was a large rock nearby Addison could use to dispatch him quickly and quietly—though how to reach him without his knowledge was the real problem.

He briefly considered pulling out the Beretta and shooting him in the head, but he dismissed that as cheap. It would be a classless act after a long career of perfect hits. No, what he needed was a long branch that he could procure without too much noise, and use it to quickly push the man over and out of the tree before he had a chance to act. While there were several nearby, they were far too flimsy for his purpose. The most suitable of the lot required him to move several yards away from the tree to retrieve it, and with each step, sure and silent as a dancer, he moved closer to his goal. A small twig snapped and he froze in place as he watched Carson for signs the man heard him.

He needn't have worried, though, as the fat man never moved from his position, so intent was he on watching the road. Retrieving the large branch as quietly as he could, Addison moved back to the tree where Phil held watch. His movements were glacially slow now, since there was no room for error. Once under the man again, he lifted the scope to his eye to check the cabin one last time for movement. From this angle the fireplace no longer obstructed his thermal imaging, and it was clear that Jason still lay motionless on the floor. If the man stayed that way for another few minutes, this would all be over soon. *And once completed, I am shed of this client for good.*

Addison placed the scope back in his pocket, and then lifted the branch, inch by inch, into position behind his target. The angle required him to use great force to unseat his target. *As fat as he is, though, once he's in motion the outcome is assured.* With one swift motion he pushed the branch as hard as he could into the back of the man's head, and was rewarded with the sight of a rifle flying loose from the fat man's hands as he scrabbled for purchase on the side of the tree. Gravity had other ideas, and the would-be sniper slipped from his perch and fell to the ground with a hard and muffled thud. The instant Addison saw the man lose his balance, he dropped the branch, picked up the rock, and ran to the other side of the tree. Straddling his first victim he raised the rock high, ready to bring it down hard to crush the man's skull.

Phil grabbed his head with one hand, and raised the other in a feeble attempt to stop the killing blow, said, "You're not congressman Henderson," and then promptly passed out.

Addison, for the first time in his career—and for the briefest of seconds—hesitated. And that was all it took.

†††

Miles saw the man fall out of the tree to his right from the corner of his eye, and swung the rifle in that direction.

"Son of a bitch was gonna snipe me," he said.

He saw a man rise from the underbrush, holding something over his head, and Miles lined up the cross-hairs on the man's chest. *Center mass!* His daddy screamed in his head. *Don't go for the head-shot.* He let out a breath and started to squeeze the trigger. Suddenly, light spilled from the open door of the cabin, distracting him for just a fraction of a second, and his hand jerked slightly as he fired the rifle. Still, the man in bushes went down, and Miles swung the rifle around again to line up a shot on the other man standing in the doorway.

†††

Jason stood on the porch, holding the handgun in this right hand, and heard the crack from the rifle. The sound of a body hitting the ground came from his left, and he turned immediately in that direction. When he awoke shortly before, he knew his only job was to open the door, but hearing his uncle fall was more than he prepared for.

"Uncle Phil!" The scream barely left his throat when he sprang from the porch to run to where he heard the man fall.

†††

The man from the cabin ran no more than twenty feet before Miles' second bullet slammed into his body, dropping him to the ground in a heap. Miles detected no movement, but he had to be sure. Standing up from his firing position, he held the rifle in front as he stepped over the tree and walked across the clearing toward his enemy.

This was the final act that would open the path before him. Eliminate Jason Callahan, and the way was be clear. The smile that spread across his face made the frozen muscles ache, but he bore the pain. He was happy for the first time in years.

†††

Phil sat up and rubbed his head, surprised to still be breathing. Beside him was the man he had seen just before passing out, a neat bullet hole punched through the jacket near his shoulder. He didn't know exactly what was happening anymore, but the one thing he was sure of was that Jason was in danger. Leaning forward, he managed to get to his knees, then finally to his feet. He raised his still-throbbing head to look across the clearing toward the cabin, and what he saw there chilled him to the bone. Jason was on the ground, motionless, with Henderson walking toward him with a large rifle in his hands, his clear intent to administer the coup de grâce.

Realizing there was no time to find his rifle, Phil pulled his knife and charged Henderson in a full throated scream.

"Bastard! Get away from him!" Phil ran as hard as he could, but he knew there was no way to reach the man before he could take aim and fire. Just as the gun was raised, Phil threw the knife with all the strength and skill he could muster, only to watch it bounce ineffectively off the man's coat. What it didn't do in damage it made up for in distraction, as Henderson, in his attempt to dodge the keen blade, allowed Phil to continue to close the gap unmolested.

Still twenty feet away, Henderson gathered his wits, aimed, and fired in a smooth motion that hit Phil in the thigh. Momentum, however, was on his side now, as his mass propelled him forward and he slammed head first into the man's chest. Both fell to the ground in a tangle of arms and legs, Phil having the upper hand for only a moment. Henderson, like Jason, was younger and in better shape, and quickly took control of the struggle by digging a finger into Phil's gunshot wound. The pain lit up his brain, and Phil released him in agony. Henderson responded by scrambling atop the larger man, grabbing Phil's head and began pounding it repeatedly against the ground.

Just as he began to pass out from the pain and abuse, something heavy fell across his prone body and the pounding stopped. Then he felt no more.

†††

Addison stood over the two men, the bloody stone still in his hands, and wondered about this new development. Jason was nearby, likely dead from a gunshot wound. Carson was bleeding from a leg wound and unconscious, and Congressman Miles Henderson—Addison's apparent client—was on top of the big man. He reached down and separated the two men. Both were breathing, but Addison knew he couldn't allow that to continue. The only question was what to do next.

His shoulder was killing him, but that could wait. The bullet was a high-velocity round and had made a clean hole through-and-through near the collar bone. He was still bleeding, but no major arteries were severed, and no bones broken, so he pulled some of the fiberfill from the hole in his jacket and shoved it into the wound. He looked at Henderson and snorted in derision. *The idiot should have used a hollow point.* He shook his head, *Amateurs.*

Examining Mr. Carson, he saw the damage was much the same as his own. There was enough flesh there that hitting anything vital would have been a complete accident. He pulled more fiberfill from his jacket, shoved it in the holes, then tore a strip of cloth from the bottom of the man's shirt to tie it up. He stood back to survey his work and nodded his head. It would do for now.

Next, he walked over to Jason, knelt over the body, and confirmed what he already knew. The man was dead. From a gunshot wound, of all things, and now this situation needed cleaning up. Addison stood, turned, and walked back to the two unconscious combatants, and made his preparations.

†††

Carl stood silently on the path far out of view of everyone in the clearing, watching the events unfold. Clothed in heavy hooded coat and pants, he stood perfectly still in the cold air with both hands shoved into the coat pockets. The hood was pulled up over his head, and the only motion was the steamy breath drifting out and up from underneath that hood. As he watched Addison rise after checking Jason's body, Carl pulled back his hood and then removed the worn Dallas Cowboys cap. The steam rising from the top of his head made him look like he was evaporating into the air.

Messy, but it'll do, he thought.

He shook his head, turned back to the path leading to the main road, ran bony fingers over his tightly trimmed hair, then replaced the baseball cap he was holding.

"Yes, sir. That'll do, indeed," he said softly, then walked away.

TWENTY-SIX

"That's a question, brother, with a lot of answers."

Jason screwed up his mouth and tossed a log into the fire. "Am I dead, for starters."

"Oh, hell yeah," he grinned down at Jason, full of mirth. "The man plugged you clean through the heart, I think. And on the run, too. Hell of a shot." He winked at Jason, and clapped him hard on the shoulder, "You done good, brother."

"All I did was get myself killed. Probably Uncle Phil, too."

His brother sat beside him and shook his head, "Again… my body." He smiled, and said, "What you did was stir the pot. You changed the variables just enough to allow the joker in the deck to make a play." He looked at the ceiling like he expected something to be there, "And that's all the consensus expected you to do. It was the first time we ever got the other man involved, and that made all the difference in the world." Staring at the ceiling and rubbing his chin, he said, "We're still not sure how that happened, but we're not looking a gift-horse in the mouth on this one." He smiled again, and looked over at Jason to catch his eyes, "Game's over, and I think we won."

"You think? You mean there's still some doubt?"

"There's always doubt. It's why we have the consensus. There are no absolutes here, only probabilities waiting to collapse into reality."

"So what…"

†††

"…happens now?"

Phil sat looking at the man who was sent to kill him. The man who instead saved his life and bandaged his leg. He looked over at his nephew's body, trying desperately to remember that Jason said no one ever died—they just started over. He desperately wanted to believe that. As his eyes pooled, he wanted to believe that now more than ever. The truth for Phil, though, was that in this reality—the one he called home—he had no family left. All he had in the world was family, and now they were gone… murdered by a madman.

"Well, sir, you get to do something none of my targets have ever been able to do." Standing beside Henderson, he looked Phil up and down, his face a mask of stone, "You get to make a choice."

"Is it 'bullet or knife,' like 'paper or plastic'?" He smiled thinly at the man he knew as James Newton, and said, "I choose for my nephew to not be dead."

Addison turned and looked at Jason's body, watching the steam rise as it rapidly shed its heat. "I am truly sorry about that. Knowing how things are turning out in the end, I would have preferred that he lived."

"Well, that's comforting." He looked away from the man, not wanting him to see his pain through the bravado.

"Yes… well, what I'm asking you is how you want" he gestured at the unconscious man on the ground, "Mr. Henderson, here, to die."

Phil turned his head back to the psychopath on the ground in front of him, his eyes flashed, as he said through clenched teeth, "Painfully."

The killer shook his head, "I don't think you understand. I have to clean this mess up. Since you don't know my name, and provided you stay out of my affairs, I can let you live," he nodded at Jason, "seeing as my primary target is dead." He turned back to Phil, "But I have had enough of this client, and now that I know he is a congressman, and he's completely tainted this scene, I'm afraid I have to terminate our working relationship." He smiled tightly at the man on the ground, "And in my business, that means rolling it up so nothing leads back to me." He shook his head, and said, "Luckily for you, the process is cleaner if I allow you to live." He snorted primly, "Two bodies I can easily explain. Three," he shrugged, "that's more of a problem."

Phil, still confused, just remained silent. It was all too much for one day, and now this man wanted him to decide... what?

"I can snap his neck, drag him to the gully a few hundred feet on the other side of the cabin, and throw him in to make it look like an accident."

"Or...?"

"Or I can get Jason's gun and use his hand to shoot our friend in the head." He looked from Jason, to Miles, then back to Phil. "My preference is for the gun. While the gully will look like an accident for Mr. Henderson, that doesn't explain away Jason—and while I can handle that, I am quite sure that is not something you want to see."

Phil considered that, and, guessing what that meant, he had to agree. "So we just stage it to look like they killed each other?"

The assassin nodded, "I believe that's the best option for all involved, yes."

"But what possible motive could they have had for coming up here to kill each other?" Another thought struck him. "What do I tell his...?" he whispered to himself.

"It doesn't matter." James watched Phil for a second, and he was sure the assassin was assessing the need to kill him after all, when he said, "You will see. There will be a lot of speculation in the news, but in the end, without witnesses, it will just become another mystery. Another conspiracy theory for the tinfoil hat crowd." He waved his hand dismissively, "This is America, after all."

Phil considered all James said, and after a while, nodded his head. A weight was finally lifted from his shoulders with that motion. "I guess we'd better git to gittin'."

"Can you stand?" James reached down, offering his hand for help. After a second or two of searching the man's eyes for deception, Phil clasped the other in his own and pulled himself up.

In the end it didn't take long to stage the scene, then clean the cabin and the area of all trace of Phil and James' presence there. Phil wanted to pull the trigger, but for some reason James wouldn't allow it. As the sun began to rise, they set out down the lonely road, then performed the same task at the car. Henderson's car was too damaged to drive back, so they hiked down the mountain toward the main highway. The intersection was only a mile from the nearest convenience store, and there they waited for a car to pick them up once James made a call.

"Hey," Phil began as they waited, "I just realized that car was rented in my name."

"It's being taken care of as we speak by one of my associates, Mr. Carson." James tilted his head and shrugged, "You'd be surprised how little money it actually takes to clean up simple paperwork. Especially since you paid with cash."

By the time the car with the two men pulled up to the Jeppesen Terminal at Denver International Airport, Phil was wearing new pants and a clean bandage on his leg—both courtesy of James' associates. As he got out of the car, his companion dug through a small bag in his lap, and then leaned across the seat to the open door.

"Here." James was holding a small stack of bills in his hand, the ends flapping limply in front of him. "This should take care of your ticket and other expenses." He smiled for the first time, and Phil was no longer sure he wanted to see that again. "Don't look at me like I'm giving you a gift. It is your money, after all. I liberated it from your hotel room in D.C." Phil took the money and stuffed it into his coat pocket. "Once you get in town, go back to your original hotel. You will find that you never left… at least as far as anyone working there is concerned. Get your truck, drive home, and try to live the life you have left." A hard, flat look replaced the smile, "And don't ever try to find me."

Phil guessed this was the closest the man ever got to being friendly, and it frightened him a bit. He was not the kind of man you wanted for a friend. Phil patted the pocket with the cash, nodded his thanks, and closed the door behind him. He heard the car drive away as he walked into the terminal.

✝✝✝

"…are you saying? I can go home?"

"Of course you can go home."

"But I thought there was more to do here."

His brother looked at him like he was waiting for Jason to work out an especially hard math problem. "There is, but not for you. The reason you were the only one for the job, out of the multitude of Jasons here, is that Henderson doesn't exist in your reality. You were the only one of us with the ability to transition at will who could make that claim."

"I could still stay and help." Jason's brows beetled in concentration, his mouth screwed up, "You need all the help you can get."

"We do, and we have." The other Jason smiled at him again, then said, "When you're here, someone has to be there, and that means we are leaving an opening—one that you can't plug." He slapped Jason on the back, "Cheer up! This means you finally get to go home. For real. Back to the life you would have made for yourself before you started your journey."

Home. The word almost held no meaning anymore. *But what is waiting for me there?* Years spent wishing for home, and now he found he feared what he might find. *Fear keeps you rooted in place, boy*, Uncle Phil had told him once. *You fight fear only by constantly moving.*

"The good news is that you have a choice of where on the timeline you want to enter your reality."

"A choice? I thought that when we died we just went back to the beginning."

The other smiled broadly. "Yes, and no."

"Holy shit, brother! Please tell me that's the last time you're gonna do that."

"Probably." He shook his head, and laughed lightly. "The point is, you and I can travel back down our timeline at will. You get to pick where you want to start the recording, so to speak." He stopped laughing and said, "Gotta warn you, though, it's gonna hurt. A lot."

Jason considered that, then said, "What if I just slide sideways at my current point in time?"

His brother rubbed his chin, and said, "Well, that's a lot easier, but even with access to all the built-up memories, you'll still have some catching up to do. You would look like a complete idiot at times until you get it all reintegrated."

Jason laughed. "Wouldn't be the first time." He thought it over for a while longer, then said, "I think I've decided to just slide over. In a way, I'm traveling into the future in my reality. I kind of want to see how things turned out. Besides, I can always go back if it sucks, right?"

The other Jason's face softened a bit. "That's true. You can always go back, but Jason," he looked his brother in the eyes, and Jason could see sadness there, "once you go, you can't ever go sideways again. You'll be locked into that loop for eternity, just like most of humanity."

"I can come here, though, right?"

His brother shook his head, "I'm afraid not. From every direction, from every reality, this is sideways." He took a slow breath, "I'm sorry, brother. It's a result of the way we are dealing with Henderson. We have trapped him here—cut him off from every avenue of escape sideways or back." He shuddered slightly, "All of us on this side have the consensus, and while we do, we are able to create—but we can't go home. Henderson, on the other hand, is trapped with no means of escape and no way to create." He closed his eyes and said, "Forever."

Jason also shuddered in sympathy. To be trapped in an empty void for all eternity. It was a horrible punishment—maybe not even deserved—but their options were limited.

"What happens to the rest of him?"

"He's the only remaining part of a perfect pair. A part that was born on the great trunk. His suffering will radiate throughout every version of himself, both sideways and backward through time." His brother sighed heavily, and said, "Some may escape his fate, and a few of those may destroy their worlds, but the multiverse—all the multiverses—will be preserved."

Jason nodded at that. It was the point of this from the beginning, after all; preserve all the universes of mankind. Sacrifice one to save all. He held out his hand, and as his brother took it, he said, "I think I'm ready to go, now."

His brother nodded, and pointed out the open door to a spot in the clearing and a brilliant blue light he realized had always been there, waiting for him. He released his brother's hand and walked to the light, feeling the warmth radiate toward him. The light reached out to him, enveloping his soul in a comforting embrace like a long-lost lover. He turned to wave back at his brother, but he, the cabin, and the clearing were gone. And only darkness was left to send him on his journey.

†††

Miles Henderson stood in nothingness. A cold empty black wrapping his shoulders like a heavy cloak. All around he felt the presence of vast others—watching him. Eyes pressed against his brain—judging him. He knew he was dead in the real world, and while he would normally just move sideways or back, there were no markers to follow.

Hands and arms extended, he walked, though his footfalls made no sound. Hearing his own breathing, he knew he was not deaf, but his feet made no noise in the interaction between his soles and the surface he trod. It was then he realized he was naked, stripped of everything but his sense of self, and the all-consuming purpose of action driving him forward.

In the distance a vertical slit of light appeared, and in renewed hope he marched, then ran, as the light burst into azure brilliance. A doorway! As he drew near, he could see a shape passing through that blinding curtain. The door slammed shut as quickly as it opened, leaving nothing but a whisper of the illumination reverberating among the walls he could see like the peal of a church bell. The light only served to drive him deep into despair as it revealed the nature of his prison. To infinity in each direction the hallway stretched, doors on either side every few feet beckoned to him with the hope of escape.

He tested the handle of the door that had just recently been opened, but it was locked. The silent others—watching, waiting—assured him without words they all were.

"It didn't have to be this way, Miles."

He realized his eyes were closed, and he opened them to the light. Or maybe the owner of that voice simply decided to appear at that moment in a flash of actinic fire, burning the memory of retinas. He didn't know, nor care, which.

"And what way is that, boy?"

The small figure, wrapped in a light that dripped from him like honey, pooling at his bare feet in a puddle of liquid dreams, pointed in either direction. "Like this," mournfully. More than mere light, Miles saw what covered the boy was the flickering of probability in constant motion. All around him were the scenes of lives he never lived, shifting and moving and melding, then separating again to swirl about and fall like rain to the ground. "I warned you, and you wouldn't listen." He dropped his gaze, drew a shuddering breath, and then looked up again. "As all knew you would." The boy sighed pityingly. *Was he fading? Are my eyes adjusting?* He watched as the younger version of himself stood in silence, wiggling his toes in the liquid light at his feet.

"So this is punishment for my crimes?" Miles snorted. "How long do you think you can keep me here, boy?"

The boy looked up, sadness in his eyes, and said, "Not me... all."

"All of who, exactly?"

"Me… you…" He opened his arms embracing the darkness about them, "us," he said simply. "Miles, there are battles between the Jasons' and Miles' of the universe in a near-infinite number of realities with the single-minded purpose of allowing all of me to do what needs to be done."

"And that is?"

"To keep all of you from interfering with all of me."

Miles was sure, now. The boy was fading. Becoming thinner. Not so much transparent as less substantial.

"And what is 'here'?"

Young Miles smiled thinly. "It is the in-between. That infinitely thin wall that separates realities." The boy took a deep breath, let it out slowly, and stood straight and tall. In a voice, clear and strong, he said, "Miles Henderson, it is the judgment of the all that you remain in this place, never to leave, for all eternity."

Miles forced a booming laugh, a twinge of nervous energy invaded the edges. "So, you are to stay here and try to hold me?"

The boy shook his head, filaments of light drifting away like loose hair, "No, Miles. No one is allowed inside but you." He raised his chin, a hard edge in his eyes, "I, like all others like me, must stay on the other sides to hold the way closed."

The filaments continued to drift away, taking more and more of the boy with them. He smiled one last sad smile, then even that evaporated as the rest of him dissolved into light and slowly dissipated, leaving only a soft glow behind. The glow was condensing even as it, too, faded.

And then the voices came.

Hell, they said as one, *is not flames, or pain, or hate. It is indifference*. There was no escape, and as the last of the light faded, leaving him once again in an absolute and velvet darkness, Miles Henderson screamed.

TWENTY-SEVEN

"I**N A HURRY TO GET HOME?**" J**ASON TURNED TO THE BUS DRIVER WHO** was watching him intently. The crisp white shirt he wore, neat stitching over the pocket with the name "Carl" in blue letters, offered a stark contrast to his dark skin.

Wait. Vertigo gripped him, and he spun in place to take in his surroundings. He could feel the boots on his feet, and his shoulders slumped. Jason turned back to the man who had just spoken.

"Carl?"

"One 'n' the same, son." Carl released the steering wheel and offered his right hand to the young man. Jason hesitated as he looked around in confusion, then sheepishly grasped and shook the man's hand.

"I… I don't understand."

Carl smiled, that one gold tooth shining in the light from the instrument panel, "Not surprised." He leaned over, closer to the young man, and stage-whispered, "Frankly, son, a lot of what you know is pretty much bullshit." He leaned back, and grinned at him as one eyebrow arched upward.

Jason looked around the bus and shook his head. "I was supposed to be going home. How did I get here?"

"You got on back in Dallas," he said as he hooked a thumb behind him. "Don't you remember?"

"I remember I've seen you a lot over the last few years."

"You don't say?" The man stared straight ahead and smiled again as Jason watched him, the lights of downtown Houston flashing by as they prowled the late-night streets. "There've been many times you didn't see me, either." Carl turned the big wheel expertly to enter the main parking area of the bus station, pulled into a bay, and glided smoothly to a stop. "How about you hang back a bit so we can talk." He engaged the parking brake, the loud whoosh of compressed air waking the remaining sleepers on board, then pulled the lever to open the doors.

Jason screwed his mouth up, but said nothing. He picked up his pack, stepped up out of the stairwell, and sat behind the driver. The old man watched him in the reflection of the windshield while the remaining passengers climbed out of the bus, the smile never faltering.

When the last person exited, Carl closed the doors, unbuckled his seatbelt, and moved to sit across the aisle from Jason. The motion was fluid, and he sat with a calm grace while facing the young man. Jason tried to match that leisurely calm, but there were too many questions running through his head.

The old man looked around the cabin, ran his hand along the material of the armrest, and said, "I don't drive this bus as often as I'd like, but I come back to it every chance I get." He looked hard into Jason's eyes, "It's a simple life," then he looked away, "and it leaves me to my thoughts." He drew a slow, deep breath, and said, "I've been a bus driver, college professor, fireman, congressman, doctor… Hell, pretty much anything you can name. Been married more times than I can count. Most of the time to the same woman." He chuckled at that. "But this is what gives me the most peace and satisfaction." He grinned lopsidedly, "Probably because it was the first real job I ever had."

Jason arched an eyebrow, and said, "Just how old are you?"

"Oh, I don't think of it in years. It's more about lifetimes, and I stopped counting after a couple hundred."

His eyes widened. "So you're like me."

"Well, yes… and no."

Jason sighed as if were his final breath. "I swear to God, the next person who says that is gonna end up missing some teeth."

Carl laughed out loud and slapped his knee. A deep, rolling laugh that brought tears to his eyes. "I can understand your frustration, son."

Jason waited until the laughing subsided, sighing heavily a couple of times and drumming his fingers on the armrest, then said, "Why are we here?"

"Is that a metaphysical question, or more literal?"

Jason crossed his arms and waited, tapping his booted foot in the aisle.

Carl put his hands up, palms out, and said, "All right. We're here because it's the best place I know to have this conversation."

Rolling his eyes skyward, Jason threw his hands in the air, "Here we go. What do I have to do now?"

"Not a thing, son. You've already done your part, and admirably too. I just thought you had some questions you might want answered."

Jason snorted. "Someone's already done that for me."

"Yes, well," Carl winked at him, "that boy didn't know much more than you." He laughed again at his own joke, eyes twinkling in the light from the dashboard.

"So... who are you?"

"I'm your daddy." He smiled and leaned forward.

"Um..."

"No, boy, not in the literal sense." He waved his hands in the air, "I'm the daddy of everything you see."

"You're God. Got it." Jason edged back a bit in the seat toward the window, putting some distance between himself and the crazy man.

"I don't know from God, son, but," he watched Jason relax slightly, "I'm what you might call an engineer. I keep the gears greased, and the machine running smoothly." He chuckled lightly, shaking his head. "It's a hell of a lot more complicated than that, but you could say this is my train." He poked a bony finger in Jason's direction, and said, "And because of you, there's a whole bunch of new stations up the line."

"I don't understand."

"Of course you don't. No reason why you should" He shook his head. "You know how this multiverse works from a quantum perspective, right?" He watched Jason's face, but didn't wait for a response. "Well, for you to happen, there had to be a universe already for you to be born in." He made a fist and poked a thumb at his chest. "That one was mine."

"I don't see how that makes any difference..."

"It'll come to you in a bit," he said, the skin around his eyes creasing. "I created you. I made sure your momma and daddy got together and made you." He pursed his lips and shook his head. "It wasn't easy, either. Someday I might even tell you that story."

A million questions ran through Jason's head, but the one that bubbled to the surface first was, "Why?"

"'I needed someone to do a job I couldn't," he shrugged.

Jason nodded. "Henderson."

"Yeah, and it had to be done through free will." Carl's face softened, and he looked down for a bit, then up again to meet Jason's eyes. "About twenty years from now Henderson pretty much ends the world. I die in the Two Hour War. A lot of people do."

"Then everything ends, right?"

"In a way… but not as it was explained to you. The universe doesn't shut down just because the intelligence that created it dies. Everything continues undisturbed—the individual goes back to the beginning and relives the loop." His eyes narrowed. "We always die at the same time as that first death. The causes change, but the timing does not. You ended then, and there is just no way to keep going beyond that."

"Can't you change the future by going back to the past?"

"You would think so, but the timeline is self-correcting. No matter what you do, you will die on the same date at the same time. I couldn't just get someone to do it for me, either—that would be the same as do-in'git myself. No, sir, everyone in that dance had to be there for their own reasons." He grinned hard, as if a frown hid behind. "Best I could do was fiddle with everyone's motivations."

"So…?"

He sighed and scooted to the edge of the chair. "I can't change my fate, but someone else could. Someone like you… part of a perfect pair." His eyes narrowed slightly, and he said, "Your brother was supposed to be the one to get it done, but he cocked it up somethin' awful his first time out, so the job fell to you."

"So I was just plan 'B'?"

"Well," he said, his gaze drifting to the floor. "I got other irons in the fire, but I figured you were the best shot."

"And once we removed the threat of world annihilation from the timeline—the cause of your original death—you could continue past that point to some future death." Jason looked up at the man eaning forward, watching him. "Is that it?"

Carl clapped his hands together once, the sound like thunder in the silent cabin of the bus. "Indeed," he said with unforced gravity, as if Jason had made a great discovery. "You gave me at least another twenty years." He reached across the aisle and patted Jason's knee. "Not to mention saving a few hundred million other lives."

"Are you kidding me? All of this just so you could have another twenty years in your old age?"

"Hey, don't knock it until you've lived the previous seventy a few thousand times." He shook his head and said, "It's more than just more life for me, though. I told you earlier… I'm the engineer on this train. I not only keep things running, I put them on the right track." His eyes narrowed. "I found a timeline once where Lincoln never got assassinated," he whispered. Just one.

"That's not possible," Jason said, shaking his head.

"Damn unlikely… but not impossible. My granddaddy was alive when the man was president, and things had to go *exactly* the same for him and my daddy to make another me in that universe. Right down to fertilizing the same eggs with the same sperm."

"But…" Jason began.

"It was a completely different country, Jason, but my family was far enough removed from major events for things to work out for me." He nodded his head and smiled wistfully. "The man served four terms as president, then was appointed to the Supreme Court by the next president. True civil rights came to this country nearly a hundred years earlier than what you know." He shook his head, "I spent one whole lifetime there, but haven't been able to find my way back since."

Jason raised an eyebrow, "That doesn't make sense. If you found it once, you should be able to go back."

"I don't think I found it by accident. And I don't think it's a coincidence that I couldn't find it again."

Jason sat back, shocked. The man sitting across from him was the closest thing to God in this universe, and he just told him someone manipulated *his* travels. This was all too much. *Why is he even telling me this?* Jason thought.

"There's more for me to do upstream, and I am going to need every extra minute to get to it all. As you've found out recently, events don't just unfold, son. Someone's always out there creasin' the paper." His face softened. "You'll do it yourself someday." The old man shrugged "It's why we are who we are."

"But how do you know it worked? How do you know there's another future for you?"

He laughed and slapped his knee. "Where do you think I just came from?"

†††

Phil climbed into the row of open seats and sat by the window. He wasn't so large he needed to buy two tickets—yet—but he was grateful for the chance to spread out. He remembered the few times he flew as a much younger—and much thinner—man, and he hated that he was now the "fat man" people had to share a row of seats with.

Now that his Jason was dead in this reality, he had to figure out what to do with Jay. The boy was a handful, and Phil wasn't sure he was up to being a daddy to the kid. He wasn't exactly father-of-the-year material. He held out no hope the boy's remaining grandparents would take him in. They didn't have anything to do with him while Kathy was alive, nor did they offer Jason any help after she died. There wasn't much chance they would help now the boy was an orphan.

He leaned back and sighed, rubbing his face with both hands.

"Don't worry, big guy. Everything will work out."

Phil sat up and looked around, not sure who spoke or even if he was the one being spoken to. He heard a light chuckle, and he turned to the old man watching him from across the aisle, one gold tooth gleaming through a broad smile.

"What was that?"

"Just sayin' everything will be fine." He nodded once at Phil, and said, "You looked like a man who could use some buckin' up."

Phil relaxed his shoulders and sat back. He smiled, weary bones settling against the stiff seat. "I could, at that."

The man leaned over and offered his hand, "The name's Carl." He smiled again, warm rather than jovial. "I've been looking forward to meeting you, son." He reached across the aisle and patted Phil on the knee. "We'll talk later. Right now, you go ahead and get some sleep."

Phil was not the least bit shocked at the old man's statement. He spent too many years traveling to be surprised anymore. The old machine rattled as the engines roared to life, and the plane taxied toward the runway. Phil settled in to try and sleep, closing his eyes against the world. "Any idea how long the flight is?"

The man smiled, scratched his head through the cap he wore. "Longer than you want… but not as long as you might think."

"Story of my life, man." Phil leaned against the window, closed his eyes, and allowed sleep to take him.

†††

"*You're* the asshole who's been yanking me around the whole time!" Jason's face grew warm, but the anger wouldn't rise above a tepid annoyance. Too much had happened.

"Not the first nine or ten times" Carl said. "That was all you. I had a hell of a time tracking you down, too." He grinned. "I don't have your uncle's gift for sifting through the various alternates." He shifted uncomfortably in the seat, old joints crackling like someone twisting bubble-wrap. "I was almost too late. The Jason in the body I put you in wasn't handling it so well."

"I gathered," Jason said through a yawn. "So, am I finished?" He sagged in his seat, eyelids heavy and threatening to close.

"That's a loaded question, boy." Carl screwed up his mouth as his brow furrowed. "There's a lot of life left, if that's what you mean." He shook his head, "But that ain't what you meant, is it?" His face softened. "Nothing is ever *finished*, son. This is an ongoing and long-term project set in motion when modern man was still young." He smiled sadly, "It will continue long after I'm dead, too. I'll continue to do the work, of course, but most of it will pass on to others like us."

"I just want to go home," Jason sighed. "*My* home. My life." He looked up at Carl, and said, "Is that possible now?"

Carl's eyes twinkled again and he clapped his hands together. "Well, of course it is. You don't have to start your part right away. That's the beauty of it, boy. You can live a full life—hundreds of them—before you join the party." He rubbed the stubble on his chin, which turned into scratching his neck. "I think it's time we sent you back up the line."

Jason's head tilted, and one eyebrow arched. "You mean forward in time? I thought that wasn't possible."

"You can always go wherever you've already been, son." Carl 's brow furrowed. "Thought you knew that."

"But—"

"But nothin', boy. Time is not an arrow, it's a loop. You can go to any point on that loop right up to the time of your eventual death. Forward, back, sideways… it doesn't matter. Everything is all open to people like us."

"Well… not sideways anymore," Jason said softly. "At least not for me."

The old man smirked. "Whatchu talkin' 'bout, Willis?"

Jason's eyes widened. "My brother told me—"

"Oh hell, son. Didn't I say that boy don't know much more than you?" He laughed and shook his head. "It's true you can't go sideways anymore… *right now*. But after the point of Henderson's death, everything opens up again for you if you want."

"I can go anywhere?" Moving sideways was a completely different proposition when you had control over it. There were possibilities he desperately wanted to explore.

"Sure, but I thought you wanted to go home?"

Jason stopped mid-thought, and his shoulders slumped. He was tired of all his travels, and he realized that all he wanted was his own life again.

Carl nodded silently as if he understood, and raised his eyes skyward, tapping the side of his head with a bony finger, as he said, "I recommend seven years from where we are right now." He leaned forward and smiled, "But you go ahead and do what you want."

Jason snorted once. "Sure, why not? That was pretty much where I was going when you hijacked me." He grinned weakly back at the man. "Will I see you again?"

Carl chuckled lightly, a soothing baritone burbling. "You never can tell," he said with a wink. And then he did something Jason didn't think possible—he reached out with a steady and gentle hand, and *pushed* Jason through the fissure in the wall.

†††

Jason woke, memories integrating in a slow tumble. He luxuriated in the soft bed, comforted by the knowledge his life was, at long last, his own. Now aware of his surroundings, felt the bed beneath, the large and fluffy comforter over him, and smiled in warm satisfaction. He smelled the clean, fragrant air, breathed deeply, then stretched in cheerful satisfaction. No day could be bad when it started this way, and he lay still while the accumulated memories folded into his own like whipped cream into a chocolate mousse. There were so many changes from what he was accustomed to that he wondered how this could possibly be his life. He ventured to peek from beneath the covers to check his surroundings.

Sunlight streamed in through the curtains, falling on the bed in waves, while a fan turned lazily overhead. That fragrant smell was stronger now, and he had just determined to discover its origin when it appeared before him in the shape of a woman.

"Are you going to lay in bed all day?" She was buttoning a white silk blouse as she exited the adjoining bathroom. She sat on the bed, grabbed one of the pillows, and hit him squarely in the face with it. "We have to get moving, Jason. We're supposed to be at your mom and dad's by noon."

Jason reached across his body, grabbed her arm, and pulled her on top of him. "We've got plenty of time, Kat," he nodded at the window. "The sun's barely up." He kissed her then, caressing her face with his free hand. Her blond hair cascaded down across her shoulders, falling on his face and tickling his nose. She had always been the most beautiful woman he had ever met, never failing to surprise him. The morning glow took full control of him now, and he held her tighter, promising far more than a kiss if only she would crawl back under the covers with him.

She pulled away, laughed. "Jason, we don't have time for that." She smiled at his feigned look of hurt, and seemed almost on the verge of reconsidering when the door burst open.

"Daddy!" Both his daughters crashed into the room, six-year-old Lisa jumping directly onto his legs, while four-year-old Laney crawled over the hope chest at the foot of the bed. They bounced up and down, squeals of "Get up, get up!" raining down on his head.

"Hey, hey, hey!" He sat up, using one of the pillows as a shield, "Give me some time, okay?" He looked at his wife, now standing beside the bed and clearly enjoying herself. "Why did you ever teach them how to open a door?"

Katherine smirked at him, then shrugged her shoulders and said, "Seemed like a good idea at the time."

The two girls, blond and pretty like their mother, and wearing matching dinosaur pajamas, eyed their parents. In unison they rolled their eyes, then pummeled their father with the remaining pillows.

After dragging himself from the warm embrace of the bed, he took a long hot shower. For the first time in years, he cried for the loss of little Jay. He could visit, but the boy could never be a part of *this* life. That Jay would never know his sisters—*or* his father. By the time he climbed out and dried off, the tears had been spent, replaced by a growing joy for the life he was always meant to have.

†††

Jason sat at the bistro-style table in the outer room of their hotel suite, eating a light breakfast and chatting with his family. Breakfast had to be light—today was Thanksgiving, after all—and he couldn't remember ever feeling so happy. This was his life, the one he left behind all those years ago, and he was only now coming to terms with the fact that it would be his for the rest of his days.

Over the past summer his tenure application was approved, and he was now an Associate Professor of physics at Princeton. He had waited until his first opportunity to visit his parents before he told them, and it was fitting that it fell on Thanksgiving. His daddy had at last scraped together enough money for a down payment on a new home—"Finally, one with a yard," his mom said—and he was anxious to see the place. It had always been his dream to get them out of the trailer park, but the old man had twice refused his offer of help.

"You two ready to go see granny and pawpaw?" He turned his head to look behind, as the two girls grinned and nodded vigorously from the back seat of the rental car. "Okay," he nodded to open door on his right, "and if your mom will just get settled, we can go." He smiled at his wife and raised an eyebrow. She sat next to him in the passenger seat with her door open, and scanned the interior of the car, taking a mental inventory of everything they had or needed for the drive.

She looked up, stopped her pre-flight check, and closed the door. "Fine, but if we forgot anything, I'm just going to go buy another one."

"Fair enough." He winked at her and started the motor. The drive to the new house wouldn't take long, so it didn't really matter if they forgot anything, but it was never a good idea to question Kat's planning and preparation. She was like her daddy that way, and hadn't changed much from their days in high school when she kept a tight leash on his study time. He knew he never would have made it through his first year of college if she hadn't been there cracking the whip. It helped that he loved it.

"All right, passengers, prepare for liftoff." He put the car in gear and pulled out of the hotel driveway. "I guess we better git' to gittin'."

EPILOGUE

THREE YEARS. PHIL DIDN'T HAVE THE LUXURY OF GOING BACK IN time like his nephew, so he was methodical in his approach. Still, it took three years and more slips through the wall than he could count before he was completely satisfied. In this reality, James—or whatever the assassin's real name was—was right. The story flared bright for a time, with many conspiracy theorists coming out of the woodwork with their wild accusations or claims of "false flags," but in the end it all amounted to nothing. The story died with a whimper within months, and the world got back to its business. It seemed that one man, even a congressman, was not essential to the workings of the world.

Miles Henderson was no longer a threat. In every reality he had observed where the man still existed, he was either a drooling, babbling fool, or completely catatonic. Many committed suicide within days of the event in the mountains, while the rest had slipped slowly into insanity. There were, undoubtedly, others that Phil would never know about for sure, as he could not slip through to every reality where Henderson existed, but every reality he visited convinced him the others had been neutralized as well. The most telling thing was that in no reality was the man mourned, or even missed. There had been no great funeral processions, or even an emotional outpouring from the nation. He simply hadn't mattered.

Phil still didn't understand everything that Jason told him before he died, but he knew that whatever had happened inside the wall destroyed the man who killed his sister and his nephew. He shuddered to think what could do that to a man. *How would you drive every version of a man so over the edge he became no more than a quivering sack of meat? What could you possibly do to a man inside that wall that he could not undo for himself?*

His eyes narrowed. "No more than the bastard deserved," he said, the hard edge of hate still there after the years.

Still, the idea crept into his brain from time to time that no man deserved such a fate. It left no room for redemption, no hope of change. There was a certain symmetry to guilt and punishment, fall and redemption, that transcended simple justice or revenge. There was no symmetry to this. This was punishment without end. Better to have killed them each to a man and be done with it. That was at least humane. If Jason was right, however, it just allowed Henderson to start over, and Phil knew from experience that the results would be the same over the long haul. In the end he decided the consensus that Jason's brother had spoken of had reached the only possible conclusion, and the results, at least, bore them out. The world was safe from one more madman.

The years of searching, though, were not just for confirmation of Henderson's defeat, but also to find the nephew Phil allied with. There were a large number of realities where Jason was also catatonic—or worse, dead—but the fact that few of those he met seemed to know anything of the wall was disturbing. At last, he decided to travel all the way back up to the cabin in the mountains to search for the veil through which Jason passed three years ago. Those intervening years were no kinder to Phil than the previous fifty, but he managed to make it up the steep slope without dropping dead from exertion.

When he arrived, the shadows of that night so long gone hit him solidly in the gut, driving even the will to breathe from his chest. The light chill in the air did not come close to matching the cold of that night, but he shivered nonetheless, while the trees stood in stony silence guarding the perimeter of the clearing. The feeling of death was pervasive and difficult to shake, regardless of the fact that three years erased every scrap of evidence of their presence. Even now, in broad daylight, the place was forbidding and lonely—no bird-call or soft susurration of crickets to be heard anywhere within walking distance of the clearing. He walked the perimeter, trying to remember the exact spot where Jason lay as he died. As he did, he passed through a very different spot. Cold, unforgiving, and full of greasy despair, he recognized it as the place where Miles Henderson breathed his last. *But that means...* he turned toward the cabin, walked ten steps and collapsed to the ground as the vertigo of Jason's passing hit him. *This was the place!*

Without thought of planning or goal, Phil sat in that spot on the hard ground, slowed his breathing, and closed his eyes. In seconds he was inside the wall following that faint trail of Jason's slip. For the first time in his memory, he felt the presence of others watching his movements, but it didn't matter. They could watch him until hell itself froze over—and probably would—but he was sure they had no interest in his actions. There was but one purpose here—finding Jason—and determination drove him ever forward, following that thin line through to the other side.

He opened his eyes to find he was sitting in his old recliner, Jason smiling and sitting across from him on the couch holding a beer. The man was dressed in a tailored suit and expensive-looking shoes. On his wrist was what appeared to be a gold Rolex, though one of the smaller, less gaudy models. Across the room, near the television, a video camera was set up on a tripod with the little red light lit up to show it was recording. Jason smiled crookedly, picked up a second can from the coffee table, and tossed it to his uncle. "Thought I'd save you a trip to Jersey." He grinned, and said, "Trust me, I did you a favor."

"How...?"

Jason laughed. "You come to see me at my office at Princeton a couple of days from now. I just jumped back a few and beat you to it." He cocked an eyebrow at Phil's confusion, "I'm special, remember?"

Phil laughed back, "Son, I've known that since the day you were born." He sat forward in his recliner, set the can on the table and tapped it a few times. As he popped the top he looked across the way at the boy, now a man, and smiled warmly. "You teachin' up there?"

"Yeah," Jason said. "Physics and some quantum chemistry. I mostly do research, though."

"Of course," Phil said with a nod. "'Bout what I expected after all those talks we had."

Both men raised their cans in salute, each taking a long pull, then settled back in their seats. Phil watched his nephew over the rim of his beer can, the quiet confidence he saw a far cry from the last time they both sat here.

Phil pointed with his chin toward the video camera. "What's with the setup?"

Jason chuckled to himself, and said, "Oh, that. This Uncle Phil doesn't like me very much. He doesn't believe me about the stuff I can do—thinks I'm nuts—and he won't take any of my help, either. He says I 'put on airs' and don't remember where I came from."

"Sounds like an ass," Phil said through a grin.

"Ya think?" Jason took a sip of his beer, then said, "I'm just recording this for him so he can see I'm telling the truth." He winked at his uncle, and said, "And before you go home, I want you to give a complete accounting of everything that happened to us when we saved the world. I'll play it back for him after you leave."

"Won't help."

"Maybe not, but it's worth a shot."

"You seem to have done well for yourself over the last three years." He eyed the watch, then looked back to Jason's face. "A bit much on a professor's salary, don't ya think?"

His nephew swirled his can for a second, then took another drink. "It's not all salary. There's research grants and release time as well. Plus Kat makes a fair sum at her job."

"Uh huh." Phil's eyes narrowed.

Jason watched his uncle for a second, then leaned forward again and said through a wink and a grin, "Let me tell you how day trading works for a time traveler."

9 781732 122000